WILD CARDS

INSIDE STRAIGHT

WILD CARDS

INSIDE STRAIGHT

Edited by

George R. R. Martin

Assisted by

Melinda M. Snodgrass

And written by

Daniel Abraham

Melinda M. Snodgrass

Carrie Vaughn

Michael Cassutt

Caroline Spector

John Jos. Miller

George R. R. Martin

Ian Tregillis

S. L. Farrell

This edition first published in Great Britain in 2013
by Gollancz
An imprint of the Orion Publishing Group
Orion House, 5 Upper St Martin's Lane,
London WC2H 9EA
An Hachette UK Company

This edition published in Great Britain in 2013 by Gollancz

1 3 5 7 9 10 8 6 4 2

A CIP catalogue record for this book
is available from the British Library

ISBN 978 0 575 13418 8

Typeset by Deltatype Ltd, Birkenhead, Merseyside

Printed and bound by CPI Group (UK) Ltd,
Croydon, CR0 4YY

The Orion Publishing Group's policy is to use papers that are
natural, renewable and recyclable products and made from wood
grown in sustainable forests. The logging and manufacturing
processes are expected to conform to the environmental
regulations of the country of origin.

To Kay McCauley, ace agent,
who always deals us winning hands

Editor's Note

Wild Cards is a work of fiction set in a completely imaginary world whose history parallels our own. Names, characters, places, and incidents depicted in *Wild Cards* are fictitious or are used fictitiously. Any resemblance to actual events, locales, or real persons, living or dead, is entirely coincidental. The works contained in this anthology are works of fiction; any writings referred to within these works are themselves fictional, and there is no intent to depict actual writers or to imply that any such persons have ever actually written or published the fictional essays, articles, or other works referred to in the works of fiction comprising this anthology.

DANIEL ABRAHAM
Jonathan Hive

1: Who the fuck was Jetboy? Posted Today 1:04 am
HISTORY, JETBOY | REFLECTIVE | 'THESE ARE THE FABLES'
– THE NEW PORNOGRAPHERS

Who the fuck was Jetboy?

My grandfather tried to tell me when I was too young.
I didn't get it. A flying ace, he said, from before there was
the wild card. I could never get my head around that. How
could you have any ace – much less one who flew – before
there was the wild card? And that all happened back
during the Great Depression, which was right before
Napoleon who took over after Rome fell. My grandfather
hadn't kissed a girl yet when Jetboy died. That was forever
ago.

My sense of history has gotten a little more nuanced
since then. I know there was a Middle Ages, for instance.
I understand that women existed before Christina Ricci,
though I'm still not entirely sure why they bothered. I've
read all the underground R. Crumb comics about the
Sleeper. My dad told me stories about the Great and
Powerful Turtle. My fifth grade babysitter – who smoked
pot and sometimes forgot to wear her bra – told me lurid
tales about Fortunato, the pimp ace who got his powers
from sex. I saw Tarantino recycle all the tropes of Wild
Card Chic, trying like a lifeguard on amphetamines to
breathe new life into them.

When I drew my ace, I thought it was the coolest thing
ever. I wasn't Jonathan Tipton-Clarke. I was Jonathan
motherfuckin' *Hive*. I was hot shit. I was the kid who really

3

could sting like a bee. Let me assure all of you out there
that nothing but nothing stops bullies picking on you
like being able to turn into your equivalent mass of small
wasplike stinging insects; it shuts those rat bastards *down*.
I figured I didn't need to go to school or worry about how
a swarm of wasps was going to pay for an apartment. I was
sixteen and an ace. I was God.

Maybe that was why Grandpa always wanted to talk
about Jetboy. Jetboy, who didn't have any powers. Jetboy, who tried to stop the wild card from coming into the
world and failed.

Jetboy (I thought, through all my youth and adolescence
and most of my adulthood to date) was a great big loser
who died half a century ago. But here's the thing: He was
a hero to my grandfather, and my grandfather was not a
stupid man.

When Grandpa started junior high, there were no aces
in the world. When he started high school, there were. He
was alive when the virus hit. He read about the 90 percent
that drew the black queen. He heard rumors of the first
jokers back when people still hid them away like they'd just
crawled out of a David Lynch flick. And he saw the first
aces. Golden Boy. The Envoy.

How can I imagine that change? How do I, or anyone in
my generation, put my mind back to think what it would
have been like in a world without jokers, much less a jokers'
rights movement? A world where we didn't think that aliens
existed? Where phones had actual dials, and no one locked
their car doors?

It's hard – it's always been hard – to look back at that
kind of simplicity and ignorance and not sneer. We know
better now. We know *more*. We were raised on President

4

Barnett. We saw pictures from the Rox war. We always knew that if we happened to be around when two aces started fighting each other, they might bring the building down, or cut us down with laser eye beams, or turn us to stone without even meaning to; we could die at any time, in any way, and there was no way to protect against it. You couldn't expect us to get choked up over a guy who fell off a blimp before our parents were born.

Most people my age think of history as being divided into two essential halves: before the Internet and after. But there was a shift before that, and maybe there have always been shifts, back through history. Maybe every generation has seen the world change forever, and we don't know only because we weren't there.

Ace or not, I grew up. I went to college. I got a degree and trust fund that I'm rapidly spending down. I write a few magazine articles, and I'm working on a novel. I'm an ace, and that's great. But I'm a journalist, too – or will be when I catch a break. Being able to turn into wasps won't help me meet deadlines or pick the right words or forgive a cent of my electric bill. So, maybe what Grandpa was trying to tell me sunk in after all. Or maybe I missed his point and made up one of my own.

Here's the best I've got, folks:

Jetboy was the end of a world. He was the last man to die before the wild card came, and his age died with him. He is a symbol whose meaning I will never understand, except in the way I've come to understand King Arthur, JFK, and all the other beautiful losers of history. He will never mean to me what he did to my grandfather, and not because I'm more sophisticated or smarter or more jaded. It's just that the world's moved on.

To me, Jetboy's a reminder that there have always been people – a few – who fought for things that mattered. And (cue the violins, kids) that maybe being a hero isn't just about whether you win. Maybe it's also about whether you die memorably.

How's that for a Hallmark moment?

2 COMMENTS | POST COMMENT

♠

DARK OF THE MOON

Melinda M. Snodgrass

Somewhere off to her right gunfire erupted.

Anywhere else in the world people would flee that sound, but here in Baghdad it was just one theme in the symphony of celebration. The sharp chattering of a machine gun set a high-pitched counterpoint to the deep bass booms of rockets. A shower of golden sparks hung in the night sky, and edged the needle-like spires of minarets like a benediction. The sparks seemed to fall in slow motion. The light from the fireworks briefly lit the faces of the crowd. Men whirled and danced. Tears glinted on their cheeks, and their mouths stretched wide as they chanted for their Caliph.

Kamal Farag Aziz, the new president of Egypt, had come to Baghdad to submit himself to the Caliph and make his nation one with Syria, Palestine, Iraq, Jordan, and Saudi Arabia, under the restored caliphate. In Cairo, Baghdad, Damascus, East Jerusalem, and Mecca, the masses celebrated. In Lebanon, Qatar, and Kuwait, the leaders of the few remaining sovereign Arab states were shivering.

Lilith pulled the edge of her *shimagh* across her nose and mouth. Partly it was to disguise the fact she was a woman, but it also kept the dust, raised by thousands of shuffling, stamping feet, from choking her. Only in Iraq could you smell the rich, moist tang of water and reeds, chew on grit, and endure nighttime temperatures in the high nineties. Her robe clung to her body, and she felt a trickle of sweat inching its maddening way down her spine. When Saddam had lived in the palace the acres surrounding the building had been given over to lush gardens. The Caliph had chosen not to take water from Iraqi farmers, and allowed the gardens to die.

From her vantage point near the palace wall Lilith could see the looming bulk of the palace. The white marble walls were washed in a kaleidoscope of colors as the fireworks display continued. A man dressed in snowy white robes and *keffiyeh* stepped out onto a third-floor balcony. He paced, rested his hands on the carved balustrade, peered down into the crowd, paced again, and vanished back into the room.

Idiot, Lilith thought. *Get yourself killed by a stray bullet.*

She waited until one particularly spectacular fireworks display lit the sky and every head craned back in that particular kind of amazement unique to yokels. Then she swept the folds of her *dishdasha* and *jalabiya* around her body and felt that strange, internal *snap*, as the surface beneath her sandals changed from dirt over concrete to less dirt over polished marble.

Prince Siraj gaped at her. He was handsome, but his smooth round face and the bulge of a belly against his robes showed the dangers of sufficient food for a Bedouin. No matter that the royal house of Jordan had been out of the desert for four generations. Two thousand years of subsistence living was bred deep in the bone, and it whispered constantly that this meal might be the last for a long, long time.

'Are—' He coughed and tried again. '—Are you the one Noel sent?'

'You better hope so.' Lilith stepped into the room. A breeze off the Tigris stirred the white fabric of the mosquito netting that swaddled the bed. An elaborate mosaic of multicolored stone covered the floor. It depicted King Nebuchadnezzar hunting waterfowl in the rushes. But of course, Saddam had been a secularist. Lilith wondered how long until the Islamic purity patrols of the Caliph would destroy this art.

'I have your clothes.' Siraj lifted the folds of black material from the bed and thrust the *abaya* and *burqa* into her hands.

She pulled off the *shimagh*, and her waist-length black hair tumbled free. Siraj stared at her. At five-ten, Lilith was a couple of inches taller than the prince. Her only worry was the silver eyes, legacy of the wild card, but fortunately the Muslim requirement of modest downcast eyes for women worked to her advantage.

'Noel said you were in school together?' she asked as she dropped the tentlike garment over her body. With one of her blades she cut discreet openings in the material that she could reach through.

'Yes. At Cambridge. We were great, good friends. He loves our culture.' The sentences emerged in agitated little bursts of sound.

'Would a friend put you in this position?' Lilith asked. The mesh was disconcerting to look through, and the veils reduced her peripheral vision. She felt naked beneath the layers of cloth.

'I can be a bridge,' the prince said as he paced around the room. His hands kept clasping and unclasping. 'Between our two worlds.'

'It's just one world,' Lilith said, then added, 'Do you have the map?'

'Yes.' He handed her a piece of paper, and hurriedly pulled back his hand when their fingers brushed.

Lilith wondered at the avoidance. He had been educated in England, and lived for long periods in the West. Perhaps it was just the proximity of the Caliph that had him jumpy. She looked down at the paper. It looked like a cross section of a honeycomb. 'A little hint would help. You know, insane religious nutters sleep here,' Lilith said.

Siraj flushed at her drawling British delivery. 'He changes rooms … frequently.'

'Well, that's … irritating.'

'He's become increasingly paranoid.'

'Understandable. He was nearly assassinated by his sister.' She gave Siraj a bright smile, then realized he couldn't see her features. *Ridiculous culture.*

Siraj plunged on as if she hadn't spoken. 'Even though I'm on his council, I think … well, I think he doesn't trust me any longer. It started when the Righteous Djinn arrived. The Djinn disapproves of Western education. He thinks it taints us.' The hand washing had become even more fervent. 'You mustn't fail.'

'Relax. Tonight you have a pro.'

The prince looked around as if expecting the walls of the room to collapse in upon them. 'It may not be as easy as you think. The Djinn accompanies the Caliph everywhere. He is enormously strong, and he can become a giant.'

'Good thing we're indoors.'

Her light response didn't please Siraj. 'Since you find the Djinn unworthy of concern, you might remember that there is also Bahir.'

'I'm very aware of Bahir.'

But it didn't stop the nervous flow. 'Bahir can teleport. Many an enemy has been surprised to find his scimitar suddenly behind them. It's the last surprise they have before they're beheaded.'

'Little flamboyant, don't you think? A gun would be easier and far more certain.' She was very aware of the pistol strapped to the inside of her thigh.

'Well, yes, it's a stereotype, but it's also symbolic. The street loves it.'

'All that symbolism is why the Arab has found himself despised and dismissed.' Lilith looked at the map again. 'I can't just go teleporting into rooms hoping to find the Caliph. Do you have any idea where he'll be?'

'He's at the banquet now,' the prince said, 'with the Egyptians. Aziz.'

Kamal Farag Aziz. Egypt's new strongman had come to power when the meddling Americans had forced a free election that swept out the secularists in power and swept in the fundamentalists of Ikhlas al-Din. 'Is your absence going to be problematic?'

Siraj shook his head. 'I took ipecac. No one doubted I was sick.'

'Ah, ipecac. Every British schoolboy's delight.' Lilith paced. 'Well, I can't crash the party.' The folds of the *burqa* twisted around her legs. 'Is the Caliph a typical male? Is he going to stay with the boys 'til dawn?'

'He is a serious man, not given to frivolity.' Siraj paused.

Lilith seized on the thoughtful look. 'What?'

'He is close to Nashwa, his first wife. He often shares his triumphs with her.'

'Good thing I'm a girl.'

'What are you thinking?'

'That I've always wanted to see the inside of a harem.'

♣

There were a pair of soldiers on guard outside the door to the women's quarters. Their dull dun uniforms were brightened by the presence of the green kerchief tied at their throats. Their eyes swept across her and dismissed her in a blink.

In a thick country accent, Lilith said, 'The Caliph has sent this for his beloved wives, but the Caliph, great is his glory, will not mind if his brave and loyal soldiers sample a few of the delicacies.'

They echoed her words of praise, and Lilith held the tray while the young men helped themselves to sugar. She noticed they both had dirty fingernails. Lilith then slipped under their arms and tapped lightly on the door. The heavy panel fell shut behind her, cutting off the bass rumble of male voices.

The large room she had entered was lovely, but not grandiose. Through a whitewash of paint she could make out the faint colors of a mural that had once graced the left wall. The air was redolent with the smell of rosewater and orange oil.

Two women stood at the window, peeking through the curtains at the continuing fireworks display. Red, blue, gold, and green light washed across the fabric and their faces. One was enormously pregnant – her face was swollen and her fingers puffy. From the way her belly hung, she looked to be within days of delivery. The other woman was at that midpoint in a pregnancy when a woman seems to glow.

Curled up on a couch was a much younger woman – late teens, maybe early twenties. She was far prettier than the other two, and not just because she didn't look like a gravid cow. She flipped the pages of a French fashion magazine with such rapidity that she couldn't actually be absorbing anything. Her lower lip thrust out, and a frown furrowed the golden skin between her brows.

Lilith offered the food tray first to the pregnant women. They grabbed at the sweets with greedy fingers. She moved to the young wife. The girl took a small slice of melon.

Lilith took the chance. The worst it would earn her would be a slap. 'I went to school in Paris,' she said softly. 'Before my father sent the family home.'

'Your accent,' the girl said. 'You sound Saudi.'

'I'm from Kuwait.' There was a wealth of emotion in the final word. 'Have you been here long?'

'Three months.'

'You must be homesick.'

The girl started to cry.

'I'm sorry, mistress. Would you like me to leave?'

The girl's hand clutched at Lilith's sleeve. 'No, tell me about Paris.'

Lilith mingled her actual visits to the city with evocative scenes from movies. She talked of the restaurant boats draped with lights sliding beneath medieval bridges, and setting the reflection of Notre Dame in the water to dancing; of strolling through the outdoor stalls on the left bank of the Seine where old men with hunched shoulders and shabby jackets peddled even older books. To Montmartre, where children fed the pigeons, and aspiring artists painted the famous church. Lilith took her rapt listener past the open doors of bakeries where the smell of bread and pastries hung so rich and heavy in the air that you could practically chew it.

The young wife's eyes held excitement, but also resentment. Lilith wove a tale of her own frustration with an autocratic father who had been inspired by news of the rise of the new caliphate, and had sent his family home so her brothers could be part of this renaissance of Islam. 'While he stayed in Paris,' the young wife said, and a touch of acid laced the words.

Lilith shrugged. 'Yes, but he's a man. So are they all, except for our glorious Caliph, long may he live and reign.'

'Yes, he is a good man,' the girl admitted.

'What is he like? Have you spent much time with him? Is there a chance he will come by? I would love to see him. I've only seen him at a distance.' Lilith rushed the questions and statements, giving the girl no opportunity to answer.

The wife laughed. 'No, sorry. He won't come. He always sends for one of us.' The lush lower lip protruded again. 'And it won't be me. Not tonight. He'll want to talk to Nashwa.'

Nashwa, late forties, first wife of the Caliph, and mother of his son and heir, Abdul-Alim. Daughter of a prominent Yemeni business-man. 'I will go and offer her refreshments,' Lilith said. She stood and gathered up her tray.

'She's in her room,' the youngest wife said, and pointed vaguely down the hall. Lilith started away. 'By the way, I'm Ameera. What's your name?'

'Sura,' Lilith answered, and enjoyed the private joke. It meant to travel at night.

♥

'*How dare you*? You knock and receive permission before entering.'

Jeweled beads on the edge of the headdress emphasized the black frown that twisted the older woman's face. Nashwa was far from a beauty. In fact she was plain, and her voice clanged rather than lilted. She had to be the wife of the Caliph's heart, otherwise he would have divorced this hatchet-faced woman.

Lilith didn't respond to the rebuke. She crossed the room in four long, fast steps, grabbed the woman's arm, and forced it up behind Nashwa's back, immobilizing her. Lilith then pictured the room in the Uffizi Gallery that held the collection of Roman busts, and took them there.

There was that dislocating moment of dizziness and extreme cold. The stone floor beneath her slippers gave way to the softer sag of wood. Nashwa screamed in her ear. Lilith released the woman, wrapped her hand in the folds of her *burqa*, and gave the frame of a large painting a tug. Alarms began their shrill-throated cry.

Lilith teleported back to Nashwa's room in the Baghdad palace. The Italian police would hold the woman for hours. By the time they accepted her story and affirmed her identity she would be a widow.

Back in the room Lilith threw off her drab black *burqa* and donned one of Nashwa's. It was still black, but the material was of top quality and it was shot through with metallic silver thread. She settled the headdress over her hair and felt the sapphires and pearls jiggling cold and sharp against the skin of her forehead. Over it all she tossed the outer robe that shrouded even her eyes. Lilith sat down to wait.

♦

Three hours passed before she was summoned.

The Caliph had sent four guards to escort his chief wife. She might be a mere woman, but the guards were obsequious because she was the Caliph's woman. *Chief wife. The mother of his eldest son.* Nashwa wielded bedroom and pillow power. Lilith touched the knives that rested in sheaths on her thighs and the small of her back, and the gun she had for insurance. They turned down another hallway. This one was narrower still. Three floors below, Lilith could faintly hear the rumble of male voices and the wail of musical instruments. She caught a whiff of roasted lamb and cinnamon. Her stomach grumbled. Lilith promised herself dinner and a glass of cabernet as soon as she was back home.

They went up a narrow staircase. Two soldiers led the way. Two walked behind her. They were now on the top floor, and the roof and ceiling radiated the heat accumulated from the day's sun. Sweat trickled slick and sticky between her breasts and down her back. She longed to scratch at the itch beneath her bra strap.

How dreadful to be the ruler of much of the Middle East and have to live in such discomfort because you're so afraid.

One of the soldiers tapped on a closed door. There was a muffled response. The door opened, and the soldiers bowed Lilith into the room. The door fell shut. Someone behind her had closed it, but she was in blinders from the layers of clothing and veils. She concentrated on what she could see through the mesh that covered her eyes.

The room was small, whitewashed, its walls adorned with flowing script. Verses from the Koran. *Yes, it looks like the bedroom of a religious wingnut*, Lilith thought. A narrow bed and a side table with a glass water pitcher were the only furniture. Oddly, the bed didn't rest against the wall. It was pulled out a few feet, and there was the cut of a door in the plaster. *Bolt hole.*

She heard the footfalls of the man who had closed the door behind her and turned to greet him. But it wasn't the Caliph. It was the Righteous Djinn. He was taller and younger and broader. The lips exposed between the black beard and mustache were thick and moist, and he sucked at the lower lip like a child contemplating a knotty problem. Oddly, his eyes were gray.

He was still normal size, but quite large enough for Lilith's taste. He wore boots beneath the traditional white robes, and she wondered if the clothes enlarged with him, or if he ended up a thirty-foot naked giant.

'Honored One?' the Djinn said, but it wasn't a greeting. A query hung in the words.

I'm supposed to do something, Lilith thought, *but I don't know what. Oh, bloody hell.*

'Lady, we must speak.' His voice was a bass rumble, and he had a peasant's accent. 'I must know that you are … yourself.' It was one of the better euphemisms for mind control that Lilith had heard, but it didn't help her situation.

It had been only a delay of seconds, but it was enough.

The Djinn's face hardened with suspicion. He lunged forward. Lilith danced back, and caught her heel on the trailing hem of her *burqa*. The Djinn managed to get one arm around her waist. He was frighteningly strong. The pressure drove the hilt of the knife sheathed at the small of her back deep into her skin. He ripped away the concealing veils to reveal her silver eyes. '*Abomination!*'

Lilith tried to teleport and found the power retreating like a wave, while lethargy blanketed her limbs. Now she understood how Sharon Cream, Israel's strongest ace, had been subdued. A wild card power was at work here.

She felt the first licks of panic. She pushed them away. It was the fear that killed you. She forced herself to analyze. The ability to drain her power was probably a mental power. They required concentration. Concentration could be broken.

A warm sense of well-being flooded her body. Rather than fight it, Lilith allowed herself to go completely limp.

The Djinn gave a grunt of satisfaction. The full lips were lowered toward her mouth. She reached through one of the cuts in her *burqa* and closed her hand around the butt of her small pistol. His mouth was on hers. The reek of his breath caught in her throat. *Pig.* She pulled free the gun, pressed the barrel against his elbow, and pulled the trigger. The report echoing off the walls was almost drowned out by the Djinn's bellow of agony. The most painful injury to the human body had once again worked its magic. The injured arm fell limp to the ace's side. Lilith drove the heel of her boot down onto his instep, then spun away. The Djinn swung his good arm, and clipped her gun hand. The pistol went flying and she fell to the floor. Her legs were flaccid. His eyes were wild, curses emerged in a staccato roar, and the arm dripped blood as he charged down on her. With the last of her strength Lilith gathered her power, felt the *snap*, and teleported just as she heard the door crash open and the confused bellows from the guards.

She ended up in one of the hallways she had traversed only a few moments before. She would have only seconds before the alarm would be raised through the entire palace. Quickly she pulled out the map. It was time for a bit of misdirection. They would be looking for a woman. *So, let's give them women.*

Snap. She was in the laundry where women labored in the heat. Lilith grabbed two of them, swept the folds of her *burqa* around all three of them, and teleported away. The women's screams set her ears to aching as they appeared in a first floor hallway. The marble walls amplified the sound. There were male shouts and the thunder of booted feet running toward them. As Lilith teleported away she heard the chatter of a Kalashnikov, and a woman's piercing scream. She couldn't believe her luck. They had actually opened fire. Panic had clearly gripped the palace. It could only help her.

Lilith grabbed two more serving women and two of the dancers who were eating in the kitchen. She used them to season the stew of growing confusion. A stitch sent white hot pain up Lilith's side, and her shoulders and back were aching. It hadn't been easy controlling the hysterical, struggling women. She rested against a wall in an alcove and waited for her breathing to slow. She heard a high and querulous tenor voice call out. *Abdul the Idiot has taken command. Perfect.*

'Lock down all the gates. No. Wait. Not until the military arrives. Turn on all the lights in the gardens.'

'That will kill our troops' night vision, my prince,' another voice warned.

'Oh, yes. Well, issue night goggles.'

'They have night goggles,' came another voice.

'Oh, yes, right.'

'Shouldn't we stay with your father?' another asked.

Which implies the Caliph has changed location, Lilith thought.

'No. We must find the crusader assassin.'

Lilith teleported back to Prince Siraj's room.

He gave a shout of alarm then relaxed when he saw her. 'What's happening? Have you done it? I heard gunshots.'

'Pandemonium. No. Yes,' Lilith said. 'How much does the Caliph love Nashwa?'

'A lot.'

'Is he a coward?'

'No.'

'Thank you.' Lilith teleported away, certain now where she would find him.

♠

The Caliph whirled as the pop of displaced air announced her arrival.

In the dimly lit bedroom the green glow that emanated from his body was apparent. His black hair was flecked with gray and his beard had two long streaks of silver that ran from the corners of his mouth. He was dressed in white robes and she could see the line of puckered brown across his throat where a sister's knife had once failed to cut deep enough. Then he had only been the Nur al-Allah, and the restoration of the caliphate had only been a dream.

The Nur's eyes telegraphed the lifting of his pistol. Lilith seized a pot of face powder off Nashwa's dressing table and flung the contents into his face. He jerked his head to the side, and spoiled his aim. But it had been a near thing. Lilith felt the heat from the muzzle flash across her face, and the report set her ears to ringing. There were female screams from beyond the door.

She ran for the bed. As she passed the door she slammed it closed and threw the bolt. It wouldn't hold for long, but she only needed minutes. Jumping, she landed on the mattress and used its spring to increase her speed and the height of the jump. She lashed out with her foot as she arced over the Nur's head, and caught him hard on the jaw. With her trailing foot she kicked his hand and wrist, and felt bones snap.

The second kick had the desired result – he dropped the gun – but it wrecked her trajectory and she fell harder than she'd hoped, onto her hip. Clenching her teeth against the pain, Lilith rolled to her feet and drew a knife from the sheath strapped to her leg. The Nur shook his head, trying to throw off the effects of her first kick.

Lilith rushed forward, but he turned to face her and drew the ceremonial dagger he wore in his leather belt. The hilt might be jewel encrusted, but the blade was all business, and a good deal longer than Lilith's knife. They circled each other in the knife fighter's hunched and forward-leaning stance.

'Who sent you?' His voice was rough, like an old crow. Once it had been liquid velvet and had enthralled thousands.

'The world.' Lilith shifted sideways as he made a quick lunge. She slapped aside his hand, and let her knife slide up his arm to cut the tendon above his elbow. The wound made it almost impossible for him to keep hold of the knife. Thundering kicks set the bedroom door to shivering.

'You can kill me, but you cannot destroy what I've built here.'

'You're right. But we can own it.' She allowed a tinge of her accent to color her perfect Arabic. It had the desired result.

'Infidel! Crusader!' He lunged for her again.

'Don't forget imperialist.' She kicked a small ottoman in front of him. It tangled between his feet, and he went crashing to the floor. She let him get to his knees then darted behind him, drove the knife into his chest, and tipped it upward searching for the tough muscle that was his heart. The steel found its mark. Blood, warm and sticky, poured across her hand, and its tangy, sweet scent filled the room.

The bedroom was off-limits to security cameras. She had to find some way to shift blame. *Five for one.* She remembered the old motto of the Black Dog and his joker terrorists. The Djinn had seen her eyes. Knew she was a wild card.

The door was almost down. 'The Black Dog sends his greetings,' she shrieked in a high-pitched voice. For an instant the blows on the door stopped, then renewed with increased fervor.

Lilith picked up the Nur's pistol, and teleported away. She needed four more victims. The final misdirection.

♣

JONATHAN HIVE

Daniel Abraham

2: JONATHAN HIVE SELLS OUT!

Jonathan went over the release form again, flipping the paper back and forth. The time he'd spent trying to parse memos from Senate campaigns just didn't help much when it came to these West Coast entertainment wonks. The whole point of the exercise, after all, was to get something he could write about. If the first thing he did on day one was sign away his rights, he might as well go fill out an application at Starbucks and be done.

He looked up and down the parking lot. Great silver buses and trucks filled the place, sound equipment and shoulder-mounted cameras making their way to the secular cathedral of Ebbets Field on the backs of scrungy-looking technicians. A folding table had been set up with a tarnished coffee service and a few boxes of donuts. Several of the other prospective contestants were milling around, trying to size each other up.

'Is there a question I can help you with?' the flunky asked through a practiced smile. She was early twenties, long-faced, and mean about the eye. Normal-looking people who lived in the beauty pits of Hollywood too long seemed to get that feral I'm-not-a-supermodel-but-I-might-kill-one look after a while.

'Oh,' Jonathan said, whipping out his own smile, 'it's just ... I'm a journalist. I have this blog, and I don't quite know what I can and can't talk about there. If I did get on the show, I couldn't really afford to take however many months just *off*.'

'Of course not,' the flunky said, nodding. 'This is just the release for the tryouts. If you're chosen for the show, there's a whole other process.'

Which didn't even *sort* of answer Jonathan's question. He smiled wider. They'd just see which of them could nice the other to death.

'That's great,' he said, shaking his head. 'I just had one or two tiny questions about the wording on this one?'

'Sure,' the flunky said. 'Anything I can help with. But it is the standard release.' Meaning *move it, loser, I've got a hundred more like you to get through.*

'I'll make it quick. I really appreciate this,' Jonathan said. Meaning *suck it up, jerk, I can stall you all day if I want to.*

The flunky's smile set like concrete. Jonathan killed half an hour niggling at details and posing hypothetical situations. It all came down to the same thing, though: If he wanted in, he'd sign. If he refused … well, the field was full of aces who were there for the express purpose of taking his place. He kept up the tennis match of cheerful falsehoods until the flunky's smile started to chip at the edges, but in the end, he signed off.

He sidled over to the coffee and donuts just long enough to confirm that he didn't want anything to do with either, and then a vaguely familiar blond guy with a clipboard rounded them up and led the way across the tarmac and into the entrance of the ballpark. They were divided into ten groups and then each was led to a camera and interview setup, where a small bank of lights was ready to make him and all the others glow for the camera. Of his group, he got to be the lucky bastard who went first.

'Don't worry about the camera,' the interviewer said. 'They just want to see how you come across through the lens. Just pretend it's not there.'

She was much prettier than the flunky, dressed a little sexy, and willing, it was clear, to flirt a little if that made you say something stupid or embarrassing for the viewing public. Jonathan liked her immediately.

'Right,' Jonathan said. The five-inch black glass eye stared at him. 'Just like it's only you and me.'

'Exactly,' she said. 'So. Let's see. Could you tell me a little bit about why you want to be on *American Hero*?'

'Well,' he said. 'Have you ever heard of *Paper Lion*?'

A little frown marred the interviewer's otherwise perfect brow. 'Wasn't that the ace who—'

'It's a book,' Jonathan said. 'By George Plimpton. Old George went into professional football back in the 60s. Wrote a book about it. I want to do something like that. But for one thing, football's for the football fans. For another thing, it's been done. And for a third, reality television is for our generation what sports were for our dads. It's the entertainment that everyone follows.'

'You want to ... report on the show?'

'It's not that weird. A lot of guys get into office so they can have something to write in their memoirs,' Jonathan said. 'I want to see what it's all about. Understand it. Try to make some sense of the whole experience, and sure, write about it.'

'That's interesting,' the interviewer said, just as if it really had been. Jonathan was just getting warmed up. This was the sound bite fest he'd been practicing for weeks.

'The thing is, all people really see when they see aces is what we can do, you know? What makes us weird. These little tricks we've got – flying, or turning into a snake or becoming invisible – they define us. It's doesn't matter what we *do*. It just matters what we *are*.

'I want to be the journalist and essayist and political commentator who also happens to be an ace. Not the ace who writes. This is the perfect venue for that. Just getting on the show would be a huge step. It gives me the credentials to talk about what being an ace is. And what it isn't. Does that make sense?'

'It does, actually,' the interviewer said, and now he thought maybe she was just a little bit intrigued by him.

One step closer, he thought. *Only about a million to go.*

'Okay,' she said. 'And Jonathan Hive? Is that right?'

'Tipton-Clarke's the legal last name. Hive's a *nom de guerre*. Or *plume*. Or whatever.'

'Right. Tipton-Clarke. And what exactly is your ace ability?'

'I turn into bugs.'

♥

American Hero was the height of the reality television craze. Real aces were set up to backbite and scheme and show off for the pleasure of the viewing public. And it was hosted, just for that touch of street cred, by a famous celebrity ace – Peregrine. The prize: a lot of money, a lot of exposure, the chance to be a hero. The whole thing was as fake as caffeine-free diet pop.

And yet ...

He'd woken before dawn in his generic little hotel room, surprised by how nervous he felt. He'd eaten breakfast in his room – rubbery eggs and bitter coffee – while he watched the news. Someone tied to Egyptian joker terrorists finally assassinated the Caliph, a Sri Lankan guy with a name no one could pronounce had been named the new UN Secretary-General, and a new diet promised to reduce him three dress sizes. He'd switched channels to an earnest young reporter interviewing a German ace named Lohengrin, who was making a publicity tour of the United States to support a new BMW motorcycle, and then given up. He dropped a quick note to the blog, just to keep his maybe two dozen readers up to speed, and headed out.

The subway ride out to the field had been like going to a job interview. He kept thinking his way through what he was going to do, how to present himself, whether his clothes were going to lie too flat to crawl back into when he had to reform. He'd half-convinced himself that his trial was going to end with him stark naked. He could always pause, of course. Leave a band of unreclaimed bugs just to preserve modesty; like a bright green insect Speedo. Because *that* wouldn't be creepy.

Now, actually sitting on the benches the Hollywood people had put out for them and watching the lights and cameras and the milling, he was starting to feel a little less intimidated. He and the other contestants were in four rows of benches just inside the first-base foul line. The three judges – Topper, Digger Downs, and the Harlem Hammer – sat at a raised table more or less on the pitcher's mound. The invisible mechanisms of television production – sound crew, cameras, make-up chairs, lousy buffet – were kept mostly between home plate and third base. The great expanse of the outfield was set aside for the aces to prove just how telegenic they were.

Which, you could say, varied.

Take, for instance, the poor bastard whose turn it was at present. He had his arms stretched dramatically toward the small, puffy clouds, and had for several seconds, as his determined look edged a little toward desperate.

'What are we waiting for?' Jonathan whispered.

'Big storm,' the guy beside him – a deeply annoying speedster by the name of Joe Twitch – muttered back. 'Maybe a tornado.'

'Ah.'

They waited. The alleged ace shouted and curled his fingers into claws, projecting his will out to the wide bowl of sky. The other aces who had made it through the interview were sitting on folding chairs far enough away to be safe if anything did happen. The morning air smelled of gasoline and cut grass. Joe Twitch stood up and sat back down about thirty times in a minute and a half.

'Hey,' Jonathan said. 'That cloud up there. The long one with the thin bit in the middle?'

'Yeah?' Joe Twitch replied.

'Looks kind of like a fish, if you squint a little.'

'Huh,' Twitch said. And then, 'Cool.'

The public address system whined. The Harlem Hammer was going to put the poor fucker out of his misery. Jonathan was half sorry to see the guy go. Only half.

'Mr. Stormbringer?' the Harlem Hammer said. 'Really, Mr. Stormbringer, thank you very much for coming. If you could just ...'

'The darkness! It comes!' Stormbringer said in sepulchral tones. 'The storm shall *break!*'

An embarrassed silence fell.

'You know,' Jonathan said, 'if we wait long enough, it's bound to rain. You know? Eventually.'

'Mr. Stormbringer,' the Harlem Hammer tried again, while

behind him Digger Downs pantomimed striking a gong. 'If you could … ah … John? Could you take Mr. Stormbringer to the Green Room, please?'

The vaguely familiar blond guy detached himself from the clot of technicians and walked, clipboard in hand, to escort the man out of the stadium. Jonathan squinted, trying to place him – café-au-lait skin, a little epicanthic folding around the eyes, blond hair out of a bottle.

'Aw, man,' he said.

'What?' Twitch demanded.

Jonathan gestured toward the blond with his chin. 'That's John Fortune,' he said.

'Who?'

'John Fortune. He was on the cover of *Time* a while back. Pulled the black queen, but everyone thought it was an ace. There was this whole, weird religious thing about him being the antichrist or the new messiah or something.'

'The one Fortunato died trying to fix up?'

'Yeah, he's Fortunato's kid. And Peregrine's.'

Joe Twitch was silent for a moment. The only thing that seemed to slow him down was trying to think. Jonathan wondered if he could buy the guy a book of sudoku puzzles.

'Peregrine's producing the show,' Twitch said.

'Yup.'

'So that poor fucker's working for his mom?'

'How the mighty have fallen,' Jonathan said dismissively. A new ace was taking the field – an older guy, skinny, with what appeared to be huge chrome boots, a brown leather jacket, and a '40s-era pilot's helmet, with straps that hung at the sides of his face like a beagle's ears.

'Thank you,' the Harlem Hammer said. 'And you are?'

'Jetman!' the new guy announced, rising up on the little cones of fire that appeared at the soles of his boots. He struck a heroic pose. 'I am the man Jetboy would have been.'

'Oh good Christ,' Jonathan muttered. 'That was sixty *years* ago. Let the poor fucker die, can't you?'

Apparently, he couldn't.

Of the constant stream of wannabes presenting themselves to the world, Mr. Stormbringer had been the worst so far, but the guy who called himself the Crooner hadn't managed to do much either. And Jonathan's personal opinion was that Hell's Cook – a thick-necked man who could heat up skillets by looking at them – was really more deuce than ace, but at least he was a good showman.

And there had been some decent ones, too. Jonathan's bench-mate, Joe Twitch, had made a pretty good showing and also managed to be so abrasive it was clear he'd be a good engine of petty social drama. The six-five bear, Matryoshka – who split into two five-eight bears when you hit him, and then four five-footers, and so on, apparently until you stopped hitting him – had been decent. The eleven-year-old girl carrying her stuffed dragon had seemed like a sad joke until she made the toy into a fifty-foot, fire-breathing, scales-as-armor version of itself. She'd also had a bag of other little stuffed toys. Even Digger Downs had dropped his comments about wild card daycare. Jonathan was willing to put even money she'd make the cut.

Jetman finished his presentation to polite applause, and the blond – John Fortune – appeared at Jonathan's side.

'Jonathan Hive?' Fortune asked.

'That's me.'

'Okay, you're up next. We're going to be filming from cameras two and three,' he said, pointing at a couple of the many setups in the stadium. 'The judges all have monitors up there, so if you have the choice, it's better to play to the cameras than the people.'

'Great,' Jonathan said, mentally remaking his presentation. 'Okay, yeah. Thanks.'

'No trouble,' Fortune said.

'Any other advice?'

Fortune looked serious for a moment. He was a good-looking kid, but maybe a little lost around the eyes.

'You're the guy who turns into wasps, right? Okay, the guy on camera two is really afraid of bees, so anything you want to do up close to the lens, go for camera three.'

'And that one's camera three?'

'You got it,' Fortune said. Jonathan redid his routine again.

'Cool. Thanks.'

Jonathan took a deep breath, rose to his feet, and walked forward to the clear area that Jetman had vacated. Jonathan nodded to the judges, flashed a smile at the other aces, and stepped out of his loafers. The grass tickled the soles of his feet.

'Anything you'd like to say? No? Well, then, when you're ready,' Topper said.

It felt like breathing in – the comfortable swelling of the chest and rib cage – but it didn't stop. His body widened and became lighter; his field of vision slowly expanded. Distantly, he could feel his clothes drop through where his arms and legs had been. A couple bugs were tangled up in them, left behind like nail clippings.

Jonathan rose up above the crowd, seeing them all at once through hundreds of thousands of compound eyes. Hearing their voices even over the hum of his wings. He had no particular form now, and the joy of flying, the freedom of his swarm-shaped body, thrilled and vibrated in him. He hadn't really cut loose in days. He had to focus and think about his routine. He brought his multiform attention to bear on the crowd, picked a woman sitting in clear view of camera three who looked game, and sent a tendril of wasps to her. When they landed on her lap, he could see her stiffen, and then as he moved the tiny bodies to spell out words, relax slightly.

It is okay. Do not be scared.

He covered her in a bright green, crawling ball gown, then burst back up into the air and sped to the end of the stadium and back, circled around, and then it was time for the grand finale. It was hard to consciously form his body, and his kinesthetic sense was fairly rough, so he sent a couple wasps to sit on top of camera three and concentrated on the view through their eyes.

Slowly, carefully, he adjusted the swarm into a smaller, tighter, angrily buzzing mass. When the insects were thick enough to block the daylight, he moved. It was like dancing and also like trying to balance a pencil. The swarm that was his flesh took shape – huge, floating, ill-formed letters. EAT AT JOE'S.

He took the swarm back to his fallen clothes, the insects crawling into the spaces within the cloth and pushing gently out to allow another few wasps in and then more and more as the bugs congealed again into flesh. He was tired and exhilarated. He took a bow to the polite clapping. The judges asked a couple of questions – yes, the wasps could sting; there were around a hundred thousand wasps in the swarm; yes, if he flew through insecticide, he would get viciously ill. Digger Downs called him Bugsy, the Harlem Hammer asked about his blog (an extra couple thousand hits if that made it to the final cut), and it was over. He walked back to his seat on the benches.

'Nice,' Joe Twitch said.

Someone gently tapped Jonathan's shoulder. The woman he'd volunteered for his demonstration. She looked different, now that he could only see her from one angle at a time.

'Hey,' Jonathan said, smiling.

'Hey.' She had a nice voice. Sexy. 'Jonathan Hive? That's what you call yourself? Well, Bugsy, if you ever try to feel me up like that again, I'll kill you. Okay?'

The woman's hand vanished in a burst of concentrated flame like a blowtorch and then popped back. She smiled, eyes hard, nodded once, and went back to her seat.

Jonathan turned back to Joe Twitch.

'Oops,' Twitch said.

'Yeah. Oops,' Jonathan agreed.

'You get that often?'

'What? Death threats?'

'Bugsy.'

'Oh, that. Yeah.'

« ll next »

AMERICAN HERO | EXCITED | 'AMERICAN IDIOT' – GREEN DAY

Well, it's official. I'm in. It's almost midnight, but this isn't getting posted until tomorrow sometime. As part of the deal with the network, I'm letting a guy in the legal department vet my blog posts while I'm on the show. Everyone wave to Kenny! (Hi, Kenny!)

[ED: Hi everyone – Kenny]

I've just gotten back from the getting-to-know-all-about-you party with my teammates. Chateau Marmont. Very John Belushi-died-here Hollywood chic. All the contestants were present, and there's twenty-eight of us, so grab your scorecards, kids. It's gonna be a bumpy ride.

I sat next to the Candle, whose ace powers appear to involve looking like his hair's on fire, across from the fattest woman I've met in recent memory – the Amazing Bubbles. I'm told that she stores kinetic energy as fat, and was apparently dragged behind a Cadillac before coming to the party, because, oh, my, God. The only one bigger than her was a Southern Baptist preacher in a bariatric wheelchair who calls himself Holy Roller and weighs in at six-hundred-some pounds. Neither of them turn out to be on my team, so I'm just hoping some of the challenges we're facing involve getting into an elevator.

(On a personal note: Yes, Grandpa, Jetman made it on, and your cap lock key's stuck again. Ask Gramma to fix it for you.)

After serving us dinner and recording all our conversations and interviewing each of us separately, we got assigned to teams. It wasn't quite the Sorting Hat, but it had some of that feel. Big ramp-up by Peregrine to each announcement, clapping, cheering, smiles – everyone has a drink, and then the next one up. By the end we were all pretty tipsy, so I imagine we made total assholes of ourselves, pouting and preening for the cameras. Frankly, I was too drunk to remember the details. I'll just have to catch it when it broadcasts, same as the rest of you.

I've been assigned to Hearts because God forbid the media ever do anything with the wild card virus that isn't a pun. There are three other teams: Diamonds, Clubs, and Spades. We all hugged and learned and grew and pledged to work together as a team until it stops being convenient.

Then we all piled into a limo and rode to our new secret lair. I shit you not. Secret lair.

It's an old mansion all tricked out to make Big Brother cream himself. Cameras everywhere but the bathrooms (and no bets that there aren't a couple undocumented features there, too) and a little confessional where we get to gossip and backbite to our dearest, closest confidant: everyone in the freaking world.

Let me introduce the contestants, Johnny. Team Hearts is:

Drummer Boy – aka Michael Vogali. Yes, *that* Drummer Boy. Percussionist for Joker Plague, seven-foot ohmigod, six arms, more tattoos than a biker's convention. He spent the whole dinner signing autographs and chatting up an ace who everyone called Pop Tart, but not to her face. Since I don't listen to Joker Plague and I'm not a thirteen-year-old fangirl, I was unaware that he has six built-in tympanic regions on his chest. Yes, he is his own drum set.

Wild Fox – aka Andrew Yamauchi. Nice enough fella. Apparently can do something with illusions that's all very thematically appropriate if you know a lot more about

Japanese mythology than I do. He'll be easy to identify when you watch the show. He's the one with the great big poofy fox tail. Seriously. He has a tail.

Curveball – aka Kate Brandt. Nice-looking girl next door. Anything she throws, she can not only control in flight but detonate on impact. She was showing off a little at the dinner and wound up exploding a water pitcher with a grain of rice. She may have been just an ee-tinsey bit drunk. In all fairness, though, she's pretty cute when she's drunk.

Earth Witch – aka Ana Cortez. Another of our carefully ethnically diverse team with, sex-appealwise, a lovely personality and great sense of humor, I'm sure. She can dig holes in the ground with her mind. Yes, I'm not making this up. One of our superheroes is a ditch digger of Mexican extraction. I'm not sure how this got by the Hollywood liberal politically correct establishment, but I think it's funny as hell. No disrespect intended; some of my best friends are vicious racial stereotypes.

Hardhat – aka Todd 'T.T.' Taszycki. Lest we be accused of not having some good old salt-of-the-earth, blue-collar types, there's Todd. A lifelong construction worker, Todd can create temporary girders with his mind. I'm not sure how he's going to play on the tube, since I haven't heard him speak a single sentence yet that was fit for broadcast. Anyone who thinks of the network as 'a damn friendly bunch of cocksuckers' is okay by me. (Hey, Kenny, can we say 'cocksuckers' on the Internet?)

Gardener – aka Jerusha Carter. She plants things. They grow. Gardener, get it?

And, of course, myself.

Now for the predictions:

First one out is going to be Gardener. Be serious.

'Stop, foul villain, or I shall carpet your lawn with giant daffodils!' How useful is that?

Drummer Boy is also going to be out within the first round or two. The guy's a rock star. One little thing to tweak his ego, and he's outta here.

And for evil team dynamics, keep your eye on Earth Witch versus Curveball. Earth Witch isn't the kind of girl that gets asked out to the dance, and Curveball ... well, like the poet said, everyone has a secret hatred for the prettiest girl in the room.

There's gonna be blood. Count on it.

80 COMMENTS | POST COMMENT

♦

from: Becca
to: Michael Berman
re: *American Hero* promo copy

Hey, Mike.

Here's the promotional copy and head shots for the *American Hero* print campaign, for your approval. Please get your tweaks and changes back to me by the 17th. Thanks. (There's two head shots for Tiffani, you'll notice, one normal and one where she's gone diamond. Let me know which one you want to use. Oh, and Alan wants to tint Toad Man green in his head shot, though it's my understanding that he's only green as a toad. What do you say?)

There will be four broadsheets, one for each team. We'll be slapping them on buses in the top twenty media markets, as well as the El in Chicago, the NYC subway, and most major airports. We'll also be using them as full-page ads in *People*, *Us*, *Entertainment Weekly*, *Daily Variety*, *Hollywood Reporter*, *Aces*, *TV Guide*, *Rolling Stone*, *Vanity Fair*, *Parade*, and assorted Sunday supplements. If Drummer Boy survives the first few cuts and makes a good run, I might be able to get him the cover of *Rolling Stone* as well.

We're also planning a major giveaway of promotional T-shirts the week that *AH* premieres. Each shirt will have the picture of a contestant on the front, with the team slogan and emblem on the back. The idea is one to a customer, so we can track the demand and get a better idea which contestants are most popular. And the deal with Burger King's about to close, so we'll also have a line of special promotional cups. Be the first kid on your block to collect all twenty-eight. We'll be tracking those, too.

Plus, we're lining up some regional media in the home markets of each contestant – print features, local television, etc. When the time is right, *Maxim* and *Playboy* have both expressed interest in doing photo spreads on some of our female contestants. *Maxim* has Jade Blossom at the top of their list, but Hef wants Curveball. Must be that whole girl-next-door thing. Maybe you could have Peregrine talk to her. *Playboy* worked for Peri once upon a time. I think my father still has the centerfold hanging in the garage. (No one seems to want Toad Man or Holy Roller to take off their clothes, can't think why.) So, take a look and shoot these back to me ASAP.

luv,
Becca

HELP IS WHERE THE HEARTS ARE.

ANA delves deep. Stone and soil, clay and sand,
they're all putty in her hands. She's the
EARTH WITCH!
Ana Cortez
Las Vegas, New Mexico

KATE's the all-American girl with the all-American arm. She'll zip
it past you or throw it through you. Nobody can hit
CURVEBALL!
Kathleen Brandt
Portland, Oregon

MIKE's large, he's loud, he's pierced, he has six arms and attitude
to spare. He'll rock you and he'll roll you. Let's hear it for
DRUMMER BOY!
Michael Vogali
On Tour, the World

Keep your green thumb, JERUSHA has ten green fingers. Mighty
oaks spring up from tiny acorns at her command. Here she is, the
GARDENER!
Jerusha Carter
Jackson Hole, Wyoming

JONATHAN bugs out at the first sign of trouble,
but he still packs a nasty sting. He's
JONATHAN HIVE!
Jonathan Tipton-Clarke
Washington, D.C.

T.T. walks the high steel and builds them strong and straight.
He's tough, he's tall, and he takes no crap off nobody. He's
HARDHAT!
Todd 'T.T.' Taszycki
Chicago, Illinois

Seeing isn't believing when ANDREW is around, so best not believe your eyes or your ears or your nose. Only the tail is real with

WILD FOX!
Andrew Yamauchi
Fresno, California

WHO WILL BE THE NEW AMERICAN HERO?

EVERYONE WANTS TO BELONG TO THE CLUBS!

BUFORD hails from down the swamp. Some say he's just a good ol' boy, but he's got him one mean tongue. Folks go green when they see

TOAD MAN!
Buford Calhoun
Loxahatchee, Florida

JAMAL takes a licking and keeps on ticking. Shoot him, stab him, burn him, and he'll be back for more. No one can stop the

STUNTMAN!
Jamal Norwood
Inglewood, California

The best-laid plans develop hiccups when PAUL's around. He makes men cry 'Gesundheit,' and women cry 'Oh, yes, oh, yes, oh, yes!'

SPASM!
Paul Blackwell
Denver, Colorado

PEARL knows all the secrets of the sea, and speaks the language of the dolphins and the whales. Go deep with

DIVER!
Pearl Olsen
Honolulu, Hawaii

TOM soars above his ancient lands on proud, strong wings, watching, guarding, remembering. Look, up in the sky, it's

BRAVE HAWK!
Tom Diedrich
Benson, Arizona

HALEY floats like a butterfly and hits like a piledriver. Light as a feather in the wind, hard as a ton of steel, that's our

JADE BLOSSOM!
Haley Mok
Redondo Beach, California

THADDEUS will knock you down, roll over you, and save your soul. Cry hallelujah, brother, and pray you don't get in the way of the

HOLY ROLLER!
Rev. Thaddeus Wintergreen
Natchez, Mississippi

WHO WILL BE THE NEW AMERICAN HERO?

♠

TROUBLE COMES IN SPADES.

That girl CLEO gets around. *Pop*, she's here, *pop*, she's there, *pop*, she's just behind you. Watch out for

CLEOPATRA!
Cleonida Simpson
Montgomery, Alabama

RACHEL has the bestest collection of stuffies anywhere. They're all so soft and cute and cuddly, just like the

DRAGON HUNTRESS!
Rachel Weinstein
Bayonne, New Jersey

An iron man from the Iron Range, WALLY has steel in his fists and a furnace for a heart. Rust never sleeps and neither does

RUSTBELT!
Wally 'Rusty' Gunderson
Mountain Iron, Minnesota

The KING is the mystery man from down along the border. Where is he from? What can he do? Who dares to look beneath the mask of

KING COBALT!
Name unknown
Somewhere in California

There's never a loser when ROSA deals the cards. Diva or demon, snake or lion, even death itself, they're all in the hands of

ROSA LOTERIA!
Guadelupe Maria del Rosario Garza
East Los Angeles, California

ALI likes to dust things up. The girl has got a little devil in her. From the land of Elvis and the Living Gods comes

SIMOON!
Aliyah Malik
Las Vegas, Nevada

JOHN burns bright by day and night in half a hundred hues. Let those who hide in darkness cower, and beware the light of

THE CANDLE!
John Montano
Durango, Colorado

WHO WILL BE THE NEW AMERICAN HERO?

––––––––––––––

THE DIAMONDS ARE OUR WORLD'S BEST FRIENDS.

MICHELLE is always blowing bubbles, but best not stand
too close when they start bursting. She's
THE AMAZING BUBBLES!
Michelle LaFleur
New York, New York

HOWARD is the man that Jetboy would have been. He's seen
The Jolson Story, but his own tale is just beginning. Make way for
JETMAN!
Howard Hawkwood
Philadelphia, Pennsylvania

IVAN is full of surprises. Like Mother Russia, the more you
pound on him, the more you have to deal with. He's
MATRYOSHKA!
Ivan Kazakova
Brighton Beach, New York

MEGAN was dirt-poor growing up, but now she's learned
to shine. A regular diamond in the rough is our
TIFFANI!
Megan McKnee
Boone, West Virginia

JOE be nimble, Joe be quick, Joe can snatch your
candlestick. You better bring your best game if
you want to go one-on-one with
JOE TWITCH!
Joe Moritz
Baltimore, Maryland

EMILY is the fastest grrl on wheels. Don't blink, or you'll miss her whizzing by. There, that's her, that

BLRR!
Emily Paige
Sunnyvale, California

Don't you dare call RAJ handicapped. His servants wouldn't take kindly to it. Step aside and clear a path for

THE MAHARAJAH!
Raj Chaturvedi
Seattle, Washington

WHO WILL BE THE NEW AMERICAN HERO?

CHOSEN ONES: I

Carrie Vaughn

The three-story brownstone burned. Tongues of fire crawled out of every window, waves of heat and clouds of smoke billowed up, choking the nighttime air. Shouts of residents trapped inside sounded over the roar of flames. People leaning out of windows, begging for help, were shadows against a backdrop of red fire. A nearby fire truck sat abandoned. Hoses hadn't even been hooked to the fire hydrant.

Ana stood on the curb and watched the inferno. Even a dozen yards away, the fire pressed scorching fingers against her face. She drew a breath and coughed at the dry, soot-filled stench. Horror at the sight froze her into inaction. This was too much. This was impossible. They didn't expect her to actually *do* anything, did they?

'We don't have any powers that can handle this,' said Drummer Boy, squinting at the glare of the flames. 'Unless somebody here is invincible and forgot to tell anyone.'

The joker Drummer Boy was over seven feet tall and had six arms. All of them were lean, powerful, and covered with tattoos, along with much of his torso – which contained a set of tympanic membranes. He really was his own drum set, and he usually went shirtless to show it off. He managed to stand with all six arms akimbo, hands lined up on his hips. With his shaved head, scowling expression, and firelight glinting off his skin, he seemed like a monster from legend.

Curveball, the pretty nineteen-year-old with a perfect figure and blond ponytail, brimmed with energy. 'Let's stop bitching and do this thing.' She dashed forward, toward the blaze.

She's crazy, Ana thought, hanging back by the curb.

The others – Hardhat, Gardener, Hive, Wild Fox, and Drummer Boy – followed Curveball. No one got close before the heat drove them back. It came off the building in shimmering walls. The air itself seemed to burn.

Hardhat reached out, seeming for a moment to paint his hand across the air. Along the wall in front of him, a structure appeared: one by one, glowing yellow I beams morphed into existence. They stacked into a scaffold that climbed to a second-story window, where one of the victims leaned out. But he couldn't convince the guy that the phantom I beams were real and would hold his weight if he climbed onto them.

'Come on, you fucking cock head! Get your sorry fucking ass down here! Jesus Christ!' he hollered. The victim kept shaking his head.

'I'll get him.' Drummer Boy ran for the scaffold. Using all six arms, he made short work of climbing the beams, and once at the top, braced himself while reaching for the victim. He winced away from a blast of sparks that poured from the window. The sparks, if anything, encouraged the man to take Drummer Boy's hand and allow himself to be coaxed from the window.

One down, at least. The flames seemed to be climbing higher, and the shouts from within continued. Drummer Boy helped a second victim climb from the window. Two rescued. Maybe this would turn out all right after all.

Ana's heart was racing, and she was just standing there. She clenched her fists, watching, praying. It was all she could do.

From inside, sounding over the crackle and roar of flames, a baby started crying. The sound was piercing, and jacked the tension to a new level.

Gardener pulled a handful of something from the leather pouch at her belt and flung it toward the building. Seeds. They instantly took root in the concrete and grew at a terrific rate. In minutes, vines sprouted and climbed, sending out leaves and tendrils, anchoring on the brick wall. Following Hardhat's lead, she used living vines instead of conjured steel.

Before the vines reached the first window, however, they blackened and caught fire. The plants collapsed into ashes.

'Damn,' she muttered.

'You got anything in there that can shoot water?' Wild Fox asked.

'There aren't any plants that shoot water,' she said, scowling at him.

Meanwhile, Hive rubbed his hands together in preparation of – something. His expression was uncertain, however. 'Maybe I can do some scouting. Find out where the people are so we don't waste any time searching.'

His outline fuzzed. Then, his shirt and pants collapsed, and in his place a swarm of tiny green wasplike insects hovered. The swarm maintained the outline of the man – a disturbing, wavering form, rather than anything with human features – and raised a nebulous, buzzing arm in salute. Then, he scattered. The swarm broke apart, zoomed to the building, and entered through three different windows.

'Is that bastard going to be okay?' Hardhat asked, staring. He'd built a second scaffold by another window and rescued a third victim.

In only a second, almost as quickly as they'd entered the building, the swarm returned, tendrils of insects shooting out of the windows and dropping to the ground. There, they coalesced, crawling together to form the shape of a man, kneeling and naked. 'Bugs and smoke ... don't mix,' he managed, coughing.

Wild Fox pointed. 'Dude, you know you're naked?'

Regaining his feet, Hive glared. 'Thanks very much. I might have missed that little fact.' With a bout of angry buzzing, his hip region snapped out of existence, to be replaced by a Speedo band of writhing insects. He went to retrieve his clothing.

'I bet the girls love that,' Curveball said, smirking.

He leered. 'You could find out.'

'We don't have time for this.' She drew a pair of marbles out of the pocket of her shorts. Then she wound up for the pitch. She threw with that odd softballer's pitch, the underhanded swing and snap. The marble flew, faster than a softball, faster than any thrown object had any right to fly. It burned through the air, glowing yellow, before impacting on the front door. The wood shattered with the force of an explosion. She threw the second one at a ground-floor window. The impact left a jagged hole in the side of the house.

'Great,' Hive said, deadpan. 'Now we can see the fire even better.' She glared at him.

Exposure to more air only made the flames larger and more ferocious. The baby was still crying.

Curveball turned to Ana. 'Earth Witch, you try something. We've got to do *something*.'

Ana shook her head. She wasn't going to open a hole in the ground just for the sake of doing something and run the risk of undermining the whole building. They hadn't been too successful so far, but that would take the cake of failures.

She said, 'Maybe we could try the fire hose.' Stupid idea, yeah. That didn't mean they had to stare at her like she was an idiot – like they were doing now.

Curveball and Drummer Boy glanced at each other, then ran to the hose and fire hydrant. They wrestled with it for a minute, without making progress. Buttoning up his shirt, Hive helpfully observed, 'I don't think you're doing that right.'

'Then you do it, Bugsy!' Drummer Boy said. He dropped the hose, which he'd been hoisting with all six hands.

The heavy nozzle yanked out of Curveball's grip. 'Hey!'

'Shit,' Drummer Boy muttered. 'Here, let me try.' Using brute force, he manhandled the nozzle into place and managed to wrench open the valve on the hydrant. The hose filled, writhed, and twisted out of their grip, spraying a sheet of water across the pavement.

'Watch it!' Hive shouted as a tail of the spray caught him.

'Stop standing there and help!' Curveball shot back.

Grabbing hold of the nozzle and pinning it down while Curveball attempted to wrestle with the hose, Drummer Boy muttered, 'This is great. This is just great.'

The baby's crying seemed to get louder.

They managed to maneuver the fire hose in place to spray water at the blazing windows, but by this time the flames were monstrous, engulfing the building. Shouting continued to emanate from within – more people needing rescue. They didn't have much time, and the minutes dragged painfully.

Then Curveball said, 'Oh my God.' She cupped her hands to her face and shouted, 'Hardhat! He's gonna jump! The guy's jumping!'

From one of the third-story windows, a man was climbing over the sill. Hardhat came running. 'Where?'

'To the right!'

Drummer Boy dropped the hose and made a dash for the window, as if he could actually catch a falling body, but it was too late. Hardhat only laid one of his I beams down before the victim landed.

'Motherfucker!' Hardhat shouted. Drummer Boy gave an angry shake of an arm.

They had no way of getting inside. They couldn't pull anyone out.

'Would somebody *do* something?' Curveball yelled. She kept saying that.

Hardhat, sweat and soot smearing his face, turned on her. 'What the fuck you want me to do? Blow pixie dust out my ass? I've *been* doing something!'

Gardener tried to step in. 'Arguing isn't going to help anything.'

'At least we're good at *that*,' Hive said, and he actually smiled.

Then they all started shouting at each other.

Some team, Ana thought.

'Maybe I can make it look like we're doing a good job,' Wild Fox said, flicking his fox tail. Suddenly, another Wild Fox – a young Asian guy with floppy black hair and a quirky grin, fur-covered fox ears, and a luxurious fox tail poking out the back of his jeans, swishing like a banner behind him – ran from the building, carrying the latest teen pop star in his arms. She wrapped her arms around his neck and planted dozens of kisses on him.

Ana looked at him. 'I thought your illusions don't show up on camera. That isn't going to help us.'

He frowned. 'Crap.' The vision before them popped out of existence.

Then, an air horn blared. The flow of water from the fire hose slowed and stopped, cut off from another source. Floodlights snapped on, drowning the area in blazing white light. The seven Hearts squinted against the glare.

Inside the building, the fires died as the feeds from gas nozzles shut off. Four people walked from the building – perfectly safe, uninjured. They were stuntmen, wearing protective suits and helmets. A fifth climbed off the stunt mat set up at the side of the building. Hollywood magic at its finest. They removed their masks and smirked at the seven aces as they passed. The three who'd actually been rescued weren't any less accusing.

From a side doorway leading into the Hollywood backlot, a woman emerged. She wore designer jeans and a fitted, cream-colored blouse. With her statuesque frame and long brunette hair, she was already stunning, but one feature stood out above all the others: her wings, mottled white and beige, spectacular even folded back.

Peregrine crossed her arms and regarded the seven would-be heroes, who avoided her gaze. 'That was a little underwhelming. But I think I'll save any more criticism for the judges. Go home and wait for your next call.'

A half-dozen cameras captured the failure from every angle.

Team Hearts had their own Humvee for use during the show, tricked out and painted with their logo. The marketing gurus had thought of everything.

Hardhat drove, and for a long time no one said a word.

Finally, Hive broke the silence. 'Well. That could have gone better.'

Crammed into his seat in back, Drummer Boy snorted a laugh.

After that, the seven passengers glared silently out their own windows. The camera planted in the dashboard captured an image of profound disappointment, and it would play on millions of TV sets for all the world to see.

♠

Ana Cortez – Earth Witch, so-called – thought through the scenario again and again, and wondered what she could have done. Dug a hole. Dug a ditch. Undermined the building. And what good would that have done? None. Now the team had lost, and one of them would get voted off.

Almost, she wished she'd get the boot so she could go home and forget about all this.

Team Hearts headquarters was a sprawling West Hollywood manor, with a gated driveway, stucco walls, a luscious lawn and flourishing garden – the kind of place that played well on television and promoted the fantasy of a Southern California paradise.

All of it was just a backdrop for the drama.

Curveball – Kate Brandt – stormed from the garage into the combined kitchen and dining area. In her, the stunned disappointment of their failure had changed to fury. Jaw set, she turned on her slower teammates.

'They should have given us some kind of warning. If we'd been able to plan—'

Hive laughed. 'That's the whole point. We're not supposed to plan. We're supposed to face the unknown. Battle the unexpected.' Arms raised, he flashed his hands to emphasize his sarcasm.

'I thought they'd start with something small,' Andrew Yamauchi, Wild Fox, said. His tail revealed his disappointment, hanging almost to the floor. 'Rescuing kittens from trees or something.'

Hardhat – T.T. Taszycki – leaned against the counter. 'Makes you wonder what the fuck is next, don't it?'

Hive just wouldn't let up. 'Look at it this way – that farce back there was highly entertaining. It should get us a lot of air time.'

Curveball turned on him. 'Would you shut up? There was nothing entertaining about that! We were awful!'

Curveball and Hive faced each other down across the too bright kitchen, and any friendly sparks that had lit between them over the last week vanished. The others lurked around the edges of the room. Even Drummer Boy, all seven feet of him, managed to slink out of their way.

Jonathan Hive was too slick. He had a studied detachment, a journalistic objectivity that went a little too far – he was always an observer. He'd put himself on the outside, and he was used to commenting on everything.

He regarded Curveball and said with wry amazement, 'You're actually taking all this seriously, aren't you? That's kinda cute.'

He'd failed to observe that she'd already taken a marble out of her pocket and gripped it in her fist.

Ana spotted it. 'Kate, no—'

Too late. Curveball wound up her pitch and threw the missile at him.

'Whoa!' His eyes went wide, and his shoulder – where the marble would have struck – disintegrated with the sound of buzzing. The cloth of his shirt collapsed as the flesh dissolved into a swarm of tiny green particles, which scattered before the marble as he flinched away. A second later, the hundred buzzing insects coalesced, crawling under his collar and merging back into his body. The marble didn't touch him, but hit the wall behind him. A faint insect humming lingered.

To her credit, Curveball hadn't thrown the marble hard. She hadn't put all her anger into it. It would have only bruised him. But it did embed itself in the wall behind Hive and send cracks radiating across the paint.

He glared at the wall, then at her. 'I guess this would be a bad time to ask if you, ah, wanted to have dinner with me. Or something.'

She stomped out of the kitchen and through the French doors to the redwood porch. A moment later, Drummer Boy followed her. No doubt another camera would capture them and whatever heart-to-heart conversation they were having.

Back in the kitchen, Hive shrugged away from the wall, straightened his shirt, and for once seemed uncomfortable that he was the center of attention. Without a word – uncharacteristically without a word – he hunched his shoulders against their stares and stalked to the back of the house to hide away in his bedroom.

Seemed as good a plan as any, Ana thought, and did the same.

Break to commercial.

♣

This was all Roberto's fault.

A month ago, back home in New Mexico, Ana lugged bags of groceries into the trailer where she lived with her father and brother. Seventeen-year-old Roberto lay stretched out on the sofa, reading a magazine and watching the evening news in Spanish.

'You should watch in English,' Ana said. 'They want you to speak English in school.'

'Being bilingual looks really good on the college applications. It shows I'm in touch with my roots. They like that. Makes 'em look all multicultural.'

She unloaded the bags on the kitchen counter, shoving aside a newspaper, mail, and other trash. Roberto immediately sat up and protested.

'Hey – you're supposed to look at that!'

'What?' She'd started unloading groceries: cans and boxes in the cupboard, hamburger and juice in the fridge.

Roberto grabbed the newspaper and shook it at her. 'This – I put it out so you'd see it.'

'See what?' she said, losing patience.

'*This*!'

She took the paper and looked at the half-page ad he held in front of her.

Wanted: Contestants
AMERICAN HERO
Auditions in Seven Cities:
New York, San Francisco, Chicago, Houston, Miami,
Denver, and Atlanta
The Search for the Next Great Ace Begins!

The ad was simple, but the words screamed with purpose – somebody's crazy idea. What was Roberto thinking?

'What's this?' she said.

'*Ana*,' Roberto said, clearly exasperated. 'The next great ace? They're talking about *you*! You have to go to the audition.'

She shoved the paper at him and went back to the groceries. She had to get dinner started. Maybe Papa wouldn't feel like eating, but if he did, she'd have supper ready.

'Ana!'

'I don't have time. I can't take time off work. I can't get to Denver. Besides, they're not talking about me. I dig holes, that's all I do. There'll be people there who can do big things. Flashy things. Fireworks, you know? They won't want me.' She was just *la brujita*.

She expected more whining from him, her name spoken in an almost screeching voice. She didn't expect him to turn quiet, and very, very serious.

'You're wrong. The things you can do – you're an ace. You could move the world if you thought of it. You have to try. It's your chance to get out of here.'

Get out of here? She'd never even considered it. Roberto had the better chance of that. And someone had to take care of Papa. 'Roberto. I can't.'

'Ana. You have to.' A tricky smile grew on his face. 'I already called Burt. He gave you the week off. I got Pauli to loan me his truck. I'll drive.'

This was definitely a setup.

♥

They left the night before the auditions, packed a cooler with sodas and sandwiches, and stopped at a rest area near Pueblo to get some sleep. Before dawn, they continued for the final three hour drive to Denver. Ana spent most of the ride listening to Roberto's chatter.

'So maybe you don't make the show. But even if you do nothing else but dig wells for the rest of your life, you can do better than Burt. You oughta be getting paid more than what he's paying you.'

Burt didn't pay well, but he paid under the table, saving everyone a lot of trouble. She put away as much as she could for Roberto and college.

'I hear you can make a ton of money in off-shore oil rigs. You should try that.'

'I don't think I could do that kind of drilling.'

'You could try, couldn't you? Or maybe houses. You could dig foundations for all the houses they're building around Albuquerque. Don't you think?'

It was flattering, how earnest he sounded. He should have been the one born with the ace. He'd have made better use of it. 'Maybe,' was all she said, and he finally dropped the subject.

When they arrived at the stadium at around 8 A.M., the parking lot was already full and a line stretched along the sidewalk. She and Roberto stared, amazed. At first, she'd been surprised auditions were being held at the football stadium – surely, that many people wouldn't show up.

'Wow. This is crazy,' he said.

Even a brief glance at the line revealed that these were potential contestants, not spectators. Ana saw a woman with four legs and diaphanous green moth wings, a seven-foot-tall man with long, sharp-looking quills sprouting along his head and down his neck like a Mohawk, and another man with green skin and glittering red eyes, faceted like gems.

Among them stood dozens who looked entirely natural – but what could they *do*?

Roberto said, 'You get signed up. I'll find somewhere to park.'

She didn't think she'd have the guts to stand in that line without Roberto backing her up. But he'd gone through all the trouble to get her here. He'd be disappointed if she chickened out. She climbed out of the truck and watched her brother drive away.

A petite Asian woman holding a clipboard and wearing a headset with a microphone marked the end of the line. She had tribal tattoos crawling up both arms. Ana couldn't be sure, but they seemed to shift, literally crawling. She tried not to stare.

She asked Ana for her name, then asked, 'What can you do?'

'I dig holes,' Ana said.

The woman raised a brow, but gave a tired shrug as if to say that wasn't the worst thing she'd heard all morning. She handed Ana a square of paper with a number on it – '68.' 'All right, Ana, we'll be getting started soon. We'll have chairs set up for you on the sidelines. When your number is called, you'll talk to the judges, then show us your stuff. You need any props? Any kind of target or anything?'

Dazed, Ana shook her head. 'Just some ground. Some dirt.'

The woman smiled. 'You'll have the whole football field. Assuming it doesn't get blown up before you get in there.'

Denver was the second-to-last audition. The woman seemed to be speaking from experience.

Secretly, Ana sort of hoped the whole thing blew up before she got in there. She shouldn't have had that sandwich this morning. Her stomach was churning.

People were still joining the line. The guy in front of Ana was practically bouncing, rocking on his feet and gazing all around him with a face-splitting grin. He was about her age, twenty-one maybe, a clean-cut white guy with thick brown hair.

'This is so cool,' he said. 'This is going to be so cool. I so totally can't wait to do this.'

'What do you do?' she asked.

'It's a secret.' His grin turned knowing.

What could any of these people do, and how did her power compare? She was from a small town in the New Mexico desert. She'd never met another person infected with the wild card virus, and here she was, surrounded by them. Sixty-eight of them. More, because the line now stretched a dozen people behind her. A woman with feathers for hair. A young boy whose fingers were long, boneless, prehensile.

She was just another person in the line. It was almost a comfort.

Ahead, the line shifted, shuffling forward in the way of crowds. A renewed bout of nausea gripped her stomach.

Where was Roberto? It was going to be okay, she told herself. She'd dug a thousand holes in her life. She could dig this one, then go home.

She rubbed the shirt over her chest, feeling for the medallion she wore around her neck. It was the emblem of Santa Barbara, patron saint of geologists, miners, and ditch diggers, the image of a gently smiling woman with a chalice in one hand and sword and pickax in the other. Her mother had given it to her before she died, many years ago now. Most of her life, but Ana still remembered. So she wasn't on her own. A part of Mama was with her.

The wild card had killed Mama – she was a latent, and it finally killed her when Roberto was born. Ana carried that part of Mama with her, in her power.

Please, Mama, get me through this.

◆

The production company offered water, sodas, and sandwiches for lunch, and Ana forced herself to eat. They didn't want anyone passing out before they had a chance to show off. That was what they called it, showing off. To Ana, it had always just been her job.

Some of the normal-looking people weren't aces at all. They stood before the three judges, glaring dramatically, and nothing happened. Ana caught one of the exchanges.

The lead judge – at least the one who talked the most, the journalist, Digger Downs – asked the man, 'What is it you do?'

'I can control your mind.' He grinned wildly.

Downs stared back. 'Is that so?'

'Yeah. And you're going to let me on the show. I'm going to be one of your contestants, and I'm going to win!'

'Right. Sure. Next, please!'

'Hey, wait—'

Security hustled him away before he could get in another word. The auditions continued. For every dozen duds or fakes, someone came along who left the audience gasping.

Early on, a woman who called herself Gardener – slim, black, and intense – trailed a handful of seeds on the ground, in front of the judges' table. Instantly, they grew into trees, towering conifers that left the judges in their own little forest. Auditions halted for an hour while one of them, the strongman Harlem Hammer, up-rooted them and cleared them away.

Later, a good-looking, dark-haired guy in his twenties stepped onto the field and flexed his fingers. Donning a cocky grin, he flung out his arms like he was throwing a ball, and a stream of glaring blue flames jetted from his hands and struck the frame of a gutted car. A layer of frost and icicles formed on the metal, even in the midday heat. Then he fired yellow flames at the pile of Gardener's uprooted trees, which caught fire. Assistants were on hand to put out the flames with fire extinguishers. Finally, he faced the judges, hands raised, and he was on fire. His head and hands burned with writhing purple flames, and he was smiling, unharmed. He called himself the Candle.

This was exactly what Ana meant when she told Roberto there'd be flashy stuff here.

'Sixty-seven!' one of the production assistants called, checking her clipboard.

'Sixty-seven, Paul Blackwell!'

'Yes!' the guy in front of her exclaimed, then dashed for the field. He hadn't been able to shut up about how cool his power was.

For a long moment, nothing happened, and Ana wondered if he was another one of those nats who claimed vast mental powers. Then, one of the judges – Topper, the former government ace – sneezed. And sneezed again. And couldn't stop sneezing. Then the Harlem Hammer sneezed. Both of them were incapacitated, wracked with violent seizures of sneezing.

And Downs – he gripped the edge of the table, caught in some seizure of his own. He wasn't sneezing, but his eyes rolled partway back in his head, and his body twitched, almost rhythmically. *Oh my*, Ana thought.

Paul Blackwell crossed his arms and regarded them with a satisfied grin.

'Jesus Christ, would you stop that!' Downs shouted. The seizures stopped and the three judges slouched over their table, exhausted.

Topper wiped her nose with a tissue and said angrily, 'Mr. Blackwell—'

'I am *Spasm*!' the guy said, punching both arms into the air.

'Fine. I think we've seen enough of your – I hesitate to even call it an ace—'

'Hold on, not so fast,' Downs said, and Topper rolled her eyes. 'Er, Spasm. You say you can do this sort of thing to anyone?'

'Yes, sir!' he said, grinning. 'At least, so far.'

The three judges leaned together to confer, and a moment later Spasm left the field, grinning. Downs scratched a note on the paper in front of him. Then the production assistant called, 'Sixty-eight! You're up! Ana Cortez!'

Ana's heart raced. This was it. Finally. She spotted a guy up in the stands, waving both arms wildly. Roberto, among the spectators. He seemed so happy. The sight of him settled her.

Smoothing her hands on her jeans, she went to face the judges. The three looked so with-it, so assured of themselves. They'd recovered quickly from their encounter with Spasm, and their gazes were almost bored. Who could blame them? Surely they'd seen everything by now.

Downs asked, 'What is it you do, Ana?'

She'd said it a hundred times by now. 'I dig holes.'

'You dig holes.' His expression was blank.

'Yeah.'

'Well.' He shuffled some papers in front of him. 'Let's see you dig a hole.'

She stood alone at the edge of the field, a hundred yards of green spread before her. She'd never had an audience like this – not since she was little, digging mazes in the playground, when all the neighbors gathered and whispered, *brujita, es una brujita de la tierra*. This crowd didn't make a sound. The silence marked thick anticipation.

She closed her eyes so she couldn't see them.

Kneeling, she touched her medallion, then put her hands on the ground.

Had to be big. Something flashy. The holes she dug for work – nobody could see how far down they went. So she had to do something else. It didn't need to be precise, no one here was measuring. Turn the hole sideways, and dig it fast.

Now.

Particles moved under her hands, the dirt shifting away from her. The ground rumbled as it might in an earthquake. It vibrated under her, no longer solid, sounding like the soft roar of a distant waterfall. She opened her eyes just as a trench raced away from her. In seconds a cleft opened, splitting the earth to the opposite end zone. A hundred yards. Wide and gaping, it was four feet deep, angled like a steep canyon. Earthwork ridges piled up on either side, and a gray film of dust floated in the air above it. She'd cracked open the earth like an egg.

A few spectators coughed. The air was thick and smelled of chalk. She breathed out a sigh. Her heart was racing, either from the nerves or the effort. Her hands, still planted on the ground, were trembling, like they still felt the vibrations of the earth. She brushed them together, wiping the dust off.

Still, no one said anything. Ana didn't know what to do next. Stand up, she supposed. Go home. She'd shown them her trick, done what Roberto wanted her to do. Now he could take her home, as soon as the judges told her to leave.

The judges were staring. Ana realized: the whole crowd was staring, wide eyed, eerily silent.

She stared back for a long time before Downs pointed his pen at her. 'You're in.'

When he met her outside, the first thing Roberto said to her was, 'Told you so.'

♠

The next week passed in a haze. The production company took care of everything – plane tickets, schedules, publicity. Even a stipend. She gave the whole check to Roberto. They weren't going to have her pay anymore, at least not until she got back. She assumed she'd get back quickly – that she wouldn't win.

The production assistant with the tattoos, who called herself Ink, wanted to know what Ana's name was. The show seemed to have hundreds of assistants, each with their own little task, clipboards and cell phones never far away.

'Your ace name,' Ink explained. 'What we're going to call you on the show.'

'I don't have an ace name,' Ana said – then realized she did. She always had. She'd just ignored it.

'Well, we need to come up with one. Any ideas?'

'*Brujita—*' she started to say, then changed her mind. That was a name for a little girl. If she was going to do this, she ought to do it right. '*La Bruja de la Tierra*. That's what people call me.'

Ink frowned. 'That's kind of a mouthful. What is that, Spanish?'

'Uh, yeah.'

'What's it mean?'

'Witch. Witch of the Earth.'

'Earth Witch.' She scribbled on her clipboard. 'Yeah, cool, that's great.'

She walked off before Ana could argue.

♣

She'd grown up in a rickety trailer home at the edge of the desert, surrounded by Mexicanos like her, yet marked as different by her power, always the odd one. Now, suddenly, she'd been plucked from her old life and set down in a new one.

She certainly wasn't the odd one here.

At the meet-and-greet party in the dining room at a fancy old hotel in Hollywood, the contestants met each other for the first time and learned their team assignments. All of it was being filmed. *Don't look at the cameras*, Ana kept telling herself.

After a while, she almost forgot they were there.

She recognized the Candle, Gardener, and even Spasm from the Denver audition. Spasm waved at her across the room, hoisting his drink in salute. Everyone else was new, and she tried to figure out who they were and what they could do. There was Diver, the woman who had real gills. Rustbelt, whose skin was iron, whose touch could turn a car to rust, and who clanked when he moved. Then there was Drummer Boy, already a star as the front man for the band Joker Plague. Hard to miss, at seven feet tall. Not to mention his six arms. Ana felt even smaller among these – sometimes literal – luminaries.

Of course, she was put on a team with Drummer Boy – who immediately announced that he preferred to be called 'DB.' Then there was pretty blond Curveball. Ana was small and drab beside them. *Well, I'm not going to last long before they vote me off.*

'You look kind of nervous,' someone said. Startled, Ana turned to find Curveball – Kate was her real name – standing beside her.

'Yeah,' Ana admitted, 'aren't you?'

Kate shook her head, and her gaze gleamed as she looked around, taking in the old architecture and the crowd of people. 'No, this is exciting. I can't wait to get started.'

'So, I guess we're all on the same team.' A man in his mid-twenties, with scruffy brown hair and an amused expression, sidled up to them. He had his hands shoved in his pants pockets.

'You're Jonathan, right?' Kate said.

Jonathan Hive offered his hand for shaking, which she did. Ana was prepared to slink into the background, but he noticed her and shook her hand as well.

'Some of us seem to be a little more comfortable with this than others.' Jonathan nodded at Drummer Boy, who was signing autographs for some of the crew.

With all those tattoos and that oddly shaped torso with its living drums, it was hard to look away from him. He seemed to enjoy being the giant in the room. He especially seemed to welcome the attention of the women. *American Hero* was blessed with – or rather, the producers had been sure to choose – a stunning selection of beautiful women, of almost every ethnicity. With six arms, Drummer Boy could flirt with all of them – resting a hand on one woman's back, another on a different shoulder, while touching a strand of hair of a third.

The hair in question belonged to Cleo – or Cleopatra – who could teleport herself and whatever she was touching short distances, leaving behind a *pop* sound, as air rushed to fill the empty space. In response to DB's touch, Cleo laughed and sidled up to the joker, tucking herself by his side. Already, Ana had caught her new nickname among the production assistants: Pop Tart.

'Hey, is that Peregrine?' Kate said, and Ana turned to look.

It was, emerging through a hallway from another part of the building, followed by a lanky young production assistant carrying a clipboard and a cup of coffee. The talk show diva and perennial celebrity's wings fluttered slightly as she turned and addressed the assistant. Ana couldn't hear, but the exchange seemed odd – overly familiar, maybe. One hand on her hip, Peregrine pointed a finger, and the assistant nodded meekly at what turned out to be a lecture.

That wasn't a boss dressing down a subordinate, Ana realized. That was a mother admonishing her son.

Peregrine took the cup of coffee from him and turned her attention to another member of the crew, and the production assistant came toward them. He had coffee-and-cream skin and light, curly hair. Young, maybe twenty, his boyish face nonetheless had a tired look.

'Hi, I'm John Fortune,' he said. 'Looks like I'll be the traffic cop this afternoon. Let me show you where we need you to stand for the shoot.'

It took a half-hour for him to break up the party and herd everyone to where they needed to be for the publicity photo session.

John asked, 'Anything else you need? Is everybody okay?'

'I think we're fine,' Kate said, returning his smile. She looked around for confirmation. 'Yeah?'

'Great. We'll start in a couple minutes.' With a mock salute, he left them.

'I'd watch out for that guy,' Hive said to Kate. 'Charm, multi-ethnic good looks – you may be doomed.'

'Oh yeah?' she said.

'Yeah, I saw the way he looked at you.'

'Kind of like how you're looking at me?'

Hive quickly glanced away and pursed his lips. 'So what if I am?' Kate blushed, and Hive sighed. 'Whew, we haven't been here an hour and we're already making great TV drama.'

Another half-hour passed while the crew adjusted the lighting.

'Just like being on tour,' Drummer Boy muttered. He was nevertheless smiling.

'This show business stuff must be old hat to you,' Kate said, looking up at him.

'Old hat with a new twist. The scenery here's way better.' He winked at Kate, who actually giggled.

Oh, this was going to be a long day, Ana thought. She was so out of her league.

A man Ana recognized from the audition detached from the mob of crew and regarded them all, a lord surveying his domain: Michael Berman, a network executive on hand to observe the proceedings. He was in his thirties, slick and intense. Even Ana could tell his suit and tie were expensive.

'This is fabulous. Thank you all for helping make this a reality. I can't wait to see what happens over the next few weeks. And I'm sure I can count on you to make this the best show possible.' He rubbed his hands together with obvious glee.

'Is it a competition or entertainment?' Hive said with a smirk. 'The world may never know.'

'I don't think I like that guy,' Kate whispered to Ana.

Ana had to smile. 'I know what you mean.'

♥

The meet-and-greet was at the hotel, but the actual unveiling of the teams for the premiere of *American Hero* took place on a Hollywood sound stage that looked like a night club, all dark glass and chrome, touched with blue neon.

Peregrine was the emcee. In her fifties now, she was as poised and beautiful as ever, and her wings framed her perfectly. She wore a black strapless evening gown that shimmered gold when she turned, and her hair lay in loose waves around her shoulders and wings.

'Welcome to the first of what promises to be twelve weeks of excitement, astonishment, heartbreak, and – we hope – heroism the likes of which you have never seen. We've searched the country for undiscovered aces, for great powers, and for people who have the potential to change the world. This is *American Hero*.'

Then came the theme song, a pounding, blood-stirring rock anthem that would no doubt be hitting the charts in weeks to come. Peregrine introduced the judges, two who in their younger days had been beloved aces in their own right: Topper, wearing her trademark tuxedo and top hat, from which she could pull any manner of items, and the Harlem Hammer, the massive, super-strong ace who had been coaxed out of retirement. The third judge knew his aces – had reported on them for *Aces!* for going on twenty-five years. Who better to judge the up-and-coming generation?

Thomas 'Digger' Downs spoke seriously, regarding the camera as he would an old friend. 'After sixty years of living with the wild card, you'd think we couldn't be astonished anymore. That we couldn't be amazed. We've seen alien invasions, madmen with the power to take over the world, plagues of crime that steal away your very mind, strangers who can peer into your soul. Women who fly, men who lift tanks, deformities that strain our definition of what it means to be human. We've seen witch hunts, assassinations, politics run amuck, the world brought to the brink and back. You'd think that surely we'd seen it all.

'But I can tell you that we haven't. Over the last few weeks I've traveled from one end of the country to the other. And I have been amazed.'

He introduced the next segment: highlights from the seven auditions, potential contestants who tried and failed – sometimes to the great amusement of the audience – and those who tried and astonished.

A dozen concrete walls shattered.

A dozen cars rose from the ground, or disintegrated, or burst into flames.

A dozen bone-shattering falls were survived. A dozen aces flew to the tops of nearby buildings.

The sequence of clips paid special attention to the ace, Curveball. The show's editors were already deciding who their heroes were.

She threw a baseball with an underhanded snap. Her whole

body seemed to pop like a spring, and the ball flew, faster than any major league pitch. It glowed yellow, then orange, scorching the air it passed through.

Then it turned. Hand outstretched, Kate guided it. As if it had a mind of its own, it flew around an overturned bus, back through a maze of twisted rebar, and slammed into one of the stacks of concrete blocks that served as a makeshift wall.

The wall shattered with the force of an explosion. Concrete and dust flew in all directions and the sound rattled the seats all over the stadium. When the air cleared, the wall was gone. Disintegrated. The missile – a simple baseball, everyone was sure to note – had destroyed it.

Downs's prediction was right: The audience at home was astonished and amazed, and they couldn't wait to see more.

'Now,' Peregrine said, donning her brightest smile yet. 'Meet your new American Heroes!'

Twenty-eight contestants joined the winged beauty on stage, standing in groups of seven with their teams: Hearts, Spades, Diamonds, Clubs. It was glorious – lights flashed, music swelled, and it sounded like cheering.

Ana was caught in it all like a deer in the headlights, a tight smile locked on her face. Drummer Boy punched six hands in the air, and Wild Fox's tail flashed sparks as it twitched.

Amidst the thrills, elation, and chaos, Jonathan Hive tapped his wrist.

'All right, kids, check your watches,' he said. 'Your fifteen minutes starts now.'

◆

A week later, the party was over.

Four teams gathered on the same stage, which now served as the field of judgment. Behind each team, as part of the backdrop, was its logo: Hearts, Spades, Diamonds, Clubs.

No one knew what to expect, so the atmosphere was beyond tense. It crackled. The last time they'd stood here, the mood had been celebratory: They were the chosen ones, they'd been anointed.

Now, they had failed. They'd had their first trial, and they didn't feel good about it.

One team – Clubs – held itself differently. Their frowns were a bit more smug, their backs a bit straighter. Before any of them saw the replays, they could all guess who had won this round.

In fact, the replay of Team Clubs' assault on the burning building couldn't have been any more glorious if it had been scripted.

Stuntman did the impossible: ran into the burning building by the front door. Nearly invulnerable, he couldn't burn. He made three trips, pulling out four 'victims,' including the doll programmed with a digital recording of a crying baby. His clothes were scorched to nearly nothing, but Diver was on hand with a coat from the fire truck to cover him. The others had been more successful operating the fire hose. Jade Blossom increased her density, making herself an anchor to brace the nozzle. The water dampened the fire enough to clear a path in the front entryway. Two more people rescued. Brave Hawk, who manifested illusory brown-black hawk wings when he flew, had been able to pull another three victims out of upper-story windows, including the one who had jumped. The flier snatched him out of the air. And Toad Man, turned into his giant toad form, managed a particularly gruesome rescue by snatching the tenth and final victim out of a window with his thirty-foot-long, viscous tongue. All ten victims rescued.

Spades and Diamonds didn't achieve quite so spectacular a victory, but they each had their moments. On the Spades side, the Candle used his multipurpose, colored flames to build a glowing red ladder to the second-story windows. The victims within climbed to safety. Metal-skinned Rustbelt withstood the flames enough to save a couple of victims from the ground floor. The team, however, suffered a drawback when Simoon, in an attempt to quell the fire by blasting it in her whirlwind form, only succeeded in fanning the flames. Their rescue effort ended with five victims saved.

Diamonds fared better. The Maharajah, the easily overlooked man in the wheelchair, had telekinetically animated a half-dozen firefighters' coats from the truck and marched them into the burning house to rescue three victims. Matryoshka had split into four smaller versions of himself, and they controlled the hose as a well-coordinated unit. Their flier, Jetman, rescued several victims from the upper floor. Unlike Brave Hawk, though, he'd failed to catch the man who'd jumped. They'd rescued seven victims.

On the other hand, the editing on the replay of Team Hearts' trial brought to the fore every mishap, every wart, every fault. Hardhat's success was reduced to a second or two, making the highlight of the sequence Curveball, Drummer Boy, and Hive yelling at each other, Hardhat and Gardener fruitlessly running around searching for victims to rescue, and Earth Witch and Wild Fox doing absolutely nothing. At least the many bleeps punctuating Hardhat's speech got a few chuckles.

For a moment, all was quiet. The judges' weighty silence was worse than any criticism. The Hearts gazed back hopefully, as if they might escape.

Topper shook her head, and it was like an ax falling. 'Aren't you taking this seriously? Do you know how many people would be dead now if that had been a real fire?'

Seven, Ana thought. Seven people, even if one of them had been a fake baby.

The Harlem Hammer continued. 'Half of you just stood there. You gave up before you even tried anything because you couldn't figure out how to use your powers. You think it's all about your aces? And you didn't even try to work together.'

Then Downs inserted his own vitriolic assessment. 'You guys aren't a team, you're a preschool! I wouldn't trust you to look after my hamster!'

Ana could imagine watching this on TV at home, and how exciting it must be. How gleeful the audience would be, watching Downs cut them to pieces. But even if she'd had a chance to respond, there was nothing she could say. They weren't wrong about any of it. Her cheeks were burning at the reprimands. Kate's gaze was downcast, her jaw tight, as if she clenched her teeth.

All the groups were quiet, quivering with tension. Maybe they had imagined what it would be like to lose, what the judges might say to them, but they hadn't imagined anything like this.

When Topper announced that Team Clubs had won immunity for the first challenge, no one was surprised. Clubs' members gave each other high fives and hugged in celebration, but didn't cheer. They looked relieved rather than smug.

Peregrine spoke solemnly, like this was an execution and not network television. 'Hearts. Spades. Diamonds. Each of you will now return to your headquarters, where you'll decide who from your team to discard.'

♠

One of the judges accompanied each team to officiate the discard process. Just when Ana thought the evening couldn't get worse, Hearts was blessed with the presence of Digger Downs, who seemed far too gleeful in his role as the 'bad' judge.

Her stomach was in knots, which were tightening with every breath. On the drive back, she and her teammates kept glancing at each other, sizing each other up, making calculations: Who should go?

She wasn't worried so much about herself. What she really hated was having to make a choice.

In the garage, Drummer Boy lingered by the Hummer and waved her over with a gesture from an upper arm. Uncertain, she went to him, wondering what he could possibly want with her.

His voice hushed – and for such a huge, brusque man, he could make his voice surprisingly muted – he said, 'You know who you're picking?'

Ah, that was what he wanted to talk about. 'No.'

'You worried?'

'About what?'

He gave a huff, like he thought she was being stupid. 'You didn't do squat during the challenge. That puts you in danger of getting kicked out, you know that?'

She supposed it did. 'I hadn't really thought about it.'

'You ought to be making deals,' he said. 'Trade votes. Make sure someone else gets it.'

She couldn't do that any more than she could have stopped the fire by digging a hole under the building. She shrugged. 'I don't even know who I'd pick.'

'Bugsy,' he said. 'The guy's a prick.'

'What do you get if I pick him?'

'Don't vote me off the next time we lose. It's that simple.'

Downs called from the house for them to hurry up.

'I'll think about it,' Ana said, and hurried away from the towering joker.

She didn't want to make deals. She didn't want to vote anyone off. She shouldn't even be here.

Inside the house, in the no longer comfortable dining room, they gathered around the long table. Cameras watched them; all their expressions were somber, their shoulders tense. Hands clenched the backs of chairs, or tightened into fists.

Downs handed them each a thin pack of cards. Shuffling through them, Ana found only seven cards. Each one bore the photo of a teammate.

The judge explained. 'Each of you will place the card of your choice face down on the table—'

Suddenly, a dozen small, furry creatures appeared on the table, jumping over each other, squeaking, dancing. Ana gasped, and everyone took a step back.

'What the hell!' Downs said.

'Hamsters,' Wild Fox said, grinning like he was pleased with himself. His tail gave a flick.

Next to him, Curveball huffed. 'You would have to go pissing off the judge.'

Murderous looks glared at him across the table, and the hamsters popped out of existence. Wild Fox glared back, his tail drooping.

Downs sighed heavenward. 'Let's get this over with. Hearts, play your cards.'

Curveball only considered her cards a moment before drawing one and setting it face down on the table. Jaw set, she glanced around the table, confident, meeting everyone's gaze. At least she wasn't going to let this cow her.

So it went around the table. Drummer Boy and Hardhat quickly followed, then Wild Fox, Hive, and Gardener. Then they were all looking at Ana, waiting.

Ana studied the cards in her hand, the smiling faces so unlike the ones she saw around her now. Her teammates were waiting to learn their fates, and she was delaying. But she couldn't decide.

She wondered what would happen if she put her own card on the table. After all, she never wanted to be here. She could leave just as quickly. Nobody would ever know that she'd discarded herself – unless all seven cards showed her face. That was a distinct possibility; as DB had said, she hadn't done anything. If all seven cards showed her face, she'd have to explain to Roberto why she rigged her own downfall. So that wasn't going to work.

She couldn't think rationally. Everyone here had strengths. Everyone here would be useful, given the right situation. If they ever had to look for buried treasure, Ana would save the day. She couldn't use that criterion to judge. If it was a matter of picking who she didn't want to live with for the rest of the show, she'd have to say Wild Fox. Then again, maybe Drummer Boy had the right idea.

She put Hive's card face down on the table.

Everyone slid the cards to Downs, who shuffled them, arranged them in his hand, and studied them. He gazed around the circle at the contestants, then back at the cards – then back at the contestants, pursing his lips studiously, narrowing his gaze. Curveball rolled her eyes, and DB crossed a pair of arms.

Finally, Downs spread the seven cards on the table. They all leaned forward, searching, desperate to see how it had turned out. The faces seemed to blur in Ana's eyes.

Two of the cards showed Ana. Only two – Ana felt relief. One showed Wild Fox. And four showed Jonathan Hive.

'Four of a kind,' Downs said. 'Hives.'

For all his commentary, Hive didn't have a quip ready for this. He was still staring at the cards, and the four pictures of his own face looking back at him.

Downs gazed at him across the table. 'Jonathan Hive, I'm afraid you've been discarded. It's time for you to leave the house.'

They even made a production of that, though Ana would have liked nothing better than to hide in the bathroom, the only place off limits to the cameras. But no, they all had to watch Jonathan get his bag and trek to the front door. While the cameras watched, Hive shook hands with Wild Fox, Drummer Boy, and Hardhat, while they muttered things like 'Good luck' and 'Take it easy' to each other. Gardener and even Curveball offered awkward hugs. Ana was the last to shake his hand.

'Good luck,' he said, as he had to the others. He even managed a wink right at the end.

Ana thought she'd need the luck the most.

♣

Curveball sets her expression, as if this is just another challenge, another task to be completed on the way to the prize. Her eyes gleaming, she looks at the unseen interviewer, sitting somewhere to the left of the camera, and speaks with such energy her ponytail dances.

'Hive, Bugsy, whatever – I think he didn't take any of this seriously. All he could do was make jokes. He may be a reporter, but that doesn't give him a right to stand there and make fun of everything.

'When I was little, I dreamed of winning a medal in the Olympics, or being the first girl to play major league baseball. Then my card turned, and well, so much for that. But now ... I can do this thing that nobody else in the world can do. *All* of us can. And it isn't a game. It shouldn't be just a game.

'I want to do something great, and I can't understand when people look at all this like it's a joke. When I see someone like Earth Witch and what she can do – what she *could* do if she put her mind to it, but she isn't doing *anything* – it makes me crazy.'

♥

Finally, Downs and his crew left, leaving the remainder of Team Hearts alone – with the cameras, of course.

'It just doesn't seem right,' Curveball said, flopping onto the sofa. 'Kicking him off like that.'

'That's the game. Some poor bastard had to go,' Hardhat said.

'It's kind of mean.'

'Come on,' DB said. 'You hated the guy.'

'I didn't hate him. I was pissed off at him, yeah. But that's different.'

Wild Fox said, 'Watch, next week we're going to have a challenge that'll be perfect for a thousand little flying bugs, and he won't be here.'

DB said, 'Or maybe we'll need someone to star in a cartoon and Fox Boy here will actually be useful.'

'Hey, I'm useful!'

'Oh yeah?' the drummer said.

A room-sized Godzilla appeared behind the sofa, complete with ear-splitting squeals and flames shooting out of its toothy mouth. Everyone jumped. It didn't matter that Ana's rational brain told her it was just another one of his illusions. She dove behind a chair to hide. Kate screamed and fell off the sofa.

Wild Fox laughed, and Godzilla disappeared. This was going to confuse the TV audiences so much ... they couldn't see the illusions, only people's reaction to them. Maybe that was enough.

DB crossed all six arms. 'Great. When we come up against Mothra, we'll call you.'

'Would you guys stop fighting?' Kate said, picking herself up off the floor. 'We just have to do better next time. Then nobody gets voted off.'

Hardhat raised his hands in a gesture of surrender. 'You know what? Next time, just boot me the fuck off. Then I can get the fuck away from you fucking losers and get back to my *real* job. Fuck it. I'm going to bed.' He stalked out of the room.

Funny, Ana had been thinking exactly the same thing.

◆

Ana couldn't sleep. She and Kate shared a room, and she kept waiting for her to come in and turn on the light.

She'd had trouble sleeping the whole time she'd been here, and it was more than nerves. This place didn't have the right sounds – the desert wind against the siding of the trailer, the coyotes in the distance. This place was silent, sheltered from the sounds of the freeway, well-insulated. *Cocooned*, she thought. And she felt like ripping out of it. What would they do if she left the house and took a walk?

Was it even safe, walking after dark in this neighborhood? All she knew about L.A. was its reputation, and that didn't say anything good about walking by herself after dark.

Maybe she'd just get a glass of water.

She turned on her small bedside lamp. Kate's bed was still empty. She and DB had once again retreated to the back porch to talk long into the night. It figured – not only was Ana the shy one, she was going to end up being the only one of the group who didn't party.

Creeping out of the room, she stopped when she heard voices.

'You're going to win this thing.' The bass voice belonged to Drummer Boy.

'I don't know,' said a laughing, female voice. Kate. 'I want to, sure. But the field's wide open.'

'You're just being humble.'

'And I think you're coming on to me.'

Ana dared to edge out another few inches, and sure enough, Kate and Drummer Boy stood at the corner where the living room ended. Kate leaned against the wall, hands tucked behind her back, head bowed, smiling – and blushing, probably, but she was in a shadow and Ana couldn't see.

DB cast the shadow, his huge frame looming over her.

He'd crossed all six arms over his broad chest and leaned on the wall next to Kate – very close to Kate.

He chuckled. 'Can't fool you, can I?'

'Are you going to use that line on all the girls? "Hey, babe, I think you're going to win"?'

'No,' he said. 'I won't use that line on anyone but you.'

One of his arms uncrossed, reached out, and touched Kate's

cheek. Ana had to admire the gentleness he displayed, despite his massive body and strength. He had to lean far over to kiss her, but he even made that awkward motion seem graceful. A second hand closed on Kate's waist, the third brushed her hip.

The two kissed, lightly and briefly. He paused, as if waiting for her to react, and when she didn't, he kissed her again.

Then she slipped away. Smiling, gaze lowered, she ducked away from his touch, out of the cage formed by his arms.

'Michael, you're a great guy,' she said softly. 'But I don't think I'm ready for this.'

'But—'

'Maybe when this whole thing is over. When we're not so distracted. 'Night.' She touched his cheek briefly, then left him standing there, dumbstruck.

Ana slipped back to her bed, but Kate reached the room before she could shut out the bedside light and pretend she'd been asleep the whole time. Her hand was on the switch when Kate leaned against the doorway. 'I suppose you saw all that.'

Ana shrugged. 'Just think of me as another camera.'

'Oh my God, tell me about it. This would be way more fun if it weren't for the cameras.' They weren't supposed to talk about the cameras in front of the cameras. They weren't supposed to mention the elephant in the room.

Kate flopped on her bed. Watching her, Ana sat up, cross-legged. 'Michael?' she ventured.

'He says his friends call him Michael.' Kate's smile turned into a giggle. 'Can you believe it? A freaking rock star. I wonder what he sees in me.'

Ana didn't feel inclined to point out that she was thin, blond, cute, and the center of attention. Kate didn't linger on the thought long, though.

She went on. 'What's he thinking? There's too much at stake here to go screwing around. I know everyone's thinking it, who's going to end up sleeping with who before they even think about who's going to win the show. But *God*, it messes everything up.'

'What did you guys talk about? You were out on the porch for hours,' Ana said.

'Were we? I didn't notice.'

'If you don't want to say—'

'No, it's no big deal.' Her expression turned wry. 'Mainly, he kept going on about how hard it is in the music business to meet girls who are honest. "Real," is what he said. They're all after him because he's a famous rock star. I'm like, yeah, cry me a river, Mister Gold Record.' But she was smiling, and her gaze had turned inward.

Ana said, 'Let me guess. He says you're not like all those other girls. You're "real" and he wants to get to know you better.'

'Not only that, he goes into this thing about how he flirts with all those girls because people expect it, because it's part of the rock star persona, and that he actually gets tired of it.' She smirked. 'He never seems to look tired when Pop Tart or Jade Blossom glue themselves to him.'

'Wild Fox said he heard there was a bet on that he wants to sleep with every girl on the show.'

Shaking her head, Kate said, 'I don't think he's like that. I think he was serious about not being into the flirting. Just because everyone assumes he's going to sleep around doesn't mean he is.'

'You like him,' Ana ventured.

Kate shrugged. 'Sure I like him. But do I *like* him? I don't know. Not yet.'

Everybody – even Ana – looked at Kate and saw nothing but perfect. But her furrowed brow and pursed lips revealed something more going on under the surface. Kate certainly didn't see herself the way everyone else did, and it made Ana warm to her.

Grinning, Ana hugged her pillow. 'You want to wait and see who else shows an interest.'

'What?' Kate said, laughing.

'Come on, I saw you talking to John Fortune this afternoon.'

'I was asking him some questions.'

'Yeah, asking *him* some questions, not anybody else.'

Her smile turned shy. 'Well, yeah, but—'

'But what?' Ana prompted.

'He's definitely kind of cute.'

'Who else has been making eyes at you?'

'No one.'

'Jonathan Hive?' Kate rolled her eyes. Ana listed: 'Stuntman? Spasm?' That time, she winced. Then Ana said, 'Berman?'

'Oh my God, no!' Kate threw her pillow at her, and Ana grabbed it, laughing. The pillow threw off a static tingle of energy.

They settled back, too weary to exert much effort, too wired to sleep, and stared at the faded shadows the bedside lamp cast on the ceiling.

After a moment, Ana said, 'You should enjoy it.'

'Enjoy what?'

'All those interesting men are looking at you. Enjoy it.'

Ana couldn't read Kate's expression, her thin smile, the narrowed, sleepy gaze. She seemed to be working something out.

Then her smile widened. 'It doesn't mean anything if I can't decide who to look at back.' She glanced over. Now *that* was a wicked look.

'Oh, now you can cry *me* a river!' Ana threw Kate's pillow back at her, sending them both into a new fit of giggling.

For the first time since she'd arrived at the auditions, Ana started to relax.

♠

Days passed. No telling when the next challenge would arrive – when the alarms would scream, when they'd all pile out of the house to the Hearts' Hummer – and how stupid was it being Team Hearts? It was way too cute, way too obnoxious, like they were an ad for Valentine's Day – and they'd fight about whether they had enough gas or who could read the GPS locator correctly. At least Ana'd been able to do that much for the team – reading GPS coordinates was part of her job back home. Thank goodness Hardhat had been able to drive their monstrosity of a vehicle. Wouldn't that have been embarrassing, failing as heroes to the point of not being able to get the car started – all on national TV.

Ana thought she didn't care. But really, she'd prefer *not* looking like an idiot on national TV.

After supper she went out to the backyard. The sky had turned dark, and the air had cooled, though it still smelled tangy, metallic. This whole city smelled like an industrial work site. At home, even after a day of working around oil rigs and diesel fuel, she could walk away from it and smell real air – hot, dusty, but real. She was homesick.

You can bag the whole thing, a voice whispered … a small, devilish voice. *Do something really stupid next time, get yourself voted off, and that'll be that.*

But Roberto would know. Roberto would never let her live it down if he thought she'd thrown the contest.

Over the last week, Kate had spent hours in the backyard throwing things at makeshift targets, practicing. Maybe she had the right idea. Ana touched the medallion under her shirt.

She left the porch and sat cross-legged in the middle of the lush green lawn. Closing her eyes, she buried her fingers in the grass, pressing down to the roots, to the earth. The soil here wasn't like the desert – this was softened by the vegetation, by constant watering. This would be easy to dig. She could even feel what *wasn't* dirt – gas lines, sewer lines. She could dig around them.

She could drill a hole straight down, hundreds of feet. She could open a furrow ahead of her. Make it as deep or wide as she liked, limited only by the space available, though she'd never dug much more than a backhoe could do in an hour or so of work. She'd limited herself. She didn't want to cause too much trouble, do too much damage, so she'd always stayed within the boundaries of the sandbox, whatever sandbox she happened to be in.

This had all started in the sandbox, on the playground. If she'd grown up in a city full of concrete and asphalt, she might never have discovered her power at all. That might have been better.

Absently, without effort, she made little holes, because she couldn't think of what else to try. Scooped out handfuls of earth. They didn't even make a sound. Then, she dug two holes at once. Two dimples formed, one on either side of her, each with a mound of scooped-out earth beside it. Well, she'd never done that before. So she tried three. Hands in the grass, laid flat against the ground, she could feel the infinite particles of it spread all around her. They moved at her command. She clenched her hands and thought of digging – three holes, then four. With a faint sound of ripping grass, as the soil under the lawn tore free, a circle of holes appeared around her. A dozen of them, all at once. Patterns in the earth. She shifted her right hand, pointed to make a trench, but instead of making it straight, she made it turn. It ran in a perfect circle all the way around her, joining all the holes.

She hadn't played with her power like this since was she small. She barely remembered. Her father had put her to work tilling the neighbors' garden patches almost as soon as she'd dug her first hole.

'You are *really* making a mess.'

Hands on her hips, Kate stood at the edge of the porch.

Sheepishly, Ana brushed off her hands. The yard looked like gophers had struck: Dozens of mounds, holes, and trails marred the whole lawn. *Great*, she thought. *Now they're going to start calling me Gopher Girl.*

'Sorry,' she said.

'Don't apologize,' Kate said. 'It's kinda cool. But can you do anything else?'

Ana shrugged and glanced hopelessly around the damaged lawn. 'I'm trying to figure something out.'

Kate left the glow of the porch light and came into the dark, picking her way around piles of dirt and finding a spot of grass near Ana to sit on. 'Not that there's anything wrong with digging holes. If you did something like this under a building you could bring the whole thing down. Or a bridge, or a car, or ... or anything. You could stop anyone by digging a hole under them.'

She could dig a trench around herself a dozen feet wide and no one could ever reach her. 'It's all just digging. It's never going to rescue someone from a burning building.'

'Tell me about it,' Kate said. 'You dig holes, and I blow shit up. Hey – if this hero thing doesn't work out, maybe we can start a business: "Team Hearts: Demolitions and Excavations."'

'"Environmentally friendly,"' Ana said, and they both giggled.

Then Kate looked around, studying the lawn, turning serious. She put her hand on one of the mounds of dug-out soil and squeezed her fist around it, letting dirt run through her fingers.

'What is it?' Ana said.

'Just thinking. Look at all these piles. What if you tried to make piles of dirt, instead of just digging? Think about filling in the space instead of digging it out. Does that make any sense?' She wrinkled her forehead, which made her look particularly young and studious.

Dios! It was so obvious!

It couldn't possibly work. 'I don't know. I never looked at it that way.'

'Well, can you try it?' she asked eagerly.

All her life her father, the neighbors, everyone, said – dig this, put a trench here, drill a new well. Never *build*.

She held her hand flat to the ground, fingers splayed, *feeling*. Build, make – positive space, not negative space. Feeling the earth under her hand, she reached for it, gathered the particles to her – not for shoving them away, but bringing them together. It almost felt backwards. Make the mound of dirt instead of the hole.

Before her, the earth came alive. It moved, crawling like a million tiny insects, swarming together. A lump formed, then grew into a mound, then a tower, a cone of brown earth rising from the lawn. All around the tower, the level of the ground sank, as the dirt in the center rose. Reverse ditch digging.

The tower reached a height of two feet before Ana pulled her hand back and clutched the medallion under her shirt. Her heart was racing, and her eyes were wide. If she'd been able to build a tower outside that burning building, she could have saved someone.

Kate's face brightened with an amazed smile. 'That's so cool!'

'Yeah,' Ana said. 'Wow.'

'You could do anything, I bet. Bridges, tunnels, castles – hey, have you ever worked with sand?'

Ana laughed. 'No – I've been in California over a week and I still haven't seen the ocean.'

'That's crazy.' Kate's gaze was unfocused, still clearly thinking of all the ways Ana could use her power. 'You know how during a big earthquake the ground is supposed to ripple, like you can see the waves moving through it? What if you could do something like that – make your own earthquake and knock down an entire army or something.'

The image horrified Ana. She gave a nervous shrug. 'They're not going to be putting us against armies. I hope I never have to do anything like that.'

'Nice to know you could, though. If you had to.' Kate beamed at her, as proud as if she had the power herself. Her smile was clear, brilliant. Honest.

'Why are you helping me?' Ana said abruptly, and regretted it. She didn't want to sound ungrateful, not for Kate's help. Not for her friendship.

Kate shrugged, looking briefly confused, like she really didn't understand the question. Like she hadn't considered. 'Because I want to help.'

'But you see how it is,' Ana said, nodding toward the lighted windows of the house. 'They – the judges and them – all talk about teamwork, how we're supposed to work together. But we're all competing against each other. In the end, we have to turn against each other. We have to vote each other off. It doesn't help you at all if I – I—' She stumbled a moment, at first uncertain what to say. 'If I'm stronger.'

Again, for just a moment, Kate seemed young – a kid in a pony-tail getting ready for softball tryouts. 'If we win the next challenge, then nobody gets kicked off. That's the way I want it. The more you can do, the better chance we have of winning. It only makes sense.' Her smile brightened again, and turned sly. 'Besides, when it's the two of us in the finals, it'll be one bitchin' catfight.'

The two of them fighting each other? No, it wouldn't be like that. The only word Ana could think to describe it was ... *fun*. Her and Kate in the finals? That would be the best thing in the world. Alight now with possibilities, her power tingled in her hands, limitless. Her imagination built castles of earth, dug moats, moved mountains, continents.

She wasn't sure she'd ever want to change the world that much, though. It was enough to have control over her little corner of it.

And so, feeling strong, feeling mischievous, she moved the little square of earth Kate sat on. Tipped it back like a lever.

Letting loose a shriek, Kate fell back, rolling head over heels. She landed hard on her backside, and for a regretful moment Ana was afraid she'd been hurt – a broken bone or twisted joint – and it would be Ana's fault.

Kate blinked and gained her new bearings. The lawn where she'd been sitting looked lumpy – that was the only sign anything had happened. It was enough of a sign.

'Oh, you *bitch*!' But she was laughing when she said it. Then her hand closed on a nearby clod of dirt.

Ana knew exactly what was coming next. She reacted before the clod left Kate's hand. Hand on the ground, she whispered a quick prayer – and up rose a wall of earth, a protective swell like a soldier's quickly dug foxhole. Ana put it between her and Kate and nestled down to hide. Not that it helped, because Kate's thrown projectile – glowing yellow-hot and throwing off sparks – flew over the barrier and came zipping straight into Ana's hiding place. She squealed and rolled out of the way as the clod dropped hard to the ground just short of where she'd been sitting. Kate hadn't been aiming for her. Still, the missile kicked up a spray of dirt that pelted Ana.

Kate ran, dodging around Ana's foxhole, and her hand held another missile. Ana waited for her; Kate took aim, wild laughter glinting in her eye.

'You surrender?' she said.

Ana tried something new – that's what this was all about, after all – and once again felt for the ground under Kate's feet, but instead of rocking it, or digging it, she made it climb. She was getting better at making these mounds, these towers. She made the soil flow and creep over Kate's shoes, up her ankles – then held it.

'What the—' Kate jerked her feet, kicking them free. The earth wasn't hard and didn't hold her long, but it gave Ana time to scramble to the other side of her shelter. *Imagine what I could do with more*, she thought. If she could build the earth up around someone's whole body, bury them up to their necks so they couldn't move at all …

Now Kate had marbles in both hands. 'That's it. No more Miss Nice Guy.'

Suddenly Ana was in a war zone, dodging bullets that pounded into the ground all around her, zooming in from all sides. They weren't very big, and none of them came right at her – this was, after all, a game. But they kept her from fleeing, locking her into a small space on the lawn, and she was laughing at the dirt flying everywhere, at Kate's wild expression, and the increasingly chaotic state of the lawn.

They both turned to the sound of the back door opening. DB and Hardhat emerged, rushing to the porch railing to look over the lawn. Ana tried to catch her breath. Kate, also breathing hard, her hair matted with sweat, joined her.

Hardhat frowned at them with a look of bafflement. 'Christ, what the fuck are you two doing?'

Ana and Kate looked at each other. Ana, a gleam in her eyes, said, 'Demolitions and excavations?'

Kate burst out laughing, Ana joined in, and the two of them fell against each other, hysterical.

DB shook his head, and Hardhat said, 'You're damn lucky we don't have a fucking damage deposit on the line for this place.'

♣

The guys seemed just as taken with Ana's newfound ability. As they trailed inside, Hardhat mapped out great plans for their future exploits. 'I can totally fucking see it – you dig this big motherfucking ditch, like a moat, see? Like if we had to protect something – then I'll build a bridge, or a tower, or—'

Kate laughed. 'She can build a bridge! She can build us a tower and no one could touch us!'

DB nodded thoughtfully. 'Yeah. It's pretty cool.' As usual, his six hands were tapping to an unheard rhythm. Sort of. The rhythm seemed a bit off tonight, as if he were distracted. He kept watching Kate.

'Just wait,' Ana said. 'The next challenge will be at the top floor of a skyscraper. No dirt.'

'Well, aren't you Merry fucking Sunshine,' Hardhat said.

Kate was now staring back at DB. The drummer's patter faltered. 'Michael, is something wrong?' Kate said.

'Uh – no. I was just—'

'I'm talking about the drumming. You're all out of synch. I just wondered if something was wrong.'

DB froze. Too late, he started again, tapping a pair of hands on his knees, but it looked more like nerves than his usual accompaniment. Kate was tight – the beats were off. There wasn't a rhythm, just noise.

Kate picked a throw pillow off the arm of the sofa.

'Oh no, no—' DB said, holding out all six arms in defense.

Kate hurled the pillow at him. It hit his shoulder with a thump, and DB glimmered, then disappeared, leaving Wild Fox curled up on the sofa. The illusion had been destroyed.

'Geez, Curveball! No fair! You totally suck in a pillow fight!'

She stood over him, a second pillow in her hands. 'You're covering for him. What's he up to?'

'I'm not covering. I just wanted to see if you could spot it. And ... you can. So there.'

Wild Fox was not a very good liar.

Kate said, 'I wouldn't put it past you, but you're way too nervous to be just pulling a prank. What's the deal?'

Glowering, Wild Fox crossed his arms. 'He said he wouldn't vote me off next time if I covered for him.'

'So what's he doing?' She wouldn't let up.

'I don't know, I didn't ask!'

The phone by the kitchen bar rang. Wild Fox jumped for it, but Kate cut him off and beat him to the handset.

'Hello? Why, hello Cleo. No, Wild Fox isn't here.' Kate was looking right at him. 'I'd have thought you'd want to talk to DB.

He seems more your … speed. Oh, you *do* want to talk to him? Yeah, he's here.' Wearing a catty grin, Kate handed the set to Wild Fox.

Sullen now, Wild Fox shook his tail, and the illusion shimmered back into place. It was almost like a heat mirage, or a mist in the air. He rippled, then he was DB, all six arms and deep voice.

'Yeah?' he said at the phone and glared at Kate. After a moment of listening, he replied, 'Yeah. Okay.' Then hung up.

'So he's with Pop Tart.'

'I don't know, I just said I'd cover for him. I'm supposed to say I'm going for a walk and then come back in five minutes with Wild Fox. I mean me.'

'Then you'd better get going,' she said. That catty smile was starting to turn vicious.

Wild Fox/DB left, almost running, slamming the door behind him.

Hardhat stared at her. 'What the fuck was that all about?'

She just shook her head. 'This is so high school.'

He turned to Ana for explanation, but she shrugged. 'I don't know, but I'm betting on fireworks in five minutes.'

'Then let's bring the popcorn,' he said.

They all stood at the door, when DB and Wild Fox walked in, right on schedule. Kate, Ana, and Hardhat waited, leaning on the walls in the foyer.

DB froze when confronted with the faces looking at him. He threw a glance over his shoulder at Wild Fox.

The shorter joker grinned sheepishly. 'Sorry man. I'd have pulled it off, but apparently I got no rhythm.'

Ignoring them, DB barreled through the foyer without a second glance. Kate followed him, calling, 'Hey, *Michael.* You get lucky, or what?'

He turned on her, and for a moment he really did look like a monster, filling the room, hunching his shoulders and bracing his arms like he wanted to punch rocks. Kate stumbled back a step.

'Yeah, I did,' he said. 'Not that it's any of your business.'

This was when the screaming match started. Kate liked him, Ana knew. But maybe not enough to let this go. Or maybe too much to let this go. Ana readied herself to tackle Kate if she decided to throw something. She had that look, like when she lost her temper at Hive. Except this was worse.

But Kate didn't have anything in her hands. She didn't get mad, didn't scream, didn't cry. Very quietly, very calmly, she looked square at DB, and her face was a mask. When she spoke, her voice was low, cutting, like a scalpel. 'You really are just trying to get every woman here into bed before the show's over, aren't you? I had you figured out from the start.'

She walked out of the room.

The silence turned suffocating. Ana, Hardhat, and Wild Fox stared at DB like he was a train wreck.

Wild Fox said, 'Dude, I'm totally sorry—'

DB went after her, where she'd fled to her room. 'Hey, wait a minute. Kate!' His voice boomed.

Ana, in her turn, ran after him. She couldn't hope to get to Kate before he did, but she tried.

DB leaned against the frame of the door to their room, six arms forming a cage around it. If Kate came out, she'd fall into his embrace whether she liked it or not.

'I don't want to talk to you!' Kate's muffled voice came through.

'Come on, what did you expect me to do? I wasn't going to sit around *waiting*—'

'Oh, please!'

'Maybe you'll think twice about playing hard to get next time!'

Ana sidled up to the door. 'Hey Kate, can I come in?'

After a moment, the door knob clicked, unlocked.

DB was tall, and Ana wasn't. She slipped under his lowest arm and got in place to shoulder open the door. She turned the knob, but DB stuck a hand out, shoving the door, bracing it open when Kate tried to slam it shut from the other side.

'Stop it!' Ana turned on him, glaring.

His lips pulled into a snarl. 'I'm talking to Kate here!'

'She doesn't want to talk!'

He was immovable, a tree, a mountain. He could muscle his way in if he wanted, and they couldn't do anything about it. He really seemed as if he meant to.

'This is our room. You can't come in!' Ana said.

The plywood door cracked, then crunched as DB's hand went through it.

'Hey!' Kate shouted from inside. DB stepped back in apparent surprise, six arms raised in a gesture of innocence.

Ana slipped in and slammed the door shut. She grabbed one of the chairs and pushed it against the door. Like that would keep him out.

But DB didn't try to get in again. 'Bitch!' he hollered instead. 'Earth *Bitch*!'

After that, the hallway was silent.

Ana sighed at the splintered hole in the door. Somehow, she found the edge of her bed and sat. She didn't have any earth to use inside. She wouldn't have been able to stop him if he'd really wanted to get in.

Kate was sitting on her own bed, looking as shell-shocked as Ana felt. Her gaze turned downward, to her hands resting in her lap.

'Maybe I should talk to him. Do you think I overreacted?' Kate asked. Ana automatically shook her head, though she honestly didn't know. Kate ran her hands through her hair. 'I fell for it. I can't *believe* I fell for it. Big famous rock star hitting on me, and what do I think? "Wow, he really likes me." I'm such an idiot.' She threw herself back on the bed and stared at the ceiling.

Ana's heart was still pounding hard. She'd spent an hour in the backyard discovering how much she could do with all these fantastic powers. And now she was learning about her limits. Inside the house, she was useless. And she couldn't say anything that would make Kate feel better.

'You're wrong about him,' Ana said.

'No, I'm not. Just wait, it'll be Diamonds House he sneaks back from next.'

'Yeah. But he's not going after every woman on the show. He's never looked twice at me.'

Kate glanced at her, distracted from her introspection. Then, she laughed. 'Is he really that shallow?'

Ana was fairly sure he wasn't, but on this matter, she couldn't argue.

'Don't worry about it, Ana. He's totally not worth it.'

♥

More cameras invaded the next day. Like Ana could be bothered by the presence of more cameras. But these came with complications.

John Fortune opened the door to the house without knocking. 'Hey – John here! Anyone home?'

'Yeah.' Ana came out to meet him from the kitchen, where she'd been snacking. She'd been taking advantage of the food she didn't have to buy or cook herself. That was probably what the cameras would show – round-faced, unsvelte Ana, always eating. 'What's up?'

'We just stopped by to do some interviews. Where is everyone?'

'I thought you guys check the footage every day.'

'We haven't gotten to last night's yet.'

She said, 'There was kind of a blow up. Big TV drama, as Bugsy would say.'

'Then it'll be a good time for interviews, won't it?' Michael Berman, all smiles, pushed his way in past the couple of crew who were lugging equipment. 'Is Curveball around?'

Ana felt her gaze darken, her expression shutting down. Getting protective. Kate did not need to be talking to this guy today. 'No.'

'Are you sure?' Berman persisted.

'Yeah.'

John, always diplomatic, stepped between them. 'We've got five other people here to interview. Maybe DB – he's always ready to talk. We'll be setting up on the back porch.'

Oh, not the backyard ...

'Uh, yeah, about that,' Ana said, fidgeting suddenly. 'That may not be such a great idea. I'm not sure you want to go out there.' What was she going to tell them? It wasn't like she could hide it, they'd see footage of the whole thing.

'Why not?' John said – and headed straight for the back door.

Ana followed him. Even from the window the churned-up soil and mounds of earth were visible. How was she going to explain this? Maybe she could put it back the way it was. Flatten the ground, talk Gardener into planting some grass ...

'Holy shit!' John stepped onto the porch.

Quickly Ana said, 'I – I was sort of ... practicing.'

When he turned to her, though, he was smiling. 'That's a real mess out there.'

'Yeah, well. The craters are Kate's.'

John just kept grinning. 'Oh man, I love you guys.'

♦

Drummer Boy dwarfs his chair, dwarfs the surroundings. He fills the frame, so that it's hard to tell if it's a trick of the camera that makes him seem huge or if he really is that big. All six hands are in motion, tapping the arms of the chair, tapping the air as if working imaginary drumsticks, or just twitching to an unheard beat.

His expression changes in response to a question. He glares, evoking the punk rock persona that made him the front man for the hottest band going. When he speaks, all six hands clench.

'You want to know who I think should win? Who the <beep> cares! This whole thing is bogus. Everyone who says I'm just here to get publicity for the band? They're right, 'cause that's all this show is good for. Cheap thrills and shameless self-promotion. It sure as <beep> isn't about heroics. Maybe Kate's right. Maybe I should just worry about getting all the hot chicks here into bed and let the show take care of itself.' He laughs, then, but the sound is bitter. 'All of 'em except *her*. 'Cause if she wants a reputation as the Ice Queen, that's fine with me.'

A rare look of uncertainty darkens his gaze for a moment, as if he's realized he's said too much. But the expression only lasts for a heartbeat, to be replaced by his usual, solid glare.

JONATHAN HIVE

Daniel Abraham

FIRST AMONG LOSERS

Jonathan sat at his laptop and didn't write. The cursor blinked.

Well, I've been voted off.

He backspaced to the beginning and sat, tapping his hands on the kitchen table. It was smaller than the formal dining table big enough to house almost thirty people. This one would only fit ten or twelve, even though there were only three of them in the great rambling mansion they called the Discard Pile.

Or, colloquially, Losers Central.

The thing about Hollywood is that it's made up of total fakes and posers. Television is brimming over with people who have the depth of mud puddles and the compassion of sex-starved piranhas. I'm actually glad to be off the show. Delighted. Seriously.

He highlighted and deleted it.

The problem was how to deal with the public in a way that acknowledged the humiliation of having gotten booted in the first round without actually losing face. It wasn't a simple thing.

'Hey!' Joe Twitch said, 'Isn't this place fucking great?'

Jonathan looked up. 'Joe …' he began.

Twitch held up a hand fast enough to make a whooshing sound like some cheap kung fu sound effect.

'I know, you buy the whole "we lost" thing,' Joe Twitch said. 'But I'm telling you, they're gonna bring us back. Like later in the show, we're gonna go back in. Why else are they keeping us in this kick-ass mansion, eh? Butlers and maids and everything. There's a pool.'

'Joe,' Jonathan said. 'We lost. They're keeping us around because they think we're amusing. We're a fucking sideshow.'

'That's what they want you to think,' Joe Twitch said. 'But you wait. You'll see. These shows do it all the time. Bait and switch, they call it. Or hey, bait and twitch. Get it? Twitch and … Ow!'

Twitch slapped himself fast enough to make a little popping sound where the air rushed back in behind his arm, and Jonathan felt one of his wasps die. It was a small price to pay.

'Can't you keep those things under control?' Twitch asked. 'Fucker stung me.'

'Sorry. Sometimes a few just slip out,' Jonathan lied. 'You should put something on that welt, though. I think they have something in the bathroom.'

Joe Twitch vanished. The laptop stayed the same.

Some people might say we've lost. I think of it as being differently victorious.

[Backspace.]

John Fortune came into the kitchen with a couple of grocery bags on each arm. He smiled and nodded to Jonathan.

'Hey,' Jonathan said. 'How's it going?'

'Pretty good,' Fortune said, hauling the sacks up to the counter-top. 'Just got a little snack food for you guys. And a new controller for the video game console. King Cobalt broke the last one.'

'He gets excited,' Jonathan agreed.

'At least he's having fun, right?'

Fortune started unloading the food, stocking up the refrigerator and pantry.

'How's it going?' Jonathan asked.

'What?'

'The show. You know, the next challenge. The teams.'

Curveball, he didn't say.

'I think things are going pretty well,' Fortune said. 'They don't really let me in on much. Just do this, get that. But Peregrine seems happy with things. And Berman's as happy as he ever gets.'

'Berman?'

'Network guy,' Fortune said. 'He was at the Chateau Marmont. Armani suit.'

'Twentysomething, visibly without conscience, hitting on all the women in descending order by cup size?'

'That's the guy,' Fortune said. 'I have the honor of delivering his dry cleaning to the office next.'

'Lucky you,' Jonathan said.

'It's a job,' Fortune said, crushing the now-empty grocery bags into little wads and dropping them in the compactor. 'Anyway. Sorry they voted you off. It's got to suck.'

'I'll survive,' Jonathan said. 'Thanks, though.'

Fortune turned to leave and Jonathan popped a wasp free from his skin and sent it skidding out after him. Fortune was driving a Saturn sedan about three years out of date. Not a car that screamed status. Through the wasp's eyes, Jonathan steered it into the pocket of a jacket hanging in the backseat, then waited.

If he wasn't going to get to play the game as a contestant, he could at least play it his way. Through the wasp, he felt the car vibrate into life and pull away. He shifted his attention back to the laptop.

Fire. Why did it have to be fire?

[Backspace.]

You might think I'd be bitter. Here I am, embraced by a team of people – yes, the noun in question is team – and they drop me the first chance they get. But what you don't see on your television is all the behind-the-scenes stuff. Why did they kick me off when Earth Witch and Wild Fox were just as powerless? Well, folks, it's because

Jonathan stared at the screen for half a minute. [Backspace.] For half an hour, he kept at it and ended up where he'd started, with a blank page.

The car stopped, the suit jacket shifted. Jonathan turned his attention back to the wasp, crawling out of the pocket and taking wing.

Berman's office was beautiful in a studied, artificial way. His secretary exuded both competence and pheromones, and (Jonathan assumed) was fucking Berman on the side in exchange for a future in the industry. Fortune nodded to the woman, who responded with familiarity and pity and waved him through the door. The wasp followed.

Berman sat at his desk. Two older men and a severe-looking woman with gray at the temples were sitting in chairs that made them look shorter.

'Just hang that stuff in the closet, okay, John?'

'Sure thing, Mr. Berman,' John Fortune said.

'Okay,' Berman said, 'So the Turtle's out for week six?'

'And Mistral refuses the new terms,' one of the men said. 'It's the adversarial thing.'

'Detroit Steel has signed, though,' the woman said. 'And I have a call in to Noel Matthews.'

'Really?' Berman said. 'The magician guy? Couldn't we get a real ace? Thanks, John! I owe you for that. Really. Take care.'

The door closed behind Fortune. Berman clicked his tongue. 'Poor fucker,' he said. 'I wouldn't have hired him, except as a favor to his mother. Kid's a dumb fuck; but at least he's a nice dumb fuck. Okay, so let's get back to the kraut. His agent's being a total … Jesus fucking Christ! Shit, that hurts! There's a fucking bee in here!'

Wasp, motherfucker, Jonathan thought, as he steered the small body up to the air vent where he could still hear. Below him, the executive and his staff were running around waving papers and looking for a first aid kit. It made the day better.

'Hey,' King Cobalt said. 'I have a new controller for the game console. You want to play?'

The Mexican wrestler ace was smiling so hard, Jonathan could see his cheeks pouching out under his mask. Jonathan felt the refusal welling up at the back of his mouth, but paused. At least the guy was having fun.

'Gimme a minute to finish this up,' he said. 'Then, sure, I'll kick your ass if you want.'

'You can try,' King Cobalt said and lumbered back toward the front room.

« ll next »

Posted Today 3:34 pm

AMERICAN HERO, DISCARDS | TRIUMPHANT | 'WE ARE THE CHAMPIONS' – QUEEN

Yes, I have been voted off the team, but I still kick ass at Gran Turismo. I would say more, but King Cobalt has insisted upon a rematch, and I must rest my gaming thumbs.

92 COMMENTS | LEAVE COMMENT

♠

CHOSEN ONES: II

Carrie Vaughn

The alarm rang at eleven A.M. A video conference call piped into the Hummer's drop-down TV screen gave Team Hearts its second mission. It wasn't a rescue this time, it wasn't a disaster. It was a treasure hunt.

Peregrine's image told them: 'You must retrieve the contents of a locked safe. The safe is located at the end of an obstacle course. Your entire team must reach the end of the course before you may attempt to open the safe. Deliver the contents to me, tonight, at the *American Hero* headquarters, for your chance at immunity.'

The video display went black, and the members of Team Hearts stared at the screen.

'Cakewalk,' DB said. 'No problem.'

'Famous last words,' Hardhat countered.

In fact, the obstacle course wasn't difficult. They followed their GPS tracker instructions to an abandoned industrial lot. There they found a maze built with concrete walls winding through the yards and buildings. Wild Fox commented, 'Sure be nice to have a bunch of flying bugs to give us a view of this.' Everyone shushed him. Drummer Boy hoisted himself to the top of the wall, which was only (from his perspective) about ten feet tall. He helped everyone else up, and by following the wall to the end, bypassed the maze entirely.

Next, they encountered about five acres of genuine military

obstacle course: coils of barbed wire laid in the dirt, high walls to traverse – the works. After bypassing the maze, they decided that was the right strategy for the rest of it. Gardener's vines tangled with the barbed wire, and as they grew they lifted, pulling it out of the way, creating a path. Hardhat built steps over the walls, Drummer Boy's strength helped lift people over, and Curveball's explosions broke through a couple of obstacles. They were on a roll. After the last challenge, this almost easy success felt wonderful. But Ana was still waiting for her chance to do something.

At the other end of the obstacle course, they found a concrete drainage tunnel, large enough that even DB could walk inside without ducking.

'This thing just keeps going, doesn't it?' Curveball said. Like all of them, she was sweating under the summer sun, streaked with dirt, and visibly tired.

At the end of the short tunnel was a locked iron gate.

'I'll blow the lock,' Curveball said, tossing a pebble in her hand. 'No problem.'

DB glowered. 'I think I've got this one.'

'But this'll be easier—'

He'd already put his head down, hunched his shoulders, and charged. All six arms pushed against it. The bars buckled, but didn't break. Grunting, his mouth twisting in a rictus of effort, he tried it again, digging his feet into the ground, slamming his bulk as a living battering ram against the barrier.

Ana expected the lock to pop, the bars to break, something. But the sound she heard was crunching, a ripping felt as a vibration under her feet – like rock breaking.

The gate's hinges exploded free of the concrete in a shower of dust and debris. The rest of them ducked back, sheltering their faces with their arms. Somebody coughed.

DB dropped the gate in front of him. It landed with a thud. Chunks of concrete still adhered to the hinges.

'Like you said. No problem,' he said hoarsely, rolling his primary shoulders into place, brushing off the effort.

Curveball didn't even look at him as she stalked past, stepping carefully in between the bars of the gate. The others filed after her. Ana waited until last, trying to think of something to say. Something that wouldn't sound trite, or wouldn't inspire him to take a swing at her. Not that she thought he'd really hit her, but right now he looked like nothing so much as a primordial creature from a forgotten jungle, hunched over, hands clenched into fists, hooded gaze staring after the blond princess he could never have. It might be best to simply creep away silently, and hope he didn't notice.

'Thanks,' she said. A simple *gracias* always helped smooth things over.

He growled and marched after the others.

The tunnel opened into a space that looked like an arena: a bowl-shaped park with grassy sides sloping down to a pond some fifty yards in diameter. The surface was dark, opaque. No telling how deep it went.

A flag fluttered from a buoy bobbing in the center of the pond – bright red, X marks the spot. The prize lay somewhere under the surface of the water.

'Well, shit!' Hardhat said. Ana could already hear the bleeps on the final cut.

'Diver on Clubs'll have this all tied up!' Diver, the woman with gills, could breathe underwater.

Despite the maze, the obstacle course they'd succeeded in traversing, despite making it this far with the sort of flair the judges had to appreciate, the game did seem fixed at this point.

'Maybe it's not that deep,' DB said. 'Maybe I can wade in.'

'Dude, can you even swim?' Wild Fox asked.

'Dude, does it matter?' the drummer shot back.

The water lapped almost imperceptibly along a sandy stretch that led out from the tunnel. DB went straight into the pond, shoes, clothes and all, until the water was up to his ankles, then up to his knees. He continued, dragging against the water, all his arms out for balance.

Then, abruptly, he disappeared. Sank straight down and out of sight. Kate gasped, hand over her mouth.

A second later he came back up, sputtering, shedding water everywhere.

'It drops off,' he reported, gasping for breath. 'Three feet deep, then straight down. I don't know how far it goes.'

He returned to shore, and they stood in a line, staring out at the water, potential heroes with no ideas.

Gardener reached into her ubiquitous pouch. 'Maybe I can get some vines growing, pull the thing up to the surface.'

'We don't even know what the fuck it is,' Hardhat said. 'We're just assuming it's right under the buoy.'

'You have a better idea?' she said, glowering at him.

'It's better than nothing,' Curveball said. 'We can think of something else in the meantime.'

The conversation continued, but Ana was only half-listening. She was looking at the sand – the ground, the earth – and following it to where it touched the water. And continued, under the water. The soles of her shoes touched the sand, and she could feel the lines of earth spreading under the water. Maybe twenty, twenty-five feet. She'd dug wells hundreds of feet deep. This was nothing. She touched her medallion, mouthed the words *por favor*.

She could feel the whole area, the hills sloping up to where they butted against concrete walls. She could bring those hills down if she wanted.

'I think I can do it,' she heard herself say, and felt herself step forward, toward the edge of the water, before she realized what she was doing.

DB laughed. 'What? What do you think you're going to do? Hey – maybe you can dig a canal, drain the water. If there were any place to drain it to. And you could dig a swimming pool while you're at it! But hey, we've already got one!'

'Would you shut up and let her try!' Kate said. DB actually shut up.

Ana knelt by the water's edge. She buried her fingers in the sand. Only her knuckles and the tendons – tensed, straining – were visible. She reached into the earth. *Watch this, Roberto.*

The hills around them started crawling, the grass rippling. The ground traveled in waves, a subtle, miniature earthquake, creeping ever downward.

The surface of the water rippled, vibrating, like someone was shaking it. Then, the water lurched, splashing with a sound of crashing waves, and was displaced, pushed out, flooding the arena. Ana ignored the stream of water, several inches deep, flowing around her. She was bringing the earth to her.

The bottom of the pond rose to the surface.

The one large pond became dozens of puddles scattered around the whole of the arena. In the middle of the arena stood a brand-new island rising a few feet above the water. With a last shuddering of earth, a bridge formed, a stretch of thick mud leading from Ana to the island. Her hands were now sunk in mud.

In the middle of the island stood a safe, a two-by two-foot square of heavy steel with a handle on the front, and on top of the safe rested a round red buoy, its flag tipped sideways and dripping.

All of them were standing in water now, but no one complained.

Ana sighed, opened her eyes, and looked on what she'd wrought. She tried to be surprised, and found only a sense of resignation. This was what she was. Earth Witch.

'Holy fucking shit,' Hardhat said. His jaw hung open.

A hand touched her shoulder, and she looked up, startled. Kate stood there, frowning with concern. Ana sat back, relaxed, and her arms hung limp.

'You okay?'

Ana smiled. 'Yeah. I'll be okay.'

Wild Fox tried to cross the mud bridge, but his feet sank to above his ankles almost immediately. His tail stiffened and twitched, and he hurriedly backed away. He had lost a shoe and had to reach back for it. 'Okay, not cool.'

Gardener already held a handful of seeds.

She tossed them, and they rained down to the start of the bridge – and grew. Giant lily pads opened and spread like carpets across the length of the bridge, digging roots into the mud, solidifying it.

They crossed the bridge, walking on the squishing green carpet, and discovered they still weren't finished, because they had to break the thing open. Without a word DB tackled it, wrenching at the handle, pulling at the crack that marked the door, pounding at the steel sides. He could bend steel bars, but he couldn't dent this. He glared at the thing as if it had offered a personal insult.

He went at it for five minutes before Kate cut in. 'Let me try. Please?' Her tone was flat.

Six arms loose at his sides, DB stepped back.

Kate already had her missile in hand, cupped to her chest in preparation for her pitch. 'Everyone stand clear,' she said, and she herself backed onto the edge of the bridge, with the others fanned out behind her.

We're a team, Ana thought. *We really are.*

Kate snapped her pitch, and Ana never even saw the marble leave her hand. Only a streak of light blazed – a shooting star – and the streak swerved, slamming straight into the combination knob and locking mechanism. The thing sparked and shattered, pieces zipping in all directions. The safe's door swung open.

They'd done it. No numbing failure this time. No sense of shame. For a long moment, they didn't seem to believe it.

Then Wild Fox cheered. '*Yes!*'

Miniature fireworks flew around him, red and gold light bursting, flowering, and falling. That was a cue, and they all let loose, a cathartic release. Hardhat hugged Earth Witch, Wild Fox grabbed Gardener's hands and spun her in a circle – and Kate hugged Drummer Boy. He lifted her clear off the ground, and they were both smiling.

They settled down long enough for DB to gesture at the safe and say to Kate, 'You want to do the honors?'

Curveball retrieved their prize: a hand-sized velvet box with a gold heart inside.

♣

Hardhat parked Hearts' Humvee in its spot outside the *American Hero* studio and cameras captured every move. They were still soaked and dirty from the challenge, but their mood was high – electric. Wild Fox couldn't sit still. His tail twitched manically.

'We're going to win. We're totally going to win. They totally can't rag on us this time.'

'We still don't know how the other teams did,' Kate said. 'If the others got into their safes, then the judges get to call it.'

Secretly, Ana thought Wild Fox was right. They had to win, after all that. She was still wrung out after rearranging the entire arena, and even that was a new feeling. She couldn't tell if the fatigue was physical – or simple mental shock at what she had done. *You can move the world*, Roberto had said. What if he was right?

They were the first to arrive. The other three parking spaces were empty. That could only be a good thing.

John Fortune met the group at the stage entrance, swinging the door out and holding it open for them. 'Hey! Welcome back,' he said.

'Hi, John,' Kate said.

'I just watched the playback. You guys were awesome. Really awesome.'

'Really?' Kate said, smiling, blushing a little. She turned almost shy.

'Thanks.'

DB hissed at Kate, 'That guy's just kissing your ass.' Everybody heard the mock whisper.

John ignored him. 'I know I'm not supposed to tell you how you did beforehand, but I have to say, the look on Digger's face when he saw what Ana did? Unbelievable.'

Ana felt herself blush.

The door pushed open wider and Berman shoved himself into the group. He spared the slightest of glances for John. 'Hey kid, why don't you find me a donut and coffee or something.'

'Actually, I'm supposed—'

'It'll only take a minute. Go,' Berman said, smiling over gritted teeth.

'I'll see you guys later,' John said, squeezing past Berman to reenter the soundstage.

DB laughed. 'Captain Cruller's on a mission.'

'Michael, shut up!' Kate glared at him.

'You don't have to stick up for him like that,' he said.

'I'm not—'

Berman butted in. 'Curveball, my God! That was fantastic! This all comes so easy to you, you know that? You're a natural.'

Ana found herself looking around for an escape route, but the executive was only interested in Kate. Came right at her, hand outstretched. Somehow, Kate overcame the reflex to offer her own hand to shake, and Berman turned the move into an open-armed gesture of welcome.

'Thanks,' Kate said, frowning. 'But we all did it. No one can fault our teamwork this time.'

'Of course, of course,' he said, but his look turned just a bit sour when he regarded the others.

DB crossed all six arms.

'And that's a great point. That was a really important element when we were putting this together, and you know – I'd love to get your opinion on it sometime, maybe—'

This time, Ana butted in. Really, this had to stop. Kate looked like she was getting ready to throw something.

She angled Kate toward the door. 'Hey, are there really donuts in there? 'Cause I'm starving. We missed lunch.' She threw Berman a smile and a glare as they pushed past him. The team followed, like she hoped they would.

Berman's voice echoed after them. 'I need to speak with Peregrine. You kids take it easy.'

'*That* bastard's kissing your ass,' Hardhat said, after they'd left the sun and entered the darkness of the building.

'Thanks for the save,' Kate said.

Ana grinned. 'Teamwork, *chica*.'

♥

They waited in catering, some on chairs, some pacing, all of them growing more nervous. Ana and Kate sat side-by-side, looking out over the back end of the set; struts and lights and cables hung everywhere, people in headsets and clipboards wandering back and forth. The dark underbelly of Hollywood magic.

'We have to win this one,' Kate said. She leaned forward, elbows on knees, glaring at nothing in particular. She smiled when John looked their way and waved at them.

Ana's own nervous twitch found her tracing the outline of her Santa Barbara medallion under her shirt. It was almost a form of prayer. But she wasn't praying to win the task.

Please, God, get me through this. Get me through the next hour without going insane.

'We did the best we could,' she said to Kate. 'Whatever happens, happens. I'm still happy.'

'Whatever happens will be exactly how they rig it to happen,' DB said. He was pacing back and forth along the wall, glaring like a caged animal. He nodded to where the three judges had arrived – Berman was already talking to them.

Ana hated to think that DB might be right.

Team Spades arrived, and they looked smug. Crap. They'd succeeded at their treasure hunt, too. The six Spades teammates ranged out and regarded them, from the two bombshells Pop Tart and Rosa Loteria, the iron-skinned Rustbelt, Simoon and the Candle, on down to the show's youngest contestant, eleven-year-old Dragon Girl. 'Hey, it's the big losers,' Rosa said. 'You guys didn't actually get anything done this time, did you? You gave up early, right?' Her grin was gloating.

Ana glared at her. People had expected the two of them – both Latinas – to bond, but Ana didn't much like Rosa. She'd never met anyone so brazen.

Before anyone could respond, Pop Tart vanished, reappeared next to DB, and gave him a smile and wink. 'Hey, honey, will I see you around after the show's done?'

DB had the gall to glance at Kate before saying, 'I don't know. Maybe.'

'Hmm, we'll have to see about that.' Pop Tart ran a finger down the uppermost of DB's arms before turning to follow the rest of her team to the stage.

Kate pointedly, fiercely, ignored the exchange.

Dragon Girl – Rachel – smiled cheerfully and waved. 'See you guys later.'

Ana waved back halfheartedly.

'We're so screwed,' Hardhat said.

Ana and the others were only slightly encouraged when the Clubs and Diamonds arrived, looking glum.

Kate leaned over to Ana. 'How could Clubs have gone bust? They've got Diver, this should have been a piece of cake.'

'Maybe they'll show it on the replay.'

The evening only grew more agonizingly tense. Finally, they were called to the stage. It'd all be over soon.

This time, Peregrine's gown was a magnificent royal purple, sleek and tailored in all the right places. She knew just how to stand to make sure the slit up the side showed off her legs to best advantage. Her hair shone and her smile glittered.

Once again, she welcomed them onstage for their reckoning. Three more of them would be eliminated – discarded – tonight. This was serious. This was war.

First came the replay segments, and Peregrine showed the failures. The other teams had fliers who had made short work of the maze. The obstacle course hadn't slowed the teams much either. But the water had proven formidable.

Team Diamonds hadn't been able to retrieve the safe. Matryoshka split, then split again, until eight little versions of the ace – stupid little versions, since they divided the original's intelligence between them – attempted to swim to the safe. They only ended up floundering like wind-up tub toys, until Tiffani herded them together and coaxed them into reforming. The Maharajah sent his telekinetic servants in the form of shirts, but they hadn't been strong enough to carry the safe back. Finally, the Amazing Bubbles had tried blasting water out of the pond. She grew thinner and thinner as she released more energy, and managed to empty about half the pond when the air horn sounded, calling an end to the task. The sun was setting by then. Of the performance, Topper observed wryly, 'At least you're persistent.'

All the contestants watched Clubs' attempt with interest, because the team's dejected demeanor could only mean that they'd failed. But how? When they found the lake, their expressions were triumphant – water! Diver's element. They acted like they'd already won. Diver leapt into the water to confirm the prize's location, and with her help Toad Man made easy work of pulling it to the surface.

Then they stalled. They poked at the safe, pounded at it, prodded it, rolled it, jumped on it, pried at the handles, fiddled with the combination. Stuntman tried hitting it, but he was indestructible, not superstrong. When Brave Hawk tried lifting the safe, thinking to fly with it and drop it from a height, his wings disappeared. He had strength *or* flight, but not both. Holy Roller even climbed up the side of the arena, pulled himself into his massive human ball shape, and threw his substantial mass down to crash into the safe like a bowling ball. He managed to tip it over, sprawling over it, vaguely resembling a beached whale. Nothing. The longer they couldn't open it, the angrier they got. It was like watching a troop of monkeys. They degenerated into yelling at each other, and even the preacher on the team couldn't keep peace between them.

'That could have been a whole lot better,' said the Harlem Hammer, in polite understatement.

Even Topper couldn't put a nice spin on it. 'I'm disappointed. You all showed such promise last week.' She shook her head, and the weight of shame settling on Team Clubs was palpable.

Downs worked up to his own commentary, glaring at them for a long moment, then raising his hand dramatically to tick off items on his fingers. 'No points for effort. No points for style. *Nothing* for teamwork. And absolutely nothing for the least awe-inspiring performance I've seen yet. Which is sad, 'cause you guys were that close.' He held thumb and forefinger nearly together. 'That close to beating this challenge. And you flushed it.' He scowled as if seriously, intensely, and personally disgusted by them.

The mood lightened as they moved on to the successes.

Dragon Girl carried the day for Team Spades. She'd had Shamu tucked in her backpack. The girl put the stuffed souvenir into the water, and a full grown killer whale burst forth. The whale swam a circuit of the pond to show off, dove to retrieve the safe, and spit it onshore at Dragon Girl's feet. Rustbelt had only to touch it to dissolve the metal into a pile of rust, leaving the prize for the taking.

It would be up to the judges to decide this one.

'And now, Team Hearts,' Peregrine said. 'Let's watch.'

There was Ana's feat in replay, almost as impressive on the screen as it had been in person. The hills fell, feeding earth to the island that rose from the middle of the pond, displacing a flood of water, massive geological action slipping by in seconds. Watching it, Ana could hardly believe it herself. *She'd* done *that*?

Topper actually smiled. 'Earth Witch, that was an amazing piece of work. I can't wait to see what you pull out next.'

Downs – the worst of them, the most irascible, impossible to please – drew out his moment, tapping a pencil, acting like he couldn't find the words. He was playing this for suspense. Then he said, 'If I ever hear you say "I just dig holes" again, I'll kick your ass myself.'

There was some laughter at that, and Ana flushed with relief. *I survived.*

Curveball's crack at the safe – simple, elegant, effortless – was the perfect end to the replay. Hearts hadn't just succeeded at the challenge. They'd made it look easy.

Harlem Hammer delivered the verdict this time: 'Team Spades, you got lucky. If Dragon Girl hadn't had that particular stuffie in her sack, what would you have done? On the other hand, Team Hearts pushed their abilities to the edge. They're mastering their powers, and they're doing it as a team. For that reason, tonight's victory and immunity go to Team Hearts.'

They cheered, all of them together, and hugged, a chaotic mass of people – with a foxtail stuck out and waving. DB waded into the middle and picked up Kate with one set of arms and Ana with the other. They squealed with surprise and laughter as he lifted them into the air.

Grinning fiercely, Kate leaned over and spoke across the top of DB's head to Ana, 'I'll see you in the finals!'

◆

Hearts House had a party that night, because they didn't have to stand around the table and pick cards. Didn't have to kick anyone out. Music played – Wild Fox put a Joker Plague CD in the stereo, which immediately endeared him to Drummer Boy and made up for all his pranks. The drummer entertained them by adding live accompaniment, tapping the membranes on his torso and pounding out improvised rhythms.

Drinking sodas, Ana and Kate watched from the kitchen bar.

'Winning feels pretty good, doesn't it?' Kate said.

'Yeah,' Ana answered. In fact, the whole world had opened up.

'It only gets better from here, I bet,' Kate said. Her smile fell, though, as Drummer Boy made his way over to them. The song had ended, and after grabbing a beer from the fridge, he veered to the bar, throwing a glare at Ana like he wanted her to leave.

He wasn't going to scare her off that easy.

Expectantly, the two waited for him.

'Hey,' he said.

'Hey,' Kate said back. Ana waved. Again, he gave her that glare. She kept smiling like she hadn't noticed.

He ducked his gaze, which almost made him look sheepish, and said to Kate, 'I was wondering if you maybe wanted to take a walk or something. Or just go out back and talk. To celebrate. I'll sneak you a beer.' He showed off the beer bottle in one of his left hands.

She smiled thinly. 'Still trying to get me into bed?'

His expression showed a moment of hesitation, like he was trying to decide which way to play this. Then he decided, offering a broad grin. 'You can't blame a guy for trying.'

'Yes, I can.' Her smile cut like glass.

DB walked away, draining half the beer.

Kate blew out a breath she must have been holding. The front door opened; Kate looked over her shoulder at it. Wild Fox and Hardhat were stepping outside.

'I was sort of hoping John would stop by,' she explained to Ana, then took a long drink of soda to hide her expression.

The next time the front door opened, Ana was in the fridge getting more sodas, but she heard Kate hiss, 'Oh my God!'

Ana looked. 'What is it?'

A man in his late thirties had just come in, a white guy with sun-streaked blond hair and stunning blue eyes. He stuck his hands in his jeans pockets and looked around like he was lost.

'Is that Brad Pitt?' Kate said. 'That looks like Brad Pitt.'

It certainly did. Despite her whispering, the actor heard her. When he saw Kate, his blue eyes lit up and he came over.

More Hollywood magic. Ana was glad she had a front-row seat for this.

'You're Curveball,' Brad said. 'I recognize you from *American Hero*.'

'Yeah,' Kate said, nodding and gaping.

'I heard there was a party, so I thought I'd stop by. Is that okay?'

'Yeah. Sure. Cool.' Kate was still nodding. 'Um ... can I get you a Coke or something?'

'Sure. That'd be great.'

Kate took one of the cans from Ana's hand and handed it to him. His famous grin widened.

Ana studied the actor – the well-known actor who just happened to show up on their doorstep. She wondered ... and decided she had to try it. If she was wrong, she could apologize and go back to being the socially awkward member of the team with no harm done.

She put her hand on his shoulder and shoved. Brad Pitt disappeared in a shimmer of light, leaving Wild Fox holding the soda. He cringed, trying to maintain his charming smile. But he couldn't pull it off like Brad could.

Kate took a moment to register the transformation. Then, she shouted, 'Oh, you son of a bitch!'

'Hey, I was just having fun! Don't throw anything, don't throw—' He ran, and she chased him, cocking an empty can like she really was going to throw it. Last Ana saw, they went over the sofa and out the back door.

Ana sighed. Now *that* was going to play well on TV. She didn't know if the contest was going to get better, but it was certainly going to get more interesting.

♠

Of all the contestants, Earth Witch still seems the most nervous in front of the camera. Like an underground creature that's suddenly been pulled into the light, which somehow seems an appropriate metaphor for her. But now, at the moment of her great victory, she's smiling. She's sitting a little taller, and her face is flushed.

She shyly ducks her gaze. 'Yeah, of course it feels great to win the challenge. But I don't think I could have done what I did without the rest of the team backing me up, you know? It sounds corny, but I feel like they really believed in me. I couldn't disappoint them, especially Kate. What else can I do?' She shrugs, purses her lips in thought, then shakes her head. 'I don't know. I'll have to work on that. Right now, I think I'm going to see what I can do about winning this thing.'

♣

JONATHAN HIVE

Daniel Abraham

BETTER THAN TELEVISION

'ST – *hic* – OP THAT!' Joe Twitch yelled.

'It's not me,' Spasm said with his shit-eating frat boy grin. 'Seriously, just because I *can* do that doesn't mean every time you get the hiccups, it's because of me.'

'Bu – *hic* – llshit,' Twitch said, pointing an accusing finger at the newcomer. The camera crew was eating the whole thing up with a spoon. 'Just be – *hic* – cause you think I moved your – *hic* – junk out of that room *hic* …'

The new round of losers had arrived that afternoon – Blrr, who was probably as fast or faster than Twitch, but only when she was wearing her rollerblades; Spasm, who had taken the bedroom across from Joe, only to find his things transported to a smaller, more distant room (to leave the first room available for one of the women, it was assumed); and Simoon, the girl who could become a dust storm. It was just an hour past dinner, and things had already devolved into a shouting match.

Jonathan was secretly pleased. Another few days with just King Cobalt and Joe Twitch, and he would have lost his mind.

Plus which, Simoon had taken the bedroom across from his.

Jonathan sat on a couch in his bedroom, trying to avoid his fellow inmates. He could hear the argument between Twitch and Spasm coming in from the hall. In the front room, the television was yammering on about events in Egypt; antijoker rioting was causing problems, the Egyptian army was threatening to impose a curfew, and the new UN Secretary-General was using the whole thing as an opportunity to show he could handle the job. There was a special report coming up on how the new Caliph, Abdul, had ordered all his brothers strangled, and whether that was going to be a stabilizing move politically, just in time for a switch to *Entertainment Tonight*. King Cobalt was obsessive about watching the entertainment news on the show. Blrr was probably going around the block for the three thousandth time that hour. And Jonathan just sat there, staring off into space. He had his arms folded so that no one was likely to notice that his right thumb was missing, small green wasps crawling over his skin where it used to be.

His attention, you could say, was elsewhere.

♥

The beach wasn't empty, even at night, but it was close. There were only a few college-age kids down by the pier, an old lady walking a dachshund with a frilly pink leash, and Drummer Boy sitting near the water with his middle pair of arms propping him up and his upper and lower pairs wrapped gently around someone. The wasp, bright green in daylight, was hard to see by the moon; the sound of its wings was muffled by the surf. So it could get in pretty close.

'We probably shouldn't be here. You know. Like this,' she said. 'We're enemies, after all.'

Jonathan recognized the voice: the woman from Team Spades who pulled cards from a Mexican tarot deck and got a different power with each draw. Rosa Loteria. That was her name.

'Whatever,' Drummer Boy said. 'It's just a game.'

'I guess,' Rosa said. 'They're going to get rid of me. So then it won't matter, right?'

'Why do you think they'd lose you?'

'They don't like me,' she said. 'Especially Cleopatra. She finds out I'm out with you ...'

'Who? Pop Tart? She won't care,' Drummer Boy said. 'That's over.'

'I thought maybe,' Rosa said. 'I'm sorry about that.'

Ah, Jonathan thought. The oh-poor-you approach. Ham-handed as seduction techniques go, but it wasn't like Drummer Boy was what you'd call a difficult lay. Still, the man was quiet for long enough that Jonathan and Rosa both started rethinking her tactics.'Why did you do it?' she asked. She traced the ink on one of his arms with her fingertips. 'Get on the show, I mean.'

'I thought, you know, if I won … I thought maybe I could make a difference. You know, really do something.'

Oh *puh-leeze*! Jonathan thought, but Rosa shifted around in the cage of Drummer Boy's arms. Her face tilted up to gaze into his eyes. The hush of the waves almost drowned out her words.

'You don't need this. You can make a difference now.'

He kissed her. Because of *course* he did.

'It's not like that,' Drummer Boy said. 'The band … the band's great. They're really great guys. And we've cranked out some wicked shit. It's just that I thought this would be a way to, you know, talk about the music. What it does. What it *means*.'

Rosa kissed him again, so the negotiation was going pretty well so far. Back at the Discard Pile, Jonathan propped his legs up on the couch. From here on in, things were going to get predictable.

Together, they walked out to the edge of the surf, the near-invisible wasp overhead at a discreet distance. They said something more that he couldn't make out, and then Rosa slipped out of her clothes, Drummer Boy did the same, and they dove together into the water. So that was it. Show's over. He took his wasp up into the salt-rich, thick air, spun around the beach a few times until he found the camera crew who'd been following the couple, and then headed the wasp back to the Discard Pile.

The incident might be good for a line or two when it came time to write the book, something about how the famous aces get all the sex maybe, or the total lack of privacy. Or exactly what the hell a *loteria* deck was anyway, and what kind of sad-ass power someone might gain from drawing *El Pescado* or *El Melon*. Nothing much more than that.

One fishing expedition officially a bust.

Jonathan shifted his attention.

♦

'You're really going to add a lot to the show,' Berman said. 'I tell you, we had quite a furball working out the rights with your agent. She's a *machine*.'

They were on the deck of what Jonathan assumed was Peregrine's house. Los Angeles spread out below them like a fire. Peregrine herself was just inside the huge glass wall, looking classy and talking to a young woman who Jonathan was pretty sure he'd seen on a magazine cover. Out here in the open air, it was just Berman and this other guy.

'Thank you,' the guy said. It came out like *tank you*, with very round vowel sounds. The wasp on the rail buzzed by for a closer look. Natural blond, blue eyes. German accent. It rang a bell. Something about BMWs. 'But what does this mean, furball?'

'A disagreement. A little dustup. Nothing serious. Just that she really knows her stuff.'

'Genevive is a very smart woman,' the German guy said.

'She sure is,' Berman agreed with a smile.

He hates her, Jonathan thought, or he is fucking her. Or both. He made himself a mental note to find out which.

'The guest aces episodes are going to be central to the show. Really central. And having someone of your stature gives the whole thing a sense of that international respect. That's what we want. A real demonstration that *American Hero* isn't just about America.'

The penny dropped.

Lohengrin. He was the guy who could generate a suit of medieval-looking armor and a sword that could cut through more or less anything. All very Neuschwanstein. He'd made a big splash a few years ago over something, but it had only played for about five minutes on American news.

So what exactly was it he was doing here? He had to be the Kraut Berman had been talking about before.

'I wanted very much to help promote heroism,' Lohengrin said. 'There is not enough of it in America.'

'I'm glad you feel that way, too,' Berman said.

The wasp landed on the rail, just a few feet away. Still close enough to hear and see.

'When am I to meet with the team that I am to lead?'

'Ah,' Berman said. 'That's actually changed a little. The part where you *lead* the team was just preliminary brain-storming. No, what the network settled on was having you face off *against* the team. Part of their task will be getting past you.'

Because American Hero *isn't just about America*, Jonathan thought. It's also about beating up foreigners. Lohengrin's expression told him that he'd drawn the same conclusion.

'Genevive didn't mention that change?' Berman said, oozing apology without actually offering one. Lohengrin smiled coolly. Jonathan saw Berman flinch when the sword appeared in the German ace's hand, and flinched himself when the sword darted at his wasp. It felt like being pinched.

He hoped the display had proven Lohengrin's point. He didn't have a backup wasp there, though, so he'd never know. It was a bummer. That angle might have been juicy.

♠

The wasp in the fold of Curveball's purse took to the air as Jonathan's attention inhabited it. It took a moment to get his bearings.

'I ... I don't really talk about it, you know,' Fortune said. The bar roared dully behind him, half a hundred conversations running in parallel. The décor was unfinished wood, painted ductwork, and odd signs and objects epoxied to the walls in lieu of actual character. 'I spent most of my life with Mom trying to keep anything from setting off the virus. She's great, you know. I mean I really love her.' He paused. 'That's not something guys are supposed to say about their mothers, is it?'

'Probably not,' Curveball agreed. 'But it's okay. I know what you mean.'

Curveball and John Fortune, sitting together in a booth at the back of some unholy Bennigan's clone. There didn't seem to be a film crew nearby. Either they were really well-hidden, or John

Fortune had used his connection to the show to sneak Curveball out of the panopticon. And if that wasn't reason enough to go out with a guy, Jonathan wasn't sure what would be.

The wasp high on the wall edged down, keeping its green carapace hidden behind the fake antlers and 1950s outhouse humor. Jonathan tried to make out what the body language was saying; Fortune with his hands on the table, a little slumped over, Curveball sitting forward too, leaning on her elbows. Listening, but not flirty. She had her hair down. It was the first time Jonathan had seen her without her ponytail.

'And then, when I drew an ace ... when I thought, you know, it was an *ace*. I don't know. It was wild. Everyone was calling me the savior, or else the antichrist. And the thing with my dad. The thing with Fortunato.'

Fortunato dying to save me, he didn't say. Now that Fortune laid it out like that, Jonathan could see how there'd be a certain amount of couch time called for.

'Intense,' Curveball said.

'Yeah. Yeah, intense. And now,' Fortune shrugged, 'it's all over. You know? I used to have guards around me all the time. And then I was one of the most important aces in the world. And now I'm Captain Cruller.'

Curveball shook her head, shifting her hand from the opposite elbow to the beer bottle in front of her. Dos Equis. Jonathan would have thought she was a wine cooler girl. 'That's Drummer Boy,' Curveball said. 'Blow him off. He's a dick.'

And dicking away, even as we speak, Jonathan thought.

'He's not wrong, though,' Fortune said. 'I mean it's weird being ordinary, you know? Not being anyone in particular.'

'Maybe you should get on a TV show,' Curveball said.

The wasp was in a pretty good position to see Fortune's face while that sunk in.

'Shit, I'm sorry, Kate. I didn't mean anything about you guys. I wasn't ... I didn't mean to slag on you.'

'No, it's okay. I mean, apology accepted, but it's not what I was thinking.'

'What was?' Fortune asked.

She looked up, half-smiling a question.

'What were you thinking?' Fortune asked.

Curveball frowned, picked up the beer bottle, drank a little, and put it down with a thud. Fortune let the silence stretch. If it had been a manipulation, it would have been a good one. The poor bastard was sincere, so it was even better.

'I'm thinking about the reasons we all came to this thing,' she said. 'Drummer Boy, Earth Witch. Me. It's been fun, and I've met a lot of people who are really great. And some that aren't so great. But the thing that ... the thing that's weird in me? I want to win. I came here and I thought, *whatever. I'll try and we'll see what happens*, but I'm around everyone, and it's like it's important. I want it. I want to be the American Hero.'

'And what do you think about that?'

'That maybe we can never be special enough to be happy,' she said.

Ooh, deep, Jonathan thought. But Fortune was nodding and smiling.

'Can I tell you something? You have to promise not to pass it on,' Fortune said.

Curveball raised her eyebrows.

'I tried to get my power back. After ... after what happened. I thought maybe I could get it back and control it. Since my dad ... since Fortunato fixed me.'

Curveball shook her head. Someone at the bar shrieked with laughter that sounded as fake as the ambiance. Curveball's hands were on the table now. There were probably six or eight inches between Fortune's hands and hers – flirting distance, maybe. Or maybe not. Jonathan was having a hard time getting a good read off the interaction.

'I tried everything,' Fortune said. 'Meditation, hypnosis, acupuncture. Rolfing.'

'You're kidding,' Curveball said with a laugh that managed to be warm and sympathetic.

'Seems kind of stupid now,' Fortune said into his drink. Jonathan couldn't be sure, but he thought the guy was blushing.

'Maybe,' Curveball said. 'I get it, though.'

'*I don't care if John fucking Fortune gets his powers back!*'

On the couch at Losers Central, Jonathan felt a wave of vertigo, suddenly uncertain of where he was. Someone was talking about Fortune. And she sounded pissed off.

He stood up, tucking the hand with the missing thumb into his pocket.

'No!' the voice said again. A woman's voice. 'No, I'm not. They voted me off the show, Mom. I'm *off*. I'm stuck with all the other losers.'

Jonathan walked to his doorway. Across the hall, Simoon's door was ajar. He could just make out her sand-colored skin and black hair as she paced.

'Yes, he's here sometimes. But it's not like …'

A faint treble yammer, a voice on the other end of a telephone connection, buzzed like a mosquito. Jonathan came closer to the door.

'I'm American, Mama. I was born in America. I've never been to Egypt. Egypt isn't my problem. John Fortune isn't my problem. I got kicked off the show, and now I'm rooming with the most annoying guy in the world, a Mexican wrestler with a fake accent, a guy who turns into bugs, and a girl who thinks roller derby never went out of style. My career is over. Peregrine already thinks I suck, I'm not going to try to get her son to—'

The mosquito whined again. Simoon paused in the narrow strip. One hand held her cell phone to her ear. Her head bowed, and she sighed.

'I'll try, okay? If the occasion comes up, I'll try – and don't push me, Mother. Honest to God, if you give me any more shit about this, I won't even talk to him.'

The mosquito was much quieter.

'You too,' Simoon said. 'Give my love to Uncle Osiris.'

The cell phone closed with a click, and Jonathan rapped gently on the door, swinging it open an inch in the process. Simoon looked up, her eyes round and surprised. Jonathan waved, hoping the gesture was appropriately friendly and not particularly stalkerlike.

'Oh my God,' Simoon said, her brows furrowing with concern. 'What happened to your thumb?'

'Oh,' Jonathan said, sticking his hand back in his pocket. 'It's nothing. It just does that sometimes. Little bits of me kind of wander off. They'll be back.'

'Oh,' Simoon said, and Jonathan mentally removed her from the list of women who would ever, under any circumstances, consider sleeping with him.

'I was just … I couldn't help overhearing you, ah, shouting at your mother there.'

Simoon sighed and sat on the edge of her bed. She looked smaller than he'd thought. 'Sorry about that,' she said. 'It's this whole long thing.'

'The camera guys are still watching Joe Twitch and Spasm fight it out,' Jonathan said. 'You want to talk about it?'

'It's nothing,' Simoon said.

'Egypt. John Fortune. Something that wasn't your fucking problem?' Jonathan said.

Simoon shook her head, paused, looked up at him.

'Okay,' she said. 'But just between us, okay?'

'Absolutely,' Jonathan lied.

'My mom's a god. The wild card hit Egypt way back when, and a bunch of the people who got it wound up looking like the ancient gods. You know. Crocodile heads or lion bodies, that kind of thing. They called themselves the Living Gods. My mom's Isis, or, you know, an Isis. There are several.'

'She's in Egypt?'

'No. Vegas. A bunch of them emigrated and got jobs at the Luxor. My mom hooked up with Elvis when she got here, and here I am. Daughter of a god and the King, and still kicked off the show. But anyway, I have a lot of family back in Cairo. Cousins and stuff.'

Jonathan moved slowly into the room and sat on the couch there. The bed would have seemed a little too familiar. 'So how does John Fortune figure in?'

'My uncle Osiris has this thing where he sees the future. Bits of it. They don't even let him into the casino part of the hotel. Anyway, ever since the Twisted Fists killed the Caliph there's been a lot of antijoker sentiment in the old neighborhoods. And Osiris told Mom that there's some kind of amulet they gave Peregrine back in the '80s, and that it's time she got John Fortune to wear it.'

'Ah,' Jonathan said. And then, 'I don't get it.'

'It's supposed to give him the powers of Ra, whatever that means. And that's supposed to help things back in Egypt. I don't know all the details, and Uncle Osiris really likes to play how he's all mystical and wise and shit, so getting a straight story out of him is, like, good luck. It's all destiny this and fate that. But Mom decided that I should tell John Fortune about the amulet. And now she's giving me all kinds of shit about how I haven't done it yet.' Simoon shrugged like it was obviously the worst idea in the world.

'And you don't want to because . . . ?'

'I came on the show to help my career. Get some exposure,' Simoon said. 'If I go talking crazy shit like this to Peregrine's kid, what kind of reputation do I get? And anyway, after what happened to him before, he probably doesn't even want powers, you know?'

'Have you ever *tried* Rolfing?' Jonathan asked.

'What?'

'Never mind,' he said. 'Just gimme your phone for a minute.'

'Why?' Simoon asked, suddenly suspicious. *Late in the game for that*, Jonathan thought.

'Trust me,' he said.

He dialed with his remaining thumb. The connection rang twice, then a click.

'Hello?' Curveball said.

'Hey,' Jonathan said. 'Give him the phone.'

There was a pause.

'What are you talking about, Hive?'

'I don't know his phone number. I know yours from when we were all buddies and gosh-darn-it friends for life, so I'm calling you. Now slide the phone across the table, okay? I need to talk to him.'

Simoon, jaw slack with horror and surprise, made a waving motion with both hands. *Don't do this.* Jonathan gave her history's least-successful thumbs-up.

'Jonathan?' Fortune said at the other end of the line.

'Hey,' Jonathan said. 'I'm over at Losers Central with Simoon, and you need to get over here.'

'What's the matter?'

'There's a story you've seriously got to hear. And funny thing is, it's all about you and how you get ace powers back.'

There was a pause.

'Is this a joke?' Fortune asked.

'That's the funny thing,' Jonathan said. 'It really isn't. Get over here as soon as you can.'

He hung up before Fortune could say anything else, and tossed the cell back to Simoon. She didn't look pleased.

'Hey!' Blrr said from the doorway. 'We're going to make some popcorn and watch some TV. You guys want to come?'

Simoon hesitated, her gaze shifting from Jonathan to Blrr and back.

'Nah,' Simoon said. 'Next time. Bugsy and I are in the middle of something.'

Blrr looked mildly surprised.

'Nothing like that,' Jonathan said.

'Yeah, didn't figure,' Blrr said, and vanished.

'You shouldn't have called him,' Simoon said. 'That was supposed to be just between you and me.'

'I know what I'm doing,' Jonathan said with a grin. 'You'll thank me for this later.'

LOOKING FOR JETBOY

Michael Cassutt

It's supposed to be a *game*. Reality TV, the teams segregated into separate headquarters, each location infested with cameras, with competition limited to challenges. Dramatic, yes. Tears and threats, sure. But it's all *staged* ...

Yet two hands appear on the railing of the deck of the Clubs Lair. Then two more, and two more after that, and Jamal Norwood knows that Drummer Boy is here, all seven and a half feet of tattooed attitude. Why?

'It's all part of the game, Stuntman.'

'It's against the rules.'

'The only rule is, there are no rules.'

Jamal, aka Stuntman, can take Drummer Boy – more precisely, can take whatever Drummer dishes – if he had any desire to endure bounceback so soon after the last *American Hero* challenge. Instead he tries to rise from the deck chair to retreat. But he is paralyzed, as if he has just slammed into concrete from a great height.

Drummer Boy passes by, his footsteps heavy on the cedar deck.

Then Jamal hears the buzzing, sees the greenish cloud in his peripheral vision. Hive is attacking, too. This must be some joke attack, some mystery challenge, Hearts against Clubs, with the Discards thrown in for good measure. Jamal tries to turn, to see the cameras, but is still frozen.

Hive's voice speaks from the cloud. 'We're not after you,

Stuntman. We want him.' Weird; Jamal didn't know Hive could *talk* in this mode.

Jamal can already feel the fluttering at his back – Brave Hawk swooping overhead from behind, like a bird of prey.

Or, rather, prey itself. Hive's cloud envelopes him, forcing the winged Apache to flutter to a stop … long enough for Drummer to grab him with his upper arms, hold him fast with the middle pair, and start jabbing him with the lower. Brave Hawk struggles, but no one can stand up to a Drummer Boy solo, especially with Hive swarming and stinging. Jamal hears the crunch and crack of broken bones, the agonized groans. *Why is this happening? Where are the goddamn producers?*

Miraculously, even though he is blinded by his own blood, his ribs visibly broken, Brave Hawk frees himself, unleashing a kick that staggers even the giant Drummer Boy. The winged Apache climbs up the railing of the deck, about to launch himself across the arroyo when he staggers and falls forward.

A bloodied baseball rolls to Jamal's chair. 'Got him!' Curveball, the snot-nosed kid whose only talent is throwing things, smirks at the edge of the deck. 'Hey, Stuntman, you used to play ball – catch this!' Curveball raises her arm, about to fire again. But Jamal can't move! Curveball's arm whips forward and the deadly ball fills his vision.

'You're going down, Stuntman.'

Jamal blinks. *There is no ball.* No invasion by rogue members of Hearts. Just Brave Hawk standing to his left, his fake wings obscuring the sun rising over the Santa Monica Mountains.

A stupid bounceback dream.

'Thanks for the vote of confidence.' Jamal doesn't like Brave Hawk. He would have enjoyed seeing him beaten up by Drummer Boy and Hive, his head crushed by a superhot Curveball missile.

'Look at yourself. How long have you been out here?'

'Since last night.'

'When there's a perfectly good bed inside. Bad sign, my friend.'

Jamal could easily explain bounceback, the need for his body to thrash itself back into shape after being crushed by a safe that had become the object of an underwater tug-of-war between two aces. Not only would he have torn up the bed, he would have literally been bouncing off the walls. Tough on the room, even tougher on the rest of the Clubs who were trying to recover from their lackluster performance.

No, it was better for Jamal Norwood to bounceback in the open, even if it meant chills, bug bites, and hallucinatory dreams.

'What's this?' Brave Hawk bends to pick up a paperback dropped next to Jamal's chair. '*Helter Skelter?*' Clearly the Apache has never heard the title. 'You're sulking out here, killing time reading. Going. Down.'

Jamal stands for the first time in hours. Stretches. It feels so good it's almost orgasmic. 'So let me go. Why do you care?'

'A, I'm your teammate. So I need you.' One of the many things Jamal finds annoying about Brave Hawk is his tendency to state the obvious – and to break it into handy categories, as if his listeners were terminally stupid. 'B, I have a proposal.'

'A,' Jamal says, knowing Brave Hawk will miss the sarcasm, 'our team is one bad challenge from being broken into spare parts. We are not competitive, so get used to it. And B, I can't imagine what kind of proposal would interest me.' To make sure Brave Hawk notes his indifference, Jamal searches for the large drinking glass he left under the chair. Bounce-back always leaves him thirsty.

'We need to team up.'

There's the glass. Empty.

Now Jamal sees that the ever-present camera crew of three, led by crazy Art the producer, with silent Diaz the operator, has followed Brave Hawk onto the deck. All of them are yawning, resentful of the early call. 'You guys need a beverage?'

'No, no, that's okay,' Art says, flapping his hands nervously. Jamal has already noted Art's terror at any violation of the fourth wall – the entirely fictitious notion that these wild cards are really conspiring, flirting, or fighting together unobserved. 'Just pretend we're not here.'

'Too late, Art,' Jamal says. But he turns back to Brave Hawk and tries to act. God knows he's had practice. But now the brave Apache has everyone on hold while he talks on his cell phone.

The Clubs Lair sits near the spine of Mulholland Drive, surrounded by dry pines and junipers that in this hot, dry season require nothing more than a discarded match and the kiss of the Santa Ana winds to explode into flame. It hasn't happened here, yet some part of Los Angeles is on fire. Jamal can smell the smoke in the air. He coughs frequently. The pages of the paperback book blur as his eyes water.

Bounceback complete, he could go back inside the house. But he would rather bear discomfort here on the hardwood deck than share space with the other Clubs at this moment – not to mention the camera crews.

Besides, he is an L.A. native: the curves, drops, and hidden mansions of Mulholland are as familiar and comforting as well-worn sneakers. He knows, for example, that the A frame to the west belongs to a notorious Hollywood detective named after a dead musician. That the estate below him – its pool still shadowed by the hills – was where a former governor used to party with pool boys while publicly dating female rock stars.

For all its rugged beauty, the setting is anything but peaceful: the smoke, the glare, the accumulation of irritants can make the most easygoing man turn violent.

Brave Hawk finishes his call. 'My girlfriend,' he announces, as if Jamal could possibly care. 'She's been reading everything and sees other alliances being formed. She says *we* need to team up, too.'

'Wise up, Cochise. All this game strategy stuff is that asshole Berman doing some "viral promotion."' Michael Berman is the network executive for *American Hero*. Jamal has seen the Armani-clad dungeon master lurking at every audition, prep meeting, challenge announcement … seldom speaking, but clearly more in charge than the actual producers. 'And what is "everything"? Is she seeing who's going to win? What the next challenge is going to be? If your gal pal has that, let me know.'

Brave Hawk is persistent. 'You think because you work in Hollywood, you know everything, but you don't, Stuntman. You and I—' here Brave Hawk makes a completely fruity gesture of clasped hands '—we could be an awesome team!'

Jamal sees a nugget of truth in this – at least in the concept of teaming up against the other Clubs. But with this creature who looks like a John Ford Indian with wings? 'Why me? Did Holy Roller already turn you down?'

This is all the encouragement Brave Hawk needs. He leaps up on the railing of the deck. 'I never asked him! And it wouldn't work – not as well as Stuntman and Brave Hawk. We're two of a kind, man!'

Whenever Jamal hears that kind of talk from Brave Hawk, the pleasant images of his evisceration reappear. 'We're both breathing. We both got talked into this project. I don't see what else we have in common.'

Voices behind him signal the emergence of Jade Blossom and Diver from the house, both indecently perky and girly at this hour – and dressed for a swim. Diver might as well not exist – Jamal only sees Jade, her eyes, the way she moves. Her mouth. He has become infatuated with her mouth, the way her lower lip slides forward whenever she is about to speak.

Which she does, calling to Jamal, 'What are you two doing over there? Scheming?' She and Diver start laughing, flirting with the camera team. It's all a big joke. Nevertheless, Jamal wishes Jade would approach him. *They* would make a great team.

'Think about it, Stuntman,' Brave Hawk says, insistently. 'We're both people of color ...'

Jamal almost laughs out loud. People of *color*? Jamal is dark enough and has always known he was tagged as 'black,' but Brave Hawk? His wild card aside, Brave Hawk is no more ethnic in appearance than an Italian American. 'And do what? Call ourselves *The Red and the Black*?' Jamal has read the novel; he knows without asking that Brave Hawk has never heard of Stendahl.

In fact, Brave Hawk loves the phrase, jabbing his finger at Jamal like a fourth-grade teacher whose student just finished the multiplication tables. 'That's the idea. Make these producers and judges think twice before they vote us off.'

'You mean play the race card, you and me.'

'Everyone else is using what they've got. Those girls are giggling and snuggling up to the judges and camera crews. Have you seen the way Curveball's been flirting with John Fortune? Rosa and Tiffani are even worse, and Pop Tart ...'

Jamal doesn't want to admit it, but Brave Hawk is correct. He's sure he's seen Pop Tart having the kind of intimate conversations only lovers have ... with Digger Downs. 'Why shouldn't we use the tools God gave us?' Brave Hawk says.

But Jamal can already hear his father, Big Bill Norwood, the pro ballplayer, sneering. 'The baseball doesn't care what color you are. Can you hit or not? That's all.' He's heard that all his life – and unlike some of the pronouncements Big Bill has made – believes it. He knows he's put in the 'black' category, but he can't honestly say it's held him back.

'Wouldn't we be smarter to just win the fucking challenges?'

'Yeah, how is that working for us?'

Jamal barely manages to get the words through his teeth. 'I just don't see how you and I singing "Kumbaya" is supposed to stop the bleeding.'

Brave Hawk looks over his left wing at the crew – he is the worst actor Jamal has ever seen, and he's seen some bad ones – while slipping his right wing over Jamal. Even though the wings are an illusion, Jamal still feels enveloped in a smelly, scratchy blanket. 'We agree not to vote each other off, for one thing. And if we find ourselves – oh, hell, trapped underwater or buried in quicksand – we share the oxygen tank.'

Jamal can't believe that the Apache ace believes what he's saying. 'I tell you what, Brave Hawk. I will absolutely cross-my-heart promise not to club you over the fucking head with the tank. That's the best I can do.' He slips out from under the protective wing. 'Grow up, Cochise.'

As Jamal walks away, his legs finally working, he hears Brave Hawk say, 'You'll be the next one out, Stuntman.'

Jamal can't resist. Right in front of Art and the camera crew, he pivots. 'If it means getting away from you, sign me up.'

For a moment Brave Hawk doesn't react. Then, strangely, he bursts out laughing. He actually claps his hands together, like a happy infant. 'Outstanding! God *damn*, Stuntman, you're good!' Then Brave Hawk looks past Jamal to the camera crew. 'Did you guys get that?'

'Yeah,' Art says, 'but don't point us out, okay?'

'As long as you got it,' Brave Hawk says, striding across the deck, daring to slap Jamal on the back. 'Just another heated, interpersonal, real-life moment for the viewers of *American Hero*, right?'

'You suck, Brave Hawk.'

For an instant, the Apache looks wounded. 'The offer was genuine, Stuntman. I just made use of your rejection for the good of the show.'

And now Jamal *really* wants to kill him.

♥

What troubles him most is the realization that Brave Hawk is essentially correct: Stuntman has no offensive weapons, no arrows in the old quiver. He can only be reactive.

Another reason to be bitter about what happened to him.

He still remembers the night his wild card turned – far out in the Valley, so far out that the hills were rising again. It was the spring of his senior year at USC, where he was majoring in film and television. Part of the experience there was to work on everyone's student project. Who knew the pimply twenty-year-old serving as director might turn out to be the next Bryan Singer, and your ticket to a career on his crew.

The other goal was to become the first Jamal Norwood – a Denzel Washington or Will Smith for the twenty-first century. And when Nic Deladrier asked him to play the badass joker in his student film, Jamal knew – just knew – it was the first step. Deladrier was not only the most skilled of all the senior year directors, he was ambitious as hell. He had friends in the business, an uncle working at Endeavour ... this student film would be shown at festivals, and Jamal Norwood's name and face would be known throughout that strata of the business where young assistants and junior agents share bodily fluids, job recommendations, and gossip.

The script called for Jamal, dressed in a leather outfit and mask as Derek Knight – wealthy amateur astronomer who, in the 1940s, discovered the approaching Takisian ship and tried to warn a skeptical America – to leap from the top of a water tank that had been painted the same color as the alien ship.

The team had built a platform covered with foam rubber six feet below Jamal's launch point – out of frame. Jamal had practiced the leap four times, twice in daylight. He was ready to do it for Deladrier's camera.

But as often happened in southern California in the spring, it had rained that day. Not just rained Seattle-style, but poured torrentially, like a typhoon. The surface of the tower was too slick for Jamal's boots. When he made the leap, he slipped – and missed the platform.

The water tower was on a hillside. The drop to the base of the hill was, Jamal later learned, over a hundred feet. The base was jagged rock – not that he hit directly, he slammed into several tree branches before cart-wheeling onto the rocks.

What he remembered was the confusion of slipping, reaching for the platform – the horrified look on Deladrier's face as the director flew upward from Jamal's point of view.

That was followed by the roller-coaster moment of freefall – no panic, just disbelief.

Then a blinding, gasping impact, like being hit by a speeding truck. Shock mercifully suppressed the pain for a few moments. Long enough for Jamal to realize he had fallen ten stories onto the rocks and was still alive.

He couldn't be certain. He was blind, deaf, without feeling in his arms and legs. For an eternally terrible moment he thought this *was* death.

But then his vision returned, at least to where he could see the flashlights of rescuers searching for him. As the roaring in his ears died down, like the temporary damage from a heavy metal concert, he heard voices, boots crunching on brush.

A face appeared upside down above him – male, white, middle-aged, bearded. 'He's here!' a voice called, far away. 'Jesus Christ.'

The face turned away, and even through his damaged ears, Jamal could hear the man retching.

Jamal Norwood lived; his wild card had turned. He was now an ace, albeit an ace whose power simply seemed to be the ability to bounce back from extreme violence, usually within twenty-four hours. The greater the damage, the longer his recovery.

The accident changed his life in more subtle ways: in true Hollywood fashion, Nic Deladrier survived the near-disaster to land an assignment as director of *Halloween Night XIII* – and whether motivated by guilt or just the practical value of having an ace for a stuntman, the first thing he did was hire Jamal Norwood.

Jamal resisted, until the pile of money got too high – and the offers to act never materialized.

For the past five years he has gone from one gig to another, one set of gags – stunts – to another, well-paid, usually falling from a great height wearing pinhole cameras for that close close-up experience. He had been flung off a spaceship in *One Against the Legion*, dropped to the bottom of a pit and then buried under tons of cement in *Hoover Dam*, crushed by the giant stomping feet of a war machine run amok in the remake of *Kronos* ...

Such was his life. It was almost Shakespearean, for God's sake. To fall, to almost die ... and, painfully, to bounce back.

◆

Showered, with no visible signs of yesterday's damage, dressed, Jamal is ravenous. He heads downstairs for the kitchen.

The Clubs are not expected to cook for themselves, any more than they are expected to choose wardrobe. 'It's like we're back in grade school,' Spasm had sneered, first day in the place. That was before they'd lost the second challenge, and voted his sorry ass off the team.

Even so, meal times are fixed, and Jamal has missed breakfast. Nevertheless, he has been living on his own for five years and he is capable of cooking a meal. He begins searching through the refrigerator and cupboards for eggs, bacon, pans, cups, a process made more difficult because the mansion housing the Clubs has been designed for its visual imprint, not utility. To begin with, the kitchen has been painted a primary blue, a color that makes all food look unappetizing. And nothing is where it would logically be.

He has managed to locate a frying pan when Jade Blossom enters. To Jamal's immense disappointment, she has exchanged the startling bikini for a tank top and baggy shorts, as if she were off for a morning at the mall. Still, she looks adorable. 'That's ambitious,' she says, noting Jamal's obvious search for the makings of a meal. 'If you're looking for food after Holy Roller's been through here, good luck.'

'I'm just amazed the guy even fits in the building.'

'Or through the canyons.'

'They got him inside the truck. It was the truck that had to get up the narrow road.' Jamal will never forget the comic insanity of Clubs move-in day ... the face of the elderly female neighbor whose shiny Jag had to wait while the *American Hero* convoy of camera limo, Club Humvee, and moving van negotiated the hairpin curve just outside the gate. Riding with Jamal and Toad Man, Spasm had thought to have some fun with the woman. 'What do you think, should I give her a little thrill? When was the last time she popped?'

'You shouldn't distract the lady while she's driving,' Toad Man had said with great indignance, beating Jamal by milliseconds. (There were useful wild card powers, and then there were the ridiculous ones: Spasm's ability to make other people orgasm or sneeze at will struck Jamal as proof that life made no fucking sense. Jamal wouldn't miss Spasm, now that he had deservedly joined the Discards.)

Getting Roller out of the truck and into the mansion had taxed even the great minds of the *American Hero* team: ramps had been built to allow the gigantic ace to shuffle his way to the front door, but getting all five hundred pounds of the man out of the truck ... well, it took both camera crews and a lot of sweating and cursing.

'They should have used a crane,' Toad had said, in all seriousness. 'Isn't that what movie people use?'

Jamal had failed to answer, as Holy Roller began, in his best Sunday-go-to-meeting voice, to alternately berate the grips for cursing ('Gentlemen, please! To hear the Lord's name and everyone else's taken in vain on such a beautiful day! It's a shame, it is!') while alerting them to the glories of God's plan ('Join the righteous, my friends! Find the joy!') was theater no one dared interrupt.

Now, alone in the kitchen with beautiful, unapproachable Jade, Jamal is half-worried that Roller is right outside … listening … and, if listening, judging.

'Now they have to use that truck to keep us supplied.'

'Another good reason to vote him off.'

Jade shook her pretty head. 'They'll keep Roller around as long as they can. He's too much like the people watching this shit.'

'How'd you get to be so cynical, so young?'

Jade can't be more than two years younger than Jamal. 'Go to a few auditions as an actress and see what it does to you.'

Jamal realizes that beautiful Jade has no idea what he does – granted, their introductions had been perfunctory, but Jamal has since pored over the online bios. Jade obviously hasn't, or she would know that he has been on his share of auditions, too. More proof that he has no chance with her. 'Why did you join *American Hero*, then? It's really the same shit, isn't it?'

She has found a box of Cheerios and casually opens it. As Jamal looks for a bowl and a spoon, he sees Jade eating right out of the box. Not that he objects – she could put her mouth on anything he owns – but he's so hungry he's almost salivating. 'I like shows like this. *Laguna Beach*, *Survivor*, *Great Race*. They're the only thing I ever watch.'

Nothing in this cupboard. 'So you know exactly how to play the game.'

'Yeah.' She crunches away. 'They sort of cast these things. There's always the old guy, the biker, the crazy one—' and here she smiles '—the minority.'

'Only me?' Jamal gestures gracefully toward Jade. 'What about Chinese-American girls?'

'My category is hot girl. Hot girl trumps the whole minority thing.' This is as true as it is irritating. 'The other category in reality TV is freaks, but …' And here Jade smiles very fetchingly. At that instant, Jamal is lost – she can be as bitchy and self-centered as she wants, she will have to rip his heart out of his chest and stomp it. 'On *American Hero* the freaks are the majority. Which is why even a … hugely fat white man is someone they have to hold onto. Will someone answer the fucking phone? Please?'

Jamal realizes he has been hearing a chirping from the living room. Toad Man hollers that he will get it. 'Hullo,' they hear him say. 'This is Buford.'

'So you've got your strategy all figured out. Be the hot girl.'

'And let you big strong men knock each other off.'

'How am I supposed to knock these other guys off? My wild card is nothing but defensive. I take a licking and keep on ticking. Big whoop.'

Jade is still crunching. 'I thought you were the big jock!'

This is a surprisingly perceptive thing for a woman as self-involved as Jade to say. 'Who says I'm a jock?'

'You walk like a jock. You talk like a jock. I know jocks … all my brothers play sports.'

Toad Man appears in the kitchen doorway, blinking, as always, in apparent bafflement. 'Hullo. Ah, they want us. Griffith Park Observatory. Does anyone know where that is?'

Wet, glistening, still in her bikini, just out of the pool, Diver drips in the hallway. 'In Griffith Park.'

Holy Roller is at the other end of the hallway, blocking it like a cork in a wine bottle and – to Jamal's amusement – preventing Art and the camera crew for getting any useful footage. 'Praise God. Another challenge. May the Lord be with us!'

The Clubs disperse to their rooms for last-minute prep for cameras, including Jade Blossom. Jamal realizes that the woman has taken the box of Cheerios. And that he still hasn't had breakfast.

♠

Jade has come surprisingly close to explaining everything there is to know about Jamal Norwood. Forget the wild card – his life changed from what he wanted to something else long before that rainy night in 2001.

Jamal's father, Big Bill Norwood, was the best athlete in a South Central neighborhood noted for NBA stars and NFL running backs, for all kinds of major and minor league baseball players. 'No hockey players, though,' Bill used to say. 'No ice.'

Jamal was good, too, with the speed and eye-hand coordination of a world-class athlete. What he lacked was size, topping out at five-nine, 160 pounds in his junior year at powerhouse Loyola High. He could be the best basketball or football player the world had ever seen, but no scout or coach would look at him long enough to notice. That's assuming the coach's eyes noticed him at all, since he was a head shorter than his teammates.

Jamal had already experienced the humiliation of being passed over for the varsity baseball team at Loyola, even though his batting average was the highest on the team. He made the mistake of complaining to Bill one night on the drive home.

Big Bill simply shook his head. 'Forget about being a pro athlete,' he said. 'You're never going to make it.'

'But I'm good, Dad! As good as the Wilkes brothers!'

'I'm not talking about "good," Jamal! You *are* good, probably in the top five percent of all the athletes your age. I'm just saying you're never going to be a pro athlete. You've got too much going on.'

'I don't understand.'

Big Bill sighed. 'You've got too much going on *in your head*.' He must have realized that Jamal was still failing to see what he meant. 'Look, you need two things to be a pro athlete: the skills, which you have, and the right kind of brain – which you don't.'

'Are you saying I'm stupid?'

'I'm saying the opposite. I'm saying that you've got too many other things in your life to think about! What makes a kid a pro athlete is *not having* any other choices. You've got to be able to shoot hoops for six hours a day after school. You've got to bounce that ball off the step. And you've got to do it because you *can't* do anything else! Because it *is* boring. If you get bored, if you find that you'd rather go to the movies or read a book or study or even chase girls, you aren't gonna be a world-class athlete.'

Jamal mumbled something about jocks getting all the girls. 'True. But it's because the girls chase them, not the other way around.'

So he went off to USC determined to be the opposite of his father – not a jock, but an intellectual. He read Eggers and Pynchon and, yes, Stendahl. He discovered Marcel Duchamp and the Constructionists. He studied French film and Howard Hawks movies.

He even saw *The Jolson Story*.

Now *that* career had been sacrificed on the altar of the wild card.

Jamal Norwood *needs American Hero*.

♣

'Today's challenge is the Scavenger Hunt.'

Griffith Park Observatory has just emerged from a five-year-long, $90 million reconstruction. Having been dragged to the site for field trips all through grade school, Jamal feels as though he knows the place – and to his eye, it has not changed. The only difference is that you could no longer park. If he and the other Clubs hadn't been driving their *American Hero* Humvees, they'd have had to take a bus.

Not that it matters for the Clubs. They are the last of the four suits to arrive, joining the other convoys as well as the horde of production vehicles and honey wagons.

Now Jamal and the other Clubs are lined up in front of a giant emblem so flimsy it flutters in the gentle morning breeze, and some kind of flat structure, like a scoreboard, covered with a colored sheet. The aces from the other suits, from Clubs to Diamonds to Spades to Hearts, all stand in front of Peregrine, all cleverly positioned so the light is in their faces. Peregrine herself steps onto a slick plastic circle twenty feet wide, bearing the *American Hero* logo.

Jamal has been on a dozen film sets, and yet he is still amazed at the artifice. Maybe it's another sign that he is in the wrong business; he wants the characters on TV and in the movies to be *real*.

Toad Man nudges Jamal. 'Boy, I thought *we* were having tough times. Look at *them*,' he says, nodding to the five Diamonds gathering in front of the symbol for their suit. They remind Jamal of an expansion baseball team about to take the field against the Brooklyn Dodgers. Only no expansion team had ever fielded such a sad-ass player as the Maharajah, missing two legs and one arm.

The Hearts, on the other hand, look cocky. There are six of them, just as there are six Clubs. Both teams have won a challenge, and the immunity that goes with it. The Spades and Diamonds, losers both times out, are down to five players apiece.

Jamal blinks – put them out of your mind. Think like Big Bill Norwood. They are *all* the enemy.

'We have hidden five statues just like this—' Peregrine raises a golden figurine, a stylized Jetboy a foot tall '—at five different locations around Los Angeles. The team that returns here within four hours with the most Jetboys wins. It's that simple.'

'Any rules?' Drummer Boy booms, shooting a shit-eating grin down at his partner in crime, Hardhat.

'Of course,' Peregrine says. 'Just one: there are no rules.'

Most of the aces actually finish the phrase for her. Jamal can feel his heart rate rise, as it did when he walked from the on-deck circle to home plate ... or his first moment on set.

'Okay, may I present ... the Scavenger Hunt!' Peregrine pulls the covers off a giant electronic display – currently blank.

'Shit!'

'One minute, Mom. They lost the feed.' That from John Fortune, hand to earpiece, running toward a satellite truck a dozen yards away – no doubt happy to have an excuse not to be Drummer Boy's Stepin Fetchit.

'Do the locations even matter?' Diver is behind him. 'No matter what, I wind up fishing or swimming. The life aquatic. Christ.'

'Could be worse. You could be a tackling dummy like me.'

'A what?'

Jamal sighs. 'Think of a punching bag on a sled. Football players practice tackles on it.'

'Let's trade places. I bet I'd like being tackled more than you would.'

'You've got a bad attitude.'

'You have no idea.' She forces a smile.

'Okay, aces! *American Heroes!*' The board has been fired up successfully, a MapQuest look at Los Angeles County, with five beeping dots. One is in the Valley near the intersection of the 405 and Ventura Boulevard; one appears to be on a peak near Mount Wilson; one is in the middle of Beverly Hills; one is way the hell and gone in Venice, by the ocean; and one appears to be located just over the hill from Griffith Park Observatory.

Jamal has no interest in dragging his ass all the way to Venice, or up some mountainside, and – as a Los Angeles resident – knows better than to face the 405 and Ventura area at any time of day. He'd also like to avoid getting into a battle anywhere near Rodeo Drive. Who needs the attitude? Besides, he has a good idea what that fifth location is.

As Jamal watches, the screen changes, actual addresses and images popping up, to reactions that range from appreciative to confused.

The fifth location is Griffith Park Zoo.

Peregrine is posing for a trio of cameras. 'You see your possible destinations. How you reach them and how you return is up to you.' She points to a huge, ridiculous clock, complete with *American Hero* hands, that has been dragged into the center of the circle. 'When I say "go" and the clock starts, you're off.

'Any last questions?' Faux drama. Jamal finds this intensely annoying and turns away before he hears Peregrine shout ...

'*Go!*'

♥

The first challenge is the freakish mad scramble to decide which of the Clubs goes where. It takes two minutes of suggestions, argument, and actual shoving before it reaches total chaos. As Jade

Blossom and Diver tussle over which of the pair would be best suited to search in Beverly Hills, Toad Man turns to Jamal and gives a half-smile. 'This reminds me of a football huddle.'

'Yeah, but nobody is the quarterback.'

It's Holy Roller who uses his voice and bulk to restore order. 'Dammit, people!' The uncharacteristic use of profanity shocks the team to relative silence. 'Time, as they say, is a-wasting. Brother Stuntman, you know this godless city better than any of us. Why don't *you* give us some guidance – and quickly.'

Whether he likes it or not, Jamal is suddenly in charge. And the choices are obvious: 'Brave Hawk, the mountain location. Reverend, you and Toad hit that Valley spot. Jade, Beverly Hills.'

Jade's face lights up in triumph – which is bad enough, but then she elbows Diver. 'Too bad, baby' – as Jamal is forced to say, 'Diver, Venice.' Remembering their earlier conversation, he adds, 'Sorry.'

If Diver's wild card were laser eyes, Jamal's head would vaporize. 'Fuck you, Stuntman. Where are you going?'

'The zoo.'

◆

The departure is a mad scramble, and not just for Clubs. Brave Hawk flaps into the sky. A few seconds later, Jetman launches himself in a blast of smoke and flame, the echo booming off the hills. Buford transforms into a toad the size of a Volkswagen and goes bounding off, with Roller rumbling behind him. A pelican the size of a hot air balloon appears out of nowhere and flaps off to the northeast – one of Dragon Girl's stuffed toys, transformed. Is she heading for the zoo? Or Mount Wilson to battle Brave Hawk and Jetman?

Jamal hears Rosa Loteria shouting for Rustbelt to 'take the zoo!' The ridiculous-looking hoser ace jumps into a production truck and starts grinding the gears ... the whole interior of the vehicle is probably now rust. Jade Blossom grabs John Fortune's cell phone and calls for a cab. Well, she's headed for Beverly Hills.

Ever Big Bill Norwood's son, Jamal gets a good jump, running for the Humvee and sliding into the driver's seat before anyone else even reaches the parking lot. He is amused to find Art in the back with Diaz and camera in the passenger seat. 'Who did you guys piss off today?'

'You're not gonna be pointing at us all day, are you, Stuntman?' Art sounds completely beaten down.

'Sorry,' Jamal says. He backs the car out of the lot and burns, as fast as he can, toward the eastern exit.

Growing up in Los Angeles has given Jamal a highly developed sense of geography, especially of various traffic shortcuts. He finds a turn-out just beyond a tunnel and quickly passes Rustbelt's truck. 'So I'm heading for the zoo,' he says, turning to Art. 'What am I supposed to do, wrestle a fucking alligator?'

Art can't hide the smile. 'Something like that.' Another reason why he is really a bad *American Hero* producer: he's jumpy about contestants breaking the fourth wall, yet can't keep his own mouth shut.

Jamal thinks for an instant – a long, stretched, athlete-in-the-zone moment, the sort he experienced on a long base hit, a broken field run, a shot from downtown. He could win this. He feels it. He wants it.

When he reaches the parking lot at the base of the hill, near the turn to the Greek Theater and right across Vermont from the battered little Roosevelt Golf Course, Jamal pulls over. He is still a few minutes ahead of his competitors. For a moment he considers simply waiting for the parade. Why not follow the competition? Lay back, hit them from behind when the time is right? Of course, that strategy presumed Rustbelt could find his ass with both hands.

What the hell. If you're going to play the game, play it balls out. More words from Big Bill Norwood. Let the other guy react to *you*.

One, two, three – here comes a truck and a pair of Humvees. Jamal can't see who's in the third vehicle. But who cares? The cars disappear into the neighborhood and what Jamal knows is horrific midday traffic.

The standard route would take them all south on Vermont to busy Los Feliz, then east and north to the entrance to the park and zoo. But there is another way …

'Are you gonna get going, Jamal? Or should we order lunch?'

He smiles. 'Art, do you wonder why I keep talking to you?'

Art shuts up. He obviously knows his own weakness.

'I *am* going, Art. Watch this.'

And Jamal pulls out of the lot and heads left instead of right – climbing a twisty road that he knows will carry him up and over the spine of the hills to approach the zoo from the other side.

♠

Griffith Park Zoo is closed for the day – Jamal would have known that from the empty lot where school buses were usually queued up. But an *American Hero* camera crew is positioned right next to the entrance – and clearly not expecting an arrival just yet. Jamal is amused to see the crew scramble like ants. 'I guess you should have called these guys, Art.'

Jamal pulls up to the entrance – knows he's in the center of two lenses – and suddenly this is like being not only on a movie set, but as the lead. Why can't he play an American hero?

He can feel his eyes narrow – a full Clint Eastwood – as he scans the scene, right to left and back – a modified Schwarzenegger. A path has been marked with cones leading from the entrance past the row of animal habitats.

Jamal turns on the Tom Cruise smile. 'Showtime.'

He guns the vehicle forward. 'Anybody behind us, Art?'

Art simply doesn't answer.

The trip is a short one – Jamal would have to be an idiot to miss the AMERICAN HERO SCAVENGER HUNT, so proclaimed on a banner.

The idea that an idol is somehow secreted inside the zoo strikes Jamal as silly – but then, so has every challenge until now. Nevertheless, Jamal does not expect to go up against a rare Bengal tiger – and he isn't.

American Hero had built a habitat of its very own. And inside it? A brown bear, some kind of lion, a rhino – and a moat filled with snakes.

And a brand new fence that sparks and hums, electrified.

'Something for all of us,' Tiffani says from behind him. So much for getting the jump. The reflection of the brilliant midday sun precedes her. Tiffani is in full diamond mode.

Jamal has never really met the glittering Diamond girl. He wonders how many discussions there were between Berman and his production team about whether or not the ace from West Virginia had to be in the Diamond suit because of her ability to transform herself into superhard carbon.

(Then he wonders how many discussions there were about making sure Jamal Norwood, aka Stuntman, did *not* wind up in Spades.)

In her natural state she is, as they would no doubt say up in some West Virginia hollow, a purty little *thang* – red-haired, bright-eyed, not much of a figure, but a definite attitude. Jamal's early impressions labeled her a white trash trailer park babe, but that could be the accent. Being this close to her for the first time forces him to revise his opinion to a more positive one. If Jamal didn't have Jade Blossom to drool over, he could do worse than Tiffani. Though not today. Not with immunity on the line.

'You can have mine,' he says.

'And they say gallantry is dead.'

Jamal smiles. 'You made good time.'

'They had a police escort for us.' That explains it; Jamal knows there's no way his competitors could be here already, going the long way around in L.A. traffic!

That's another thing he failed to anticipate … the continued interference by the *American Hero* production team. What else have they got cooked up for him? He slips along the freshly painted safety railing – surprisingly substantial, for an *American Hero* construct – noting the various booby traps laid for the contestants. Beyond the moat of snakes, there were odd-shaped pools filled with some kind of bubbling goo – acid? Surely not. Holes in walls – would something shoot out of there? Projectiles? Or balls of flame? The ground within the habitat, where the animals were clearly not walking (fenced by some low-level electrical current?), was marked with a grid. Webbing? What would happen if you stepped on it? Would you be hobbled, bound? Or would you fall through? Roaming through this habitat … three big, mean animals who somehow managed to keep from attacking each other? (A thought that inspires Jamal to look for feeding troughs – he finds them in the shadows at the rear, piled high with disgusting substances.) The question remains, of course: where is the damned idol? Come on, Jetboy, show yourself!

Tiffani nods toward the habitat. 'Hey, lookie there.' She points with perfect fluidity of motion, surprising Jamal, who expects to hear grinding: Rustbelt is atop the cagelike habitat, the bars now looking aged, thanks to the ace's touch. And a few yards away – still outside – an honest-to-God T Rex is distracting the lion. Wild Fox is here too.

Jamal is impressed with the thought that Rustbelt must have made a hell of a leap to reach the cage. Either that, or his touch was enough to protect him going across the electrified fence.

Jamal looks for some kind of staging area, preferably one in front of a camera crew. He can still see Rustbelt hanging from the gridwork and Wild Fox's T Rex engaging the animals. The bear roars and swipes at Rustbelt, fast and close enough to send the iron yokel sprawling. 'Hey, watch it!' Rustbelt yells, his nasal Minnesota accent as annoying as a honking car. 'Geez, you could hurt a guy, ya know?' Then he laughs stupidly, as if it was all just an act for the cameras. But even from fifty yards away, Jamal can see Rustbelt's hands shaking. He drops to the ground with a clang that echoes off the walls of the habitat's caves, and starts sidling between two of the domed units, tipping over fake rocks and newly planted trees. There's no obvious way in, not that Jamal can see.

What the hell.

Jamal flings himself at the electrified fence, feels the stinging spark – the total, instantaneous clench of every muscle in his body – know that can't be good … smells his own flesh singeing.

Then he hits the concrete apron bordering the moat. He lies on his back, panting, twitching, the sun and sky whirling. He feels as though he's been flattened by a three-hundred-pound linebacker at full speed, or dropped from an airplane.

Come on, bounceback …

How long? He's not sure. He forces himself to sit up … stand up. Okay, he's still in the game.

It's not impossible to jump the moat, Jamal sees. Like most *American Hero* hurdles, it is designed to look more challenging than it actually is. A quick leap, and he's over.

Though he slips on what proves to be dirt that is so hard it's become slick. Trying to right himself, he feels as though he's pulled a thigh muscle. Fucking idiot. The injury won't do anything but throb and slow him down. The trauma isn't severe enough to trigger a bounceback. Where's the big wild card power now?

'Hey, Rusty! Look out!' Jamal turns – atop the railing, at the opposite side of the habitat from glittering Tiffani, Wild Fox has resumed his natural form, ears and tail and all, and is alerting Rustbelt to Stuntman's approach. Jamal can't even see the iron ace, though the grunting and snorting of bear and lion are clues to his location.

Suddenly Tiffani flashes into view, still outside the railing. 'Behind you, Stuntman!' she yells helpfully.

A shadow falls across Jamal. The rhino. Wham! The beast head-butts him, sending him crashing into one of the domes covering a cave. The surface of the dome is raw concrete – it's not enough for Jamal to be slammed into it, he's also scraped raw, bleeding.

And trying to avoid the rhino's feet. Miss. Miss.

Then a direct hit on his left shoulder. He can't help screaming, can't help hearing his voice echoing in the habitat.

He drags himself inside the habitat. The rhino, either satisfied by the punishment it has inflicted on the intruder, or otherwise distracted, turns away, allowing Jamal to begin to bounceback.

One new sensation breaks through the pain: this cave is the worst-smelling place Jamal has ever been in.

He sits … tests his shoulder. Completely shattered, but rebuilding. He uses the time to search the interior of the cave for Jetboy. No, nothing but bear or rhino shit.

Presently he drags himself out of the cave, emerging to a clamor of voices – Wild Fox roaring in his latest animal persona, Rustbelt yelling like a drunk at a tailgate party, Art and the other producers keeping their cameras aimed. Something is going on out of his line of sight. Fine. It gives him time to search further.

He performs a flanking maneuver, putting one of the caves between him and the snorting rhino, who seems – if possible – to be growing more agitated at the presence of multiple aces in the habitat.

In the shadows Jamal sees not only the expected foliage and the odd box or barrel – presumably filled with feed – but other obstacles, including what could only be a limbo bar.

Who is that stupid production designer again? Or is this the work of the 'writers' Jamal had seen lurking with the camera crews?

Maybe it's his experience on films, where the action is usually broken into pieces, but he feels a strange sensation, as if he is seeing his quest as it will appear on plasma screens days or weeks hence … wide-angle habitat … lion, bear, rhino … snakes in moat … face of Tiffani … Wild Fox with his ears pricked up and his tail swooshing. Cut, cut, cut!

Rustbelt kicks over a bucket of feed, starts pawing through it.

Wild Fox is in the habitat now – and he's taken the shape of the bear! Which one is the ace? Ah, the one stopping to search.

Tiffani, where's Tiffani? Got to have that eye candy, people! There she is, glittering and glowing. And to Jamal's amazement, then fury, she simply steps on the electrified wire – balancing like an acrobat as St. Elmo's Fire envelopes her harmlessly – then simply dropping to safety in the habitat.

Of course. Stuntman is flesh and blood. He gets hurt, then bounces back. Tiffani is transformed into one of the hardest substances known, a lousy conductor. A few stray volts of electricity wouldn't even curl her hair, assuming it could be curled. She shoots the camera a smile so bright that Jamal can see it from behind, the way it shines on the crew's faces.

She turns. 'Get going, Stuntman!' Cut. Cut. Cut.

Then it's Rustbelt, ducking under the sweeping paw of the brown bear. (What the fuck does he think he's doing?) Cut.

Wild Fox-as-the-bear pulls apart one of the cavelike habitats and begins picking through its contents in a very fastidious, unbearlike manner. 'What have we got here?' he says. *Shit, does he have the Jetboy idol?* Jamal wonders. *Am I screwed?* Cut.

Then Jamal himself, Stuntman, is suddenly face-to-face with a lion. For one fraction of a second, he wants to laugh at the image … black man with a lion! Like some black-and-white jungle movie.

He's been electrocuted and stomped. He can't handle being slashed. *Gotta go, gotta move.* Make it more like the football field: run, spin, stop, reverse.

His bad leg slows him as he tries to clear a casing that covers pipes and a faucet. *Wham!* Jamal hits again, not hard by Stuntman standards, but enough to knock his wind out.

Tiffani screams at the lion, causing the beast to turn – it freaks out, if a lion can freak out – at the sight of her.

Under the tipped casing, Jamal sees the damned idol, Jet-boy, lying on his back. He rolls so he can crawl toward it …

Zap. He can't fucking do it! That grid in the habitat floor – it's some kind of nonlethal weapon, a wireless taser, slowing him down! Reach, crawl, reach …

'Hey, Rusty!' He can hear Wild Fox.

Where? Jamal turns away from the glittery idol – still out of reach – can't see either Wild Fox or Rustbelt – no Tiffani, either. But they must be closing in. Three camera crews are scrambling closer.

Then there are the animals. He can smell them …

Boom! Here comes Drummer Boy, all arms and attitude, yelping as he hits the taser field, but snatching Jetboy out from under the casing before Jamal is within five feet of the thing. 'Tough luck, superstar!'

Not Drummer Boy: *Wild Fox!* As he turns, Jamal reaches out, finds his tail. He can't see it, but it's there. He gives it a yank, and 'Drummer' loses his balance, turns back into Wild Fox … and sits down in a pile of bear shit. He hits hard and loses the idol.

Jamal finally gets to his feet. Dragging himself after the figurine, he sees it picked up by Rustbelt … it instantly changes color and texture. Seeing his immunity in the Minnesotan's hands – a stocky, stupid-looking kid who acts like an ape with a hand grenade – Jamal loses his temper. 'You ruined it, hotshot!' Jamal shouts.

Rustbelt reacts as though Jamal has slapped him. And while he is distracted, Tiffani appears next to him and snatches the idol from his hand.

'Hey!' Rustbelt is even more wounded.

'Don't let her do that, goddammit!' Wild Fox snaps. He scrambles over the fence and out of the habitat. Rustbelt stands frozen as Tiffani actually poses with Jetboy, like a hostess on a game show, all glittering girlishness. 'Purty, ain't it?' Her accent is as thick as Jamal has ever heard it. He knows what she's doing. Four cameras are on her and the male aces flanking her. The first one to make a move will look like a mugger attacking a cheerleader.

With one last look over his shoulder – yes, there's the damned rhino, looking as confused as Rustbelt – Jamal joins the group in front of the cameras. 'So much for teamwork,' he says.

'Come on, Jamal, what did you expect? We can't share the idol.'

She's right, of course. They were never teammates. Jamal rejected the idea. He realizes that he resents the way she's got the idol: not from her wild card ability, which is no more useful than Jamal's, but from *being a girl.*

'You haven't got back with it yet,' Rustbelt says, the longest, most coherent sentence Jamal has heard him utter.

For a moment, the sentence seems to take shape and hover in the air … a tangible challenge.

Tiffani realizes that her feminine immunity might be in danger.

As the cameras follow, she starts running for her vehicle.

♣

Jamal has bounced back enough that his leg no longer bothers him, though his shoulder will be a gooey mess for hours yet. He easily out-distances Wild Fox and Rustbelt in the race to the vehicles. But Tiffani is ahead of him, Tiffani is pulling out, right behind an *American Hero* Humvee and its camera crew. Jamal reaches his own wheels – Art and his camera operator are already inside. Clearly they expect to record his frustration at losing to Tiffani.

It isn't until he is on the road, zipping through traffic heading south from the zoo, that Jamal begins to wonder just what he hopes to accomplish. 'How are the other contests going?'

'I hear the shopping is taking too long.' Art glances over his shoulder at the camera operator, who snickers. 'Brave Hawk whupped up on Jetman. He's already back with his idol.'

So Brave Hawk would live to fight another day. Jamal really needs to win, if only so he can spare himself a boatload of condescension from the Apache ace. This assumes, of course, that Jamal isn't voted out.

It won't be for lack of high-speed driving. Jamal has been trained, and while doing spins and turns in a controlled environment like a movie location is far easier than simply going fast, running lights and driving on the shoulder … he has the skills, and the two yokels behind him do not.

He catches Tiffani at the turn east onto Los Feliz, pulling abreast of her. For a moment she isn't aware of him – too distracted by the stares, shouts, and gestures she is getting from the cars behind and in front of her. Then she glances to her right – and Jamal has the pleasure of seeing true surprise on her face.

'There's nothing you can do, Jamal!' She isn't saying it to be mean, he thinks. And for a moment he feels bad, because he has realized how to get the idol from her.

But only for a moment. The other aces like Tiffani. She won't be voted off. Jamal, however, is on the bubble.

He can't make the move here, not on Los Feliz, with three lanes of midday L.A. traffic surging, then slowing, like gobs of sludge in a fat man's bloodstream.

Suddenly he sees an opening on the right. Tiffani's car is stuck behind the Humvee in the middle lane, but there is room to pass on the right, where, insanely, cars are parked. Zip to the right, then zip back before creaming himself on a BMW. He shoots a light – Tiffani and the *American Hero* team are now a good minute behind. Now he's able to turn onto Vermont and stop. 'Get out,' he tells Art and the camera guy.

'What the hell are you doing, Jamal?'

'Get the fuck out of here so you don't get hurt!'

Fortunately, Art is one of those people who reacts quickly. Maybe it's the look in Jamal's eyes. The producer and camera operator pile out of the Humvee. Jamal has it in motion before the doors slam.

He looks in the rearview mirror. The camera Humvee is just now making the turn, fifty yards back.

Faster, faster. He needs more time.

Past the golf course, whipping to the left. Up the hill. The glistening dome of the observatory flashes past like a rising sun.

Here! A turnout just around the edge of the hill. He slews the car around, frantic, get ready. He blinks sweat out of his eyes. This is genuinely nuts. He wants to be anywhere but here. Big Bill is right – he doesn't have the mentality for competition.

Tiffani's Humvee drives past. And without making a conscious decision, Jamal guns his vehicle right into the side of Tiffani's car, neatly T-boning it off the ledge.

Jamal feels himself go weightless, like a drop on Space Mountain or that awful, awful fall on the Nic Deladrier project. The impact of car on rock, then on Tiffani's car, is like being slammed into a brick the size of a garage door.

He is hanging in the air, in his lap and chest belt, nothing new broken, but definitely in pain, especially with his rubbery shoulder. He has smacked the side of his face, too. But the massive Humvee is intact – he is able to open the door and pull himself out.

He can smell smoke and feels dust in his throat. The light is so brilliant his eyes hurt. A breeze is starting to swirl up the canyon, a Santa Ana driven by the differing temperatures of desert to the north and ocean to the south. The only sounds are distant voices, school kids at play on fields far below, their shouts amplified by the surrounding hills.

The slope is steep. He has to hold onto the car to keep from slipping down. His legs aren't good, but he can already feel them bouncing back. Tiffani's car is ten yards farther down the slope, upright, but its body crunched, as if squeezed in a giant's fist.

And Tiffani is still strapped into the front seat – her glittering diamondlike surface smudged with dust. She is frantically trying to free herself, a process complicated by her need to scream at Jamal. 'You stupid son of a bitch!' It actually takes her several seconds and deep breaths to get the words out. Jamal merely slides to the passenger side of her vehicle and – absorbing three first-rate punches – plucks the foot-tall, rust-colored Jetboy out of the wheel well.

'You could have killed me! What do you think you're doing?'

'Winning.' He sees how trapped she is. 'When I get to the top, I'll make sure they come for you.'

He jams the idol inside his shirt because he needs both hands to get up the slope.

♥

Bounceback is working for him – he has jogged two hundred yards up the road, one turn short of the observatory lot and the finish line, before he sees – strangely – a beautiful, naked woman standing just up the hill, like Hugh Hefner's vision of Eden. It's Jade Blossom! His dream girl with the saucy mouth and amazing breasts …

He trips, his feet tangled in a rope. As he hits, he lands on Jetboy. More pain. Rolling on his side, struggling to free himself with one good hand, Jamal sees Jade Blossom transform back into Wild Fox.

Of course.

Not only have Wild Fox and Rustbelt caught him, they have help. Drummer Boy is here, too, and Rosa Loteria – which would explain the caballero reeling in the lasso that tripped him up. Adding to the fun, there is a camera crew with Rustbelt – Art and Diaz.

Jamal looks up the road. The camera Humvee has backtracked. Then the *whump-whumping* of helicopter blades causes everyone to turn. The aerial camera from the flying challenge is back now, too.

Jamal feels as though he has become Will Smith. He is the action-movie star, and this is his big finish. This is like *Bad Aces II*. Helicopters, Santa Anas stirring dust, afternoon light. All he needs is theme music.

'Come on, tough guy,' Drummer Boy shouts, easily blocking the mountain road with his flailing arms. He looks like a Hindu god on crack. As the chopper swoops south toward Sunset Boulevard and Thai Town to make a turn, Jamal hears the crunch of steps behind him. He bolts, and dodges a blow from Rustbelt.

He is surrounded. And outnumbered.

The only safe thing is to keep moving. He's faster and more mobile than his opponents. All he has to do is reach the damned finish line.

Drummer Boy picks up a rock and flings it. Jamal sees it, dodges, but here comes another one. Fuck! Without thinking, he ducks, hauls Jetboy out of his shirt – stands like A-Rod at the plate and smacks the next projectile. The impact is jarring, like hitting a baseball on a cold day.

But what takes the sting away is seeing that projectile smack Drummer Boy in the forehead. All of the ace's arms flutter like tree limbs in a gentle breeze, and he sinks to the cracked pavement. Jamal retrieves Jetboy and sprints past him. Rosa Loteria has transformed back into herself and is madly shuffling her magic cards. Using Jetboy like a club, Jamal smacks the deck out of her hands, and hears her gasp as the cards go flying. Then his path is blocked by a snarling tiger. He runs right through it, knocking Wild Fox back on his shit-smeared tail.

He can see the observatory building ahead of him. Lining the railings, half a dozen aces – Brave Hawk's pseudo wings fluttering in the breeze, Dragon Girl, Pop Tart.

And Berman, the network guy, off to one side.

It's as if the world is ganging up on Jamal.

A hundred yards to go. The camera truck is behind him. The chopper above.

For a moment, he wishes he could get to the building itself. What a perfect spot to replay the knife fight from *Joker Without a Cause*!

Jamal is hit from behind. It is the most surprising blindside tackle he has ever felt. He hits the pavement hard – chin scraped, hands raw. Jetboy flies out of his hands. Rustbelt rolls past, upset by his own momentum, his bolts sparking on the pavement. Jamal scrambles after the idol.

He and Rustbelt grab it at the same time.

For an instant they are eye to eye. 'It's mine.'

'Mine, now,' Rustbelt says.

Both of them know that Jamal can't win a tug-of-war. His wild card – never especially helpful except on a movie stage – is completely useless here. But what had Tiffani taught him? He has other weapons. Especially when he hears Rustbelt say, 'That's what you get for being a—'

The word is lost in the roar of rotor noise from the hovering chopper.

Jamal lets go of the idol. He points at Rustbelt and screams as loudly as he can, right in front of all the cameras, *'Did you hear what he called me*? What kind of racist shit is that?'

◆

'It took you long enough.'

It is early the next morning. Clubs Lair is quiet. Jamal sees Michael Berman emerging from the breakfast nook. Astonishingly, he is still dressed in his black suit and tie. The only signs that he has been up all night are a faint beard stubble that shows a surprising amount of gray, and the loosened knot of his tie.

'Didn't know we were meeting.'

'You're not that stupid.'

Jamal removes the carafe from the coffeemaker – still dirty. He smashes it into Berman's face, hearing the crunch of it, but it doesn't break …

No, no need for that. Hear the man out.

He empties the old coffee into the disposal as Berman, strangely, opens the exact cabinet where the coffee is kept. 'You didn't expect to drop that little bomb on us without experiencing a little fallout, did you?'

Jamal feels a tight smile forming. Fallout. Bounceback, oh yes. The look on everyone's face when he shouted that Rustbelt had called him 'nigger.' The rusted Jetboy idol never made it to the finish line. The whole scene fell apart, aces herded into their vehicles like witnesses to a crime. Sullen, confused silence at the Lair that night.

Silence, that is, except for Brave Hawk, who offered a pat on the shoulder. 'Told you.'

Now Berman removes the carafe from Jamal's hands and wipes it dry with a paper towel. He goes to the Sparkletts dispenser in the corner and fills it. 'What proportions do you use?'

'Excuse me?' Jamal is still in bounceback, never his best mode, and suddenly feels unsure. What is this man doing here? What is he talking about?

'What proportion of coffee to water?' Berman's expression suggests this is the most natural question in the world.

'Two to one. I mean, one to two. One coffee to two water.'

'Me, too.' With two quick moves, Berman gets the coffee-maker started.

'So,' Jamal says, 'where's the camera crew?'

'This conversation doesn't exist.'

'Fine.'

'Neither, I suspect, did that word. It can't be heard on the tapes.'

Jamal lets that statement hang in the air. 'Which doesn't mean it wasn't said. Just like this conversation – no record, but real, right?'

'That would be an interesting public debate, wouldn't it? Your word against Rustbelt's.' Berman shakes his head. 'Poor Wally. Of all the people to pick on – he's as black as you.'

'He's iron, Mr. Berman. He's not *black*.' Jamal hears these words come out of his mouth. Where did he learn to be militant? Certainly not from Big Bill. 'Is that what you want? A public argument between me and Rustbelt?'

'We've had enough of that already.' True, before the Clubs had even returned to the lair after the scavenger hunt, the blogosphere had inflated with the news of Jamal's accusation.

'So, where does that leave us?' Jamal says. 'Where does that leave me?'

Berman picks up the Jetboy idol. 'You seem to have gained a

new kind of immunity. It will be impossible for anyone to vote you out of *American Hero*.'

'Does that mean I'm the winner?' He finds the thought incredibly exciting – as if he'd just been told he was going to start in the big game.

'I couldn't possibly tell you something like that.' Which in no way means that he *isn't* the winner – the first American Hero! 'It would be best for all of us, I think, if you tried very hard not to think that. To simply play the game. By the rules.'

'I thought there were no rules.'

'The apparent rules. The rules we make up as we go along.' Berman suddenly puts his hands to his face, the gesture of a much older man. 'Do I have your promise to … play that way?'

'Yeah. By the rules we make up as we go along.' For a moment, he wishes Big Bill Norwood could be sitting in the breakfast nook. Or maybe that nasty little Nic Deladrier. How do you like Stuntman now?

Jade Blossom enters. 'Oh,' she says, her mouth forming that single syllable most prettily.

Berman stands, and a look passes between him and Jade. With utter certainty, Jamal realizes that Berman has been after Jade – and so far, unsuccessfully. Berman makes a grand gesture, midway between an introduction and a surrender. 'You two must have a lot to talk about.'

Then he leaves.

Almost instinctively, as if searching for a human touch as much as an erotic thrill, Jamal reaches for Jade.

But she raises a hand. 'Wait a second.'

Behind Jade, Jamal sees Art blinking sleep out of his eye, gesturing for Diaz to raise the camera.

'Now.' And she takes his hand.

♠

METAGAMES

Caroline Spector

'You lose.'

Are there worse words in the universe to hear?

Sure. 'You've got cancer' tops it, but the odds are low that I've got cancer at age nineteen. Right now, though, I'm a loser.

The Diamonds are losers. And we're doing it on national television. Not to mention the coverage we're getting on YouTube.com and every freaking blog in the universe.

And now we're going to Discard. Again.

I hate Discard.

'This sucks.'

That was Tiffani, and her West Virginia accent got thicker when she was mad. She was changing out of her show clothes into her sweats. I tried not to sneak a look at her, but she wasn't being shy about changing in front of me. And why would she be anyway? It was just us girls here. Her skin was the color of white oleanders, and she smelled like sweet sweat and musky roses.

'I am sick of losing challenges,' she said as she hooked her bra. 'We would have won if Matryoshka had kept control of his copies.'

'Yeah, I hate losing, too.' I didn't like the camera being on us as we changed, but there was nothing I could do about it. It was in the contract. The only time you could be alone was in the bathroom. And then you had to be *alone*. No one could come in with you unless there was a camera following. No wonder I felt like I was going crazy.

Of course, in my pre-wild-card life I'd been shot almost naked

149

by some of the best photographers in the business. Not that any of them would recognize me now. I'm big as a house.

I grunted as I pulled on my pants. I was still pretty large, even after all the bubbling in the last challenge. There had been one last hard hit before we lost, and it had plumped me up.

There was a knock on the door. Ink stuck her head in the room. She was a tiny girl with spiky black hair and tattoos writhing across her body. 'They're set up and ready for the Discard ceremony,' she said.

Tiffani glanced in the mirror. She looked amazing – her cloud of fiery hair a sharp contrast to her milky skin.

I didn't bother to look at myself. I knew I'd be disappointed.

♣

Jetman and Matryoshka were sitting at the table when we arrived. Matryoshka had recombined himself, so he was at his full intellect. Not that his full intellect was any great shakes, but he was a nice guy, and he made great pierogi. Not as good as the late, lamented Second Avenue Deli in New York, but damn good nonetheless. We were the same age, but I always felt as if I were older than him. Like a big sister.

'Come along, children,' said the Harlem Hammer. He was the one judge I actually liked.

Tiffani and I took our seats. The Hammer had a deck of cards in front of him. The Discard deck. Blarg.

I glanced at Tiffani. Her mouth was pulled in a tight line. Losing that last challenge had been horrible. We *all* hated losing.

'I think we did okay, until the end,' said Matryoshka.

Tiff shot him a look that could have melted glass. 'Well, it doesn't matter how we did up until the part where we lost, does it?' she snapped.

Matryoshka looked at her like a wounded puppy. I felt bad for him.

'I think you're being too harsh on Ivan,' Jetman said. He was slightly older than the rest of us and, because of his obsession with

Jetboy, he tended to have old-fashioned notions about things. 'He can't help getting kind of, well, er, uhm ...'

'Stupid?' I said and immediately hated myself. It was true, but ...

'I'm sorry, Ivan.'

Matryoshka shrugged. He was stoic, I'll say that for him. The Harlem Hammer tried to get us talking about the challenge, but we weren't much help. We'd lost every one thus far. Our team was pretty much decimated. And now we had to throw another person under the bus.

The cards were dealt and I slowly picked up my hand. Tiffani, Jetman, Matryoshka, and my own face stared back at me. Tiffani had plucked her card out, and it was already lying facedown on the table. She looked calm and cool, and I wished I felt as certain about whom to choose.

I doubted I would be chosen. I was the only one who had performed well on all the challenges. I figured, if the Diamonds ever hoped to win one, they needed to keep me.

Jetman had a way with gadgets and he always managed to come up with the right gizmo during challenges. And he could fly with his jetpack, which came in handy. Oh, and his guns were good, too. One shot sleeping gas and the other a net.

I fiddled with the edge of Matryoshka's card. Despite the fact that his Mini-Me's got dumber and dumber as he divided, they could be effective at overwhelming opponents. I looked at Tiffani's card. There was a slight smile on her face in the photo. It made the corners of her aquamarine eyes crinkle. She was pretty much impervious to harm, and that was great except ... well, she sucked in a fight.

I pushed that thought away. It wasn't really fair. She didn't choose to have a power with no real offensive capabilities. And Tiffani and I had been together since the Atlanta tryouts. We were the only two who had made the show from Atlanta. She'd never voted against me, and I'd never voted against her. I guess we had a sort of unspoken alliance.

I glanced up and caught Jetman looking at me. I felt a stab of fear in my stomach. Maybe he *was* thinking of putting me in the Discards.

'You need to make your selections,' the Harlem Hammer said. His voice was deep and reminded me of the Barry White albums my parents used to play. I shoved that away, too. I tried not to think about my parents anymore.

Matryoshka pulled a card from his hand and placed it facedown on the table. Jetman followed.

'What's it going to be, Bubbles?' the Hammer asked me. I couldn't put it off any longer. I sighed and picked a card. The Harlem Hammer gathered our discards, shuffled them, and made a small deck.

He turned the first card over. Tiffani's face stared up at us. I glanced at her. She gave me a tight smile, then looked back at the board.

The next card was Matryoshka. He frowned and shook his head slightly. Another card turned. Matryoshka again.

'One vote left. Is it going to be two pair or a set?'

With quick efficiency, The Hammer dealt the last card.

Matryoshka.

Tiffani breathed a sigh of relief. So did I.

Matryoshka and Jetman were already standing, shaking hands, and doing that back-slapping thing guys did to prove that they liked each other, but not in a 'gay' way. I stood and walked around the table. Matryoshka and I hugged. He was a big guy, but his arms barely made it around my girth. I felt terrible that I had chosen him, but I had to think of the team – and who would be the best American Hero.

♥

I stood in front of the bathroom mirror and stared at my reflection, depressed about voting Matryoshka off. I started thinking about all the other nice people I'd voted to discard. Blrr and the Maharajah were both really decent. Joe Twitch had some issues, though, and I knew he had pissed Tiff off.

'Michelle, you know you can't be in there for too long.' It was Ink – again.

I glowered at my reflection. I'd been using a colored hair spray to change my platinum hair to black. The shade did nothing for me – turning my skin sallow rather than the pale olive luminescence which had earned me hundreds of thousands of dollars in modeling contracts. But no one had recognized me thus far. The dark hair alone wouldn't have masked my identity – but my wild card did.

The face staring back wasn't the one I knew. The upward-slashing cheekbones, so beloved by photographers, were buried under chubby pink flesh. The sculpted jaw line that had once made my neck look even more swanlike was obscured by a roll of fat. Only my eyes were unchanged. I called them dog-shit brown. They were fringed with one of my genetic quirks – a double row of long black lashes.

I was a freak of nature long before my card turned. I'm taller than average, and my legs and arms are abnormally long for my body. In short, I was a photographer's dream. I'd been modeling since I was a child. My parents had leased me out to the highest bidder and exploited me like carnival barkers peddling Siamese twins.

But then my card had turned.

Things were different now. People didn't stare at me in the same way. And when I did catch someone's eye, now there was usually a breathtaking look of pity there.

Ink banged on the door again. 'Michelle, you have a contract. Everyone else has already done their Confessional.'

'Can't I go to the bathroom in peace?' I put the toilet lid up and let a small bubble rise on my fingertip, then let it drop into the water with a satisfying plop. It looked pretty until it hit – as iridescent and apparently insubstantial as any soap bubble. But I'd given it plenty of density, and it sounded convincingly turdlike. Unfortunately, it was heavy enough that it chipped the porcelain, but I decided that no one would be likely to notice. *That should keep Ink from bugging me for a few minutes.*

Then I felt crummy. Ink had been nice to me.

At least it still felt good to bubble. It tingled and sang in my bones and skin. Bubbling pulsed through my blood and throbbed like another heartbeat. Sometimes I thought I'd go crazy if I didn't get to bubble more often – but the bubbling made me skinnier, and I couldn't afford to be recognized.

'Are you okay?' Ink sounded worried.

'What's going on?' I heard Tiffani ask.

I flushed the toilet and opened the door.

'You're supposed to do a Confessional after Discard,' Ink said. She had changed her tattoos, and they scrolled across her arms like a crazy Mayan tally board.

'Are you okay?' Tiffani asked. She gave Ink a pleading look. 'Can you guys give us just a few minutes?' If she had looked at me the way she was looking at Ink, I'd've agreed to anything. 'Just have them turn on the shower cam. We'll keep in range. I mean, it's the bathroom. How far are we going to go?'

Ink snorted. 'Fine. You have five minutes, and then I'm coming in with the whole crew.'

Tiffani and I went back into the bathroom and closed the door. The light on the shower cam blinked on.

'Okay, so why are you so depressed?' Tiff asked.

I sighed. 'I guess it's mostly getting rid of Matryoshka. He was a great guy. He didn't deserve to go.'

Tiffani glanced in the mirror, then stuck her tongue out at her reflection. 'I hate the way I look,' she said, then turned back to me. 'Listen, this is a competition. There are rules, and we have to play by them. If we lose challenges, we lose teammates.'

There was a towel on the floor, and I picked it up and began folding it. 'I know, I know. I just don't get why we've been losing every challenge. I mean, we all try so hard. I just hate that we have to vote people off.'

Tiff grabbed a brush from my basket of toiletries on the counter. She closed the toilet lid, then sat me down and started working on my hair. 'I don't understand why you keep making your hair black with that crappy spray dye. You've got nice hair under this mess.'

She sectioned off a chunk and started to braid it. It felt good to have her hands on me, even if she was just doing it out of habit. She had a bunch of sisters, and she'd told me they'd always braided each other's hair.

The braiding was relaxing. 'I've been feeling bad since Blrr,' I said. 'Joe Twitch was … well, after he stripped you naked in like five seconds, I wasn't going to have him in the house anymore, but Blrr was a good kid and a great housemate.'

'Her power was useless without the right conditions,' Tiffani said as she started braiding the other section of my hair. 'The other teams are all thinking the same way. Who's good in challenges, and who you can't stand to live with. Though how any one could live with Stuntman is beyond me. He's such a jerk.'

Tiff tied off my braid. I stood up and looked in the mirror. I used to love the way I looked in braids, but not now. They just made my face look rounder.

'You don't like them,' Tiff said sadly. 'It's not them. It's my face.'

Tiff stood on tiptoe and gave me a quick kiss on my cheek. 'There's nothing wrong with your face, Michelle.'

I blushed and looked down. I didn't know if she felt the same way about me as I did about her, but my cheek was burning where her lips had touched it.

There was a hard bang on the bathroom door. 'All right, you guys,' Ink said. 'We're coming in.'

The door swung open, and the floating camera crew started to file in.

'We were just leaving,' Tiff said as she slipped past them. I couldn't slip past anyone anymore and had to stand there, like an idiot, until they backed out of the room.

◆

The sound guy clipped a mic onto the neck of my hoodie. I sat in the Confessional chair and started pulling the braids out of my hair.

'You don't need to do that.' Ink had changed her tats again. Now there were a series of typewritten questions on her arms. But she had kept the Mayan images on her face and legs. 'They look nice. You're one of the prettiest girls on the show.'

I shrank back in the chair. Well, as much as my girth would allow me to. No one thought I was pretty anymore.

'So, why do we always have to drag you into doing your Confessionals?' Ink asked.

The red eye of the camera blinked on. They were rolling again, sucking me into that meat grinder. I looked at Ink so I wouldn't have to look in the camera again. It didn't love me anymore. 'I know I haven't done as many Confessionals as everyone else. I guess I just didn't have much to say.'

A disappointed expression slipped across Ink's face. I knew I was making her job more difficult, but of all the things we did on the show, this was the one that made me most uncomfortable. Tiffani loved Confessional. I don't know why. The Maharajah had started calling her the Little Nun because she was always in there. So we had all called her that – until the Maharajah got voted off.

'So, what do you think about the other contestants, now that we're getting close to a reshuffle?'

I noticed that the end of one of the ties on my hoodie was frayed, and I started to worry it. My hands had been so beautiful. Now the nails were ragged and the cuticles raw. I heard Ink make a throat-clearing noise, and I knew I had to answer her.

'I guess ... I guess I like most of the other players.' I glanced up and saw Ink frown at me. 'I mean, I like my teammates. The ones that are left. And I think Dragon Girl is sweet, even if she is, you know, kinda young to be on the show.'

'What about Rosa Loteria?'

I looked away from the camera. I wished she hadn't asked about Rosa. 'Well, I don't know her all that well,' I said. 'I've only really seen her at press stuff.'

'But how do you feel about her?'

I sighed. I had to talk – it was in that damned contract. 'I don't think she cares about being a hero. She only cares about making money and being famous.'

'And that's bad, right?'

I looked up at the camera this time. 'No, it's not bad to want those things. But this isn't about getting money or being famous. It's about being a hero.'

'Do you think Tiffani is heroic?'

'I think she tries to be.' I assumed Tiff felt the same way about *American Hero* that I did. She had had my back. She'd told me she had never voted against me, not once.

'Well, what do you think a hero is?' Ink asked.

'It's not just acts of physical courage. What's a hero, if you can't trust them to keep their word? What's a hero, if they would betray a friend? What's a hero, if they think of themselves before anyone else?' I looked Ink straight in the eye. 'That's not being a hero. Anyone can do that. We all do that. But a hero tries to do better.'

I dropped my head again, and my hair covered most of my face. I scrunched down into the chair and didn't say anything else. After a few minutes, Ink told the camera crew to stop rolling.

'You did great, Michelle,' she said.

'You're supposed to be calling me Bubbles,' I reminded her. She gave me a funny smile.

♠

'What're you working on now?' I asked.

Jetman was in the garage tinkering with yet another of his gadgets. Since the Maharajah had been voted off, Jetman pretty much kept to himself.

'I'm not sure what it is yet,' he replied. 'Things just ... *change* as I'm working on them.'

He started looking for something in his toolbox, and I handed him a Phillips head screwdriver. He grunted and took it from me. Sometimes I hung out with Jetman when he was gadgeting. Whenever he couldn't find something in his toolbox, I gave him a random screwdriver. It seemed to work. Or maybe he was just humoring me.

'You know, I thought you were going to vote me off during Discard,' I said.

'Actually, I was thinking about voting Tiffani off,' he said. 'But then I thought you might get pissed.'

It took me aback. I would never get pissed at Jetman for voting the way he wanted to. I told him that.

'Yeah, I realized that,' he said. 'But I knew that you and Tiff were planning to get rid of Matryoshka after the last challenge. So I figured, go along to get along.'

I leaned against the bench running along the west wall of the garage. I was baffled. 'But we didn't ha—'

'*C'mon, Diamonds*!' Tiffani yelled from the end of the driveway. 'We're going on a mysterious ride.'

'Our master's voice.' Jetman wiped his hands on a greasy rag. We went outside, and he pulled the garage door shut behind us. There was an SUV limo waiting for us. Tiff was already inside, and Jetman and I piled into the spacious backseat. It was roomier now that there were only three of us left on the team. 'Where do you think we're going?' I asked.

Tiff shrugged. 'Reshuffle. After all, all the teams have lost at least two players.'

'I hope it's a reshuffle,' Jetman said. 'We can't afford to lose anyone else.'

♣

The limo took us to the Warners back lot, where *American Hero* was taped.

We piled out of the back of the SUV, and Ink led us through one of the soundstages to makeup.

Peregrine was standing under a spotlight, arguing with one of the directors about her lighting. 'I'm telling you, if you don't put a decent filter on that thing I'm going to look like a crone,' she said.

'Peregrine, my goddess,' the director replied. 'You will never look like a crone. I don't care how hard you try.'

Peregrine gave him a lethal glare. 'Shameless flattery is one way to get around me, but don't think I'm not going to notice if you don't fix that.'

Ink left us at the makeup area backstage. We were used to doing the whole makeup, blocking, hurry-up-and-wait routine that was part of the show taping.

The hair and makeup guys finished with us, and we took one last good look in the mirror.

Jetman looked as if he'd had no makeup done at all. He was a kinda plain-looking guy, but they'd made his skin perfect, as if a blemish had never been allowed to mar his face. And Tiffani ... well, she was as beautiful as ever. It was a pity she was so short. Had she been taller, she would have made a great model. I took a quick glance at myself. My eyes did look great, and they did bring out the best in my skin – as much as they could, given how crappy my black hair made it look.

Ink finally came back. 'Okay, guys,' she said. 'We'll be taping a short segment with Peregrine.'

When we arrived back onstage, the Hearts were sitting in a row of director's chairs. Three empty chairs faced them. Hearts had won the most challenges; there were five of them, and only three of us.

We sat in our chairs. Mine gave a loud groan. I heard a Heart laugh, blushed, and hung my head.

'Asshole,' I heard Jetman say softly.

Peregrine swept onto the stage. When I'd been younger, I'd really admired her. Not only was she a great model, but she still went out and did things with her wild card ability. I guessed she must be in her fifties now, but you'd never know it. She usually wore very revealing couture gowns, but today she had on long palazzo pants, a gold-sequined halter top, and four-inch-high sandals. Her wings fluttered behind her, making her look like a disco angel. 'Are we ready to shoot this?' she asked.

'We're rolling,' said the director. 'Start anytime.'

'Welcome to *American Hero*,' Peregrin said, looking into camera one. 'We're halfway through the competition, and we've lost quite a few of our heroes. But some of the teams have fared better than others.' She turned to camera three and her wings fluttered. 'I know that some of the players here think we might be reshuffling the teams tonight.'

There were groans from the Hearts.

'But we've decided to keep the suits separated for now.'

The Hearts gave a small cheer. 'However,' Peregrine continued, 'our Diamonds team has not done well, and they are at a distinct disadvantage. So we've decided to let them draw one member from Hearts to even the teams up.'

There was stunned silence from the Hearts, and then an angry murmur bubbled up. 'You've *got* to be kidding!' shouted Drummer Boy, jumping to his feet. '*We're* being penalized because *they* suck?'

Curveball placed a hand on one of Drummer Boy's lower arms. 'Calm down. It's just part of the game.'

'It's bullshit,' he said.

I glanced at Tiff to see how she was reacting. There was a Mona Lisa smile on her face. 'Do we have to choose now?' Tiffani asked.

'No, you have twenty-four hours to decide. We'll be bringing you back tomorrow night for the pick.'

'And cut,' came the director's voice.

Peregrine cupped her hands over her eyes and squinted up at the lights. 'Did you put the filter on that spotlight?' she asked.

♥

'So, who do you want to bring over from the Hearts team?' I asked when we were back in the limo.

'Drummer Boy,' Tiffani said at once. 'He makes the most sense. He's the most powerful player on their team.'

Jetman opened the fridge in the limo bar and took out a beer. 'You think he's more powerful than Hardhat or Earth Witch?' he asked.

'Well, how handy is making steel thingamabobbies?' Tiffani asked. 'Are we really going to need a trench anytime soon? And Wild Fox? Don't even get me started on how crappy his power is.'

'We could take Curveball,' I suggested.

Tiff made a face. 'Michelle, you and she have almost the same power. Why would we duplicate that? We've got to get someone who'll work well with our team.' She leaned forward and touched my leg. 'Taking DB will demoralize Hearts. It'll break up their alliances. And if he's got any showmances going, it'll stop them, too.'

'Showmances?' Jetman asked.

'You know, when two people on a reality show become romantically involved for the duration of the show. Sometimes they stick – like Boston Rob and that joker chick from *Survivor*, what was her name?'

'Amber,' Jetman replied. 'She looked like she was a big chunk of amber. She even had bugs stuck in her skin. It was pretty gross, but I guess you never know what's going to float someone's boat.'

Tiff gave Jetman a big smile. 'They won the money because they had this amazing alliance. I heard one of the PAs say that Drummer Boy's been making time with every willing girl on the show. Ever since Curveball dumped him, that is. And they may be getting back together after that little scene when we were taping.'

Aside from Curveball calming him down at the studio, I didn't really see much going on. But, honestly, I'm bad about picking up on that who's-doing-whom stuff.

'I just don't get all this intrigue,' Jetman said. 'I think Drummer Boy's a conceited jerk.'

'He's a big guy, though,' Tiff said. 'He could probably be handy in a brawl. Besides, if we lose again, we can get rid of him instead of one of us.'

I had to admit, Tiffani's plan sounded good, especially the last part. I hated the idea of one of the last three Diamonds going home.

◆

Jetman was fixing breakfast in the kitchen the next morning. He'd started doing that after we lost our first challenge. His cooking was a bit uneven – and he couldn't seem to make breakfast without dirtying every dish in the house.

He was just scooping eggs into a serving bowl when I came in. 'Morning, Bubbles,' he said, passing the eggs to me. 'You want pancakes or waffles this morning?'

I looked at the table. A stack of bacon and about twelve sausages were piled on one plate. A large bowl of fresh fruit salad sat next to it. There was a basket overflowing with pastries – croissants, cinnamon buns, kolaches, and muffins.

'Uhm, I think I can find plenty of stuff to eat. You really don't need to make anything else.'

'Oh,' he said. I turned toward him and saw a hangdog expression on his face.

Crap.

'But you know I can't resist your pancakes,' I said. Actually, his pancakes were really bad. But he brightened and pulled another bowl out of the cabinet.

I sat down, put the bowl of eggs on the table, and loaded my plate with pastries, bacon, eggs, and fruit.

'Remember, you've got pancakes coming,' he said.

'Herummm,' I replied around a mouthful of food. My wild card power made me fat, but otherwise, I could eat anything I wanted and stay skinny.

Tiffani straggled in a few minutes later. Her face was sleep-swollen. I thought she looked adorable. With her kimono-style robe wrapped around her, she appeared tiny and delicate.

'Pancakes, Tiff?' Jetman asked.

'Gah, no,' she said. 'Just coffee until I can get my heart going.'

'Breakfast is the most important meal of the day.'

'And caffeine is my drug of choice. Don't get between me and my fix.'

I poured her a cup from the carafe on the table, put three sugars and a dollop of cream in it, and then passed it to her. She took a long pull and smiled at me. I felt my stomach flip-flop.

'I'm glad you're all up,' said Ink as she sauntered in with one of the mobile crews. 'The producers think all the heroes need a break from the competition.'

Tiff took another hit off her coffee. 'How about three days and four nights in Jamaica?' she said.

'No can do,' Ink replied. 'We're shooting "Diamonds Pick a Heart" tonight.'

'So, what's the "break"?' I asked, using my ironic air quotes.

'You have a choice,' Ink replied. 'You can have a thousand-dollar shopping spree, a trip to Disneyland, or a spa day.'

'I'm guessing this isn't an off-camera event,' I said.

'Nope. It's going to make for some great footage. But you do get out of the house for the whole day. And, even better, no press obligations and no workouts.'

Jetman and Tiff both looked chipper at that. Neither of them liked working out.

'I've always wanted to go to Disneyland,' Jetman said as he ladled pancake batter into a pan. 'I think I'd like to do that.'

Ink smiled at him. It was a great smile. 'You'll be getting the VIP treatment while you're there. I think you're going to have a wonderful time.' She turned toward Tiff and me. 'And what are you two going to do?'

'I'd like to go shopping,' Tiffani said. 'I've never even seen a thousand dollars in one place. But I don't want to go alone.' She looked at me hopefully.

I was torn. I had plenty of clothes – even if most of them didn't fit me anymore. And Disneyland sounded like fun. So did having a spa day. But Tiff gave me a pleading look, and I couldn't resist. 'I guess I'll go with Tiffani,' I said.

Ink looked disappointed. I guess they hoped we'd each take a different 'prize' so there would be more diverse footage to work with. 'Be ready in half an hour.'

♠

The Beverly Center wasn't as swank as Rodeo Drive, or as trendy as Melrose Avenue, but there was a great variety of stores. We decided to start at Bergdorf's and work our way through the mall from there.

'Oh my God,' Tiffani said, stroking a bright red cashmere wrap. 'You've got to feel this.'

I smiled. I couldn't remember the last time I'd been that excited about shopping. After all the modeling, I'd started to hate clothes. I usually wore inexpensive off-the-rack stuff and some of the nicer pieces that the designers would send around. That was one of the perks of the job. I had loads of status symbol accessories that were only mine because some designer thought Jill Blow would covet his $500 sunglasses because she saw me wearing them in *In Style* magazine.

Tiff picked up the price tag and blanched. 'It's four hundred and fifty dollars. Every bit of clothing my sisters and I bought last year didn't cost that much.'

Without thinking, I said, 'You're kidding.'

Tiffani rubbed the cashmere against her cheek. 'Nope. When I said we were poor, I meant *real* poor.'

'I thought there was just "poor." '

She laughed and carefully put the wrap back on its shelf, then ran her hand across the rainbow colors of the rest of the shawls. 'We never went to see movies. They cost too much money. We didn't go out to eat. We never had cell phones, or clothes that hadn't been worn by someone else first. Or an inside toilet.'

I stared at her. 'You're kidding. How did you find out about *American Hero*?'

She laughed. 'Honey, everyone has a TV. Even the folks without indoor plumbing.'

We wandered over to the perfume counter. Tiff took a bottle of Joy 1000 off the tester tray and spritzed a little on her wrist, then sniffed. She held her wrist under my nose. The heavy aroma of jasmine and roses wafted up. 'It's okay,' I said. 'It's just not my cup of frothy cappuccino.'

Tiffani sniffed her wrist again. 'Mmmmm, I think I like it.' She glanced around for a salesgirl. One rushed over. I think she noticed the camera following us.

The salesgirl gave us a bright smile. 'How can I help you?' she asked.

'How much is this?' Tiffani asked.

'Do you want the perfume or the cologne?' the salesgirl asked, putting bottles on the counter.

'Uhm, I'm not sure.'

I leaned over and whispered in Tiff's ear. 'Cologne will be cheaper, but doesn't last as long as the perfume.'

'Tell me the price on both,' Tiff said.

'The perfume is one-hundred and sixty, the cologne is seventy-eight.'

'Does it buy you dinner, too?' Tiff asked. She looked between the two bottles, then put them both back on the counter. 'I do want to get some things for my family. If I've got anything left, maybe I'll come back.'

The salesgirl plastered on another toothy smile. 'Certainly. We're here until nine P.M.'

Tiffani was already wandering toward the shoes. The salesgirl leaned over the counter. 'Are you from *American Hero*?' she asked softly. 'Is that *Tiffani*?'

'Yep.'

'Do you think you could get me her autograph?'

It stung. I was used to being the person who was singled out. 'Just a minute,' I said, taking the paper and pen.

I walked to Tiff, who was looking at a pair of Stuart Weitzman sandals. '*Three hundred dollars* for a pair of shoes?' she exclaimed. 'Seriously, do people here just like pissing money away?'

'If they were Manolos or Jimmy Choos, they'd be a lot more expensive,' I said. I picked up a pair of Dolce & Gabbana pumps and contemplated them for a moment. At my current weight, I'd snap the delicate heel in no time.

'But these aren't even all that pretty.'

'It's fashion,' I replied, putting the pumps back on their display stand. 'Hey, the salesgirl at the perfume counter would like your autograph.' I pulled the pen and paper out of my pocket and handed them to her.

'Really?' Tiff said, glancing in the direction of the perfume counter. She looked surprised and thrilled. 'I didn't think she even recognized us.'

I smiled at her excitement. 'Don't be silly,' I said. 'You're a star.'

She beamed up at me. I wanted to kiss her. I hated that she grew up poor and didn't have nice things. I wanted to give her everything she'd missed and everything she desired.

We finally ended up at the Gap, a few doors away from Bergdorf's. Tiff had a ball picking out sweaters, jeans, shirts, and coats for her siblings.

'So,' I said as Tiffani handed over her prepaid Visa card to the clerk. 'Got any money left over for yourself?'

'I doubt it,' she replied. 'But it doesn't really matter. And I'm glad I found that sale rack.' She looked over at me. 'Why haven't you bought anything?'

I jammed my hands into my pants pockets. The only thing I'd seen during our shopping that I wanted had been an ultra-stretchy track suit. It was made of some micro-fiber I'd never heard of and had a beautiful drape and wasn't shiny. But it was also fantastically expensive, and I didn't want Tiffani seeing me spend my whole amount on one thing. Besides, I had a better way to spend my money.

We grabbed Tiff's bags and headed for the door. But just outside the store there was a crowd blocking our way.

'I wonder what's going on?' Tiffani said. Then the cameras started clicking, and we realized that they were waiting for us. '*Tiffani! Over here!*' shouted one excited preteen. Her friends squealed when Tiff looked their way. 'Oh my God, she *looked* at me!'

Tiff walked over and said hello to them. Another wave of squealing was set off. I stood there, feeling awkward.

'Are you the Amazing Bubbles?' a gawky boy wearing an over-sized T-shirt asked me.

'Yes,' I replied. 'I am.'

'Would you sign my shirt?'

'Sure,' I said. One of the clerks handed me a Sharpie and offered to hold our packages while we were signing autographs. 'Front or back?' I asked.

He turned around. 'Back.'

I signed his back – 'The Amazing Bubbles.' He turned and gave me a big grin, so I held my hand out and made a baseball-size bubble. I released it, and it floated over to him. He caught it and held it in his hands for a few seconds before it popped.

A few more people asked me for autographs – but when I was

finished I saw that Tiff was not only still signing, but that even more people were gathering around her. I decided to slip off and take care of the shopping I wanted to do while she took care of her fans.

When I returned, I was surprised to see that the crowd was even bigger than before. And then I realized why: Tiffani had turned to diamond. The lights in the mall were hitting her and bouncing off her faceted skin, making rainbows on the walls. As she moved she twinkled. She shone like a star. It was bittersweet. I was accustomed to being the one people noticed, but I couldn't begrudge Tiff the attention. I could see her grinning. She was beaming, and so excited.

'Bubbles,' I heard her say. 'Where's Bubbles?'

'I'm here, Tiff,' I said loudly.

'Come here!'

'I can't. You're surrounded.'

'Make a hole!' she yelled. The crowd parted and she ran to me. 'This is the Amazing Bubbles! You're going to be hearing a lot about her.' She grabbed my hand with her long, cool, diamond fingers and dragged me into the center of the crowd. 'Show the people what you can do.'

I felt my face grow hot, and I knew I was blushing. 'This isn't the place ...'

She gave me a little poke in the arm. 'Stop being so shy. One more little bubble won't hurt.'

I couldn't say no to her. And I was touched that she had dragged me into the center of her throng of fans. I turned my palms up and felt the electric sensation surge through them. I released a stream of hundreds of multi-size bubbles toward the ceiling, very Lawrence Welky. They caught the lights and shimmered, then vanished.

'It's so beautiful,' I heard someone say.

'Bubbles will sign any autographs you want,' said Tiff. She gave me a big grin, then took another piece of paper to sign. A group of Japanese tourists thrust autograph books at me and I signed them all. Then I posed for photographs with them. I guess I got caught up in the moment, because by the time I realized things were getting out of hand, it was too late.

The first thing I noticed was how loud it had gotten. I glanced around and saw that the crowd had swollen. I got up on tiptoes. The crowd was now at least fifteen people deep. We were standing next to the railing, and I saw that there were people lining up on the stairway and gathering on the lower level, too. Some of them were text-messaging. Others were taking photos.

I whispered in Tiff's ear. 'We need to get out of here. The crowd is getting kinda big.'

There was a slightly dazed expression on her face, as if the attention from the crowd had made her drunk. Then she shook her head, and she was back. 'How do we get out?'

'Tell them to make a hole again,' I replied.

'*Make a hole!*' she yelled.

A couple of people close to us shuffled away, but the rest of the crowd was so intent on getting closer, it pushed them back at us. An angry shout came from the rear. Parts of the crowd moved then, and I saw a gap.

I grabbed Tiffani's wrist and pulled her toward the opening. It helped that I was taller and bigger than her. It was easier for me to make people get out of our way. I heard a noise from below and glanced over the railing. People were pointing at us and running up the stairs. I knew we needed to get out of the mall fast.

There was a street entrance in Bergdorf's, but I didn't like the idea of pulling a big crowd into that store. Then I saw a small side exit between the Body Shop and Furla that we could slip out of quickly. We ran for it, with the camera guys hot on our heels. It was weird, but people rarely get in the crew's way.

We burst through the doors at street level and I looked around for the limo. They'd dropped us off at the Bergdorf's end of the mall, so I figured they should be nearby. Tiff was giggling. She gleamed in the afternoon light. 'Oh, my gosh,' she said with a half-laugh, half-hiccup. 'This is so wild.'

'You should power down,' I said. 'You're like a Christmas tree right now – all lit up.'

'You got it, boss.' I didn't have to look back to see that she had changed back. I could feel her soft flesh in my hand instead of the cool hardness of her power.

I saw the limo then. It was stuck in traffic on the opposite side of the street, with the cars trying to turn into the parking garage.

'There's the car!' Tiff yelled. She pulled her wrist out of my hand and started across. I heard a rumble, looked to my left, and saw a tourist bus coming. There was no time to say anything, to warn her to diamond up. I just leapt out and shoved her out of the way as hard as I could.

Then the bus hit me and I stopped thinking about anything else.

My body ballooned. Part of me realized this was good – we had a challenge coming up, and the bigger I was, the better. As I flew through the air, I heard the squealing and hydraulic hiss of the bus brakes. My body felt oddly weightless – until I crashed into the back window of a parked Lexus. The impact from that landing made me even bigger. I lay for a moment in the confetti of broken glass. It wasn't that I hurt, I just couldn't figure out how to move quickly at this size. Being hit by a bus, even if it didn't kill you, was disconcerting.

I rolled off the Lexus and safety glass rained onto the pavement. The bus driver was already out of his vehicle and coming toward me. 'Holy crap!' he said. 'Are you okay?'

Glass tinkled off me. 'Just a little shook up.'

'Michelle!' Tiffani ran over to me. She was diamond, thank goodness. Then she was brushing glass from my shoulders and making little *tsking* noises as she examined my torn pants and jacket. 'Well, these are hopeless,' she said. 'Good thing you've still got your spending money.'

My hands were itching, and I burned to bubble. It was always this way after a big surge of fat. By now, the limo had gotten free from traffic and was pulling up alongside us. One of the PAs jumped out. 'Are either of you hurt?'

'Nah,' Tiffani said. 'We're built wild card tough.'

There was a tap on my shoulder and I heard, 'A thousand pardons, but is this your purse?' One of the Japanese tourists was holding out my bag.

My heart sank. I'd brought my favorite purse on this excursion, and now it was much the worse for wear. 'Yes, it's mine,' I said, taking it from her. 'Thank you for bringing it back.'

'Oh, if I had a purse this wonderful,' she said, 'I would be heart-broken if anything happened to it.'

Tiff looked at my purse, then at the tourist. 'It's a handbag. What's so special about it?'

'Oh my, that's a real Hermès Birkin,' the tourist replied. 'And if I'm not mistaken, it's a very rare color as well. In Japan, they sell for almost two million yen.'

Tiff's eyes bugged out. 'Two million for a purse?!'

'Tiff, that's in yen,' I said. 'The conversion rate is, like, totally insane.' I wasn't about to tell her that at retail in the states, Birkins could cost from $15,000 to $50,000. Which was also completely insane.

'Okay, I confess, it's not a real Birkin,' I said. I hoped my lie would mollify Tiffani.

'I'm certain that is a real Hermès,' the tourist said. 'There are certain distinguishing signs …'

Why did I have to run into the one Japanese tourist with perfect English and an eye for overpriced accessories? I felt terrible. Tiffani had grown up so poor.

The crowd was swelling, traffic was backed up behind the limo, and I'd managed to dent the front end of a bus as well as destroy a Lexus. Our day of fun was rapidly turning into a gigantic horror show. I was trying to figure out what to do when Tiffani grabbed my hand, stood on tiptoe, and whispered in my ear. 'We can't fix any of this,' she said. 'Let's get in the car and let the PA sort it out.'

'I can't just leave,' I said. 'This is my fault. And how on earth will he be able to handle all this?'

'Please get in the car, ladies,' said the driver. Normally, the drivers didn't talk to us – unless we initiated the conversation. 'If I come back without you, it's my job.'

I was torn. The PA was clearly in over his head, but I didn't want to get the driver in trouble. Reluctantly, I allowed Tiff to pull me into the limo.

♥

Tiffani and I sat in the Jacuzzi. Tiff was wearing an itty-bitty bikini and I wore the Big Girls Special. I might as well have been wearing a muumuu. We could hear Drummer Boy banging around inside the house. He was massively pissed at being taken off the Hearts team.

When we all got back from the taping – what a fun car ride that was, what with Drummer Boy alternately sulking and making snide remarks – Tiff suggested that she and I should grab a couple of bottles of wine and hang out in the backyard until things inside quieted down some.

'Wow, he's got some stamina,' I said. 'He's been in there banging around for at least an hour.'

Tiff took a drink of her wine, then wrinkled her nose. 'You'd think this stuff would taste better. Actually, I think he's playing. Sounds like Tommy Lee's drumming.'

'Well, I can't taste anything,' I said. 'After two glasses my mouth's kinda numb. Yeah, you know it does sound like he's drumming in there.'

Tiff got up and reached for the wine bottle. Water sluiced off her, ran down her back, and between her legs. I closed my eyes. It was too distracting. I imagined sliding my hand between her legs, and that didn't help anything. I opened my eyes and Tiff was filling my glass up. 'So,' she said, as she settled into the water again. 'What's the story with your purse?'

I groaned. I'd hoped we wouldn't end up talking about it. 'Okay, I'll explain it,' I said. 'But you have to promise that you'll keep it a secret.'

She looked at me with limpid eyes. 'Of course. That's what friends are for.' Her tongue darted into her wine glass. And that made me take another big drink. I leaned closer to her, hoping that between whispering and the noise of the Jacuzzi, they wouldn't have good enough sound to air what I was about to say.

'I'm not Michelle LaFleur,' I whispered. 'I mean, that's my real name, but I work under the name Michelle Pond. I'm a model. I mean, I was a model. I started young. You know, I was the OshKosh B'Gosh girl for like five years when I was a kid.'

'You? A model?'

I laughed. It did sound ridiculous, given my current appearance. 'I know, it seems goofy, doesn't it?' I said softly. 'I was in demand, and since I never went through an "awkward" stage, I kept working solid from the time I was two years old until well, just about now.'

Tiff adjusted the top of her bikini. I tried not to stare.

'Anyway, I pretty much did it all,' I said. 'Runway shows, fashion modeling, the works. And I had a great career, except that I was working like a dog and not seeing any of the money from it.'

'I can barely hear you,' she said, scooting closer. She dropped her voice lower as well. 'But if you were working, where did the money go?'

And there it was. The question that I dreaded. The reality of my life that was so bitter to me, I could barely stand to think about it, much less talk about it.

But there was Tiffani with such sympathy in her eyes, and the wine made me feel disconnected from myself. I drained my glass for Dutch courage.

'Well, that's the embarrassing part.' I put my glass on the side of the pool. 'My parents both quit their jobs to be my full-time manager and agent. I worked nonstop. Worked like a mule. All that stuff normal kids get to do, I got to pretend to do in commercials and pictures.' As I talked about it, I felt queasy. 'For a long time, I didn't want to believe what was happening. But when I was fourteen, I figured out how to get into their computer, and I saw their accounts.

'By law, they were supposed to be putting away a certain amount of my income for when I became an adult. But I could see that they hadn't done that. Not only that, but there were these accounts set up overseas.' I closed my eyes and swallowed. 'They had been stealing from me for years. I should have had enough money to have my own life when my modeling career was over. Go to college, start a business. But they had been spending most of it and hiding the rest. My own parents stole everything from me.'

For a moment it felt like it had been the first time I'd realized what they'd been doing. Like someone had kicked me in the stomach. There was a terrible lump in my throat, and I closed my eyes and thought I might start crying. I felt Tiff's hand stroking the back of my neck. 'You poor child,' she said. Her accent made her voice honey-smooth. 'I've never heard of such a thing!'

I snuffled and knuckled my eyes to keep the tears at bay. When I thought I had myself in hand, I looked at her.

'You've lived a kinda sheltered life,' I said quietly. 'Money makes some people subhuman.'

She poured the last of the wine into my glass, then handed the glass to me. 'What did you do?'

'I was only fourteen when I found out. It took me a year to get a lawyer who would take me seriously. We filed for my emancipation and sued my parents. I won my emancipation suit, but by the time we got a judgment they'd fled the country. We managed to seize one account, so I wasn't completely broke, but most of that money went to pay my lawyer.'

Tiffani leaned closer and I could smell her scent even over the chlorine. 'And then your wild card turned and you can't work anymore?'

'Oh, I could work,' I said. 'If I bubbled down to my normal size, I could probably have plenty of work. But then I couldn't bubble.'

She frowned. 'You mean, you could make a nice living by wearing pretty clothes and getting your picture taken, but you're here?'

I sighed. I knew she wouldn't understand. Being poor drove her. She wanted to give her family what they'd never had. But her family would love her, no matter if she won or not. Mine had never loved me. I was just a payday for them. 'I guess that's one way to look at it,' I said. 'But the bubbling, it's changed things for me. I can do something worthwhile with this power. Modeling doesn't do anything but help sell stuff.' I lifted my hands out of the water. They were pruney. 'Not only that, but I'm nineteen. That's practically ancient in the modeling world. And I was getting sick of seeing the things the girls would do to stay thin and keep working.' I picked up my wineglass and drained it. It felt good to finally tell someone.

Tiff sipped her wine and stared off into space. 'But what does that all have to do with your purse?'

I'd forgotten all about the purse. 'As I was packing up my stuff before I left my parents' place, I noticed my mother's closet door standing open. I couldn't believe what I saw in there. She had, like, five of those Hermès purses. This was how she was spending my future – on freaking handbags. So I took them. I sold off all but one, and that's my emancipation bag.

'Mommy got me back, though. After the decree came down in my favor, I got a box from them. It was all my stuffed animals. They'd been ripped apart and the stuffing was pulled out. It was carnage in that box.'

Tiff choked back a giggle. 'They killed your stuffed animals?'

I gave her a little push on the arm. 'Stop! You make it sound so ... goofy. I loved those stuffed animals!'

She had taken a drink of wine, and it spurted out of her mouth as she laughed. 'Oh my god – that's so *lame!*'

I tried not to laugh. I did love those stupid stuffed animals. I loved them every bit as much as Dragon Girl loved Puffy.

'What's the party about?' Drummer Boy walked up to the edge of the Jacuzzi. He thumped out a complicated pattern on his chest with his lower pair of arms.

'There are only two of us here,' Tiff said. 'That's hardly a party.'

For a moment, he stopped thumping and raised all of his arms over his head. It made his chest and abdominal muscles flex. I rolled my eyes and then looked at Tiff to see what her reaction was. She gazed at him with lowered eyelids. It was an appraising gaze.

'Is there room for me? Or is the fat chick taking up too much space?'

Tiffani laughed. It was throaty and made me shiver. 'There's plenty of room for everyone. This tub is huge.'

Drummer Boy shucked off his pants. He was naked underneath. The producers were going to love this. He hopped into the tub and settled himself across from us.

'So, are you two an item?' he asked. 'Like "Fat Chick" and "Rhinestone Lass" – BFFs?'

I blushed. But Tiff just playfully splashed some water at him. 'Yes, you are so smart. Two women in a tub always means that they're lesbians. And if this were a porn film, we'd just be waiting for you to be the man-meat in our girl sandwich.'

He grinned at her. 'Works for me.'

'I'm outta here.' I wasn't going to stay while he insulted me and flirted with Tiff.

'You sure, Michelle?' Tiffani asked. 'There's plenty of room. And I'm sure DB will play nice.'

'I never play nice. Where's the fun in that?'

I grabbed my beach towel, wrapped it around me, and went upstairs to my room.

I'd just finished changing into my pajamas when there was a knock on the door. I could still hear Tiff and DB laughing outside in the Jacuzzi. When I opened the door I was surprised to find Ink standing there.

'Hey,' I said. 'Is anything wrong?'

She crammed her hands into the pockets of her jeans. 'I heard about the incident at the mall today and I wanted to see if you were all right.'

'Of course,' I said, feeling a bit nonplussed. 'I'm the girl that can take getting hit by a bus. It was no biggie, really.'

'Ah.' Ink frowned and shook her head. 'Well, I'm glad to see you're all right. Just checking in.'

'Uh, okay.' I stood there for a moment, at a loss for what to say next. 'Well, I'll see you tomorrow.'

She looked as if she wanted to say something else, but then she just said, 'Goodnight' and left.

◆

The clanging of the challenge alarm woke me up. I fumbled for the alarm clock and groaned when I saw the time: five A.M.

I threw on my usual challenge outfit: stretchy, baggy sweatpants, a long-sleeve XXL T-shirt, and a hoodie. They were extremely tight on me this morning. The run-in with the bus had fattened me up. As I ran downstairs, I pulled my hair back into a ponytail.

No one was in the living room, and the front door was open. I figured I was the last one out, and trotted as fast as I could at my current size to the waiting limo. But Jetman was the only other teammate in there.

We sat in the back waiting for another twenty minutes until Tiff and Drummer Boy came out, with Ink and the mobile crew following behind them. A slippery, sick feeling went through me.

It was still dark when we got to the studio. The guard waved us through the gate, and we were dropped off at makeup. I guess they wanted to get going on the challenge quickly, because there was none of the usual hurry up and wait.

We were hustled to the set. The full challenge-taping crew was there. The bank facade was lit up like the Fourth of July. The director came over to us. 'Good morning, Diamonds. Ready for today's challenge?'

'Ready for anything,' Drummer Boy said, hitting what sounded like a rim shot off his chest.

The director gestured toward the set. 'Here's the story. A bank robbery is underway. Your challenge today is to free the hostages, take care of the henchmen, and defeat the ace that's running the show.'

'Who's the ace?' Jetman asked.

'Well, that's part of the challenge. You won't know until you get in there.'

That made me nervous. There were lots of aces and some of them had powers that weren't immediately obvious. Mind-control powers were what worried me the most. They could take over and have us at each others' throats if we weren't ready for it – and maybe even if we were.

'Ready on the set,' came over the loudspeaker. Immediately there was silence. And then: 'Action!'

There was the sound of explosives from inside the bank. Then the *rata-tat-tat* of a machine gun. Even though I knew it was just effects, it got my adrenaline going.

'So what's the plan?' Tiffani asked. She looked up at Drummer Boy as if he had all the answers.

'I think we need to get the hostages out first,' I said. Jet-man nodded.

'Sounds good to me,' Tiff said. 'Bubbles, do your stuff.'

I let a bowling ball-size bubble loose at the front door, which exploded like a cheap firecracker. Bits of wood and glass flew across the street. 'Tiff and I should take point. We're invulnerable to projectile attacks.'

'I'm going aloft,' Jetman said. 'I'll come in from behind.' He hit the power button on his jetpack. It sputtered, then the engine caught. It made a putt-putt noise, like an anemic Vespa, but it took him airborne in seconds.

Smoke rolled out of the opening I'd made. Tiff went diamond again, and then we ran into the bank with Drummer Boy behind us. A barrage of paint-balls hit us. They did nothing to me except create more fat. Unfortunately, Tiff was hit in the face and the paint coated her diamond surface, obscuring part of her vision.

I saw a group of people sitting in a circle on the floor. Their hands were tied behind their backs. Standing in front of them were six guys with paint-ball guns. I didn't see anyone who looked like an ace, but with aces, it was hard to tell.

Another round of paint-balls were fired at me and Tiff. 'God-damn it,' I heard her say. I glanced over my shoulder and saw that she had run into one of the prop desks. Most of her face was covered in paint. She probably couldn't see a thing.

Drummer Boy ducked behind one of the desks. If he or Jetman were hit by enough paint-balls, they'd be declared dead and out of the challenge.

I fired a barrage of bubbles at three of the henchmen who were grouped together. These were baseball-size bubbles, and I made them extra hard and dense. One guy was hit on his hand and screamed as he dropped his weapon. Another got one in the gut, and he doubled over.

I missed the third, but Jetman didn't. He burst through the front-door transom windows and fired his 'jetnet.' It whistled past my head and opened in midair, catching the lights and gleaming like a silver spiderweb. Then it wrapped around the goons and they fell to the floor.

More paint-bullets spattered me. I laughed and flung another hail of bubbles at the remaining goons. I missed one because he dropped to the floor, but the other two took direct hits to the chest. Their weapons went spinning out of their hands, and then the hostages shrieked with what sounded like real fear.

I glanced at the hostages and saw that one woman had been struck by one of the guns. She had a nasty cut on her forehead, and it looked like she would have a black eye. I knew they were extras and that they knew injuries might happen, but no one should have to bleed for a paycheck.

Jetman was hovering overhead – the ceilings were high in the bank, fifteen feet at least – and firing down at the three goons. A cloud of gas enveloped them, and moments later, they fell down unconscious. Now we could rescue the hostages. I ran to Tiff and gave her my hoodie so she could wipe the paint off her face, then I helped Drummer Boy untie the extras.

Another henchman appeared.

He was a young guy, maybe a few years older than me, maybe Jetman's age. He was maybe six-one, six-two. His blond hair was cut short, almost military style. He was dressed like the other goons, but he was unarmed. I knew I'd seen him somewhere, but I just couldn't place him.

'This sucker is mine!' Drummer Boy yelled, running past me toward the new henchman. DB had a good foot of height on the guy, plus the extra four arms. He cranked back the three arms on his right side and haymakered one at the guy's head.

Blondie didn't even flinch. As DB's fists made contact, a beautiful yellow corona ballooned around the new guy. He reached up, clamped his left hand around Drummer Boy's middle right fist, then grabbed DB's belt. He lifted DB – who weighed at least two hundred and fifty pounds – as if he were a toddler. Then he tossed him through the front window of the bank.

'Oh crap,' I heard Jetman say as he flew over to us.

'Who is that?' Tiff asked. Jetman had a look of awe on his face. I glanced down at Tiff and saw she had managed to wipe most of the paint from her face, but it had left her diamond skin less than sparkly.

'That's Golden Boy,' Jetman called down. 'The Judas Ace. He's a legend. They say he's invulnerable to harm and one of the strongest men in the world.'

My heart sank. I looked through the jagged hole where the window had been. DB was still lying in the street. One down. And Tiff would be virtually useless against Golden Boy.

That left Jetman and me.

'What about your sleeping gas?' I asked. 'We get him down with that, use your net ...'

'Oh dear,' said Tiff.

Golden Boy was already lunging toward us. Jetman zipped up to the ceiling. Tiff turned and ran to the front door. But I knew if he hit me, he'd only give me more power, so I stood my ground.

He dashed right past me toward Tiffani.

I ran outside in time to see him picking Tiff up and tossing her down the street. She shrieked as she sailed through the air. Then she landed hard and lay as still as Drummer Boy. Her power had protected her from most of the harm of the impact, but landing that hard had knocked her out. I was pissed. I knew she would be all right. But she was my friend and you don't mess with my friends.

I looked around for Jetman and saw him flying out of the hole DB had made. Golden Boy stood between us. I saw Jet-man pull his jetgun from its holster. I backpedaled so I wouldn't be in range when the gas went off.

Jetman fired. I heard the shot and expected to see Golden Boy go down in a cloud of sleeping gas. Instead, the next thing I knew, he was standing there holding the gas cartridge in his hand. Jetman's mouth dropped open. I'm pretty sure mine did, too. Then Golden Boy flung the sleeping gas cartridge back at Jetman. The pellet hit him in the chest and a blue-gray plume of gas enshrouded him. A few seconds later, he plummeted to the ground.

I winced as he landed. He was going to feel like hell when he woke up.

Golden Boy turned toward me. I knew he couldn't be hurt by

my bullet-size bubbles – his force field would just absorb them. But a bigger impact would keep him off balance. I had no hope of winning at this point, but I wasn't going down without a fight.

A bubble formed between my palms. It got bigger and heavier until it was the size of a medicine ball, and then I made it larger still. When it was the size and weight of a wrecking ball, I let it fly at Golden Boy.

It caught him in the chest. His force field bloomed, but he was knocked backward. So I powered up another bubble of that same size and weight and let it go. It staggered him as well. I could feel my clothes getting looser, but I didn't think about that. What mattered was keeping him off balance.

Golden Boy took yet another one in the chest. I felt my pants and panties slipping, and I decided to hell with them. I let them slip down to the ground then kicked them away. Now I had only my T-shirt on. It was long enough. And Golden Boy had steadied himself again.

I powered up another bubble and flung it at him. But he was ready this time, and it only made him stagger back a little.

I cast bubble after bubble at him, each progressively bigger and heavier than the last. But he came at me inexorably, like the tide moving in, until I couldn't make big bubbles anymore. I was almost back to my normal size. When I looked up, he was closing on me. I fired one last desperation bubble, and it popped against his chest like it was made of soap and water.

Golden Boy reached out, and I thought he was going to toss me like he'd tossed Tiff, but he just took my chin in his hand and lifted my face up.

'Nice try,' he said. Then he patted my cheek. 'And you'd be real pretty if you keep that weight off.'

♠

'You lose.'

Like I said, the worst words in the universe.

The only good thing was that Drummer Boy would be going home instead of one of the original Diamonds.

The ride back to our secret lair was silent. Tiffani seemed oddly calm, not pissed the way she usually was when we lost. Drummer Boy hadn't even made his usual snide remarks at me. Of course, I was thin now. More to his taste, I suppose. I was still wearing just the oversize T-shirt. My hoodie was covered in paint, and my pants were way too large to bother putting on. Luckily, a size XXL tee made a perfectly fine minidress.

Ink met us at the front door. She told us we had an hour before Discard, then pulled me off to the living room. 'There's something you need to see,' she said, flipping on the TV.

She'd paused the TiVo on CNN. My heart sank when I saw the graphic. *American Hero Contestant Famous Model.* There were side-by-side pictures of me. One was from a *Vogue* cover I'd done the year before and the other one was my *American Hero* headshot when I was at my most bubble-ready.

'Shit,' I said.

'Do you want to see the rest of the story?'

'Ooooo, I do!' DB grabbed the control from Ink.

'... *Hero* contestant, "The Amazing Bubbles," turns out to be none other than Michelle Pond, a well-known model whose private feud with her parents became tabloid fodder when she filed for emancipation at age fifteen.'

DB flopped on the couch and looked from the TV to me. 'I thought you were just trying to be all Goth and spider-farmerish with that black hair.' He gave me the once-over. 'So, are you a real blonde?'

I wanted to punch him.

'How on earth did this get out?' My voice quavered.

'Someone leaked it,' Ink said. 'But, you know we're going to show today's challenge footage on the show. It would have come out then, anyway.'

I nodded. I had realized when I couldn't stop Golden Boy and had bubbled down to my real size that someone would figure it out. In a way, I guess I was relieved.

'Pond's agency, Cavullio International, has informed CNN that Pond's appearance on *American Hero* violates the terms of her contract with them and that she is no longer with the agency.'

My mouth dropped open. I'd been with Cavullio since I was eight. I'd brought them massive amounts in fees. The sons of bitches.

'Bad break,' DB said. To my amazement, he wasn't being sarcastic. He sounded genuinely sorry.

Tiffani came in and watched some of the report. She gave me a little pat on the back. 'It's going to be okay. Aren't there plenty of other agencies out there?'

She was right. I just couldn't believe that my entire life was coming apart on CNN. 'We've got Discard,' I said woodenly. 'I'm going to go take a shower.'

♣

Digger Downs was our judge for this Discard. I wished it was the Harlem Hammer again, but the judges were rotated. Downs wore a nice brown pinstripe suit that he managed to make look rumpled and seedy. The makeup department had tried to make him look less dissipated, but it hadn't worked.

'Looks like the Diamonds lose again,' he said as we sat down. 'And then there's the drama of Bubbles here. Or should I say Michelle Pond? I see you've gone back to your roots.'

I gave him a look that I hoped would turn him into cinders. Unfortunately, it just made him giggle. 'Yes, Mr. Downs,' I said with an insincere smile plastered on my face. 'I have gone back to my natural hair color. It did take a while to wash out that spray dye. And thank you for noticing.'

It actually felt good to have that dye out of my hair, but Digger made it seem almost pornographic. What a creep.

He gave a ratty smile to Drummer Boy. 'So, Drummer Boy, how do you feel about your new team?'

'They suck,' he replied. 'But I didn't exactly do great in the challenge, so I don't want to be unfair to them.'

'Are you worried that as the newcomer to the team, you're vulnerable?'

DB shrugged. 'You never know how these things are going to work out.'

I had to admire his coolness. It was obvious that his head was on the chopping block. He'd been beyond stupid in the challenge, and he wasn't a real Diamond.

Digger dealt out the cards. Once again, Tiff pulled her choice out immediately and laid it facedown in front of her. Drummer Boy also made his selection quickly. I pulled DB's card out and put it face down.

Jetman was the only one who hadn't pulled a card yet. I saw him looking at the three of us and I was baffled by why this was difficult for him – unless he was breaking the Diamonds alliance. I hated to think that. He slowly pulled a card out and slid it across to Digger.

Digger collected the rest of the cards and shuffled them. He cradled the small deck in his hand. 'Time to see who stays and who goes,' he said.

He flipped the first card over and placed it on the table. The Amazing Bubbles. My pudgy face smiled up at me. *Figures*, I thought. *No doubt, Drummer Boy would like me out.*

The next card was flipped. Drummer Boy. He frowned, but what did he expect? 'One-to-one so far,' Digger said.

He turned the third card. It was Tiffani. I looked at Jetman. He gave me a calm, steady look. Had he really voted for Tiffani? Or had Drummer Boy voted for her? Had he voted for me? All I knew was that Tiff and I were voting for DB. Then Digger flipped the last card.

The Amazing Bubbles.

'And the pair takes the lady out,' Digger said.

My hands began to shake, and I slipped them into my lap. I knew I must look shocked, and I was.

'Tough luck, Bubbles,' Digger said. 'So, will you be going back to your modeling career now?'

I pushed away from the table and stood up. Everything seemed to be moving in slow motion. I could almost feel the cameras zooming in on my face. They would want to see the pain.

Jetman came around the table and hugged me. He whispered in my ear. 'I voted for Tiffani, Bubbles. She made an alliance with

DB. They wanted me with them, but I wouldn't play ball. Screw the metagame. I won't play like that.' He squeezed me tighter. 'And I knew you wouldn't believe she was stabbing you in the back.' He let me go then. I stood there like a deer in the headlights.

Tiffani had betrayed me.

Drummer Boy was shaking my hand. 'No hard feelings, Bubbles. It's just a game.'

Tiff was standing behind him, but I couldn't look at her. I didn't want to talk to her, or hear her excuses. I just turned and went to my room.

♥

I was shoving the last of my clothes into my bag when I heard a knock on the door. 'Michelle, it's me.'

It was Tiff. A wave of nausea swept over me.

'I'm not in the mood,' I said.

'Look, I'm not going to apologize for voting you off,' she said through the door.

I jammed my last piece of clothing into my bag and yanked the zipper closed. 'Well, thank goodness for that,' I replied. I felt as though I might throw up.

'It's just … I mean … I just got your presents.'

I'd forgotten the presents. I'd taken the money the show had given me and spent it on Tiff for the things she'd wanted but hadn't bought for herself. I'd had Bergdorf's send the packages with the perfume and cashmere shawl around to the house. I felt like an extra-special idiot.

'You know, I never asked you to spend your money on me,' Tiff said. 'And I never promised you anything.'

I went to the door and yanked it open. 'I know you didn't promise me anything. I gave you those things because I thought you would like them. Because you spent the money you could have spent on yourself on your family instead.' I took a big breath. My entire body was shaking now. 'Don't think that makes me less pissed at you. You did something rotten and underhanded.' I wanted to slap her.

'I know I let you down,' she said, giving me a pleading look. 'I just didn't have any other choice.'

I grabbed my bags off the bed. Then, as I brushed by her, I said tightly, 'There are always choices, Tiff.'

She called after me, but I ignored her.

♦

The Discard Pile was stunning. At least, if I was going to hang with the losers, it would be in top-notch style.

The living room was large – it had to be. Eleven of the discarded *AH* players were already living there. Twelve now, with me. And two more were on their way.

I discovered that every time there were new Discards, the house members threw a party.

A very loud, drunken party. It was just what I was in the mood for.

After several glasses of champagne, I asked the Maharajah to show me to my room. I unpacked, then went back down. The party was in full swing. Joker Plague's new album was cranked to eleven, and everyone was dancing like it was the end of the world. I grabbed a bottle of champagne and got out in the middle of it all.

♠

Light streamed hot and heavy through the bedroom windows. I opened one eye. I wasn't dead, but felt as if I could do a remarkable facsimile of it. With a groan, I rolled over. Or I tried to. Ink was asleep next to me. Naked.

I glanced down at her body. It wasn't covered in its usual tattoos. Her skin was the color of milky tea. There was a tangle of dark hair between her legs, and her breasts were small and tipped with delicate brownish-pink nipples. I tried to remember how we had ended up in bed together. But the throbbing in my head made it impossible.

I sat up. The room tilted for a moment, then righted. Now I felt ravenously hungry, but I knew it wasn't just for food. I needed to be fat again. I needed to be able to bubble.

'You're awake,' Ink said, stretching.

'Uh, yeah,' I replied. I wondered if Ink would bail on me when I got back to my Bubbles size. Or if she would bail anyway. I couldn't remember if we had professed anything other than drunken lust.

'You were pretty drunk last night,' Ink said, making her the Queen of Understatement.

'Yeah,' I said, rubbing my face. 'I don't remember a lot after we all started dancing.'

Ink stretched again and I wanted to run my lips across her firm belly, then kiss and nibble in the dark thatch of hair between her legs. I had a brief memory flash of musky flesh and sweet, soft hair against my mouth.

'Well, you'd already consumed an enormous amount of champagne before I got to the Discard Pile,' Ink said. 'The party was going full tilt, and you dragged me into the middle of the dancing. Then you told me I was your "Asian Princess." And after that, you carried me up here and we more or less canoodled until we both passed out.'

I moaned and hid my face in my hands. I was mortified. Why on earth had I called Ink my 'Asian Princess'?

'I am so embarrassed,' I said.

'Why? I thought it was hilarious.'

'When … how … did you end up here? In Discards, I mean.'

Ink rolled over onto her stomach. Her bottom was a perfect peach shape. I dimly remembered nibbling on it.

'I've been lobbying to be the PA for the Discard Pile for a while. I knew you were going to be on the chopping block and I wanted to stay close to you.'

I felt a hot blush go up my face.

'But, but, I didn't know you liked me … you know, like that.'

Ink laughed, and her bottom quivered. *That's really distracting*, I thought.

'You can be kinda dim about some things, sweetie,' Ink said, looking at me coyly over her shoulder.

'Uhm.' Then I blurted out, 'You didn't sleep with me just because I'm skinny now, did you?'

Ink giggled. 'No, I wanted to sleep with you even when you had that horrible black hair and that big, delicious ass. In fact, I kinda like the idea of a girlfriend who can be any size. Variety is the spice of life and all that.'

'Oh.' I hadn't thought of that. Come to think of it, a girlfriend whose skin had infinite moods might be pretty amazing, too.

Ink rolled onto her side, then grabbed my arm and pulled me close. I hadn't expected her to be so strong.

'Let me show you how much I like you.' She slid her hand down my arm. Then she put her hand between my legs and began to stroke me. She leaned forward and rained nibbly kisses on my mouth. 'Next time we do this, you're going to be bigger. I want your flesh – all of it.'

I tried to think of something to say, but I was at a loss. And everything Ink was doing felt so good that soon I gave up thinking at all.

♣

'I just don't know how she could do it,' I said. Ink was pulling her pants on, and I stared at her perfect bottom for a moment.

'Tiffani doesn't look at it the way you do.' She grabbed her bra and slid it on. 'Besides, you can't dwell on it. You've got to think about where you're going to go from here.'

I flopped back on the pillows. I was a failure. I would never be a hero. I'd wanted to do something good with my power. I'd wanted to make a difference. Now I was washed up.

'Are you wallowing over there?' Ink pulled her tight T-shirt over her head.

I put my hands over my face. 'No … yes … maybe.' I knew Tiffani had screwed me over, but part of me still couldn't believe what had happened. 'Maybe DB got to her. Jetman said they had an alliance. Maybe DB lied to her.'

Ink came over and stood at the end of the bed. 'Okay, enough of this,' she said, looking extremely annoyed. 'Stay here. I'll be right back.'

♥

'I had a feeling you would be making excuses for Tiffani, so I had this copy made.' Ink pulled a DVR out of her bag and slipped it into her laptop. The DVR clicked and whirled. Then a QuickTime window opened, and I saw Tiffani sitting in the Confessional room. A marker appeared in the lower corner: CONFESSIONAL #30 – DIAMONDS – TIFFANI

She was looking directly into the camera, her heart-shaped face framed with a corona of auburn hair. I wanted to hate her, but I couldn't.

'Of course I'm playing a game,' she said with a slight smile. 'Everyone here is playing a game. And if they're not, they're just not paying attention.

'Look, this isn't about who would be the best hero. It's about being good TV. When Rupert won a million in an online poll on *Survivor*, no one complained. He couldn't cut it in the game, but the audience loved him. There's nothing wrong with that. This is America. We vote on things – that's the way we do it.'

She smiled at the camera again.

'I know I'm not the most powerful ace here. My power is goofy. I can turn my skin into a diamond-hard substance. That and three bucks will get you a latte at Starbucks. And yes, I know what Starbucks is. I may be a hick from West Virginia, but those things are everywhere.

'Anyway, I would be a great American Hero because I have "The Package." I'm pretty. I have the whole rags-to-riches angle. My power looks cool, but it's non-threatening.'

A voice came from offscreen. I recognized it. Ink's voice. 'What about Bubbles?'

Tiffani shrugged. 'I know that Michelle likes me. And I like her, too, just not in "that" way. And besides, Michelle takes this all way too seriously. She actually believes in the whole "hero" thing. What a goober.'

'Anyone you would like to be involved with?'

Tiffani blushed. 'DB. I admit it. He's gorgeous. He's famous. He's rich. What's not to like?

'Look, I'm playing the game. In the beginning, I allied myself with a strong player who I knew would be loyal to me. That was Bubbles. But she's too powerful, and I knew eventually I would have to get rid of her. So, when we had the chance to add DB to the Diamonds, well, I just combined the thing I wanted with the thing I needed.'

I hit the pause button. I didn't want to see any more. Had she been making a fool out of me the entire time?

Ink took me by the shoulders and gave me a shake. 'Look, Tiff didn't care about being a hero. You did. But the show wouldn't have made you a hero. You're going to make yourself one.'

'How?' I felt stupid and used, and anything but heroic.

She put her arms around me. 'Well, we've gotten tons of e-mails from gay and lesbian teenagers sent care of *AH* to you. Most of them thanking you for being such a great role model – and some suggesting things that I'm pretty sure are illegal in all fifty states. They love the fact that you didn't hide the fact that you're gay. And that you didn't hide the fact that you were interested in Tiff. That's being a role model. That's pretty heroic.

'And then there were the big girls, gay and straight, who wrote in saying that you made them realize any size could be beautiful as well as powerful.'

She let go of me and gave my hair a playful yank.

'And there are also all kinds of offers to endorse products, and plenty of agencies that want to represent you, if you decide to get back on the modeling merry-go-round. But I know you, and that's not what you're about. Now sit here, read these e-mails, and stop feeling sorry for yourself.' She marched out of the room.

So I spent the next couple of hours doing what she said. And she was right. I could do something to make a difference.

I opened my hand and concentrated on bubbling. A grape-size bubble appeared, and I let it float to the ceiling.

I needed to get fat again. One of the Discards would no doubt be happy to pound the heck out of me until I plumped up. And after that, well …

The future was bubbling up.

◆

JONATHAN HIVE

Daniel Abraham

ALL THE BEST STORIES START 'THIS ONE TIME WE WERE REALLY DRUNK, AND ...'

'Seriously,' Jonathan said, 'is there nothing going on in the whole fucking world besides this show?'

'Probably,' Gardener said as she leaned down to get another beer from the cooler on the coffee table, 'but who really cares?'

The Discard Pile was getting more and more crowded with each passing week. With every new addition, Jonathan was more and more grateful he'd lost early and gotten his pick of bedrooms. Earlier this week, Spades had won their challenge, foiling Detroit Steel and his gang of bogus bank robbers, but Golden Boy and henchmen had handled the Diamonds. The Hearts had yet to face their own rogue ace, but the evening's entertainment was watching the daily footage of Clubs getting their collective clock cleaned by the Aryan poster boy, Lohengrin. The studio was even providing the pizza.

It wasn't a formal party, just a bunch of failures drinking cheap beer and talking smack about people who'd already done better than they had, and getting filmed so that every shitty thing they said could be used as a voiceover for the home audience.

'Here it comes,' King Cobalt said, pointing at the big plasma screen. 'Watch this part.'

It was the same fake bank that Detroit Steel had failed to rob the day before, or one so much like it as to make no difference.

Lohengrin stood in the entrance in glowing white armor. The

sword in his hand looked cheesy by comparison. The studio had made him use some kind of special effects prop instead of the actual force sword he could conjure from nothing.

'Hey,' the Maharajah said, 'Lohengrin. Can that really cut through anything?'

'*Ja*,' the blond, brawny ace said from the far end of the couch. 'Steel, stone. Anything.'

'You want another beer?' Simoon asked him.

Jonathan watched their guest of honor waver between his love of beer and his disgust at the American interpretation of the word. He held up a hand to decline.

'Would you guys *watch*?' King Cobalt said, frowning under his mask.

On the screen, the preacher, Holy Roller, had become a near-perfect sphere, barreling down toward the bank like a huge Baptist bowling ball. The Lohengrin on the screen struck a heroic pose and brought his sword to bear.

The impact was intense. Lohengrin was blown back through the door into the bank – they'd already seen the footage from the interior cameras – and Holy Roller bore a stripe down his midsection that showed where the sword would have cleaved him nearly in half had it been real. With a visible sigh, the enormous ace played dead. And then a moment later, Lohengrin appeared again, unbloodied and unbowed. The Discard Pile cheered. Lohengrin grinned and ran a hand though his hair. 'It was a very strong blow,' he said, as if apologizing for his victory. 'The priest is a formidable opponent.'

On the screen, Toad Man and Stuntman were circling around to attack Lohengrin from both sides. They'd all seen this from a different angle before, too.

'Look!' King Cobalt said. 'Here it comes!'

The doorbell rang.

'Pizza's here!' Diver shouted. 'Who's got the money?'

Jonathan caught a glimpse of Fortune trotting up from the back of the house, digging for his wallet.

'Don't forget to tip him,' Spasm yelled. Fortune nodded. Jonathan didn't think anyone else caught the little flash of anger in the kid's eyes. Jonathan rose and picked his way across the crowded floor and through the cameras trained on the Discards. He caught up with Fortune in the atrium, signing a voucher. A stack of pizza boxes sat on the side table.

'Want a hand with that?' Jonathan asked.

'Sure,' Fortune said. 'Thanks.'

The kitchen was as wide as a cafeteria. There was room to lay out all the boxes, lids open, and cheap paper plates besides. The fluorescent lights buzzed; Jonathan had heard two of the sound guys bitching about it.

'How's he taking it?' Jonathan asked.

'Who?' Fortune asked.

'The new Ku Klux Klan spokesmodel,' Jonathan said. 'Rustbelt.'

Fortune hesitated. 'Not so well,' he said.

'You think he really did it?'

'Stuntman said he did,' Fortune said. 'So it doesn't really matter, does it?'

'Reality television,' Jonathan said, like he was saying 'jumbo shrimp.'

A shriek and a peal of laughter came from the front room. Then King Cobalt's voice saying 'Watch this part.' Jonathan dropped a slice of pepperoni onto a plate and handed it to Fortune.

'Thanks,' Fortune said, 'but I can't. It's for contestants.'

'Did you tip the delivery guy?'

Fortune stared at him.

'So, why can't I tip you?' Jonathan asked. 'Come on, this is all bullshit anyway. Have some food.'

With a half smile and something between a cough and a laugh, Fortune accepted the plate.

There had to be a way, Jonathan thought, to bring the subject up that was more graceful than *So, did you track down that magic amulet yet*?

'So. Did you track down that magic amulet yet?' Jonathan said, wincing.

Fortune looked uncomfortable. Before he could come up with a polite evasion, Lohengrin appeared in the doorway, a little shame-faced.

'Excuse me,' he said. 'Is there any other beer?'

'Sorry,' Fortune said. 'That's all the studio got.'

'We are the losers, after all,' Jonathan said.

The German ace's expression fell. Jonathan suddenly remembered Fortune and Curveball safely out of range of the cameras, and the plan, such as it was, sprang into Jonathan's head full-formed. Which was to say actually, about half-formed, but that was enough to start with.

'I bet our man Fortune here knows some good bars, though. Right?' Jonathan said.

'Um,' Fortune replied.

'Do you?' Lohengrin asked, his face a mask of longing.

'Well ...'

'Come on,' Jonathan said. 'We'll sneak out the back.'

Lohengrin's smile was brilliant. Fortune hesitated for a long moment. He certainly wouldn't have done it for Jonathan, but Lohengrin was a guest of the show, the kind of guy that Berman and Peregrine wanted to keep happy.

'I'll buy the first round,' Jonathan said. Lohengrin's eyes seemed to shine.

From the front room, Spasm yelled, 'Hey! Where's Captain Cruller? Chop chop, man. We're hungry out here.'

'Okay,' Fortune said. 'Let's go.'

♠

Here was the thing: writing a book meant finding something to write about. Sitting on the couch while Spasm talked about how he could have done better and King Cobalt shushed everyone was not the stuff of high drama. John Fortune – the guy who used to be an ace, whose father died, who wanted nothing more in the world than to regain his status and honor – was. But Fortune was also reticent and private and trying hard to make the best of his situation. And, in all fairness, if they'd been calling Jonathan by names like Captain Cruller and Fetchit the Wonder Gopher, he'd have been keeping a low profile, too.

What Jonathan needed was friendship. Shared confidences. The details of Fortune's situation that would make the whole thing spring to life when he wrote it up. It was the perfect counterpoint to the aces on the show – if there was just a way to get the man to relax and open up.

A way like, say, *lots* of alcohol. And a few other people to open up and tell stories on themselves first.

What the hell? It worked for the guys who sold videos of girls exposing themselves.

'So,' Jonathan went on, 'there I was, in the girl's locker room, nothing but a towel on. And Christy had this huge can of bug spray and this look in her eyes like she was just daring me to try and get away.'

Lohengrin chortled and gestured to the waitress.

'That can't have gone well,' Fortune said.

'Yeah, we pretty much broke up after that,' Jonathan said.

'I had *einen* lover when I was at school,' Lohengrin said. 'She was beautiful. Like a goddess. But she had another boy she was with as well. He tried to hurt me one night. With a knife. I had my armor, of course, but because of how he attacked, I had nothing else. I had to try to calm him while he keeps stabbing at me.'

Lohengrin made sad little stabbing motions and shook his head.

'Why didn't you use your sword?' Jonathan asked.

Lohengrin shrugged. 'I felt pity for him. He was just a normal boy and I was ...'

Lohengrin gestured at himself. It should have been a statement of conceit: *I was the mighty Lohengrin against whom no mere nat could hope to compete.* But something about the guy made it seem okay. Lohengrin was an ace. It made a difference.

'I didn't ever really date,' Fortune said. 'My mom was always afraid that something might happen to me, turn my wild card. She had private investigators follow me. I had bodyguards to make sure nothing ever happened to me.'

'Wow,' Jonathan said, mixing sarcasm and sympathy in his tone, 'and the girls didn't go for that?'

'That is hard,' Lohengrin said. The waitress arrived, sweeping the empty bottles from their table and putting down fresh ones like she'd trained for Cirque de Soleil.

'I don't know,' Fortune said. 'It was just my life. It was the way things were. And then when the card did turn, and I thought it was an ace …'

Jonathan clapped Fortune's shoulder. The pathos of the guy's life was amazing. Or possibly Jonathan was drunk enough to be getting sentimental.

'Did you ever get your mom to tell you about the amulet?' Jonathan asked.

'What amulet?' Lohengrin asked, as if Jonathan had coached the guy. Now Fortune had to tell the story, and in doing so remind himself of the hope that Simoon had brought him. The powers of Ra, whatever they were. A fate, a destiny. Something better than running trivial errands in the cocaine economy of Hollywood.

'You must find this thing!' Lohengrin said when Fortune had finished.

'I can't,' Fortune said. 'Mom doesn't know where it is. Or at least that's what she says.'

'You don't believe her?' Jonathan asked.

'I don't know. Maybe it's true. Or maybe she's just so in the habit of protecting me from things that … you know, it's just what she does. Maybe she has it in her safe or something, and just doesn't want to risk it.'

'And what about you?' Jonathan asked. 'Would you risk it?'

Fortune looked sour. There were the beginnings of tears in his eyes. How desolate it must be, Jonathan thought. How empty. To have been an ace, to have been important. Fortune was carrying not only his father's death but also the dragging weight of being no one in particular. It was the saddest thing Jonathan had ever seen.

Okay, he was definitely getting maudlin now.

'I can open safes,' Lohengrin said.

Jonathan and Fortune both stared at him.

'Any safe. Just like this,' Lohengrin said and snapped his fingers.

'Aren't Berman and your mom wining and dining the new guest ace? Noel whatsisname?' Jonathan asked. 'The stage magician guy they brought over from England?'

'She's … yeah, she's out. How did you know that?'

'Heard someone talking about it,' Jonathan said, not mentioning that he had been a wasp at the time.

'I thought the magic was his ace power,' Lohengrin said.

'No, he's just a stage magician,' Fortune said. 'He's got the wild card, but that's just his shtick. Or anyway, that's what he says.'

'But—'

'The point is,' Jonathan broke in, 'her house. Is there anyone there?'

'No. My dad … my step-dad, I mean. Josh. He's out of town all month. But—'

'It's perfect,' Jonathan said. 'Come on. Let's go take a look!'

'Guys,' Fortune said. 'Look, I really appreciate that you want to help out, but … but …'

'You must find your destiny,' Lohengrin intoned, his hand on Fortune's shoulder. 'If God has need of you, and this is the path your honor demands, you *must* go. You *cannot* do less. And I will aid you, if I can.'

It should have sounded cheesy, but the fucker really pulled that Arthurian shit off. Jonathan felt genuinely moved.

'Yeah. What he said,' Jonathan said. 'Let's get the check.'

♣

Through one set of noncompound eyes, Peregrine's house looked more impressive. The Beverly Hills address matched with the mission-style architecture and the Spanish tile roof. The lawn was lush and green. He half expected to see Marilyn Monroe slink out of the house with a martini glass in her hand. Which was, he supposed, exactly the effect the architect was shooting for.

Jonathan pulled the car carefully into the driveway, stopping well before the garage door. That was the trick of driving intoxicated; allow lots of room for error.

'It is beautiful,' Lohengrin said, leaning forward until his forehead almost touched the windshield. Maybe the crazed German bastard was a sentimental drunk too. It was endearing. Jonathan tried to turn off the engine and discovered he already had.

'We shouldn't be doing this,' Fortune said from the back seat.

Jonathan found the button.

All four doors unlocked simultaneously. The sound was like a prison door slamming closed. Jonathan grinned and got out of the car. The others followed him. Lohengrin was humming something martial as they went up the sculpted concrete path to the door. Fortune started behind them both, but hurried to catch up, as if he wanted to protect the house from them.

'This is just ... okay, be careful in here, okay? This is my mom's house. I don't want you to—'

'John,' Jonathan said. 'We aren't high school kids sneaking into the liquor cabinet and downloading porn. We're grown men searching for a pariicuiar answer to a specific question.'

Fortune hesitated.

'We will do you no dishonor,' Lohengrin intoned. 'I swear it.'

That was apparently the trick, because Fortune took a key out of his pocket, unlocked the door, and stepped in. While he disarmed the alarm system, Jonathan took in the house. A black stone fountain burbled to itself in the entryway. The decor in the main rooms was chic and clean, with high ceilings and open spaces. He could almost see Peregrine rising from the couch and stretching out her wings. A glass wall led out to the deck he'd seen before, through other eyes.

'Come on,' Fortune said, heading down a hallway to their left. 'Let's get this over with.'

Jonathan walked after him. The art that hung tastefully from the wall was beautiful, one piece commenting subtly on the next. The air smelled like his grandmother's house in Virginia, the air conditioning doing something arcane that reminded him of cucumbers. The architecture itself made him think of television sets – everything a little too spacious and a little too clean, and everything, *everything*, in place. Jonathan tried to imagine what it would have been like growing up in a world like this, a climate-controlled childhood. And nothing anywhere that referenced Peregrine's past as sex symbol and lover of the half-black, half-Asian pimp-turned-ace-turned-monk-turned-martyr Fortunato.

Lohengrin paused in the entryway, swaying slightly. His brow was furrowed in intense concentration.

'What's up, big guy?' Jonathan asked.

'John's powers. His old powers,' Lohengrin said. 'He almost destroys the world, *ja*?'

'Yeah,' Jonathan agreed. '*Time* magazine did a whole thing on it. Bunch of people thought he was the messiah or the antichrist, or whatever. If Fortunato hadn't come in, it would have been ugly.'

'*Ja*,' the German agreed. 'And we are helping to get his powers back?'

Jonathan blinked. 'But,' he said. 'That stuff. Back at the bar. His destiny …'

Lohengrin nodded in agreement but still frowning. 'I may have been wrong,' he said.

'Huh,' Jonathan said. And then, 'Hey, Fortune?'

Peregrine's bedroom. Extra-wide king-size-plus bed with raw silk sheets, a skylight on runners that could open to let someone in or out if they could fly, tasteful bedside table and lamp with the latest issue of *Variety* open to an article about *American Hero*. But no John Fortune.

'Fortune?'

'In here. Dressing room.'

It was like a walk-in closet the size of an apartment. Dresses, coats, shoes, suits, sweats, a dresser devoted to undergarments. And a table with a jewelry case that would shame some department stores, complete with vanity mirror where John Fortune was sitting, hands flat on the table, jaw set, eyes focused and determined. He looked like the world's most desperate drag queen getting ready to suit up.

A steel safe door two feet square gazed out from the wall at shoulder height like high-security Dadaist art.

'Fortune?' Jonathan said. 'Hey, the Lone Grin here had a point that might be worth just kicking—'

'All her jewelry is in there,' he said, nodding at the safe. 'Necklaces, amulets, beads. Whatever.'

'Yeah, but ... you see, we were wondering if maybe getting back your powers ... I mean the last time you had 'em—'

'I know what happened. I was there.'

'All we meant was, the stakes are a little—'

'You just thought of that now?'

Lohengrin raised a hand like a kid in school. 'It was me,' he said.

'Yeah,' Jonathan said. 'I didn't really think of it.'

'Well, I did,' Fortune said. 'It's okay. I'm good with it.'

'That's great,' Jonathan said, 'but I'm not sure—'

'Step off, okay!' Fortune shouted. '*You* are the one who wanted to try this, right? I didn't ask you to poke into my life. You took that on yourself. *You're* the one who came up with the bright idea of hauling me up here and digging up this amulet. I'm just Captain Cruller, the guy who used to be famous for letting his own father fucking *die*! You hold up a chance for me to get that back, and then you want to talk about it? If you ladies are getting cold feet, go stick 'em in something hot!'

Fortune's face flushed red, and his breath sounded like a bull's.

'You are right,' Lohengrin said. 'I gave my word to help in this. I will not fail you.'

'Um, hello?' Jonathan said. 'What about maybe destroying the world?'

'I have given my word,' Lohengrin repeated. 'Honor demands I do this.'

'Honor demands *what*? How fucking drunk *are* you?'

But Lohengrin had already put out his hand. The blade that appeared in it glowed with a soft, pure light. The German turned to the safe and with a flick of his wrist carved a hole in the steel door and part of the surrounding wall. John Fortune yelped and sprang forward.

'What the fuck!' he shouted.

'I opened the safe,' Lohengrin said, as if that wasn't obvious. 'Is what we came for, *nein*?'

'You *broke* the safe,' Fortune yelled. 'You didn't tell me you were going to break it.'

'But ...' Lohengrin began. Fortune turned his back to them both, reaching into the darkness of the safe. The rant was going on under his breath. Jonathan caught the words 'very clever' and 'dickhead.'

He was starting to think John Fortune might not be a sentimental drunk.

Lohengrin started to pace, his wide, teutonic brow furrowed. Jonathan tried very hard to think, but there was still enough booze in his bloodstream to make things muzzy at the edges. There had been a plan when he'd started this, and he was pretty sure that this hadn't been how it had gone.

'Fuck,' Fortune said.

'Didn't work?'

'It's not here,' Fortune said. 'These ... they aren't ...'

His voice wasn't angry anymore. More sad. Fortune hung his head, and Jonathan put a hand on the guy's shoulder.

'So here's the thing,' Jonathan said. 'I'm a real asshole sometimes. I didn't mean to—'

'I am asshole too,' Lohengrin said, putting his hand on Fortune's other shoulder. Jonathan caught their reflection in the vanity mirror. With Fortune's head low and the pair of them flanking the guy, it looked like an old print he'd seen of Lancelot and Merlin supporting King Arthur.

Nice detail, he thought. He filed it away for when he wrote the book. Fortune's head came back up.

'I know where it is,' he said. Before Jonathan could think through what the words really meant, Fortune was gone. Jonathan and Lohengrin fouled each other trying to get out of the dressing room door, so Fortune got to Peregrine's study well before them.

It was another beautiful room – soft light, teak furniture, soft carpet. One wall was dedicated to images and mementos of the life of one of the world's more glamorous wild cards. Magazine covers, newspaper clippings, plaques with her name and the appreciation of President Barnett and Senator Hartmann. Three Emmy awards. A People's Choice award. Trophies and plaques detailing her charity work and other random appreciations. Pictures of her floating above the New York skyline, flying past the Eiffel Tower. Standing, wings spread and eyebrows raised, before the pyramids. Jonathan was struck by how young she looked back then. 1987. He'd been six years old.

Fortune sat on the corner of the wide, low, wooden desk. A simple loop of leather cord hung from his hand, a red bauble at its end. In the dim light, the setting looked brass. Jonathan and Lohengrin both stopped dead.

'Fortune,' Jonathan said, and licked his lips. 'You should maybe put that down. You know, just for a second.'

Fortune looked up. He was smiling. He shook his head. If they hadn't been drunk, Jonathan and Lohengrin might have found the right words to talk him back. They might have had the presence of mind to leap forward and snatch the thing from his hand. If they hadn't been drunk, they wouldn't have been there in the first place. John Fortune tossed the amulet in the air, caught it, and dropped the cord around his neck. The red stone bauble struck his chest with a low, heavy sound, and then hung there, innocuously.

Jonathan Hive stared at the thing as it shifted slightly against Fortune's shirt. After a moment, he remembered to breathe. Fortune laughed ruefully, touching the amulet with his fingertips. 'Nothing,' he said. 'Just another fairy tale that didn't come true.'

'Look, Fortune. I'm sorry. I shouldn't have—'

John Fortune started screaming. Lohengrin's mystic armor appeared, a white luminous medieval knight. Jonathan hopped back a step and then forward again. The brass setting lay on the floor, two hollow half-rounds, like a walnut shell with the nut missing. The stone was gone. Fortune was ripping off his shirt, shrieking like a girl.

'What!' Jonathan shouted. 'What is it?'

'It's inside of me! Holy shit! Get it out!'

A lump moved under Fortune's dusky skin, something forcing its way through him, up his chest, over his collarbone.

'Lohengrin!' Jonathan screamed. 'Knife! The big knife! The sword! Get your sword! Cut it out!'

'No!' Fortune cried, but whether he meant the thing crawling in his flesh or the plan to cut him open wasn't clear.

The knight shifted his attention from Fortune clawing at his own flesh, to Jonathan's trembling finger. The lump passed under Fortune's jaw, and then up through his cheek. As Lohengrin stepped forward, the sword glowing into being in his hand, the thing reached John Fortune's forehead. Something like a detonation filled the room: light and heat and a kind of shockwave that Jonathan felt in his bones though it didn't blow back his hair or his clothes. The air smelled of dust and overheated stone.

'*Mein Gott.*'

Where John Fortune had been, a huge she-lion crouched, light streaming from her like a small sun. She bared her teeth at Lohengrin, who stepped back, his sword held at the guard before him. The lioness howled.

'What the *fuck*!' Jonathan shouted.

The lioness turned to him, startled by his voice. When she opened her mouth, he saw the billowing flame in her throat. He barely had time to expand out, wasps exploding in all directions, before the blast of fire passed through the space where he had been.

The study descended into chaos. Lohengrin swung his sword, the tip cleaving pits of lathe and plaster out of the walls. Flames burst over him like water while the lioness leaped and roared. Jonathan, not sure whether to flee or try to save Lohengrin from Fortune, or maybe Fortune from Lohengrin, buzzed madly around the room.

The lioness leapt and snapped, growled and screamed. Jonathan split himself, rolling and dodging every time the lioness shot at him.

Fire, Jonathan thought as he fled out to the hallway, *why does it always have to be fire?*

Lohengrin staggered out, victim of a lucky swipe of the lioness's huge paw. The lioness followed, pressing her advantage. The screams from the beast's throat were terrible.

Lohengrin seemed to be fighting a defensive battle, keeping the lioness at bay and trusting to his armor for protection from the flames. The lioness had no such compunction. Her lips were pulled back in a snarl that would have made Jonathan certain that he was about to die if he'd been back in his human form.

With a howl, the lioness leapt past Lohengrin and into the main room. The open architecture served her. There was no way to block her path, and she was able to leap from one end of the room to the other, claws digging into the walls and floor.

'Stop!' Lohengrin shouted. 'You must stop!'

Fuck that, Jonathan thought. *Go! Let it go!* But without the benefit of lungs or a throat, all he managed was a slightly louder buzzing.

An alarm blared. Jonathan felt a few of his wasps cook off and die. And then a few more. Either he was getting worse at dodging the lioness …

No, no – the house was on fire.

In the study, flames had taken the desk and the wall of awards. The hallway was also alight, tongues of blue-and-orange flame licking at the walls and ceiling. The lioness roared again, and flames belched out, breaking off Lohengrin's armor and setting the curtains on fire.

Jonathan condensed back into human form at the front door. Another fire alarm went off, the high squeal like the house itself screaming in fear. The sound seemed to shock Lohengrin and the lioness both. Two heads – one armored, the other leonine – turned toward Jonathan. He threw open the door. 'Get out! *Now*! Out!'

For the first time, both the lioness and Lohengrin noticed the flames sheeting up the wall, the swaths of sword-slashed and burning furniture. To Jonathan's profound relief, they bolted for the door.

The lioness paused on the lawn, her head shifting from Jonathan to Lohengrin and back.

'Ah. Good kitty?' Jonathan said. The lioness howled, turned, and sped away into the night. Lohengrin took two fast steps after her, and then stopped. The lioness was already half a block away, and still accelerating. Lohengrin's sword and armor vanished.

Flames flickered inside the house. Smoke was billowing out of the movable skylight in Peregrine's bedroom. Jonathan sat on the lawn. Lohengrin stepped over and squatted down beside him.

'The house,' Lohengrin said.

'Yeah,' Jonathan said. 'We torched it.'

'Where are your clothes?' Lohengrin asked.

Jonathan sighed. 'In the house,' he said.

'Und the key for the auto?'

'In the pocket,' Jonathan agreed. 'With my wallet.'

In the distance, sirens were just starting to wail. Jonathan sucked his teeth, Lohengrin looked around, shamefaced.

'Well,' Jonathan said, 'that could have gone better.'

♥

STAR POWER

Melinda M. Snodgrass

The front doors of the bank blew into sparkling shards. Even safety glass was no match for one of Curveball's marbles. The robbers fired wildly with their paint-ball guns, and retreated as Curveball, Hardhat, and Wild Fox rushed through the doors. The paint-ball pellets bounced harmlessly off the web of glowing yellow girders that served as a shield for the advancing aces. The building gave a lurch and settled. There were screams of terror from the bank customers held hostage in the safety deposit vault.

Noel Matthews sat huddled among the bound and gagged bank customers. His henchmen were succumbing to Curveball's Nerf balls and the touch of Hardhat's girders. There was the sound of paint-ball guns firing wildly from the back of the bank. The last two of his men came stumbling into the lobby. Earth Witch pursued them, and soon had the floor cracking and dancing beneath their feet. They shouted with alarm and fell in a tumble of guns, arms, and legs. All six of his henchmen were now effectively dead or captured.

Hardhat moved to the door of the vault and gestured to the prisoners with a grandiose sweep of one brawny arm. 'Okay folks, you're safe now.'

Noel shook back the trailing curls of his long blond wig, and looked pleadingly up at the big ace. Hardhat's chest swelled and he swaggered over to Noel, pulled a utility knife off his carpenter's belt, and cut Noel's bonds. Noel pulled the gag out of his lipsticked mouth. 'Thank you,' he whispered huskily.

'No fuckin' problem. It was my goddamn pleasure.'

Earth Witch had found Noel's trademark black, snap-brimmed fedora in front of a wall of safety deposit boxes. She picked it up and frowned from the hat to the boxes. His reputation as a magician and a wild card had her wondering if he could have somehow crammed flesh and blood into a metal box.

Wild Fox and Curveball were moving to cut the ropes holding the extras who had played the bank customers. Noel flowed to his feet and stepped up behind Hardhat. With one hand, he pulled out the paint-ball gun and shot the big ace in the small of his back. With his other hand he threw a flash/bang, blinding everyone except himself, because he had closed his eyes.

Noel heard Hardhat's bellow of 'Son of a fucking bitch!'

Noel opened his eyes. A mic on its boom swung wildly for a moment, as if Hardhat's curse words had weight. The sound man grimaced and reasserted control of the long metal handle with one hand, while with the other he mopped at his streaming eyes. Everyone else in the small vault was also knuckling or covering their eyes.

Wild Fox had vanished, using his illusion power to transform into someone else. The floor began to vibrate beneath Noel's feet. He aimed carefully and shot Earth Witch in the left tit. She gave a yelp of pain.

Her cry drew Curveball's attention. '*Ana!*'

Noel used Hardhat's bulk and weight to spin the big ace and send him staggering into the gaggle of people, like a human cue ball. During the spin, Noel patted Hardhat down, located the cell phone in the ace's pants pocket, and pulled it free. There were more cries of pain as Hardhat arrived. Noel thumbed the phone to camera and swept the lens across the milling crowd. A pretty girl was revealed as the Japanese-American ace. *Quite a lot of gender bending going on here*, Noel thought with a grim smile, as he tossed away the phone and threw a handful of smoke bombs, while simultaneously shooting Wild Fox.

Noel hit the floor in a sliding dive. His last glimpse of Curveball before the thick smoke filled the room had revealed a furious frown between her golden brows. Nerf balls were going to start flying. People above him yelped and cursed as the balls struck. Even though they were soft, Curveball's power was formidable. *The mixers are going to be busy bleeping out the profanities.* People were tripping over him, and he took a pointed toe in the ribs. Time to get up and face Curveball.

Noel sprang to his feet and pulled a long piece of fur out of the waistband of his leg-hugging black jeans. The smoke had him as blinded as the aces and extras, but as he came up against people he brushed the soft fur across exposed skin. It seemed to take hours before he heard a girl's voice say, 'Fox?'

'Wrong,' Noel said and shot Curveball.

He stripped off the blond wig, walked out of the vault, gathered up the duffel bag of fake money from behind the tellers' counter, and shrugged into his trademark black leather jacket with the diamond lapel pin in the shape of a comet. It nicely covered the skimpy tank top, and the tight jeans would pass for a male's attire. He paused briefly to pluck a Kleenex out of a box on a manager's desk. He wiped away the eye shadow and lipstick. Pulling another fedora out of the jacket pocket, he set it at a jaunty angle over his sweat-soaked brown hair and walked out the sagging front doors.

Heat shimmers hung like the hint of ghosts in the air over the baking sidewalk of the Warner Brothers backlot. Sweating, red-faced studio employees had gathered to watch the fun. Noel reached into the duffel bag and flung Monopoly money into the air. He then pulled his conductor's baton from another pocket, waved it in a complex arc around him, and took an elaborate bow to the cheering crowd.

◆

The limo carried Noel from the Beverly Hills Hotel back to the Warners lot. He had dreaded leaving the rush of icy air and the chilled champagne that had waited in the room, but that was the price of celebrity. He had to go to the wrap party at the conclusion of the Rogue Ace challenges.

The sign for Mulholland Drive crawled past, and the limo crested the last big hill. The San Fernando Valley shimmered in the heat haze, and the setting sun sent flashes of brilliant light off millions of windows and acres of steel and chrome. It was as if a mad signaler were sending code on a global scale. But the code was a cacophony that no one could read. *Rather like Egypt right now*, Noel thought, and then forced his thoughts away from his real life.

The driver dropped him as close to the studio restaurant as possible. It didn't help; by the time he trod up the stairs to the etched glass doors his clothes felt damp. A PA from the show was waiting to open the door. Despite the heat, the kid still had that stunned, loopy smile that said, *I'm in Hollywood. I'm working for a television show. I have five roommates, but it doesn't matter.* Noel gave him one of his patented blazing smiles, and stepped into the marble-floored, blue lobby. There was a roar of conversation from the restaurant proper, and the blood-pulsing rhythms of a salsa band.

Nephi Callendar, the government ace who went under the *nom de guerre* Straight Arrow, was deep in conversation with Rustbelt, the Minnesota hick who looked like an ugly redesign of the Tin Woodsman for a proletarian remake of *The Wizard of Oz*. Noel shouldn't have been surprised. It was only natural that the American federals would try to recruit new aces for their Special Committee for Ace Resources and Endeavors from among the contestants.

Still, there were times when Noel's government found itself in less than perfect agreement with their American cousins. Despite his victory over the Hearts, Noel did not relish a matchup with some of the more formidable aces of *American Hero*, and Rustbelt was one of those aces. Any country with weapons made of steel, or bridges over strategic rivers, was vulnerable to Rustbelt's power.

'. . . and we have a great medical plan,' Straight Arrow was saying.

'Are you going to tell him about the Old Spies Retirement Home, too?' Noel drawled as he strolled over. 'Where's the romance, Nephi?' Noel lowered his eyelashes suggestively. The Mormon ace shifted uncomfortably at the sultry look. He knew what Noel was and he wasn't comfortable with it. *Oh my, no.*

'He's young and an ace with a *very* formidable power,' Noel continued. 'The boy wants tuxedos, martinis shaken not stirred, and trysts with beautiful and dangerous women.' He gave Rustbelt a blazing smile. 'You'd do much better joining the Order of the Silver Helix.'

'Oh. So, what's that then?' Rustbelt asked.

'The British Secret Service.'

'Wally is an American,' Straight Arrow said shortly.

Rustbelt's ponderous head, with its steam shovel jaws, swung between them.

'Ah, but we're *such* good allies. You wouldn't mind my poaching just a teensy bit?' Noel turned back to Rustbelt. 'Think about it, old man. I could sign you up right now.'

'I thought you were a magician,' Rustbelt said in his absurd accent.

Noel laid a finger next to his nose. 'Ah, that's my cover, don't you know. Travel to exotic locales, first-class accommodations. You'd love it.'

'Now that sounds like a heckuva deal.'

'He's a *joker*,' Straight Arrow snapped.

With Rustbelt's metal skin no blush was readable, but the hick shuffled his feet, setting up a tooth-grating shriek on the marble floor.

'Ace, Nephi, ace,' Noel reproved. 'One might almost think you're prejudiced.' Straight Arrow could blush. The blood washed into his face, turning his cheeks brick red. *Just one more little twist*, Noel thought. He laid a hand on Rustbelt's shoulder. 'No, Wally is an ace, and a very powerful one at that. You know, you're far and away the most interesting ace in this mix. The others are all just flash and dazzle.'

'You should know,' Straight Arrow said, and the words had to fight to escape from between his clenched teeth.

Noel ignored the SCARE ace. 'I think it's a travesty that you were voted off so early, but jealousy, alas, is all too common. We should discuss this over a drink. They have a very nice bar at the Beverly Hills Hotel. We can get to know each other ... better.'

'He's not recruiting you,' Nephi warned Rustbelt. 'He's making fun of you, and you're falling for it. Don't be a rube.' The government ace drew in a sudden, audible breath, as if trying to suck back the words. But it was far too late. He might blame Noel, but it was Straight Arrow who had uttered the insult.

Rustbelt shifted from foot to foot and the big head drooped. 'Oh, gosh – well, a guy should think about this. It's all pretty confusing. It's getting late, don't you know, so I oughta head out. ...' His voice trailed away and he bolted at a run for the doors to the restaurant. The marble cracked under his pounding feet.

The truth was that Straight Arrow had been trying to protect the young man. Nobility was always so easy to manipulate.

Nephi stared at Noel. 'You are the very devil,' he finally said. Noel smiled and took a little bow. A reluctant smile briefly touched the American's lips. 'Flint should have had you in Cairo. You're more evil and cunning than the Ikhlas al-Din. You might have prevented that mess developing in Egypt.'

It was one of those compliments that held a slap. Noel smiled. 'And how do you know we didn't engineer it?' he countered, but it was hollow, and Straight Arrow knew it.

By tacit agreement they left the lobby, stepped down the dead-end hallway that led to the restrooms, and into the men's room. 'Then you'd be incompetent instead of asleep at the switch.' Straight Arrow glanced quickly beneath the doors to the stalls. For the moment, they were alone. 'There are reports of rioting in the joker quarter of Alexandria, and whispers of wholesale murder of the followers of the Old Religion in Port Said and the necropolis of Cairo.' He blew out a breath, and ran a hand through his graying hair. 'I don't know why the imams and mullahs are reacting so violently. It's a totally made-up religion.'

'Aren't they all?' Noel asked, and watched Straight Arrow's lips thin. 'And it's not totally about religion. The Twisted Fists killed the Nur. The street is angry.'

'We've got some intelligence that suggests the Fists weren't behind the murder, but the new Caliph won't believe anything *we* tell him.'

'I don't expect Abdul will be in power for long. Prince Siraj and the other moderates will push him aside.'

'Will that stop the killing?'

Noel shrugged and leaned forward to study a blemish on his chin in the mirror over a sink. 'Probably not, but at least we'll have someone reasonable to deal with.' He decided that heat didn't suit him. His normally crisp, wavy brown hair was limp, and his English rose complexion looked blotchy and red. Even his blue eyes were ringed with red from the Los Angeles pollution.

'God, you're a calculating bastard.' Straight Arrow paused, then added, 'You and the prince were at Cambridge together.'

Noel didn't answer. It was clear the American knew that full well, and the more you talked the more you were likely to give up.

'Well, if you guys did engineer the assassination you might want to tell Siraj to get his fanny in gear. If things don't calm down pretty quickly, we're going to have to step in. We have our own interests to protect.'

Noel didn't try to hide his derisive smile. 'Oh, dear fellow, really, you shouldn't. You Yanks are always so heavy-handed. Best you leave empire to those of us with real imperial experience. We'll act, but after we have a little useless PR bleating from the UN secretary-general.'

'Jayewardene is going to the region?'

'Yes, Abdul the Idiot asked him to intervene.'

Straight Arrow shook his head. 'He's a very brave man.'

'No, he's a predictable idiot.'

They heard footsteps approaching. Noel turned on a tap and washed his hands. Straight Arrow looked over at the urinals. 'Well, as long as I'm here.'

'Yes, best you be busy or people might think we're trysting.'

'Go away,' the American ace said in a muffled voice.

It was Michael Berman who entered. They danced a bit in the doorway. 'Hey, nice work,' the producer said.

'Thank you. Did I ruin your ratings?' Noel asked.

'Nah. Nats secretly love to see aces getting their ass kicked. Especially when a nat does the kicking.'

Noel moved on.

♠

'You've got my power, right?' Wild Fox asked. 'You create illusions.'

Noel smiled enigmatically.

'You're a short-range teleporter,' Curveball said. 'Is that it?'

Noel took a sip from his crystal champagne flute. The bubbly puckered the edges of his tongue and danced in his sinuses. He was impressed. Given the age and class of most of the *American Hero* contestants, he'd expected Asti Spumante, or some other equally sweet crap.

'Nah, he's a fucking shape-shifter,' Hardhat said. 'It's the only way he could look that fucking hot. I know broads, and he was a fucking broad.'

'No. No. And no. As to how I attracted you – I'm an inter-sexed individual,' Noel said, with a happy anticipation of Hardhat's likely response.

'Huh? What the fuck is that?'

'A hermaphrodite.'

'Huh?'

'A person who has the sexual attributes of both a male and a female.'

'You gotta cock *and* a pussy?' Disgust and fascination – but definitely more fascination – laced Hardhat's words. *Hmm*, thought Noel. *I can still be surprised.*

'Precisely.'

'Uh, I need a beer,' Wild Fox said. His eyes roamed desperately around the crowded room, and he sidled away.

'Whatever you are, you're one cold *pendejo*,' Earth Witch said.

'And why would you say that?'

'You sacrificed all your henchmen.'

'They were expendable.'

'They were your men.'

'They were tools, and I wanted to win.'

'How did you win?' Wild Fox asked, drawn back despite his unease.

'Brains and cunning.'

'So you don't have any powers?' Wild Fox challenged.

'You're not listening.'

'He's saying he beat us because we're stupid.'

Noel just smiled again at Earth Witch's bitter remark. Hardhat dropped a broad, heavy hand onto her shoulder and said, 'Get the fuck over it, Ana. He knocked our dicks in the dirt fair and square.' Curveball gave him an ironic look. 'Uh, boobs ... uh?'

'You better quit while you're ahead, T. T.,' the blonde said. She looked up and saw Drummer Boy bearing down on her determinedly. He had two of his four arms folded across his chest, and the fingers on his other two arms were snapping out a nervous rhythm. 'Uh-oh.' It was meant to be under her breath, but Noel heard it. She darted away while Earth Witch tried to intercept the rock-and-roll star.

Noel drifted over to the buffet table, where he grazed and observed. Earth Witch had failed in her attempted block, so Curveball was sprinting around the perimeter of the Warner Brothers restaurant with Drummer Boy stalking after her, taking one step to every two of hers. While Noel languidly consumed an egg roll, they made three complete circuits of the room.

In another corner, sex – rather than determined virginity – was decidedly in the air. Berman leaned against the wall while Jade Blossom, Pop Tart, and Tiffani all preened and vamped. He looked like a man at a buffet, savoring his choices.

'Hey, magician.' The words were strongly accented with the distant echoes of Spain filtered through Mexico and the American barrio. Rosa Loteria stood hip shot in front of him. There was no flirt here; the blue eyes flashed a challenge at him. She clutched her antique deck of *loteria* cards in a hand.

'My dear.' Noel gave her a bow.

'You can cut the sophisticated European crap,' she said.

Noel found himself smiling. 'All right, what can I do for you?'

She jerked a thumb over her shoulder toward the Candle. His multicolored flames waved languidly around his head like a psychedelic halo. 'That *pendejo* motherfucker' (Noel reflected that there seemed to be a lot of *pendejos* present tonight) 'has been giving me rafts of shit because I drew *Los Platanos* during the challenge.'

The back of Noel's mind supplied the translation – the Bananas.

'Yes, I can see how that would be rather less than useful.' He reached out and took the deck from her. It was old, probably Napoleonic, and very beautiful. Noel began shuffling the cards. 'And you want to learn how to do this—' and after each shuffle he flipped out *La Muerta* over and over again. The opulently dressed female skeleton looked coy, as if she knew a secret. Noel found his thoughts going back to his conversation with Straight Arrow, and the situation in Egypt.

'Yeah. That's what I want,' Rosa agreed.

Noel gave her back the cards. 'I expect I could teach you, and with practice you could probably become quite proficient, but I foresee some problems. It would be unwieldy to mark all the cards, and you would be tying yourself to the most lethal of your manifestations. Depending on the circumstance, you might want a different power. To pull Death all the time might be coming on a little too strong, don't you know? Also, this is the crutch on which you hang your power.' Noel tapped the deck of cards with a manicured forefinger. 'Would you actually be able to transform if you knew you were cheating? You are Rosa Loteria, the Lottery Rose. If you removed the element of chance …' Noel let his voice trail away and raised his eyebrows.

The girl's brows snapped together in a ferocious frown. 'I can't risk losing my powers.'

'I would reach the same decision.'

'Well, crap!' She walked away, trailing Spanish like a kite tail of profanity.

Noel fixed on a vapid smile and went strolling. There was a lot of conversation about the concluded Rogue Ace Challenge, but another thread of conversation wove like a line of bright sparks throughout the party.

'... burned to the ground.' Said with breathless excitement by Diver.

'That idiot Bugsy will be behind it.' Said with Southern ice by Tiffani.

'... Peregrine's *fuuurious* with Simoon.' Said by Pop Tart, with that tickle of enjoyment at getting to observe anger and not be on the receiving end.

'... didn't find any bodies.' Said with a thread of disappointment by Jade Blossom.

'... insane with worry.' Said with compassion by the Amazing Bubbles.

'Of course, he's her itty witty baby boy.' Said with just the right amount of disdain by Rosa Loteria.

Women are always so dependable when you need news. Noel lifted another glass of champagne off a passing tray. He glanced over at Peregrine, and indeed the famous joker's smile kept jumping back into place as people walked up to talk to her. Otherwise, her eyes glittered with anger, and a strained frown ridged her forehead. Occasionally, she darted a cold glance at Simoon. Noel recalled the girl's biography: daughter of one of the Egyptian jokers who had sought sanctuary at the Luxor hotel in Las Vegas, she had a second-rate power. Wind powers had always seemed faintly silly to Noel. Of more concern was her connection to Egypt – however tenuous. He decided to find out more.

Noel moved to Peregrine, lifted her hand, and brushed his lips lightly across the back. 'Thank you, dear lady. It actually did end up being quite a deal of fun.'

Peregrine's smile was pinned back in place. 'I doubt the Hearts would agree. You defeated them pretty soundly.'

Noel looked over at Simoon. He allowed his expression to shift to grave and disapproving, then nodded sagely. The young woman clasped her hands and stared intently at Noel and Peregrine. High color burned in her cheeks. He inclined his head once more toward

Peregrine as she said, 'The weather certainly was beastly. Damn Santa Ana.' Noel once again looked over to Simoon and frowned. She came boiling out of the chair and crossed the room with a stiff-legged walk, until she stood directly in front of Peregrine.

Noel hid a smile. Once again the human capacity to assume that everything was about *you* had kicked in and had the desired result.

'What are you saying about me?' Simoon asked.

'We weren't talking about you,' Peregrine replied. Her tightly compressed lips allowed the wrinkles around her mouth to escape her careful makeup job. 'And feeling the way I do about you right now, it would be better if you weren't talking to me, either.'

'This is not my fault.'

'You told him about that damn thing!'

'And for all we know the amulet didn't have anything to do with your house,' Simoon said. 'That idiot Bugsy was there, and Lohengrin, and they'd all been drinking.'

'John was not drunk,' Peregrine gritted.

Simoon threw her hands up. 'Okay. Fine. Have it your way. Ignore how he felt having to work for his mom, and having DB call him "Captain Cruller" and everybody bossing him around. He was an ace. Now he's just … ordinary.'

The girl started to walk away. 'It was just a necklace. A piece of tourist trash,' Peregrine yelled after her.

Simoon turned around, but kept walking backwards as she yelled back, 'If that's the case, then why are you so pissed? Unless you really are afraid it was magical.'

The room, which had gone very quiet, erupted once again into frenzied conversations. Peregrine turned scarlet, and her eyes filled with tears. Noel pulled out a handkerchief and handed it to her. He murmured an apology and hurried out of the restaurant.

Oedipal issues didn't interest Noel. What interested him was a magical amulet with an Egyptian connection.

He crossed the cracked marble foyer, out the doors and down the steps. Simoon sat slumped at one of the round concrete tables outside the studio cafeteria. Nothing exemplified the economic differences on a movie lot like these two restaurants. The one Noel had just left catered to the stars and the studio power brokers. The cafeteria fed everyone else. Noel laid a hand on the girl's shoulder and produced another handkerchief. She wiped her eyes. 'Thanks. Sorry.'

'Not at all.' Noel pulled out his cigarette case. 'Do you mind?' Simoon shook her head. He lit up.

'Turkish,' the girl said. 'Uncle Osiris smokes them. I've never seen a white guy smoke one before.'

Noel tilted his hand and surveyed the cigarette. 'My flat mate at Cambridge put me onto them.'

The girl stared back down at the cracked and weathered surface of the table. The Santa Ana wind whipped her dark hair around her face. A few strands caught on the lips of her generous mouth. She pulled them free and the motion lifted her bosom. She was short and stacked, and Noel felt a brief stirring in his trousers, but he knew the likely outcome, if he should disrobe.

Noel sat down next to her on the bench. 'Would you tell me more about this amulet? You said it was magical, and I can't help but be interested.' He gave her his most winning smile. 'Call it professional curiosity.'

'I don't know too much about it, but my mom called and started pushing me to tell John about it. It's an *achet*, and Thoth gave it to Peregrine when she toured Egypt a million years ago. I guess she was pregnant, and the *achet* was supposed to be for her kid. But Peregrine never gave it to him. With everything that's going on back in Egypt, my mom and Osiris and the other old folks were all twitching out about getting the necklace to John. Mom said to tell John that it gives the wearer the strength and power of Ra – blah, blah, blah. I thought it sounded just stupid, but Mom kept bugging me and bugging me, so I finally told him so she'd shut up about it and get off my back. I need to concentrate on what I'm doing here, and now I've pissed off Peregrine, and I'm just screwed.'

But Noel wasn't really listening any longer. *Ra. The sun god in the ancient Egyptian pantheon. John Fortune seemed to have an affinity for light and fire. And Peregrine's house did burn down. His thoughts were spinning. Of course this might all just be the maundering of desperate jokers looking for a miracle, and I may be seeing connections where none exist.*

Simoon stood up. 'Well, I'm going to go back into the house. I think I've had as much fun as I can stand tonight.'

'Wait. You're sure Bugsy and Lohengrin were with him?' Noel asked.

'Well, they're missing, too.'

'You wouldn't happen to have a cell number for any of them?'

He watched a series of complex emotions sweep across her face. She pulled out her phone. 'I think I've got Bugsy's. He kept calling me for a date.'

And obviously struck out, Noel thought as he copied the number into his palm.

'Okay, I'm out of here. Thanks for the handkerchief.' She offered it back to him.

'Keep it.'

Noel watched her walk away, admiring the sway of her hips. Sparks arced through the dark as he flung away the cigarette. He dialed the number she had given him. A youthful, sleep-blurred voice answered.

''Lo?'

Noel cut the connection, and checked. His phone, courtesy of the Order, contained a GPS tracker similar to those used by 911 operators. Bugsy hadn't disabled the GPS feature on his phone. He was in the Nevada desert.

Noel called and arranged for a car to be delivered to his hotel.

♣

WAKES THE LION

John Jos. Miller

The night was dark, the ground was cold, and John Fortune had no idea where he was.

Lying on his back, he looked up at a black, star-spangled sky. He seemed to be in the bottom of a shallow gully, hemmed in by rough-hewn rocks and boulders, without a taco stand, road, car, or streetlight in sight. When he held his hands in front of his face, he could barely see his fingers. His chest felt funny, his throat raw. His body hurt all over, as if he'd just run back-to-back-to-back marathons. Even more distressingly, he was totally naked.

He lurched to his feet, wincing in sudden pain as small, sharp stones on the floor of the arroyo dug into the bottoms of his feet. 'What happened to my clothes?' he asked aloud.

There came no answer.

He lurched in a circle, dizzy and coughing. He remembered ... he remembered the skittering thing crawling under his skin, like a rat burrowing into his body. The fear that had enveloped him. There had been a man, clad in shining white, who'd tried to kill him with a sword ... *wallah*! Fire had danced all around him, and smoke blinded his eyes. Maybe the fire had taken his clothes – but no, that idea was ridiculous. He had no burn marks on skin or flesh.

Finally he remembered – he had run, bursting out of the house into the night. The feeling of freedom had been exhilarating, intoxicating. He had run for hours. *How many hours? How many miles*? He did not know. In the end he had collapsed, exhausted. *Here.*

Wherever here was.

Fortune shivered. He couldn't just sit here all night. He had to get back to Los Angeles. He was starving. He'd never been so hungry. He needed food, bad. *And clothes.* He couldn't sit around butt naked in the middle of nowhere and wait for help. Help of any kind was unlikely to find him. He'd have to seek it out.

And if that thing was still in him, he really needed medical attention.

He remembered that the thing had been scuttling toward his head. Hesitantly, he put his hands on his jaw, gingerly felt his cheeks, up around his ears and across his forehead – where he felt a lump. The thing that had climbed into his body was still in his head.

John Fortune freaked and ran. Or tried to.

He clawed his way up the side of the arroyo, sliding back down several times in a rain of gravel and sand. Once he dislodged a rock near the edge of the dirt bank that would have crushed him if it had landed on him, but somehow, miraculously, it missed when they both tumbled back to the gully's floor.

Somehow, he dragged himself up out of the arroyo. He glanced around wildly, desperately looking for something, anything that might hold a hope of aid. He was in wild, undeveloped foothills that dropped down to a plain dotted by clumps of stunted evergreens. The ground was sparsely covered by small shrubby bushes, tufts of grass and cactus, which he discovered when he brushed too near one and scratched his left leg from calf to ankle. The sudden pain acted like a pitcher of cold water thrown in his face. He tried to breathe easier. Aided by the light cast by the rising moon, he spotted a dark ribbon of what could be a road, or at least a path or trail of some kind, free of the stones that were tearing up his bare feet.

He started toward it, cautiously but quickly, eager to find some human contact, someone who could tell him what had happened to him and assure him that he'd be all right. ...

He was thirsty, and his hunger was so great that his stomach cramped like it did before his monthly blood came. The moon rising above the foothills was gigantic in the night sky. The jackals who laired in the wadis greeted it, howling. Fortune's head throbbed in rhythm with their cries. The hunger was bad, but he was used to it. He had often gone without food, when that meant that his children could be fed. Not that his sacrifices had helped much in the long run. He had lost them all, one by one. Jamal burning with fever, clutched hopelessly to his breast, nothing to feed him but the salt tears dripping from his cheeks.

The road was more of a dirt track than a highway, but it was smooth and soft on his bruised feet. The jackals didn't follow him on it, but the flies did. They weren't as bad as the flies in the marketplace, but they bothered him as they buzzed around his head, whispering, leading him perhaps back to the temple where there was shade and water and blessed rest, and ...

What was he thinking?!

These were not his thoughts, these memories of a life he'd never led. Jackals? Children? A temple? John Fortune's hands rose to his forehead, then dropped down, afraid to touch that thing that had burrowed beneath his skin and climbed to his brain. These weird memories had to be coming from it, athough ... they were human memories, and that thing had been ... a *thing*. An amulet-size bug that had been nesting in his mother's chest of drawers since before he'd been born. A scarab, a beetle, not ... *not a person!*

Fortune wandered down the path, not knowing what to think, not even wanting to think. Sometime later he stumbled upon a hardtop road. *This is more like it.*

His hopes rose higher when he saw a building settled in one corner of a lonely crossroads, unlit and seemingly deserted. Still, there was at least a chance that it might contain something useful. Some food to soothe his cramping stomach. Some water to cool his burning forehead. Maybe a phone to call his mother. Some clothes. *Some goddamn shoes.* His feet were killing him.

It was a gas station, existing somewhere in a state between abandoned and decrepit. Its roof sagged badly. The dusty pumps in front of it had not been used for years. The chair by the front door, looking as if it had been used too much over the years, was half off its rocker. It was almost inviting enough to drop onto, but Fortune wasn't sure if it would hold his weight, and the bamboo lattice seat would probably have been fairly uncomfortable on his bare ass.

The glass-windowed storefront was only slightly less dusty than the disused gasoline pumps. Encouragingly, however, of the three words – GAS FOOD DRINK – etched into its surface, only the word gas had been crudely crossed out by a couple of swatches of duct tape.

The front door was aluminum bars set between sagging screens to keep the flies out. It was locked, though it didn't look very sturdy. Fortune considered it for a moment, then grabbed the handle and yanked at it with all his strength. A low rumble sounded deep in his throat, surprising him, and his legs, back, and arms knotted from sustained effort, as the door slowly peeled away from its warped wooden frame with complaining metallic screeches. It finally came mostly clear, hanging limply by its hinges. Fortune was breathing heavily when he stepped through the doorway, but he finally felt as if he'd accomplished something, even if the B & E made him feel mildly guilty. Still, he could pay back the storekeeper, once he'd recovered his black Amex card.

Inside it was almost as dusty as out. Fortune could see rows of canned food stacked haphazardly on rickety wooden shelves, along with some loaves of bread, jars of pickles and peanut butter, and packages of cookies and crackers, and – *good God* – an old-fashioned cooler set against one wall, plugged in and humming away, a soft breeze wafting off it. He couldn't deny his sudden urge to lean his burning forehead against its metallic coolness.

He slid the cooler open, reached in, and dragged out a bottle of ice cold Coke. On the cooler's side was a built-in bottle top remover. He popped the lid, put the bottle to his lips, and drained it in a single, long gulp, shuddering as the sugar and caffeine hit his stomach.

He finished the bottle with a satisfied sigh, and noticed for the first time a wooden coatrack with a beat-up pair of bib overalls hanging from it. They looked a little rank and far too large, but Fortune was in no position to be choosy. He pulled them down from the hook and danced his way into them, hopping on the sagging plank floor as he put them on. Fortune felt better. He had clothed himself. More sustenance was within reach. Now, if he could only find some shoes ...

He looked up and saw his face framed by a cracked mirror set in the old wooden coat tree. The thing in the middle of his forehead was like a massive pimple, red and hard and shiny. It looking ugly and freakish.

The fear struck him again like a blow to the face. He panicked, scrabbled at the amulet with grimy fingers. He tried to pry it out of his forehead, but his fingernails were too short to get a grip on it – though in his blinding fright he scratched himself so badly that blood began to flow.

A knife, he thought. *A piece of glass. A strip of metal.* Anything to get that thing out of his head.

Fortune's heart nearly stopped when a car pulled into the store's rutted dirt parking lot, its headlights gleaming like monstrous eyes through the dirty storefront window. A strange, powerful hand clamped down on his brain, and he began to *change*.

The metamorphosis should have been painful, but if it was, John was too frightened to notice. His body grew massively. He felt his new overalls rip apart at the seams, as if they'd been made out of paper towels, and he was naked again. But he didn't really need clothes. He was furry all over, with a thick pelt that shone as he had once shone himself, back when he'd been an ace. He could see a ghostly reflection of his body in the dirty glass window.

A lion. Of all the crazy, impossible things in the world, he had turned into a lion.

No. Not quite. More precisely, he was a lioness ... but a lioness a lot bigger than any he'd ever seen at the zoo. And he *glowed*. He glowed like a beacon in the dark.

That was the only solace he could cling to, all he could think about if he wanted to keep his sanity. Because he no longer had any control over the body that was no longer his. He stared at the car outside, trying to speak, trying to call out – but something would not let him. Something else had taken command of his flesh, something that was growling, twitching its tail angrily, its muscles ready to leap and pounce. *Something . . . or someone.* It was furious, he realized, but it was also, underneath it all, very afraid.

Car doors opened and slammed. John heard his name called out. 'John! You in there?'

He recognized the voice. It was Bugsy. The massive figure at his side had to be Lohengrin, though he could see little but their outlines because of the headlights glaring in his eyes. The lioness tensed. She leaped, landing atop a rickety wooden shelf, scattering cans of chicken-noodle soup and beanie weanie everywhere. He felt her take a deep breath. Her lungs expanded enormously and a heat kindled in her stomach, burning like a furnace popped on by a pilot light.

'*Mein Gott!*' Lohengrin shouted. 'The lion again!'

<*No!*> Fortune screamed. He made no sound, though the word reverberated in his skull like an echo in a tiny cave. <*Don't hurt them! They're my friends!*>

The lion let its breath out in a whoosh that engendered a smoky billow of air, but no flame.

<*The big one tried to kill me with his sword,*> a voice said in his head. It had a lilting accent that Fortune couldn't identify, and was definitely feminine . . . and tinged with fear.

Her words brought back shattered memories – his first transformation, in his mother's house . . . Lohengrin . . . the sudden armor and sword . . . fire, smoke, the scream of an alarm. The house burning down around them. Crashing through a window to escape.

John would have sunk to his knees if he'd had control over his transformed body. <*Who are you?*> he asked.

<*My name is Isra,*> the voice said. <*But I am also Sekhmet the Destroyer, the champion of my people and the Breath of Ra.*> There was no doubt that it was a woman.

My God, Fortune thought, *I've got a woman in my head.* He had to be certain. <*Where are you?*>

<Once I inhabited the amulet,> Isra told him. *<For, it seemed, a long, long time. Now I am in your body. What year is it?>*

<Two thousand and seven.>

There was a long silence, then, *<More than twenty years. Tell me all that has happened!>*

<Wait, wait, wait!> Fortune thought frantically. *<How about telling me what the hell has happened? How did you get into my head? And my friends, out there—>* Bugsy and Lohengrin were peering though the storefront. *<Let me talk to them!>*

Isra shook her shaggy head. *<That is impossible. Sekhmet lacks the tongue, the voice box, to form human words.>*

<Sekhmet?> He remembered her saying the name, but it still meant nothing to him.

<The Destroyer. The Protector. The Breath of Ra.>

Still nothing. *<Well, turn us back into me, then. Let me talk to them.>*

<No.> The single word was hard, final. She hesitated a moment, then almost plaintively said, *<I was chained in the amulet for so long … so long.>*

<Well—> Fortune swallowed his anger. Isra had the upper hand at the moment, but he'd managed to retrieve his body before. He could do it again. If he could just figure out how.

<Well. Wave at them or something, to show them that it's okay. That we're friendly.>

Isra lifted a paw. Lohengrin's sword had flickered into his hand. He and Bugsy looked each other. 'What do you think?' the German ace asked in accented English. 'This time, she is not attacking. That is good, *ja*?'

'*Ja*,' Bugsy replied, 'I think that it might be all right. John, is that you? Are you … are you all right?' Isra nodded her leonine head.

<Why'd you do that?> Fortune asked. *<I'm not all right.>*

'John?' Bugsy was saying. 'Can you … ah … change back? If you want to … I sent out a few hundred wasps to find you after you busted out of Peregrine's house.' He paused momentarily. 'Ummm. Sorry about the house and all, but it wasn't us. It was the lion.' He stopped for a moment, as if realizing how lame that sounded. 'She breathes fire. Uh … you breathe fire. Really. You probably know that, though.'

'John,' Lohengrin said. 'I am sorry too.'

'Anyway,' Bugsy said quickly. 'I'm sorry it took us so long to find you. Trying to rent a car in the middle of the night is a real bitch, and you were really moving there for a while. My wasps could hardly keep up … uh … but the question is, where should we take you? Do you need to go to the hospital?'

Isra shook her head angrily, a low grumble sounding deep in her broad chest.

'We could call your mother,' Lohengrin offered.

'No,' Bugsy said, 'no, not *his* mother. *Simoon's* mother. Isis. She was the one who wanted him to have the amulet. Let's take him to her. Maybe she can … fix him or something.'

'Is she a doctor?' Lohengrin asked.

'No, I think she's a god.'

<*Isis! Yes, I must find my people. I can sense them, vaguely.*>

<*The Living Gods?*> At last, some things were starting to come together. <*I know them – some of them, anyway – sort of. The ones in Vegas. Las Vegas. Nevada.*>

<*Nevada?*> The lioness paced through the store and pushed through the remains of the door, shoving it completely off its hinges. She padded past Bugsy and Lohengrin, who turned to keep her in sight at all times. Fortunately, the rental car was a convertible. Isra – or Sekhmet, or whatever the hell she should be called – leaped lightly into the back and settled herself regally across the seat. She pretty much filled it.

Lohengrin's sword disappeared. 'I think she wants to go to Isis,' he said. He slid into the driver's seat. Bugsy took shotgun. 'Great,' he announced. 'Road trip.'

♥

The sun had been up for some time when they hit the Strip.

They could see the black glass pyramid of the Luxor towering in the clear morning sky a mile down the street to their right. John Fortune could read the utter amazement in Isra's mind as they moved past hotels and casinos, though her leonine features showed nothing but regal inscrutability. Despite the early hour the street was thick with traffic, and the sidewalks were crowded with pedestrians. Las Vegas is truly the city that never sleeps.

It was difficult to say who was more astounded – Isra, or the crowd on the sidewalks – as the rental convertible slowly cruised down the Strip. Fragments of excited conversation from the onlookers came to them:

'Holy crap, look at the size of that lion!'

'Is it real?'

'Of course it's real! Whaddya think this is, Disneyland or something?'

'It's too big to be real! And it's glowing!'

'Is it dangerous?'

'It's probably a publicity stunt.'

'That blond guy driving must be Siegfried.'

'Nah. He has tigers.'

'And look! There's Ralph! Looking good, Ralph!'

'I had no idea he was so young.'

'Wave to the camera, Ralph!'

Bugsy waved enthusiastically, while the big German remained dignified as he drove sedately to the Luxor, muttering, 'I am not Siegfried. I am Lohengrin.'

Fortune could feel Isra's growing excitement as they pulled into the Luxor's parking lot, passing a giant sphinx, a serene reflecting pool, and rows of obelisks. They stopped in front of the main entrance to the hotel, but none of the valets dared approach. Sekhmet was snorting fire in her excitement, much to the excited approval of the crowd that had gathered to gawk.

The show was only starting. The lioness leaped out of the back of the convertible and padded lightly, eagerly, back and forth, very much as if it was feeding time at the zoo. *<Easy,>* Fortune said, desperately hoping for some kind of help to arrive.

It soon did. Half a dozen of the Living Gods filed out of the main entrance to the hotel casino, accompanied by a retinue of fan-bearers, jugglers, acrobats, and other retainers. Led by the beautiful Isis, attended by fan-bearers holding ostrich feathers over her head, by a fat-bellied dwarf whose name Fortune didn't know, by jokers with the heads of a dog and a hawk. Bringing up the rear, accompanied by their own servants, were two old familiar figures – Thoth, the ibis-headed spokesman of the Living Gods, and ancient Osiris, he who had perished and then come back to life, supposedly. As usual, a cryptic smile wreathed his tight-lipped mouth.

Isis – beautiful, voluptuous, and wearing a gown that was more diaphanous than modest – was receiving most of the attention from the gathered onlookers. Especially when she bowed low gracefully and said, 'Hail, Lady Sekhmet! Your coming was foretold by far-seeing Osiris! Long have we awaited your arrival! Enter our abode!'

The onlookers burst into applause as the lioness returned Isis's bow, as elegantly as four legs would allow her, and followed the colorful procession into the Luxor's lobby. Bugsy and Lohengrin, exchanging glances, took up the rear. They were a traffic-stopper as they paced slowly, ceremoniously through the cavernous atrium and halted before the elevators. Not only was Isra reluctant to enter them, it seemed that she was too big to get into one even if she'd wanted to. *<You have to give me back control,>* Fortune urged.

Isra snarled and some of the onlooking tourists glanced about nervously.

<Come on,> Fortune said. *<You'll never fit into one of these cages.>*

Perhaps the word 'cages' did it, or maybe just the mere thought of confinement again. Whatever made Isra relinquish control, there was an unexpected, instantaneous transfiguration, and Fortune found himself standing naked in front of the elevator banks.

Fortunately, the fan-bearers acted with instantaneous aplomb and covered him – almost entirely – before the cameras in the hands of onlooking tourists could go off. All the important figures piled into the elevator, leaving their retinue to entertain the assembled crowd and deliver a spiel about the Pageant of the Living Gods, six days a week, with matinees on Wednesdays and Saturdays.

It was a tight fit inside the elevator, but with John Fortune back as John Fortune and not a monstrous lioness, they made it. Osiris punched the button and they scooted upward to the private penthouse of the Living Gods in the heart of the Luxor pyramid.

'We must have something around here that would fit you,' Isis said, as they entered the living area of a spacious suite. She rattled off some sentences in Arabic to the dog-faced god, who looked to be about Fortune's size. 'Go with Anubis. He can lend some clothes that should fit. When you return, we'll have refreshments.'

'And answers for my questions?' Fortune asked.

Isis smiled. 'Of course.'

Feeling like an idiot, Fortune borrowed the ostrich-feather fans from their bearers and followed Anubis, who seemed friendly enough (if John could accurately read his grinning canine features) but had little English. Fortune was glad to score jeans, a T-shirt, and a pair of sneakers.

By the time he returned, drinks and snacks had been laid out. Bugsy and Lohengrin were conspicuous by their absence. Only three senior members of the group – Thoth, Osiris, and Isis – were awaiting him.

'Don't worry about your friends.' Thoth hadn't changed since the last time John had seen him. His features were birdlike, with a long, sharp beak that gave his words an odd clacking cadence. 'We have set them up in their own suite where they can refresh themselves and relax. Much of what we have to say here should stay among family.'

'I'm flattered that you think of me in those terms.' Fortune balanced a plate of pastries dripping with honey in one hand and a tiny cup of coffee loaded to the top with sugar in the other. 'I've done nothing to deserve it.'

Osiris, who had little English, spoke a rapid stream of Arabic. Like Thoth, he was also little changed since Fortune's last trip to Vegas. He was brown-skinned and thin, lean to the point of emaciation, with a bald head, dark chin beard, and dark, vibrant eyes. He looked like an antediluvian rock star who ate too little and spent way too much time in the sun. Thoth translated his words into precise English, unaccented but for his strange lisp. 'We need

Sekhmet now more than we ever have. She was meant to be the greatest among our people, our champion and shield against those who would destroy us – but, as you well know, things do not always work out as they should.'

Isis took up the story. 'Isra was born in Alexandria, of a family who had for generations worked the docks. The gods certainly work in mysterious ways. Yes, they gave her great powers. But her body, ill-nourished, worn out by childbirth and a life of hard work, could not contain the tremendous energies needed to fuel them. She was forced to … to *change*, in yet another way. To shrivel onto herself, to go into a deep sleep – until one would come whose body could be her vessel.'

'You.' Thoth nodded his head like a bird pecking for bugs. 'You, who should have been an ace, you whose heritage was stripped from you. We beg you, please, to let Sekhmet live through you.'

Fortune swallowed a honeyed date, choking. 'As a parasite in my body?'

Thoth shrugged. 'Surely, more of a symbiote. She does nothing to harm you.'

'But I don't want her inside me, controlling me. Why can't she share *your* body? Or yours, or his?'

Isis looked sad. 'If we could, we would serve her. But we lack your strength.'

Osiris nodded vigorously as Thoth translated his words again. 'Surely,' Osiris said, 'you have seen the news out of Egypt.'

'Some,' Fortune said. 'I've been busy.'

'Of course,' Osiris continued. 'The whole world has been busy while hundreds of our people have been killed. And without Sekhmet to protect them, it will only get worse. Hundreds of thousands of innocents – men, women, and children – all will die. The Living Gods themselves will pass from this world, starting a new dark age that will cast its shadow across the globe. Sekhmet *must* return to Egypt.'

'Why can't she return in your head?' Fortune snapped. 'I have my own life – a job. Friends. I'm supposed to go back to college in the fall.'

Isis looked significantly at Thoth and Osiris. 'We understand. You are tired. Much strangeness has been thrust upon you. We should talk later, when you have had a chance to rest.'

'Yeah,' Fortune said. 'That's a good idea. I'm really tired. I should call my mom. Let her know that I'm all right. Something will work out, I'm sure of it.'

'Yes.' Thoth didn't look at him.

'I'll call Anubis,' Isis said. 'He'll take you to the room we've arranged for you.'

'Thanks.' Somehow John couldn't meet her eyes.

Osiris stopped him as he stood to leave, taking his hand with a devil-may-care glint in his old, glittery eyes, and barked a few sentences in Arabic.

'What did he say?' Fortune asked Thoth.

'He said,' Thoth replied, 'that he is not worried. That he knows that you will do the right thing in the end. In visions he has seen you leading a great and powerful army, bloodied but unbeaten, your heart's desire at your side.'

Anubis was waiting, like a grinning puppy. He had the eyes of a puppy, eager and trusting. Fortune couldn't look at him either. They left the Living Gods' quarters and Anubis led him down a corridor to his room, bowed down low to him, and left.

Fortune settled into the comfy chair. He had to call his mother, but later. There was still too much on his mind. He turned on the TV, turned down the sound, and dialed room service to order more food. The channel was CNN. He watched the news flicker by silently as he put in his order for steak sandwiches, fries, and a couple of milkshakes. He couldn't decide between chocolate and strawberry, so he ordered both as he watched President Kennedy and his hot actress wife receive foreign dignitaries at the White House. When a story about Egypt came on, John turned up the sound.

It was terrible. A bunch of fanatics calling themselves Ikhlas al-Din were killing jokers in Cairo – women and children as well as men. Fortune stared at the horrific images on the screen. He couldn't believe that no one was protecting these people. That the authorities were allowing this to happen. Something had to be done.

Someone … someone had to do something.

He turned off the television, unable to watch any more. The words Lohengrin had spoken before they'd burned down his mother's house came back to him. 'You must find your destiny,' the German had said. 'If God has need of you, and this is the path your honor demands, you must go.' John got up out of the chair and paced around the room. He didn't know if God needed him, but there was sure as hell a bunch of poor devils in Egypt who did.

The doorbell rang and Fortune called out, 'Yeah?'

The door opened. It was his food. A smiling bellboy wheeled it in with a flourish.

'Thanks,' Fortune muttered. He signed for it, and when the bellboy noticed the size of the tip he smiled even further.

'Thank *you*, sir.'

Fortune didn't even notice that he left. He took the cover off the dish on the cart. The steak sandwiches and fries looked great and smelled even better, but suddenly his appetite had disappeared. He wanted to *do* something, but all he could do was pace.

He thought of Kate. How he had spoken about wanting to make a difference. He did. He did want to help people. What he went through to try to regain his ace …

And now. Here was another opportunity.

Most people never got one in their entire lives. So far, he'd had two.

He could take it, or he could go back to being Captain Cruller for the rest of his life.

He flopped down into the comfy chair. He had to think. Kate … His heart's desire?

When he closed his eyes, exhaustion took him. Fortune fell asleep.

◆

He woke in the shower.

He didn't remember getting into bed, sleeping, getting out of bed, undressing, and going into the bathroom. That bothered him.

But then a lot of things had been bothering him lately, and he still felt enough residual weariness to suspect that he hadn't slept well at all. Given the events of the last couple of days, that was hardly surprising.

He felt for Isra's presence in his mind, and found her, silent, curled up like a kitten in a dark corner. He still wasn't sure what to think of her, of what her presence in his life offered him, for good and bad. He pondered as he washed his hair, soap-slick fingers slipping over the amulet that weighed like a stone against his forehead. He was getting into deep waters. Maybe deep enough to close over his head and drown him. John had no illusions about himself. He liked to think that he was reasonably bright, but he knew he was terribly inexperienced in the ways of the world. He had been sheltered and protected all his life, and he suspected that, by nature, he was a little more trusting – *all right, naive* – than most. He pondered this as he dried himself off, and went back into the bedroom to dress in his borrowed clothing.

But if he could believe in Isra, if he could trust her, she offered him the type of life that he had once tasted, and lost. Not that he regretted the loss of his ace. *Not much, anyway.* He could have done good with it, but clearly it was out of control. Whether his ace had been inherently unstable or something in Fortune himself had been tacking – training, focus, willpower – he knew that his father had sacrificed his life to save him, and perhaps save the entire world as well.

But that stage of his life was over. Isra was offering him entry onto a new stage. If he could believe her. If he could trust her.

The phone rang. He had a sudden premonition.

'John?'

'Hello, Mom.' He didn't ask her how she'd managed to track him down. Peregrine had her ways. *And her detectives.* 'Sorry, I meant to call you last night – I mean, last morning, but I guess I fell asleep.'

'Thank God you're all right.' Peregrine sounded relieved. That was good. 'You *are* all right?'

'Sure, Mom.'

'That's good.' Solicitous. 'Now I won't feel so bad about killing you.' Not so solicitous.

'Uh—'

'Do you know how worried I've been?'

'Yeah, uh—'

'Do you know that you and your idiotic friends burned my house down?'

'Yeah, uh, I'm really sorry—'

'My Emmys *melted!*'

'Mom,' Fortune said quickly, 'I'm, really, really sorry about that. But it couldn't be helped. It was the lion. She breathes fire, and Lohengrin frightened her—'

'The lion.' Ice cold. This was not good. 'I see. I hear, also, that that amulet, that thing, is in your head. I should have thrown it away years ago!'

'Mom.' He took a deep breath. Suddenly it all seemed very clear to him. 'Really, this is a great opportunity.'

'You have a *thing* in your head.'

'You don't have to tell me that.'

'How can you be sure that it's not controlling your brain?'

'What, Isra?'

'If that is its name.'

'Isra's not an "it." She's a woman. An Egyptian woman. And I'd know.'

'How?'

'I'd *know*,' Fortune repeated firmly. 'It's not as if we don't have discussions with each other. Arguments, even. It's not like she's turned me into some kind of robot or something.'

'John—' Peregrine said, anguish in her voice.

'Listen, Mom, I'm not a kid anymore. I'm grown up. You can't treat me like a kid, surround me with bodyguards, watch over me twenty-four hours a day.' Again, Lohengrin's words came unbidden into his mind. 'I've got to find my own destiny.'

'It's not your destiny, John. It's what that creature in your head wants.'

'That's not true.'

'How do you know? How can you know that?'

'Because,' Fortune said quietly. 'I wanted it, too, before I put the amulet on. I've always wanted it. I don't want to work on TV shows, fetching donuts, doing errands. I want to be someone who can do important things. Who can make a difference in the world. Like my father. Like you. You were my age when you fought the Astronomer.'

'That was different.'

'How?' Fortune asked.

'I was in control. I knew what I was doing. You – you're *younger* than I was. And maybe that's my fault. Maybe I did protect you too much. Sheltered you. But you're my son. I couldn't stand by and let something awful happen to you. And this … this Isra. We just don't know what it's doing to you. Can't you see that? We have to at least get it checked out. I can be there by seven in the morning. I've messengered a credit card and some ID. Just stay put until I get there. We'll charter a plane and have you at the Jokertown Clinic before we know it. Dr. Finn will be able to help. I know he will.'

Suddenly all of Fortune's certainty was gone. He couldn't forget the fear he'd felt when the amulet had burrowed into his body. The feeling of someone else locking him up in his own head, controlling him. It was creepy, and it was frightening.

And Isra would be with him, always. *For the rest of my life.*

'I don't know,' he said hollowly.

'I do,' Peregrine said. 'Sit tight. I'll be with you before you know it. You're my son, and I love you.'

'All right,' John Fortune he said. 'I'll wait.'

♠

It was an interminable wait.

The messenger showed up not too long after Fortune hung up the phone with a package containing fresh clothing, a black Amex card, and a wad of cash. It would be hours before Peregrine could make it up from Hollywood.

Suddenly John couldn't stand to be confined to the room any longer. He had to get out and do something. Anything.

He wandered down to the casino. There were no clocks there,

no night and day. Just color, action, lights, and noise, mindless and buzzing. He got a cup of quarters, fed some into a slot machine and pulled the handle. He watched the wheels buzz around. He got an ankh, a sphinx, a bar, a mummy. He fed in more quarters.

<Is this what you want?> Isra asked him.

Fortune dug out more quarters from his plastic cup, fed them into the slot, and pulled the handle. 'I've been wondering where you were.'

<I've been listening to you. Letting you think without intruding.>

'Thanks. That's real decent of you.' Two mummys. He won a buck. He fished the quarters out of the mouth of the return slot and fed them into the machine again.

<I know this is hard for you. But think of my people.>

'I didn't ask for this, you know.' The person at the next machine looked at him, and Fortune realized that he was speaking out loud. He didn't care.

<Many times people don't ask for their responsibilities,> Isra said. *<But they accept them. Can I share something with you?>*

Fortune shrugged angrily. 'Sure. Why not?'

The person at the next machine got up and left.

<Imshallah, I would have said once,> Isra told him. *<'As Allah wills.' But I no longer believe in Allah. I lost my faith when I lost my son Fuad. I once had children. Fuad was my oldest. I bore him when I was sixteen. He died a week before his twentieth birthday, crushed in an accident at the docks. He was my oldest, of eight, and lived the longest. He was the last one I lost. Gone. They are all gone.>*

Fortune paused in his mechanical feeding of the machine. 'Oh, God. I'm sorry.'

<I know you are. Do you want to know what it felt like?>

'No,' he whispered.

But Isra knew his mind, and knew that he was really saying yes.

She opened her memories to him, and they slammed into him like an express train. The agony of birth. The ecstasy of holding her baby for the first time. Their lives, difficult and hard, their trials and sorrows, all compressed into a millisecond of time that bit into his brain like a knife. A child dying in her arms, carried to its grave wrapped up in an insufficient cloth shroud. Put in a coffinless grave, the hard clods of dirt raining down upon the tiny corpse.

Fortune was too stunned, too overwhelmed to cry.

<Disease. Poverty. Malnutrition. They took all my children. But now, now ... > Isra's voice hardened. <Other children are suffering. My people are being slaughtered. Burnt out of their homes. Thrown out of their neighbourhoods. Being killed by ignorance and fear. I can't let that go on.>

Fortune knew he couldn't, either. And it wasn't Isra. It was him thinking it.

He put his last quarters into the machine, and for the first time relinquished control willingly. Their hand pulled the handle together, the wheels spun, and five ankhs in a row came up. Sirens started to wail.

Isra was bemused by the flashing lights and the loud sounds the coins made clattering down the shoot and spilling out and onto the carpet, but she knew the flash of silver when she saw it, and she realized what it meant. She grabbed a handful of large plastic cups that were stacked on a nearby counter and filled them with coins.

Behind them, a voice said, smooth as silk, 'You're very lucky.'

It was a woman. She was lithe and sinewy without tautness. Her simple black dress clung to every line of her body like a second skin, her long black hair swept down her back, past her waist, like a living wave. Her face was elfin, but not mischievous. It was queenly, full of a beauty that Isra could have only dreamt of. Her eyes were startling. They were silver, with odd flecks in them, gleaming like stars.

'Yes,' Isra told her. 'I am.'

The woman smiled. Her smile was dazzling and promising at the same time. Her strange eyes fastened on Fortune's and looked deep, as if she were more interested in him, in what he thought, in what he desired, than anything else in the world. She stood so close that their bodies nearly brushed. Isra set down her plastic cups full of coins. The woman smelled like a tropical night. Like languid flowers, musk, and heat.

'What do you plan on doing with your winnings?' the woman asked.

'I plan on putting them to good use.'

'I'm glad to hear it. There are many worthy charities.' She paused. 'Just one question. You're not John Fortune, are you?'

'What makes you say that?' Isra didn't like this woman. Under her own scent was another, a man's smell. The woman had been with one, and recently. But there was something else …

The woman said, 'You're not a man.'

'You read minds?' Isra asked, defensively.

'No. I read men. And you're not one.' Another smile – warm, seductive. 'I am interested in aces. And I find fire-breathing lions fascinating. Lionesses, that is.' Her sensual lips pursed. 'I can see that my curiosity is not going to be satisfied.'

'Why should it be?'

'No reason,' she admitted. She turned to go and paused for a final word over a finely turned shoulder. 'Take care of yourself.'

Isra watched her go, her snarl unheard amid the buzz of the casino's background noise.

♣

Isra took a cab to the airport, and paid the driver with coins taken from one of her cups. The Pan American counter was fairly quiet, until she dumped her winnings out all over it.

'Is this enough for a ticket to Cairo?' she asked. 'One way.'

The ticket agent, used to the eccentricities of Vegas life, counted out the coins as quickly as he could, but ended up shaking his head. 'Sorry. You're short a couple of hundred.'

She growled her frustration, which alarmed the agent somewhat. <Isra,> Fortune said. <Let me. You don't know enough about this. You'll get us in trouble.>

The agent watched, somewhat mystified, as his customer began to talk to himself. 'All right,' the young man finally decided. 'Wallah. It is in the hands of the Gods.' Then he reached into the pocket of his jacket, pulling out a passport and black Amex card, the kind without a credit limit. 'Charge it to this, please. First class.'

♥

JONATHAN HIVE

Daniel Abraham

A BAD DAY IN CAIRO

Las Vegas: the world capital of massive overstimulation. Ever since they'd arrived, Jonathan had been feeling the contact high of the city. Every time they left a casino, men and women waited to press advertisements into his hand. Other gambling establishments or sex shops or invitations to warehouse parties or the kinds of phone lines where a girl with a husky voice would describe what exactly she'd be doing to you if she was there. And, for the right price, she could be.

The air itself in the timeless elf world of the casinos was different. Jonathan had heard that they pumped extra oxygen into the atmosphere, just to keep the rollers rolling and the little, wizened women at the nickel slots pulling on the levers and pressing the buttons and moving on to the next machine. And always, everything was bright and buzzing and ringing, half-naked and fast and exciting and maybe, just maybe, the key to the one jackpot that would make everything, always be worthwhile. It was like swimming in a fever dream.

It might not help that they were very, very drunk.

'Fortune has a beetle in his head,' Jonathan said. 'That's not an accepted recipe for clear thinking.'

'*Your* head turns into bugs,' Lohengrin replied. Somehow that seemed to be a refutation.

'Wasps,' Jonathan said, and gave a little belch. 'Not beetles.

Wasps. Anyway, what does John need us for? Isis said he'll have the power of Ra. Ra, Ra, sis-boom-bah. You got Ra on your side, you don't need bugs. Did I tell you about my system for blackjack?'

They had been playing Stump the Barman. Lohengrin had never known that so many drinks were served in pineapples and coconuts, and his amazement pushed Jonathan to think of more and more obscure drinks, just for the expression on his face. Some were garnished with cherries and slices of pineapple, some with olives, some with onions. One had a shrimp in it. Their table was covered with paper parasols and tiny plastic swords. After a Slimer, a Sledgehammer, a Blue Motherfucker, a Purple People Eater, and a Sloe Screw on the Beach, Lohengrin started talking about the day at Neuschwanstein when he walked into the castle to face the terrorists. 'The gate was sealed, but I cut through it with my sword. They shot at me, but they could not hurt me. There were five of them.'

'You're not talking five wingnuts down in Egypt. You're not talking the Bavarian Freedom Front. Millions of pissed-off Muslims, that's what we're talking here. We could be killed. I *don't* have the power of Ra. Did I mention that?'

'You are an ace. A warrior.'

'You may be a warrior, *Mein Herr*. I turn into bugs.'

'Many, many, many bugs,' said Lohengrin. 'Too many for anyone to kill them all, *nein*? Why do you have this power, do you think?'

'There was this virus. Maybe you heard about it. There were aliens and a guy with a blimp and some dude called Jetboy. The guy with the blimp might have been German, come to think of it, but I won't hold that against you. I try to be well-mannered. I haven't mentioned Hitler once in all the time I've known you.'

'God,' said Klaus. 'God made the world. All the worlds. The aliens, the germs, he made them, too. Jetboy.'

'I think the press made Jetboy.'

Lohengrin ignored that, which was too bad. Jonathan thought it was a pretty good line. 'God wanted us to have these powers. You and me. He puts a sword into my hand and armors me in ghost steel, and he turns you into flies.'

'*Wasps*. Hello? Flies are gross.'

'Jonathan, my friend, why would God have given us these powers, except to protect the weak and innocent?'

'Oh *please*. Do I look like a caped crusader? Are you my plucky sidekick? God did it to fuck with our heads. Or to win a bet with Satan. He did it for the same reason he gives kids leukemia. How should I know? He's God; he doesn't explain this stuff to me. Did you miss the part where I was saying how we could get *killed*?'

'Who will help these people, if not us?'

'The United Nations. The secretary-general's flying into Cairo. Not Kofi Annan, the new one. He was on the TV in the bar when you were up in the suite screwing what's her name. Lilly of the Valley.'

'Lili Marlene. We were making love. She was beautiful, Jonathan. Perhaps God sent her as well.'

'Him or the night manager. Ask what escort service he used, you can ring her up again. I promise you, you're not going to bump into *her* in Egypt. Hey, what say we check out the Excalibur? I hear they have jousting. You'd like that, I bet.'

'Jonathan, Isis said that people are *dying*.'

Jonathan put down his drink and focused on the great muscle-bound lunk at his side.

'People are always dying somewhere in the world,' he said. 'When they're not dying in Cairo, they're dying in Timbuktu, Kalamazoo, Hoboken, Hohoswinegrunt, or some other goddamned place.'

'Hohenschwangau, but no one died there. I saved them. With *this*.' Lohengrin stood up, a broadsword appearing in his hand, white, shimmering, its edge a razor. He brought it down hard, shearing through the steel and mica table in one sudden, savage cut. Coasters, coconuts, and paper umbrellas flew everywhere.

'Great,' Jonathan said, 'that's a good argument. Beat up the furniture.'

The waitress – a blond woman in her midthirties with an expression that could stun rats at twenty yards – came up to them.

'You can put it on the room,' Jonathan said.

She nodded in a way that assured them both that she would,

while simultaneously informing them that they had had their last alcohol for the evening. All without speaking. She was very talented that way.

'How about a cup of coffee?' Jonathan asked.

She nodded again, turned, and walked away.

'We are men,' Lohengrin said. 'We are blessed among men. Our actions should be guided by what is right and noble!'

'We're drunks in Vegas,' Jonathan said. 'Our actions should be guided by vice and alcohol.'

Lohengrin shook his head. He managed to look deeply disappointed without precisely focusing his eyes.

'Do you have no dreams, Jonathan?'

'Sure,' Jonathan said. 'They just don't involve getting anointed by God.'

'What then?' Lohengrin demanded. 'What is your dream?'

'I want to be a journalist,' Jonathan said.

'And what is it a journalist would do?'

The waitress reappeared with two cups of coffee. She balanced them on the remains of the table, nodded, and walked away again. Jonathan looked at the black surface, neon bar lights and the flickering blue television screens reflecting in it. *What would a journalist do?*

'Ah, fuck you,' he sighed. 'Fine. We'll go.'

EGYPT | DEPRESSED | 'ROCK THE CASBAH' – THE CLASH

There was a time not all that long ago when I thought poverty was not having enough cash to order a bucket of fried chicken. I may have been optimistic about that. When it comes to pure human misery, pencil in the Necropolis outside Cairo for your touristy needs.

I came here from Las Vegas, specifically the Luxor. I have moved from the fantasy of Egypt to the reality. Given the choice between drinking and playing craps with a fake Cleopatra whose tits are always just offering to fall out of her dress, and walking through the slums of Cairo, I'm not sure which I'd recommend. The fake is a beautiful dream, but there's nothing like reality for reminding you just how toxic dreams like that can be. I have gone from the city of excess to the city of desperate want. The change has left me a little nauseated.

The first day here, we started at the pyramids. They were, indeed, amazing. They're bigger than you think. Start about the size you imagine them, then up it by another half or two thirds. They're huge. You can see why the idea of them made it all the way to Vegas.

But they're also not Egypt. *Egypt* came when Lohengrin was moved to charity. He started handing out euros to the beggars. We were swamped so bad it took half an hour to make it the thirty feet back to the car. If a couple of the kids got stung, I can apologize and feel like shit about it, but at the time it seemed like the only option.

Imagine being in the middle of a crowd of forty, fifty, maybe a hundred shouting kids, their hands out, pushing against each other and against you. The air smelled like

unwashed bodies and desperation, and there we were.
Westerners with money. Aces, no less. You wouldn't
think I'd have been frightened, but let me just tell you,
there's something in a hungry kid's eyes that doesn't have
anything to do with pathos or gratitude. At the time, I
thought it was just hunger. And yeah, it scared me.

That's been the signature moment of the trip – the flat,
angry eyes of hungry children. And that, boys and girls,
was just tourism. It doesn't even touch on the riots.

So, yeah … the riots.

Things were quiet the first few days we were here.
During the day we'd try to track down Fortune when we
weren't taking in the sights. At night, we pretty much
stayed in the little faded hotel room with its yellow
wallpaper and air-conditioning that smelled vaguely like
fish, watching old American sitcoms dubbed into languages
I don't speak. The fifth day there was a news brief that
broke in. It was local, and neither of us knew what the guy
was saying, so I got online and looked it up on the CNN
and Al Jazeera sites. Turned out there was a riot going on
right here, near Cairo.

A little background: After the Caliph got himself
assassinated in Baghdad, the leaders of the Ikhlas al-Din
called for retribution on the killers. And, hey, cool by me, I
say. Someone offed the president, I'd be happy to see them
strung up, and I didn't even vote for the guy. 'Root out the
terrorists and the people who shelter them.' That was the
slogan. Again, I'm all for it.

On paper at least.

The thing is, how do you know who the bad guys are? If
a Muslim kills the president, does that make all Muslims bad
guys? If a joker organization kills the Caliph, does that

mean all jokers are guilty? If the Twisted Fists are a bunch of joker terrorists and the Living Gods are also jokers, does that make them allies?

The answer is, apparently, yes.

Through the night, other riots bloomed all through the Middle East. Alexandria, Port Said, Damietta. The temples of what they were calling the Old Religion burned. There was some particularly ugly footage of Hathor being pulled from her temple by the horns. The talking heads on CNN and Al Jazeera both talked about these being 'spontaneous outbreaks.' Kamal Farag Aziz, the local Ikhlas al-Din strongman – added 'of righteous wrath,' but the basic sentiment was the same. The fans of the Caliph were mad as hell and not going to take it anymore.

We found Fortune the next day in the Necropolis. The spontaneous outbreak of the previous night had been teams of well-organized men with guns and tasers, all wearing black fatigues and black-and-green *keffiyeh*, moving through the poorest parts of the city and slaughtering whoever crossed their paths.

The Necropolis is a great, huge, sprawling suburb of the dead. Ancient mausoleums with whole families of squatters living inside. No food, little water. Squalor, though.

Yes, most of the people living there are jokers, but some are just poor. John Fortune – Sekhmet, really – showed us a lot of bodies. Most of them were new. The Cairo police were around, too, allegedly taking statements, but most of what they did was assure people that the streets weren't safe, that there weren't enough police, that the time had come for the jokers to get out of town. Their eyes were flat, just like the beggars' had been. That was when I figured out that what I'd seen in those children around the pyramids hadn't been hunger at all. It was hatred.

That night, Fortune and Lohengrin and I joined up with the local folks to patrol the Necropolis. There were a couple death squads we came across. But the graves here go on forever, and there were other groups we missed. The night after the riot, we lost another couple dozen people. They might be dead, they might have been taken prisoner, they might have done the sane thing by saying fuck this and heading south.

Okay, so why south? What's the silver lining? The jokers do have someplace to go. The farther up the Nile (which is to say south) they go, the more refuges there are for the Living Gods. The nearest big stronghold is Karnak. Already, the Necropolis is emptying. The jokers are putting what few belongings they have on carts or in grocery baskets, or tying them to their backs and walking south. There are other poverty-sick people swarming in to take over the prime gravesites, the mausoleums with the best roofs and the fewest bodies.

The Egyptian army, seeing the mass flight, is offering what protection it can on the road. Fortune's going, too. So's Lohengrin. And so, God help me, am I.

Internet access is what you could charitably call spotty out on the road. My cell phone does have upload options, if I can get a signal from a satellite. There are, I'm told, villages with land lines I could use to dial up if there's nothing better.

I may be a little scarce for a while, folks, but hang tight. This is news really happening, right now. And I'm going to tell you how it comes down.

One side note. We were getting ready to head out, Lohengrin and me, and I said something about how well

« ‖ next »

organized the 'spontaneous outbreaks' all seemed to be. I just want everyone to be very clear that it was the German guy who brought up Kristallnacht.

I wasn't going to go there.

1002 COMMENTS | LEAVE COMMENT

CRUSADER

George R. R. Martin

The shortcut is a mistake.

The road runs along the west bank, following the course of the Nile. Once chariots carved deep ruts in its surface, and priests and pharaohs and Roman legionnaires moved along it, but now it carries cars and trucks and yellow school buses. Semis belch diesel as they roar past palm trees and fields of sugar cane.

The family has neither truck nor chariot, only a pair of wire grocery carts stolen from some Cairo supermarket, piled high with clothes and toys and pots and all the rest of their worldly possessions. A small boy rides in one shopping cart, a crippled old man in the other. The mother and the father push, and from time to time the daughter lends a hand. She is twelve and already taller than her parents, a slender girl and pretty.

They have been walking for days, every day and all day, pushing the rattling carts down the two-lane road, part of the great river of refugees flowing from the delta down toward Karnak, Aswan, and Abu Simbel, stopping only at night to rest exhausted in some nearby field. All that long way they have stayed on the road, never straying far from the column. Every day Karnak is a little closer. In Karnak they will be safe, the old man promises. Their gods are strong in Karnak. Anubis will open the way for them, Horus and Sobek and Taweret will defend them. There will be food for

248

everyone, beds to sleep in, shelter from the sun – but only when they reach the temple, the glorious New Temple.

The talk along the road is that Karnak lies no more than a day and a half ahead, as the ibis flies, but the road follows the river, so when the Nile loops east the road loops as well. That is when the whisper goes up and down the ragged column, passed from mouth to mouth. *There is a quicker way, a shorter way, just leave the road and cut due south, and you'll shave twenty kilometers off your journey.* Twenty kilometers is nothing for a man in a car, but for a family pushing two old shopping carts it is a long way. The daughter's feet are blistered, the little boy is sunburned, and the father's back aches more with every step. Small wonder that they leave the road to take the shortcut.

Since the dawn of time, Egypt has been two nations, the black lands and the red. The black lands along the Nile are rich, wet, fertile, and well peopled. The red lands beyond are harsher, a sere and savage wilderness of sand and stone and scorpions baking beneath the merciless Egyptian sun.

That is where the jackals find them.

Far from the road, they sweep down upon the family as they cross a fissured plain of red stone and hard-packed sand. One has a rifle, the other two long knives. One rides a red horse, one a black, and one a dun. All wear the green-and-black *keffiyeh* of Ikhlas al-Din. They are lean men, black of hair and eye, with short beards and sun-browned skin. To western eyes they are indistinguishable from those they hunt, but they know the red lands as the family from Cairo does not. They know the red lands as only a jackal can, and like jackals, they sniff behind the herd, waiting to descend on stragglers.

There is nowhere to run, nowhere to hide, no one to hear a cry for help. The mother wraps thin arms about her daughter, and the old man begins to pray. He prays to Set and Sobek, to Hathor and Horus, to Anubis and Osiris, prays in the same Arabic tongue the riders speak. Yet, when they hear his prayer, it whips them to a fury. 'There is no god but Allah, and Muhammed is his prophet,' one cries. He springs from his horse, kicks over one of the family's shopping carts, and slashes the old man across the face, opening his cheek to the bone. The praying stops. There is no sound but for the faint buzzing of a wasp, and the soft patter of blood falling on sand baked hard as brick.

The riders dismount. The daughter, brave and pretty, pleads with them. In Cairo they have many Muslim friends, she says. They have never done any harm to the people of Islam. The jackal with the rifle answers her. 'You bow down to monsters accursed of Allah, and our Caliph's holy blood is on your hands.' He swats at an insect buzzing round his head, a wasp that glimmers in the sun like an emerald with wings. 'You would steal our lands from us, you and your demon gods. You think we do not see? We see. This is where you die. The sands will drink your joker blood.'

The wasp stings him in the neck.

Cursing, he swats at it, but the insect is too quick. It lands upon the rump of the nearest horse, and stings again. The horse rears up kicking. A second wasp appears. They fly around the jackals, darting in and out, landing on one man's nose, another's arm, stinging. One of the riders catches a wasp in his hand and crushes it between his fingers. He wipes the remains off on his pants leg, grinning. Only then does he hear the motorbike.

From the south the knight appears, bouncing over stone and sand, a plume of smoke and dust rising up behind him. Like an answered prayer he comes, his armor flashing in the sunlight, white and bright as mountain snow. Swan wings adorn his warhelm. On his breastplate shines the Holy Grail that Arthur sought and never found. When he lifts his hand a broadsword springs forth from his fingers where no sword had been before, a blade so white and sharp that for a moment it outshines the bright Egyptian sun.

'*Deus Volt!*' the knight roars as he comes on, and his cry echoes across the bare and boundless sands. The jackals break before it, running for their mounts. Only the rifleman lingers long enough to wheel his horse and fire, but when the shot rings harmlessly off the knight's white armor, he lets the rifle tumble to the sand and races away after his companions.

The knight climbs off his motorbike. His sword and helm and

armor melt away, dissolving as a morning mist dissolves before the rising sun. 'No harm will come to you,' he says, as he pulls a handkerchief from his pocket to press against the old man's bloody cheek. 'Come with me. Your gods are waiting for you.'

The brave young girl plants a kiss upon his cheek. A wasp buzzes happily around them, and all is right in the red lands, on this day, for this one family ... though, on the way south, they pass the corpses of others who were not so fortunate.

The shortcut is a mistake.

♠

Klaus looked up from the screen. 'It is good, Jonathan. It moved me, truly.' *Deus Volt*, he thought. *God wills it.* Those had been the words the old crusaders cried when they marched out of the West to free Jerusalem. He did not remember shouting those words at the jackals, or any words at all, but perhaps he would shout them next time. 'Will they read this in Germany, do you think?' It pleased him to think that his father might read about his feats. His little brothers, too.

'All over the world. You wouldn't believe how many hits I'm getting.' Jonathan was seated on an orange crate with his laptop balanced on his thighs. 'I need to find some place to buy a trench-coat. The trenchcoat guys get all the prizes. I could win a Pulitzer for this, if I only had a trenchcoat. This is a big story, and no one's covering it but me.' A wasp landed on his cheek and crawled up his left nostril. That would have vexed most people, but Jonathan Hive took no notice. 'I'm bearing witness for the world. Just call me Edward R. Hive.'

'*Ja*, only ... I do not wish to spoil your prize, but that was not how it happened. You never stung the horse. There was no horse. They drove a four-wheel truck.'

Jonathan waved off his objection. 'Trucks are boring. Horses are romantic. Some of the asswipes ride horses, right? Or camels. Would camels be better, do you think?'

'No. There was no pretty daughter either. If a pretty girl had kissed me, I would know.' Klaus tore a strip of peeling skin off his arm, frowning at the pinkness underneath. In Cairo he had slathered on sunblock whenever he ventured outside, prompting Jonathan to compare him to a housewife from a situation comedy, her face covered in cold cream. When sunblock became harder to find, he bought a straw hat off a peddler in a felucca, but his arms still burned and peeled. 'And they had no grocery carts. How could they push grocery carts across the sand?'

'They were *symbolic* grocery carts. It's a poignant image of displacement. The devil's in the details, dude. Bottom line, these numbfucks wandered off into the desert and would have died if not for us. The rest is just some frosting for the strudel. Everyone likes frosting on their strudel. That, and sex. You have to have the pretty girl, she's what sells the whole thing.'

Klaus peeled off the soiled T-shirt that he'd slept in, one of those Herr Berman had given him when he agreed to be a guest on *American Hero*. On the front was a picture of Diver, the dolphin woman. 'You could just say the mother was pretty.'

'The mother had a mustache.' Jonathan closed his laptop. Both of his legs ended at the knee, and tiny green wasps were buzzing in and out of his ragged denim shorts. His sneakers, footless, had tumbled to the ground, acrawl with bugs – a few toes' worth, at least. Thousands more were spread out over the better part of twenty kilometers on both sides of the Nile, watching everything and everyone. Even when Jonathan was with you, he could be a hundred thousand other places, too. 'And speaking of girls,' he went on, 'you were talking in your sleep last night. "*Lili, Lili, where are you, Lili?*" Barf. I can't believe that you're still mooning over a one-night stand.'

'She was more than that to me.' Klaus grabbed his jeans and shook them. A scorpion tumbled from one cuff and scuttled off. 'I dreamed I was at the Luxor, looking for her. Our suite went on and on. So many rooms, like a maze. I knew that she was lost, but still I searched, calling her sweet name.'

'I was having a nice dream, too. I was eating flapjacks with Simoon and Curveball in the Valley of the Kings. The Living Gods were making them. You should have seen Horus flip that skillet.'

'Flapjacks?' Klaus scratched at the stubble under his chin. He needed a shave. 'What is flapjacks?'

'Pancakes.'

'The gods do not serve pancakes.'

'They would if they had some batter,' said Jonathan. 'You woke me up with all your *Lili, Lili* moaning. Dude, what happens in Vegas is supposed to stay in Vegas, didn't anyone tell you?'

'You would not say these things if you had met her.' Klaus pulled on his jeans and zipped them up. 'She was beautiful.' He remembered the feel of her in his arms, the taste of red wine in her mouth when he kissed her. *And her eyes. She had the most amazing eyes.* 'The smell of her hair ... it fell all the way down her back, black as night—'

'Carpet matched the drapes, too, though mostly I was looking at her tits. You know, there *are* other girls.'

'Lili was a woman.' The first time Klaus had seen her, she had been standing under a hallway light fumbling for her room key, and something about it had reminded him of the girl beneath the lamplight in the old soldier's song, so he had asked her if her name was Lili Marlene, and she had smiled at him and said, 'Close enough.' That was all it took. He had made love to her three times that night, and when they were not kissing they were talking. Lili had been so easy to talk to, not like the other girls he had known. Klaus was sure they'd talked for hours, although the next day he could not seem to recall her telling him anything about herself, not even her real name. One moment she had been lying beside him, drinking wine from the minibar and laughing as he tried to teach her the lyrics to 'Lili Marlene' in German, but then Jonathan had come stumbling into the suite, making noise and turning on the lights, and suddenly she was gone. Klaus had only taken his eyes off her for an instant, but ...

'Oh, shit,' said Jonathan Hive. He was gazing off at nothing, and there was a distant, cloudy look in his eyes that Klaus had learned to recognize. 'There's trouble.'

'Where?'

'The Valley of the Queens. John's there.'

'I go at once.' Klaus pulled on a fresh T-shirt. This one had a picture of the Candle. 'Where is my hat?'

'Never mind the hat,' said Jonathan. 'Just *go*. I'm with you.' The meat of his thighs dissolved away, his shorts sagging empty as a swarm of green wasps filled the tent.

♣

The temperature was well above a hundred Fahrenheit.

Sand and stone shimmered in the heat. A kite circled high above the Colossi of Memnon, riding the thermal that rose from those great ruined twins. Cracked and weathered by countless centuries of sun and wind, the huge stone pharaohs still seemed to exude power. Perhaps that was why the refugees had chosen to huddle around their broken thrones.

The camp went on as far as Klaus could see, an endless sprawl of displaced humanity sweltering beneath the Egyptian sun. A fortunate few had small tents like the one Klaus shared with Jonathan, but more were sheltering under cardboard crates or heaps of rags. In Cairo, even the poorest of them had tombs to sleep in, and tourists to beg for coin, but here they were exposed to all the elements, with no one to beg from but each other.

And every day the camps grew more crowded, their residents more desperate. This was not the biggest camp, either. The one along the riverbank covered twenty kilometers, and small groups of jokers had spilled over the hills to the Valley of the Kings and the Valley of the Queens.

The boys he'd hired to watch his motorcycle sprang to their feet at his approach. 'We guard good,' announced Tut. His brother Gamel just held out a hand. Klaus dug a euro from his jeans. It was too much, but he felt sorry for the boys who had lost their mother to the knives of Ikhlas al-Din.

When he kicked the stand back and fired the ignition, the engine coughed and smoked before it caught. The bike was a fifty-year-old Royal Enfield that Sobek had sold him for seven times its worth. Every time he rode it, Klaus found himself pining for the R1200S sports bike that his sponsors at BMW had presented to him when he had signed to be their spokesman. He loved the deep, throaty growl the boxer engine made when he gunned it down the autobahn in the fast lane.

His BMW was in Munich though, and so he sat astride this relic with its bald tires, flaking green paint, and an exhaust pipe that looked to be made of solid rust. The bike's gas gauge was broken, too, stuck somewhere just above empty even when the tank was freshly filled. *I am running on fumes*, he thought. Klaus prayed that it would be enough to take him through the hills, and down into the Valley of the Queens.

'*You get them, Lohengrin!*' Tut shouted, as Klaus fed some fumes to the engine. '*You kill them good!*'

Over ground like this, he dare not push the Royal Enfield too hard. Even at a sprinter's pace it rattled so badly that he feared it might shake itself to pieces before he reached John Fortune. A nimbus of white light played about his head, took form, became a warhelm with a narrow eye slit and swan's wings sprouting from the temples. A motorcyle helmet it was not, but Klaus had faith that the ghost steel would protect him in a spill.

Turning west and south, he wove a crooked path through the squalor of the camp, bouncing past the hulk of an abandoned school bus where a dozen families now were living. Behind the bus, the carcass of a dog was turning over a cook-fire that stank of burning camel dung. A cloud of wasps trailed after Klaus, glimmering and winking in the sunlight. A joker whose face had sprouted dozens of small heads threw a rock at them as they went by, and a dark-eyed woman with a child at her breast gave Klaus a lingering look, as if to say, *You are not one of us. What are you doing here?*

Some nights Klaus would ask that selfsame question as he twisted in his sleeping bag on the hard ground, wondering if that was a scorpion crawling up his leg or just another of Jonathan's wasps. Barbarossa would mock at him for coming here, he knew, and most of the other aces of the Reichsbanner would consider him a fool. He had thought to find in them a modern Round Table, where heroes broke bread together and talked of righting wrong, but the only wrong they wished to right involved their tax rates.

'You expected more, *ja*?' Barbarossa said afterward, when he and Klaus escaped the feast for a beer garden in Heidelberg's student quarter. 'You are young. You will learn. It is all cartels and sponsors now. Mighty Euro and Mighty Dollar are more powerful than any ace on earth. They own us, *ja*.'

'Not me,' Klaus had insisted. 'My honor is not for sale.'

Barbarossa pinched his cheek. 'Keep your honor. It's your smile they will buy, your big blue eyes and pale blond hair, and these apple cheeks of yours.'

He was right, and I was wrong. His first endorsement had been a local dairy that offered him five hundred euros to say their milk helped him grow up big and strong. Klaus had resisted at first, but his mother said he should do it for the children, that milk was good for children, and maybe they could go as high as a thousand euros. That was a lot of money, so Klaus drank the milk and smiled for the cameras. Other endorsements followed, until finally he signed with an agent and she brought him BMW. He loved his motorcycle, and loved the freedom that fame and money brought him, but sometimes at night he still felt like a fraud, no different from the hollow heroes of the Reichsbanner, who took adulation as their due but never did a thing to earn it. Yet, what had he done since Neuschwanstein? Nothing but smile and sign 'Lohengrin' on pictures of himself. That was no life for an ace, or for a knight. There was no honor in it.

♥

The road wound back and forth as it made its way through the hills down into the valley known as Biban al-Harim, where the tombs of eighty ancient Egyptian queens were sunk into the dry and stony soil. Klaus was banking round a curve and wondering how long his fuel would last when he heard the sound of gunfire ahead.

Jackals, was his first and only thought. That was the name that Jonathan had given to the rabble of Ikhlas al-Din, the Muslim fundamentalists who had been swept to victory in Egypt's last election. It was not enough for them to drive the Living Gods and their worshippers from their homes. All the long way south, they had continued to hound the refugees, raiding their camps, picking off stragglers, even burning villages and poisoning wells along the way to deny them water, food, and fuel.

Even here, Klaus thought grimly, *even now*. Pale light danced around him, hardened, became breastplate, greaves, gorget, gauntlets. He leaned into a turn and accelerated, pushing the old motorbike as fast as it would go, and leaving Jonathan's wasps well behind. A little farther on, he came upon a woman clutching her child by the hand as blood streamed down her face. She flinched at his approach, and Klaus did not have the time to set her fears at ease. He screamed past her, his armor shining. The gunfire grew louder, staccato bursts that echoed off the hills. He could hear other sounds as well, shouts and screams, the roar of some great beast and the chudder of a helicopter's rotors.

The jackals had no helicopters. *The army*, Klaus thought, *the army has moved in to stop them*. For a moment he was relieved.

When the valley opened up before him, Klaus hit his brakes and swerved to a sudden halt in a spray of dust and pebbles. He let his helm dissolve for a moment to give himself a better view, but even so, it took him a long moment to understand what he was seeing. The camp down there was much smaller than the one by the colossi, and half of it was in flames, rag tents and cardboard shacks alike sending up greasy pillars of smoke into the sky. A truck was burning, too, a large flatbed with a green canvas awning. Corpses littered the ground. Through the smoke he saw armed men moving, dim shapes with automatic rifles in their hands. He heard rifles chattering, a woman wailing. Above it all the helicoper moved, firing at something on the ground.

Some of the wounded had rushed toward the nearest of the ancient tombs and were trying to tear down its steel scissors gate to seek refuge inside. Klaus saw three men appear behind them and open up, raking the refugees with bullets. Their bodies danced and jerked under the impacts, like marionettes gone mad.

And then the lioness appeared. Even from a distance she was huge, larger than a pony, almost as big as the draft horses that pulled his father's wagon up the mountain. Flame swirled from her jaws as she leapt onto the soldiers. Two fell screaming, wreathed in fire. The third she opened from throat to crotch, tearing at his intestines until the helicopter's shadow fell across them. Then she whirled to leap, but the copter was beyond her reach. Klaus saw her hammered to the ground by a stream of machine gun fire, heard her roar of pain, saw the bullets kicking up dust all around her as she turned and raced away.

Jackals do not have helicopters. Through the smoke and dust, Klaus could see the uniforms, patterned in the tan-and-dun of desert camouflage. *Not jackals. Those are soldiers. It is the Egyptian army doing this.* This time he would not be facing paint-ball guns, or the cheap Czech pistols of the Bavarian Freedom Front. The jackals had always fled before him after a perfunctory shot or two, but these men were trained and disciplined, and there looked to be a lot of them. *But none with my armor.*

At Peenemünde, the scientists had argued for months about the nature of that armor. Doktor Fuchs theorized that it was made of coherent light, Doktor Alpers suspected quantum particles, and Doktor Hahn coined the term 'hardened ectoplasm.' Klaus did not understand half of what they said, so he went on calling it *ghost steel*. Even after six months of study, the scientists still could not say with certainty whether it was made of energy or matter, but their tests did show that it was impervious to knives, axes, bullets, flamethrowers, acid, shrapnel, lightning bolts, and everything else that they could find to throw at him. The Egyptian soldiers were not nearly as well-armed as the good doktors. There was nothing they could do to harm him.

Klaus fed the motorbike a little gas and gathered speed as he went rolling down the hill. Mists shimmered around his head and became his warhelm again, its wide white wings outstretched. When he raised his hand his sword appeared, shining bright. *Today we will give Jonathan something true to blog about*, he thought.

◆

Afterward, Klaus could not have said how many men he had faced, or how many he had slain.

The smoke from the fires drifted everywhere, acrid and choking, so thick at times that friend and foe alike seemed to vanish and reappear like phantoms in a dream. Sounds echoed in his ears – screams, shouts, the whine of rifles and the chudder of the big machine gun, the chopping of the helicopter's blades, Sekhmet's terrifying roars. The she-lion was off to his right, behind him, just ahead; try as he might, Klaus could not find her. At times he could have sworn there were two of her.

He had no trouble finding the soldiers, though. The first man he slew was coughing when he emerged from the smoke, but as soon as he saw Lohengrin he raised his rifle. '*Yield!*' Klaus called out to him. 'Throw down your weapon, and I will not harm you.' Instead the soldier dropped to one knee and squeezed his trigger. Klaus saw the muzzle flash. The round struck him near the temple and caromed off. 'You cannot harm me,' he warned the man, his voice booming through his warhelm. 'Yield.' The soldier fired again, and then a third time. By then Klaus was on top of him. When he swung his sword, the man raised the rifle to protect himself, but the ghost steel blade sliced through stock and barrel and opened him from neck to belly.

Klaus did not have the time to watch him die. Other soldiers had appeared by then, and they were firing, too. He gave them all the chance to yield. None did, though a few of them broke and ran when they saw him cutting down their friends. Perhaps they did not have the English to understand what he was saying. Klaus would need to learn the Arabic word for 'yield.'

Riding through the smoke and slaughter like a ghost, Lohengrin soon lost all sense of time and place. No blood stained his ghost steel; his armor gleamed white and pure, unblemished, and his blade glimmered palely in his hand. '*God wills it,*' he remembered thinking – though, why any god would will such carnage, the white knight could not have said.

When the fighting ended, Klaus was hardly conscious of it. The fires had burned low by then, and a hot wind out of the red lands to the west had begun to dissipate the smoke. He realized suddenly that he could no longer hear the helicopter. Sekhmet had fallen silent as well. It had been a long while since he had last heard her roar. *John*, he thought.

Jonathan's wasps had found him by then. They buzzed around his head, the thrum of their wings strangely reassuring. Klaus wondered how much Bugsy had seen of what had happened here. He turned his head, searching for the enemy, but all of the soldiers were dead or fled. Klaus let his sword and helm dissolve, but kept his body clad in ghost steel. '*John!*' he bellowed, rolling slowly across the battlefield. '*John Fortune!*'

In the end it was the wasps who found him, sprawled naked by the entrance to a tomb, where he had been protecting the jokers who had taken shelter within. John was drenched in blood, but none of it was his own. When Klaus tried to lift him he gave a gasp of pain. 'My ribs,' he said. 'I think they broke some. The bullets – they melt when they touch her flesh, but they still hurt. They hit like hammers.'

'You look ghastly,' Klaus admitted.

'I just tore a dozen men to pieces with my fingernails.'

'That was Sekhmet,' said Klaus. 'She fought nobly.'

'*With my fingers!*' John's skin was damp with sweat.

He looks forty years old, Klaus thought. His face had thinned to the point of gauntness, and he had lines around his eyes that had not been there in Hollywood. The red scarab that was Sekhmet sat above his eyes like some huge blood blister, making his forehead seem to bulge the way his famous father's had bulged when he fought the Astronomer in the sky above Manhattan, a year before Klaus was even born. John's skin had darkened, too; daily exposure to the harsh Egyptian sun had browned him several shades. That made him look more like Fortunato, too.

Some of the surviving jokers had emerged from the tomb. A hunchbacked woman with snakes for fingers offered Klaus a charred and torn blanket. He wrapped it around John Fortune to stop his shivering. His smooth brown skin was covered with dark bruises. Klaus unhooked his canteen from his motorbike to give him a drink of water. 'Not too much, now,' he cautioned. 'Sip.'

Between sips, John told him how the fight had started. The

camp had been a small one, perhaps three hundred people, jokers and their families down from Port Said and Damietta. Even among the followers of the Old Religion, jokers were reviled if their wild card deformities did not mimic the old Egyptian gods, so these had chosen to take refuge in the Valley of the Queens, well away from the larger camps to the east. When word of them reached the New Temple, however, Taweret had dispatched the goddess Meret to bring them food, clothing, and medical supplies. John went with her, in case of trouble.

'When we first saw the helicopter, Meret waved to them,' John said. 'She thought it was Ikhlas al-Din we had to fear, not the army. Then they touched down and the soldiers started pouring out. We did not know what to make of that. Meret told me to continue with the food distribution and went to speak with their captain. She was walking toward them when the soldiers opened fire. There was no warning, no reason given. They just started shooting. All I could think to do was let Sekhmet work the change, so we could fight them.' His voice was hoarse.

'The captain must have been Ikhlas al-Din. A member or a sympathizer.' Klaus remembered Meret from his last visit to the New Temple. A dark, slender woman, she'd had vines and lotus flowers growing from her head in place of hair. *She was gentle, too, and even had some German. Who would want to kill such a woman?* 'It was a rogue unit,' he told John, hoping it was true. 'This mad captain – we will report him to his superiors.'

'He's dead,' said John. The scarab in his swollen forehead seemed to throb. 'I tore his throat out.'

Klaus nodded. 'We must get you back to the New Temple. Can you ride? Hold on to me. That is all you need to do.' One of the jokers helped him lift John Fortune onto the Enfield. 'Hold me tight,' he told him. 'It is not so far.'

♠

They were walking down the hill road an hour later when they heard the roar of a truck coming toward them.

Klaus had been pushing the Royal Enfield along for almost

a kilometer. Its tank had gone bone dry, but he could not bring himself to abandon it. When he heard the truck he let go of the handlebars and called up his blade and armor. He could feel the heat of Sekhmet beside him, and smell the sulfur stench of the smoke rising from her nostrils. John had changed back as soon as the bike had died, too weak to continue in his own flesh.

When the driver of the truck came round the rocks and saw them, he screeched to a sudden stop, his air brakes screaming like a chorus of damned souls. Behind the wheel, a man with the long snout and gray-green, scaly skin of a crocodile grinned at them. 'Those motorbikes go faster if you ride them instead of pushing them along,' he called out. 'So you are not dead. Good. Taweret sent me, to fetch her sister back. You can come, too.'

Klaus lowered his sword and let the ghost steel dissolve back into nothingness. Of all the Living Gods he had met, old Sobek was the one that he liked best. No more than five-six, the Egyptian had heavy shoulders, big arms thick with muscle, and the sort of hard, round belly that tells of a great fondness for beer. Where his fellow gods dressed like pharaohs in silken robes, golden collars, and jeweled headdresses, Sobek wore baggy pants, suspenders, and a stained photographer's vest. His skin was cracked and leathery, more gray than green, and what he lacked in hair and ears he made up for in teeth. They were long and sharp and crooked, those teeth, stained brown and yellow by the rank black Turkish cigarettes he smoked.

Sekhmet sprang up onto the bed of the truck, and Klaus grabbed his motorbike in both hands and swung it up beside her, before climbing into the cab next to Sobek. 'Meret is dead,' he told him, as he slammed the door. Behind them, Sekhmet curled up and began to lick her bruises.

Sobek put the truck in gear. 'We know.'

'This time it was not jackals. The army—'

'We know that, too.'

'How? Jonathan? Did he send his bugs to you?'

'He called Horus on his cell phone.' Sobek wrenched the wheel around, and sent the truck roaring back toward the river. 'They sent soldiers to the Valley of the Kings as well, and there we had no one to fight back. The generals say they sent the troops in to protect the sites against the vandals and tomb robbers who were threatening to despoil the graves of the pharaohs and their queens. Only terrorists attacked the soldiers, they say, that was how the fighting started. It was on the radio, and Al Jazeera. The Twisted Fists are the cause of all the blood-shedding.' He gave Klaus a sideways glance. 'You two are the Twisted Fists. In case you were not knowing this.'

Klaus was shocked. 'They call us *terrorists*?'

'Why not? You terrify the Caliph, I think. At night he dreams of the crusader's big sharp sword and wets his bed. In the morning his wives all smell of piss.' He laughed. 'General Yusuf has sent word across the river. Cairo wants you and Sekhmet handed over to him for trial. If we do that, he says, the rest of us may leave in peace. Leave for where, you wonder? Hell, I am thinking. Well, it does not matter. Taweret will never *hand you over*. Sekhmet is her sister, a fellow goddess. Your friend would turn into bugs and fly away, and you would make the white sword come and go *chop, chop, chop*.' Sobek drove with one hand on the steering wheel and the other slamming at the horn, one of his foul black Turkish cigarettes turning to ash between his teeth.

'What will you do?' Klaus asked him.

'Go to Aswan. Where else? There are more of us in Aswan.'

'You mean to flee?'

'Flee or fight. Serquet can summon scorpions, Bast sees well in the dark. Babi is strong as ten baboons, and I have many teeth. The rest have no powers, only funny heads. The army, they have guns and planes and tanks. Guns and planes and tanks beat funny heads. So we flee. Aswan is a good place, I am thinking. How to get there, though? That is not so easy. Taweret has summoned the gods to meet upon the morrow. You and your friend may come as well, and we will talk about what must be done.'

'*Ja*,' said Klaus, but his tone was dubious. He thought of Tut and Gamel, of the families in the yellow school bus, of the joker man who had thrown the rock at him. It was a wonder that any of them had survived the journey down from Cairo. Aswan was two hundred kilometers farther on. 'Many will die,' he said to Sobek. 'If you are forced to leave this place ... they do not have the strength. There is no food, no water. To make them march – this is murder. The world will not allow it.'

'The world is not here.' Sobek plucked the cigarette from his teeth and flicked an inch of ash out the window.

'The secretary-general has come to Cairo—'

'—waiting for the Caliph. They will have a nice talk while the freaks are dying. Later perhaps the UN will pass a resolution, and a year from now there will be sanctions, yes? The Caliph will tremble, but we will all be dead.'

Klaus scowled. It was too true. 'America—'

'—is watching television. John told us. Plastic babies burning up in fires, actors robbing banks, lies and seductions and betrayals, good stuff to watch. Old Kemel was a fool to make us gods. He should have made us television stars, and then the world might care what happens to us. But no, we are only jokers dying in the desert, and none of us will win a million dollars.'

He was not wrong, Klaus realized. By then they were passing through the camp, and Sobek was forced to slow. His truck was of the same vintage as the motorbike, but unlike the Enfield, it could not weave through traffic. Instead, the crocodile god shouted in Arabic at the people in their way. Klaus wondered if he wasn't screaming, *Gods coming through! Make way for the Gods!*

If so, no one was listening.

Klaus looked out at the people again as Sobek leaned on his horn. Aside from a few obvious jokers, most of them looked no different from the fellahin he had glimpsed working in the fields during their long trek south, or the men who had hunted them through the necropolis of Cairo. *They are all the same, all Egyptian, all poor, the ones who pray to Allah just as hungry as the ones who pray to Osiris.* 'You are so much alike,' he said to Sobek. 'Why do you fight? Why do you hate each other?'

'I do not hate Muslims,' Sobek insisted. 'My father was Muslim. My mother was Muslim. My sisters were Muslim, my friends were

Muslim, my wife was Muslim, everyone I knew was Muslim. Even I was Muslim. Not a *good* Muslim, it is true, but I always meant to make the pilgrimage to Mecca. Instead, my head began to pound one hot day as I worked a freighter, so I left the docks and went home early. My wife gave me a damp cloth to cool my fevered brow, and I went to sleep. When I woke I had the head of a crocodile.' He shrugged. 'My wife fled screaming when she saw me. She was bringing me some mint tea in my favorite cup, and it shattered on the floor and scalded me. My sisters spat on me and called me foul, my doctor said the best cure for the wild card was a gun, my father told me his son was dead. When I went to pray to Allah, the imams said I was an abomination, but Kemel – Kemel found me passed out drunk in the City of the Dead, took me to his temple, fed me on mutton and lentils, and told me that I had become a god.' He took a drag on his cigarette and blew smoke through his nostrils. 'It is better to be a god than an abomination. That is why I am no more a Muslim. But I cannot hate them, no. They are still my neighbors and my kin.'

This is so, Klaus thought, *but your neighbors and your kin, they want you dead.*

♣

It was dusk by the time they reached the Nile. Across the river, Klaus could see the lights of Luxor coming on. Over there were colorful bazaars, air-conditioned hotels, five-star cruise ships, fine restaurants, holy mosques, a modern hospital, museums full of antiquities, hot baths, and service stations with all the oil and gas a motorbike could want. Two divisions of the Egyptian Second Army had surrounded Luxor to 'protect' the city from homeless refugees and joker terrorists alike, while navy gunboats patrolled the Nile to deny them any hope of crossing. The tourist-haunted ruins of Karnak and Thebes were on the east bank as well, just north of the modern city, but those, too, had been declared off limits to the dispossessed.

Kemel, the founder of the movement to revive the Old Religion, had dreamed of restoring the ruined temples and making them seats of worship again, but the world's archaeologists and the ministry of tourism had defeated all his efforts. The ruins were too valuable as ruins; tourists were the life's blood of Egypt's economy. Denied access to the ancient sites, Kemel had instead acquired land on the west bank of the Nile, and there erected the great complex called the New Temple, three hundred acres of shrines, altars, fountains, courtyards, gardens, and statuary, with half a dozen Living Gods in permanent residence.

A heaving sea of humanity surrounded the temple walls as they approached. Most nights the priests who served the Living Gods fed whatever beggars had turned up at their gates on lentils and spiced mutton, but not on this night. The temple gates were closed and barred, the road leading to them impassable.

Cursing, Sobek swung the truck off the road and took it wide around, bumping through a cane field to the back gate. Even here the crowds were thick, and they finally had to abandon the vehicle. When the people saw Sekhmet padding toward them, her tawny skin bruised but still aglow, they parted before her like the Red Sea. Some went to their knees, while others salaamed. Klaus followed behind her, all but unnoticed. At the temple gate the guardsmen moved aside when Sobek barked at them in Arabic and snapped his teeth. They reminded Klaus of the Pope's Swiss pikemen; more ornaments than warriors, they carried tall spears and dressed as warriors of the time of Ramses the Great. No doubt the tourists loved them, but when Klaus tried to imagine them facing the soldiers he had fought today, it made an ugly picture.

Only when they were inside the temple grounds, hidden by the thick walls and velvet shadows, did the lioness halt, shimmer, and transform back into John Fortune. *He looks stronger than before*, Klaus tried to convince himself. When he spoke to Sobek in Arabic, however, he knew that it was still Sekhmet he was looking at. Sobek barked an order, and two acolytes came hurrying to help escort them to John Fortune's quarters, while two more went in search of food and water.

John's bedchamber was in the inner temple, off a corridor lined with ram-headed sphinxes where the younger priests and acolytes were quartered. Though not as large or grand as the suite that Klaus and Jonathan had shared at the Luxor in Las Vegas, the room did have a window overlooking the Nile. Klaus could see the lights of Luxor beyond the river, and the white sails of feluccas shimmering palely in the moonlight. A dozen wasps were crawling on the walls, glistening green; Jonathan was with them, watching.

'I leave him now,' said Sobek, as the acolytes were washing John and dressing him in a linen sleeping gown. 'So should you. Eat first, you will be hungry. Then go. He needs to sleep.'

It was true. The body that John shared with the woman Sekhmet had not slept since the day they had burned his mother's house down and melted her awards. Whenever John closed his eyes, Sekhmet opened them again; when she slept, he woke and took his body back. The flesh that they shared kept going night and day. It was a young body, strong and healthy, but all flesh must rest.

Now it was Sekhmet who was awake, with John asleep within. Klaus was just learning to tell the two of them apart. They spoke with the same voice, but different words. They had the same face, but not the same expressions. Sekhmet used her hands in speaking more than John Fortune ever had. *If I had spent twenty years in an amulet, moving would feel good to me as well*, Klaus reflected.

Temple servants brought them beer and bowls of lentil stew. Klaus ate it all, though he was sick of lentils. 'Sobek intends to go to Aswan,' he said, tearing at a loaf of black bread.

'Sobek is a crocodile. I am a lion.' Sekhmet had eaten only a few bites. The outlines of the scarab were plainly visible through the swollen skin of John Fortune's brow. 'With the power of Ra we might have turned them,' she said, in a weary voice, 'but we are only half of what we might have been.'

With the power of Ra, John might have turned the world to ash. Klaus kept the thought to himself. He had read enough old legends to know that it was never wise to argue with a goddess. 'The secretary-general is in Cairo. They say he helped end the fighting in Sri Lanka. If the United Nations will send help—'

'Would Germany allow United Nations peacekeepers upon its soil?' Sekhmet spoke with scorn. 'Why should the Caliph do what your German chancellor would not? The United Nations was a bad jest when I went to sleep, and now that I am woken I find it is a worse one. Even Sobek has more teeth than this UN.'

Klaus studied his friend's face. *He is John, and he is not.* 'Sekhmet, my lady – might I speak with John?'

His eyes narrowed. 'If that is your desire.' The words were curt. After a moment, though, the face before him seemed to soften. Klaus was still uncertain. 'John?'

A wan smile. 'Yes. I was dreaming.'

'A good dream?'

'Kate was in it. Curveball.' He sounded almost himself again, like the boy that Klaus had met on *American Hero*. Though John was almost two years his elder, somehow Klaus still thought of him as a younger brother, the same way he thought of Kurt and Konrad. 'I shouldn't be dreaming of her, though,' the boy went on. 'When two wild cards get together ... my mother told me of the risks as soon as I was old enough to understand. That's why she was always frightened for me whenever I did anything that might have ... whenever I did anything.'

'All mothers are fearful for their sons,' said Klaus.

'Not all of them keep a detective agency on retainer as baby-sitters, though.' John pushed a hand through his hair. 'I'm surprised Mom hasn't sent Jay Ackroyd to bring me back yet.'

'Perhaps you should go back. I did not like the way you looked today. Those bruises ...'

'They're fading.' John picked disconsolately at his bowl of lentils. 'Bullets melt when they touch our skin.'

'*Ja*,' said Klaus, 'but that is not to say they do not harm you. If you throw a rat in a canvas sack and beat on it with a club, the sack will not tear, but the rat will still be smashed. The bullets may be smashing you up inside. And if they shoot her lion with some larger round, a cannon or a rocket—'

'She'll die, and I'll die with her,' John snapped. 'You sound like my mother now. She flies, you know. That's her power. Bullets don't bounce off her the way they bounce off you. She can't shoot balls of fire or stop time or raise the dead, the way my father could.

All she can do is fly. When she was my age, she had these claws made, like big steel fingernails, and whenever there was trouble she'd slip them on to fight. She fought the Astronomer and his crazy Masons, she fought the Swarm monsters, she even came to Egypt and fought the Nur's people, with only wings and *claws*! I'm her son as much as Fortunato's. I'm not going to hide away in some monastery for fear of who I am. If I die, I die. I'm staying.'

♥

It was morning before Klaus returned to the tent he shared with Bugsy. By the time he had left John Fortune, the gates of the New Temple had been closed and barred for the night, and no amount of argument could persuade Babi and his temple guards to open them again. Klaus could have conjured up his broadsword and slashed apart the gates, just as he had once slashed apart the gates at Neuschwanstein, but he did not wish to offend John's fellow gods. Instead, he had made his apologies to Jonathan's bugs, and begged a bed for the night from the temple priests.

With his motorbike as dry as a mummy's casket, he'd had no choice but to walk back from the New Temple, shoving his way through throngs of desperate refugees intent on going in the opposite direction. The whole camp was in turmoil, and many were leaving, getting away from here as far and fast as they could. The slaughter of the jokers in the Valley of the Kings and the smoke-laced struggle in the Valley of the Queens had become common knowledge. Even Tut and Gamel had heard the tales. When Klaus came trudging up, Tut wanted to know if Lohengrin had killed them all. Gamel was more concerned about the Royal Enfield. Who would pay them now, without a motorbike to watch? 'In Aswan, I will buy another motorbike,' Klaus promised. 'A big, fast one, all shiny.'

Jonathan was blogging when Klaus entered their tent. 'The Crusader returns,' he said, without looking up from his laptop. 'The talk is you and Fortune slew the whole Egyptian army.'

'A few soldiers only. More are coming. General Yusuf—'

'—has given the gods their marching orders, I know. I'm writing about it now. It won't happen, though. Taweret will never abandon the New Temple. You can bet the farm on that.'

'I do not own a farm,' Klaus said, puzzled, 'and if the army comes, the New Temple cannot be held.'

'Course not. Which means it's time for the three of us to follow the Yellow Brick Road to Aswan. Okay, you're the Tin Woodsman and John's the not-so-Cowardly Lion, so I suppose that makes me the Scarecrow, but who's Dorothy? Hey, I've got a great name for this tremendous historical event that we've all been swept up in. Mao did the Long March, the Cherokee had a Trail of Tears, and now we've got … drum-roll, please … the *Road of Woe*!'

'The Road of Woe?' Klaus made a face.

Jonathan looked crestfallen. 'You don't like it?'

'Is stupid.'

'The Woeful Way? The Terrible Trek?'

'Is more stupid.' Klaus started shoving clothes into his pack. He had a lot of *American Hero* T-shirts. 'John says he will not go.'

'Sekhmet says John will not go, you mean. How about the Big Shlep? The Hike Through Hell? Give me a little love here, I need something memorable, something crunchy that the blogosphere will chow down on.'

'The Exodus.'

'Been done. Ten plagues, ten commandments, a golden calf. The chariot race was cool. Yul Brynner as Moses. Or was it Telly Savalas? All bald guys look alike. Charlton Heston was Pharoah, I remember that much. "So let it be written, so let it be done." Maybe Terrible Trek deserves a second look.'

'The *Second* Exodus.'

'Not bad.' Jonathan's wasps began to buzz more loudly. They did that when he got excited. 'Not great, but maybe if I tweak it … Exodus II, the Sequel. Give the knight a sausage. Hey, did you bring back any food? Anything but lentils. Bearing witness for the world is hungry work, I could use—'

The tent filled with sunlight.

Klaus threw up an arm to shield his eyes. For half a heartbeat he was blind, and when his sight came back to him there was a man standing over Jonathan Hive with a scimitar in his fist. Bugsy must have seen the menace there, because he raised his hands to protect himself. The intruder sliced them off.

Blood fountained from the sudden stumps, brighter than Klaus would ever have believed. *Red fire*, he had time to think, but even as the words were forming the red was going green. The scimitar reversed its arc and came back in a golden blur to bury itself in Jonathan's skull. '*Nein!*' Klaus cried, moving at last, too slow, too late, but instead of the meaty thunk he feared there was only a furious buzzing as the blade split apart a ball of insects and ripped through an *American Hero* shirt and a picture of King Cobalt in his wrestling mask. Wasps exploded in all directions and fled headlong from the tent, and Lohengrin summoned up his ghost steel.

The stranger turned. He was a head shorter than Lohengrin, but his arms were lean and corded, his stomach flat, his chest broad. His pants were desert camouflage, his vest Kevlar. Over it he wore a shining cloak of cloth-of-gold, fastened at his throat with interlocking green jade crescents. His skin was dark as oiled bronze, his beard red-gold. A *keffiyeh* concealed his hair. 'You are the Crusader.'

'I am Lohengrin. And you are Bahir.' The beating of his heart had slowed and steadied. 'The Sword of Allah.'

'You know of me. I am flattered.'

'I know you are a coward and a killer, a teleport who strikes down unarmed men from behind.'

'Now I am less flattered. You talk too much. Killing should be a silent business.' Bahir leapt forward.

He moved like a panther, his golden scimitar flashing. It slashed and spun and slashed again, quick as lightning. The first cut would have opened Klaus from groin to navel and the second would have taken off his head, but his armor turned both blows.

'You cannot do me harm,' Klaus said. He raised his own sword and stepped forward, putting all his weight and strength behind his swing. Bahir vanished with a soft *pop*, and Klaus went stumbling, thrown off balance. Before he could recover, the Arab was behind him, hacking at his head, once, twice, thrice. As the third cut landed, Klaus was whirling, his own blade lashing out.

Bahir leapt backwards, but not before the tip of Lohengrin's sword sliced through his kevlar vest as if it had been made of gauzy silk, leaving a long thin slash that soon turned red. 'You are quicker than you look,' the assassin said.

'*Ja.*' Klaus thrust. Bahir vanished and reappeared to his right, delivering a blow that would have taken off his sword arm at the elbow if he had not been armored. Klaus turned, and Bahir jumped again, slashed at a hamstring, and found armor there as well. Klaus swiveled. 'Stand and fight,' he boomed. 'Take off that coward's armor,' Bahir threw back.

Lohengrin chopped down with his broadsword. This time Bahir raised his scimitar in a parry. The white blade met the golden one, sheared through it like a guillotine through butter, and bit through cloth and Kevlar into the flesh of Bahir's shoulder. *A little harder and I would have his arm off.* Blood welled as Klaus slid free his sword, but his finishing stroke met only empty air.

And suddenly the tent was dimmer, as if the sun had gone behind a cloud. This time the Arab did not reappear. Some spots of blood and half a scimitar remained beside the clothing Jonathan had left behind, socks and shoes and T-shirt, cut-off blue jeans, and a pair of crusty undershorts. Klaus looked for his friend's hands, but those had disappeared as well. Could Bahir have taken them with him as a trophy? He made one last circuit of the tent to make certain the assassin was not lurking in some shadow, but found only a scorpion and a few stray wasps of Bugsy's. Finally Klaus exhaled, and let his sword and armor melt away.

It was twenty minutes before those first few wasps were joined by others, and another half hour before enough of the small green bugs had gathered for Jonathan's head to reform. His hair was plastered to his scalp with sweat and his eyes rolled back and forth, looking this way and that. When Klaus lifted the head up by the hair and set it atop the orange crate, Hive's mouth opened and shut and opened again, but no sound escaped his lips. That came later, when enough bugs had assembled to make a throat, a set of vocal cords, and lungs. 'Is he gone?' Jonathan wheezed at last. 'What happened? Did you kill him?'

'I cut him, but he fled.'

'I told you Egypt was a bad idea.' The air was thick with wasps by then, crawling over one another and thrumming noisily as green chitin turned into clammy white flesh. 'We could get killed, I said, remember?' His genitals took shape, small and shriveled. Arms and legs began to form. Thighs and calves, ankles and elbows, little pink toes with ugly yellow nails. His hands came last. To Klaus they looked no worse for having been severed, but Jonathan kept flexing his fingers and feeling his wrists, pinching and squeezing as if searching for a pulse. 'That hurt,' he said. 'That *really* hurt. Some of me died. Some bugs.'

'*Ja.*' Klaus found himself staring. 'Are those … are those your same hands? Or did you make new hands from different bugs?'

'How would I know?' Jonathan's voice grew shrill. 'New bugs, old bugs … they're *bugs*. Do you think they have assigned places, like for a fire drill? Maybe I should name them all and take attendance, so I'll know which ones are tardy.' He found his undershorts and pulled them on, one leg at a time. 'He tried to cut my head off,' he said, snatching up one sock. 'Why me? What did I ever do to him? What if he comes back?'

'He will not come back. I frightened him away when I cut his sword in half.' Klaus nudged the severed scimitar. 'See how clean and sharp the cut is? His blade is no match for mine.'

Bugsy flinched away from it. 'What if he gets another sword? What if he comes back *while we're sleeping*?' He stood on one leg and yanked his sock on. 'Where's the other sock? Did he take it? Maybe that's how he finds people, you know, like a dog. Bahir, that was Bahir, do you know how many men he's killed? He can go anywhere. There's no keeping him out. He killed a man in Paris, broad daylight, a Syrian general who'd defected to the West, he was eating a croissant on the Left Bank and suddenly this Bahir guy pops up behind him, removes his head, and takes it back to Damascus as a present for the Nur. It was in the *news*.'

'In Germany, too.' It had happened while Klaus was still at

Peenemünde. He remembered hearing Doktor Fuchs and Doktor Alpers arguing about whether such teleportation was truly instantaneous.

'I have to get back to D.C.I think I left my stove on. *Paper Lion*, that's all I wanted. No one ever tried to cut George Plimpton's head off, I would have heard about it.' Jonathan snatched up a Curveball T-shirt and pulled it down over his head, but it was one of Klaus's shirts and much too big for him – and anyway, he pulled it on backwards. HELP IS WHERE THE HEARTS ARE, declared the slogan drooping down across his spindly chest. 'Why come after me? You don't kill the press, it's in the rules. Don't they know the rules? Fortune's the one with the beetle in his head, and you're the hero with the big sword. So they come after the bug guy?'

'You blog, too. You bear witness to the world.'

'So?' Jonathan spied something. 'Oh, good, my other sock.'

'So I am thinking – maybe there is something coming that they do not want the world to witness, *ja*?'

Jonathan looked up. His eyes got very big. 'What's the German for *oh, shit*?' he said. He dropped his sock.

'Pack your things,' Klaus told him. 'We are going to the temple. John must know of this. Him, and Sekhmet.'

◆

Above, the sun blazed in the blue sky, with not a cloud in sight. Below, its twin burned bright in the still waters of the long reflecting pool that ran down the center of the hidden courtyard. Yet even with two suns, somehow the yard was cool.

In shady alcoves around its wide perimeter, the Living Gods of Egypt sat upon their thrones, listening as the argument raged on. Taweret was speaking now, the eldest of the gods resident at the New Temple, and their chief. The flesh-and-blood Taweret sat beneath a towering likeness of herself, attended by her retinue of nine dwarf priests clad in linen robes and gold collars. That flesh was gray and rubbery, her legs as thick as tree trunks, her head that of a hippopotamus, held up by a padded steel brace that kept the weight of it from snapping her neck. Jonathan had written that

Taweret looked like a fugitive from Walt Disney's *Fantasia* who had traded her pink tutu for a jeweled collar and a silken robe. Fortunately, the goddess did not read English.

'What is she saying?' Klaus asked Sobek.

'She says she is too old and fat to fight, that bricks and stones are not worth dying for.' Sobek took a pack of cigarettes out of his vest pocket, tapped one out, and lit it. 'She was here with Kemel when he built the New Temple and it has been her home for many years, but Aswan has lovely temples, too. She has spent our treasure on a cruise boat to carry us to Aswan. The *Pharaoh* docks at Luxor now, but will be here on the morrow.'

An uproar greeted that pronouncement. The child Little Isis sobbed and the grotesque four-headed Banebdjedet began to shout from all his mouths at once. Black Anubis leapt from his throne, brandishing a fist, and Red Anubis screamed at him. From the shadows at the foot of the pool came a rustle and a high-pitched ululation as Serquet edged forward into the sunlight. She had the face of a beautiful young woman atop the body of a gigantic red scorpion, and the poison that dripped from her coiled tail smoked where it struck the paving stones. Everyone began to talk at once, until Horus slapped his wings together for silence, a sudden thunderclap so loud that it set the water in the pool to rippling.

He is angry, Klaus knew. He had only to look at the god to see that. Horus began to rant at Taweret.

'What flew up his butt?' asked Jonathan Hive.

'Taweret,' answered Sobek. 'Horus says that she is a frightened old woman whose cowardice shames us all. That it took Kemel nine years to build the temple, yet Taweret will abandon it in a moment. That we must fight for what is ours.' The crocodile god took a deep drag on his cigarette. 'He is always angry, Horus. He was a pilot, a colonel in the Air Force, very famous, but now …' He exhaled a plume of foul black smoke. 'I have read how John Fortune's mother flies with – how do you say it, teke? Her wings are for steering. Horus has no teke. His wings are too big for him to fit into a cockpit, but too small to lift his weight. He cannot fly. How will he fight the army?'

Jonathan began to cough. 'Can you blow that smoke the other way?' he asked. For once, he had no wasps flitting about him.

Instead Sobek blew a smoke ring. 'I should have gone to America with Osiris,' he announced. 'I speak the English, I could be a greeter. "Hello to you, good sir, and welcome to the Luxor. Good luck with all your gambling, madam. A woman, sir? Yes, I'll send one to your room." Thoth married a showgirl. I could have done the same. I am much prettier than Thoth.' He turned to where John Fortune stood, listening in grim-faced silence. 'John, my friend, take me back with you to this other Luxor, where King Elvis rules. I wish to meet him.'

John did not reply, but Bugsy did. 'The king is dead,' he said. 'Just imposters left.'

Sobek shrugged. 'Ah, well. I am too old for showgirls.'

The wrath of Horus finally ran its course. Taweret mumbled a reply in Arabic, looking as sour as a hippopotamus can look. Then some of the other gods stepped forward to say their piece, as Sobek translated. 'Babi and the temple guard go where Taweret goes. Serquet means to stay and fight with Horus. She will summon a thousand of her small red sisters, she says. Bast says this is folly. She will go upriver on the *Pharaoh*. Min is not so sure. Unut believes we should send envoys to Cairo, to sue for peace.' He dropped the cigarette, crushed it out beneath a heel.

'My heart would stand with Horus,' Sekhmet said, in the voice of John Fortune, 'but my head knows that Taweret is right. If we had the power of Ra—'

'If we had eggs we could have bacon and eggs,' Jonathan muttered. 'If we had bacon.'

Klaus frowned. 'What does that mean?'

'It means we're fucked.'

Sobek nodded. 'Aswan is our only hope.'

'And if the army follows you to Aswan?' asked Klaus.

It was Sekhmet who answered. 'South of Aswan there is only Abu Simbel, and Abu Simbel is not large enough to support a tenth our numbers. If they will not let us be in Aswan, then the Nile must run red with blood.'

'I saw that movie,' said Jonathan Hive. 'Skip the blood, it doesn't work. Go straight to the death of the firstborn, maybe you'll get their attention.'

So let it be written, thought Klaus, *so let it be done.* He had seen that movie too.

♠

Nightfall found the three of them in John Fortune's rooms, overlooking the Nile. Jonathan was on his laptop once again, checking flight times out of Egypt. 'Fuck,' he kept saying, 'I am so dead. Aswan is the closest airport that's still open, would you believe it? And all the flights connect through *Cairo*!'

'Perhaps God does not wish for you to go,' said Klaus. 'If you leave us, who will bear witness for the world?'

'Wolf Blitzer. Katie Couric. Jon Stewart. Geraldo Rivera. Okay, maybe not Geraldo, he couldn't bear witness to his dick if he found it in Al Capone's vault.' The laptop gave a cheerful beep. Jonathan punched a key, read the screen, scowled. 'Oh, look, another girl who wants to have John Fortune's baby. This one's pretty cute, at least. Why do I even bother with e-mail? All I get is spam, and girls sending naked pictures to the two of you. What am I, your pimp? No offense to your father, John. How come none of these girls ever send *me* naked pictures?'

'You turn into bugs,' said John Fortune.

'*Ja*,' said Klaus. 'And you are very small, where women want men to be large.'

'That's cold,' said Jonathan, stung. 'I'll have you know that I'm perfectly normal, Nancy Heffermann told me so in junior high. Anyway, size doesn't matter. I could show you sites—'

'I was speaking of your heart.' Klaus thumped his chest with a closed fist. 'Here.'

'Leave him be,' said John Fortune. To Jonathan he said, 'The *Pharaoh* will take you to Aswan. From there you can a charter a plane to Addis Ababa or Nairobi, and connect to a flight back to Europe. Take my Amex card, I won't be needing it.'

'The *black* card? That's ... dude, I don't know what to say.'

Klaus could not listen to any more. He turned for the door. 'Lohengrin, wait,' he heard John say, but he was weary of waiting, tired of talk. Just now, he wanted quiet.

He found it in the maze that was the New Temple, wandering through moonlit gardens and down long marble corridors. Red lamps glowed along the walls, mimicking the light of torches. Temple guards and acolytes watched him pass in silence, and once he turned a corner and came upon Anubis, attended by half a dozen lithe young priestesses. The light was too dim for Klaus to say whether it was Red Anubis or Black Anubis, but from the way the jackal-headed god stared at him it was plain he was not wanted, so he made an awkward bow and backed away.

Finally he found himself in a cavernous hall beneath a towering sphinx. She had a lion's body and a woman's face, which reminded him of Sekhmet, but she had the wings of an eagle, too, and ram's horns coiling from her temples. She was some god, he was certain, though Klaus did not know her name. He wondered if his own god would hear, if he said a prayer to this one. His family was Lutheran, though he had never been especially devout. Church was for Christmas and for Easter. 'Father,' he said, in a soft voice, 'hear me now. We are lost.'

A pair of slender arms encircled him, and two soft hands covered his eyes. 'And found,' a voice whispered by his ear.

Klaus knew that touch, that spicy-sweet scent, that voice. '*Lili*?' he gasped, incredulous. 'Can it be you?'

'*Underneath the lantern by the barrack gate, darling I remember the way you used to wait,*' she sang. '*My Lili of the lamplight, my own Lili Marlene.*' The lyrics he had taught her. Her voice echoed in the hall, low, smoky, intoxicating.

Klaus ripped her hands away, whirled, and took her in his arms. When he kissed her, her own mouth answered him, no less hungry. The dark red lipstick that she wore looked black in the gloom of the hall, but her eyes shone silver pale. Klaus kissed her on each eyelid and then again upon the mouth, picked her up bodily, whirled her in the air. Breathless with laughter, she demanded that he put her down, and Klaus obeyed. 'You are here,' he said. 'You are truly here, in Egypt. But ... but how?'

A half-smile brushed her lips, full of mischief. 'Ask me no questions and I'll tell you no lies.'

'No. Truly. Lili, what could you be doing here?'

Her face turned serious. 'I could ask the same of you.'

That confused him. 'I came for John.'

'And I came for you.'

That made him happy. 'I have dreamed of you. But how could you know where I was?'

'The whole world knows where you are, my gallant knight. Every time your friend Hive uploads a new instalment of his blog, a million people read about your latest exploits.'

'A million?' Klaus had no idea. 'So many?'

'This week. By next week it will be ten million, if Hive is still alive. No one likes to find bugs crawling through their dirty laundry, least of all a caliph.'

'The Caliph will be pleased, then. Jonathan is going home.'

'Is he? Clever lad. He'll live to blog again. You should go with him, Klaus. And take your friend John Fortune.'

'John will not leave. The Living Gods are his people.'

'*Sekhmet*'s people, you mean.' She took his hand. 'Klaus, you are being used. The Living Gods are no more gods than the characters at Disney World. We've known for half a century that the wild card has a psychological component, so it is hardly surprising that here in the shadow of the pyramids some of those afflicted should mimic the forms of Isis, Osiris, and the rest, but to suggest that they *are* those gods ... Kemel, the man who started this cult, belongs up there with Joseph Smith and L. Ron Hubbard. Take a closer look at your new friends, love. They are very good at accepting offerings, you'll find, but not quite so apt when it comes to answering prayers.'

This was a side of Lili that Klaus had not seen in America. There it had been all wine and kisses and laughter, and secrets whispered in the dark. Now she was confusing him. He was good at fighting with a sword, but not so good with words. 'They are jokers, *ja*, I know, but the Muslims mean to kill them all—'

'*Abdul-Alim* means to kill them all, yes. He is desperate to prove himself a strong man and end the whispers that say he is a weakling and a fool. Do not paint all Muslims with the bloody brush. The situation is more complex than that. The Nur was the most charismatic leader Islam has produced since Baybars, yet it took him twenty years to unite all of Arabia and restore the caliphate. Abdul the Idiot will destroy it all in twenty months. When he falls, the rule will pass to Siraj of Transjordan, who is a moderate, a secularist, and a pragmatist. Prince Siraj is a good man. Under him, the Arabs will have peace and prosperity, the West will get its oil, and the Living Gods and their poor deluded worshippers will be left to live in peace.'

'Those that are not dead,' said Klaus.

'Those that are not dead,' she agreed. 'First Abdul-Alim must fall, however. And your presence here has only served to prop him up. Nothing unites a quarrelsome people faster than a threat from outside. Do you know what they are calling you on Al Jazeera? *The Crusader.*'

'The crusaders were brave men,' Klaus said stoutly.

'I do not have time to argue Bohemond of Antioch with you, my sweet. Just take my word, "crusader" is not a term of endearment in this part of the world. All you are doing is giving Abdul the visible enemy that he needs to stay in power. And now that Bahir has failed him, he means to send the Righteous Djinn against you.'

Klaus crossed his arms against his chest. 'I defeated Bahir. I can defeat this djinn as well. I do not fear any foe.'

'Fear this one. Eighteen months ago, the Israeli ace Sharon Cream went missing. The strongest woman in the world, they say, yet when the Mossad found her body, it was gray and shriveled, like a fly after the spider has sucked the juice out of it. Her flesh turned to dust when they opened her for an autopsy.

'The Djinn's first public appearance came a few weeks later. He lifted up an armored car and threw it forty feet. That was enough to earn him a place in the Caliph's guard, but not enough to excite much interest in the West. Strongmen are a dinar a dozen, and the Nur had other aces in his service.

'He also had General Sayyid, the crippled giant, his right hand and closest friend. Even in his youth Sayyid had struggled to support his own weight, and twenty years ago an American ace shattered both his legs to pieces. He never walked again. No one was surprised when Sayyid finally passed away. The Nur gave him a lavish state funeral in Damascus, but his casket was kept sealed and he never lay in state. Among the mourners was the Righteous Djinn, grown to gigantic size. He stood thirty feet tall … and he had the strength to support that weight.

'Since then, several of the Port Said aces have vanished under mysterious circumstances, the heroes who turned back the Israeli armies during the wars of 1948. Old now, and sickly, but still … Kopf is one who is missing. In 1948 an entire Israeli army broke and ran from him, seized by a terror no one could explain. And now we hear reports that two of the Caliph's brothers died of fear after a visit from the Djinn.

'You are seeing the pattern here, I hope. Your power is formidable, but you would do well to stay away from the Righteous Djinn, unless you mean to armor him in ghost steel.'

Klaus stared at her. 'How could you know all this?'

'I had my own encounter with the Righteous Djinn. After that … let us say I took an interest in him. Never go to battle blind, *mein Ritter*. It pays to do your homework.' She slipped her arms through his and laid her head against his chest. 'Come away with me, Klaus. I know a lovely castle on the Rhine. A roaring fire, a canopy bed, and me. What more could you desire?'

'Nothing,' said Klaus. 'When this is done.'

'Now. This moment. Kiss me, and I'll take you there.'

He wanted her as badly as he had ever wanted a woman. Yet, instead of taking her in his arms, Klaus stepped away from her and said, 'Take me … how could you take me there?'

The half-smile returned, teasing. 'I have my ways.'

Suddenly he understood. 'You are an ace.'

'I abhor that word. So crass, so common, so *American*. I prefer to call myself a *woman of mystery*, thank you very much.'

The world shifted under his feet. *Lili of the lamplight*, he thought, *our beautiful chance meeting, the night we spent making love and talking*. All of it suddenly seemed unreal. He could feel it dissolving, melting away like his ghost steel after a battle. *An ace, and here in Egypt*. 'What powers?'

'That would be telling. A gentleman *never* asks a lady her age, her weight, or whether she can fly. There are some who call me the Queen of the Night. Do you know your Mozart, love? *The Magic Flute*? No, you are more of a Wagner man, I think. *The Ride of the Valkyries, ja*? Let me be your valkyrie. I can promise you a ride that you will never forget.'

Klaus had wanted more than a ride. Klaus had wanted all of it, all of her. Now he was not sure. 'When this is done – that will be the time for us. Not now. It is like our song, like *Lili Marlene*. He wants to be with her, the soldier, she is all he thinks about, but he must go to war, he must do his duty. His honor demands it. It is the same for me.'

'You're wrong. This is not your country. This is not your fight. Go home, Lohengrin. You won't find your grail in Egypt. Only your grave.' Lili stepped away from him. 'I see I am wasting my breath. It is written on that stubborn German face of yours. *Auf Wiedersehen*, Klaus. I wish you well, truly … though, if I were you, I would start sleeping in my ghost steel. The next time Bahir comes for you, he may be in earnest.'

'Wait,' Klaus called out. 'How can I reach you? Where do you live? Your name – is your name even Lili?'

'Close enough, darling. Try *Lilith*.' And she slipped into the shadows and was gone.

♣

The noisy, crowded, festering camp that had sprung up around the Colossi of Memnon had blown away in less than three days. Only trash and night soil remained to show where thousands had lived, loved, and starved for weeks on end. Klaus would not have been surprised to see the colossi themselves rise from their ruined thrones and stride off toward the south.

"'*Look on my works, ye mighty, and despair,*'" said Jonathan, as the two of them paused for a last look. 'Lord Byron, man. I think he wrote it about these two guys. Bad boy Byron. He was like the Drummer Boy of the romantic poets.'

The *Pharaoh* had departed two days ago, carrying Taweret, most of the other gods, and almost all the priests. She was a large and luxurious boat, rated at five stars by the ministry of tourism, so the Living Gods had found room on her to take abroad five hundred of their followers. They would have taken Jonathan as well, but he did not turn up to board. 'I overslept,' Hive kept insisting. 'What, am I the first guy who ever missed a boat?' He blamed his cell phone. 'Fucking alarm never went off. If I get killed, someone needs to sue Sprint.'

Yesterday Sobek had departed, accompanied by Red Anubis, Min, Unut, Thoth, and several others. The crocodile god had managed to piece together a convoy of seventeen large vehicles: moving vans, semis, school buses, cattle trucks, flatbeds, dump-trucks, and the like. Somehow he'd struck a deal with General Yusuf and obtained petrol enough to get them down to Aswan, two hundred kilometers to the south. Then he crammed them full with children, as many as each vehicle could carry. In some cases he had to tear them from a mother's arms, but most parents were eager to find their sons and daughters a place on one of Sobek's trucks.

Gamel and Tut were among the last to climb aboard. 'We stay with Lohengrin,' Gamel insisted. 'Watch motorbike. One euro.' Klaus slammed the gate shut on his protests, and slapped the truck to send it off. The smaller children were weeping when the convoy finally began to roll. Jonathan took pictures of their tear-streaked faces with his cell phone.

The congestion was horrendous, both lanes thick with old cars, bikes, motor scooters, rusted vans and panel trucks, even taxicabs. Some drove along the shoulders, while others straddled the center line, advancing with fits and starts, bumping people out of the way. Abandoned vehicles sat rusting on both sides of the road, a few squarely in the middle. The ones that had not been abandoned quite yet were all honking angrily at the tangle of foot traffic, like a flock of huge steel geese. Klaus had become convinced that every car in Egypt had its horn wired to its brake pedal, so any stop or slowdown produced a blast of noise.

They saw four women and a boy trying to pull a horse wagon of the sort his father used to carry tourists up the mountain. Jonathan took a picture with his cell phone. They saw a mother with three infants on her back, and a man with a wrinkled old woman slung across his shoulders. Jonathan snapped them both. They even saw a thin young girl pushing a wire grocery cart as tall as she was. Inside it was a squalling infant with a missing leg, on a bed of rags. 'A poignant image of displacement,' said Jonathan, as he took the picture. Hundreds clutched backpacks, suitcases, and bundles, and all of them were shoving, stumbling into one another in their haste to get away. Some appeared to be near the point of collapse. Klaus had seldom felt so angry or so helpless as he did watching the human river flow past him. He wondered how many would live long enough to see Lake Nasser.

'It's time.' John Fortune was mounted on a l ong-necked Arabian mare, a lean red horse bred for the desert sands.

Klaus mounted up beside him on an Arab mare as black as the Egyptian night, while Jonathan climbed gingerly onto an old dun-colored gelding. Hive had his legs today, but under his *keffiyeh* both his ears were missing, along with his pinkies, ring fingers, and two toes off each foot. Klaus had not inquired about his genitals, although it struck him that Jonathan had sent out more wasps than could be accounted for with just some toes and fingers.

The horses were a parting gift from Sobek. 'They will not run out of gasoline, at least,' the crocodile god had told them. John Fortune turned out to be a skilled rider. He'd gotten a pony for his seventh birthday, he told Klaus, and had taken riding lessons all through his teenage years. 'Never rode without a helmet, though. Mom was afraid that if I fell it would trigger my wild card and turn me into a bowling ball with tentacles.'

Or a fire-breathing lion. Klaus was good with horses too, though these spirited Arabians were more temperamental than his father's huge German plow pullers.

Sobek had seen to their clothing, too, providing them with Bedouin garb better suited to the red lands than denim cutoffs and *American Hero* T-shirts. 'Hey, cool, *Lawrence of Arabia*,' Jonathan had enthused when the three of them donned their Arab clothing for the first time. In his blog he wrote that John Fortune made a good Omar Sharif and Lohengrin could pass for Peter O'Toole on steroids, but 'Anthony Quinn I'm not, though I did like him in that Zorro the Greek flick.'

The whole world was moving south, but the three of them rode north. Jonathan's wasps had seen detachments from the Egyptian Third Army moving rapidly down the Nile. They had guns and tanks and planes, just as Sobek had foreseen. Wherever they encountered jokers they shot them out of hand. With them came the jackals of Ikhlas al-Din, flying the flag of the caliphate.

'We cannot hope to win this fight,' John Fortune told them, when they stopped for a drink of cool water late that afternoon. 'There are too many of them, and only three of us. All we can hope to do is confuse them, delay them, and buy some time for our own people. We need to dart in, sting them, then turn and fly away to sting again somewhere else, like Jonathan's wasps.'

'*Ja*,' said Klaus. 'Sting and run. I understand.'

'Righto,' said Jonathan. 'But you know, sometimes when you sting someone they swat at you. Just thought I'd mention that. Sometimes all the wasps don't make it back.'

John Fortune nodded thoughtfully. 'Jonathan, it was brave of you to stay, but—'

'I overslept,' said Bugsy. 'That's all it was. I missed the bloody boat, so what the hell. Missus Hive's little bug is in. Fucker tried to cut my *head* off!' He scratched under his *keffiyeh*. 'I'm thinking tanks. If I can find some way to get *inside*, twenty, thirty wasps could really mess up a crew. Sting their hands, their arms, their faces. Crawl inside their pants and sting their dicks. I'll lose some bugs, but there's more where they came from. You think if I fly down that big cannon on the turret, I'd pop out inside the mother-fucker, or what?'

'Try it. Let us know.' John smiled. 'Too bad Rustbelt isn't with us. He's the guy you really want for tanks.'

As the sun was sinking in the west, Jonathan reported that the advance units of the Third Army had left the river. 'Where the road makes its big loop, they're cutting straight across the desert. Armored cars, tanks, infantry. Apaches, too. Fuck it, I hate heli-copers. The backwash blows my bugs to hell and gone.'

The three of them undressed in silence, and stowed their Bedouin garb in their saddle rolls. Klaus stripped down to shorts, T-shirt, and sandals. John and Jonathan got naked. By then they could see the dust of the advancing column with their own eyes. 'This is really stupid,' said Hive. 'Did I mention that? Fucking cell phone.' Then he vanished, and in his place a venomous green cloud uncoiled in the air like some huge, smoky python. John was gone as well. The horses whickered in fear when the lioness appeared, but she did not linger long. Across the sands she ran, bounding toward the foe. The swarm followed.

Klaus was the last. Against the red of the setting sun, the white of his ghost steel shone as pure as hope. On his left arm a shield appeared, in his right hand a gleaming sword. Before the light was gone, he meant to carve up half a dozen tanks.

'*Deus Volt*,' Lohengrin cried, as he strode into the red lands, following the lioness and the wasps. He was no hollow hero. None of them were hollow heroes. And this night, if God willed it, they would teach the foe that the shortcut was a mistake.

♥

Jonathan Hive

Real People, Really Dying Posted Today 11:42 pm
GENOCIDE, EGYPT | FREAKED | 'OCCASIONAL GUNFIRE'
– THE EGYPTIAN ARMY

Good news, faithful reader. I'm not dead yet.

Okay, that was it. Good news now officially over.

I've seen some of the comments in the last few posts suggesting I might not be the least racist person you know. Let me take a moment to make something clear. I think there's a lot of really great Muslim folks out there. Lots of them. There's a guy here with the head of a crocodile who was pretty devout for a long time. He's a nice fella. Cat Stevens? Love him. Rumi? That guy's poetry got me laid in college, and I shall be grateful forever.

Okay, I suck. I don't know any Muslims, okay? I didn't know any Egyptians before I came here. But it's not because I've got anything against them. Allah doesn't seem any weirder to me than the version of Jesus that the Pentecostals are all fired up about. I don't cross the street anytime I see a woman in a head scarf. I've never secretly toilet-papered a mosque. I'm a fucking liberal, okay? We love everyone but Newt Gingrich.

There's only one kind of Muslim I really fucking hate – the kind that's trying to kill me. And if they converted on the battlefield, became Episcopalians? I'd still fucking hate 'em.

The New Temple in Karnak fell a week ago. We put it off as long as we could, me and Fortune and Lohengrin. We even stopped the armored division for a while. We had some help at the end from a local ace who could summon up scorpions. Battle of the Bugs, we called it.

She's dead now.

They came in force. I don't know how many. Hundreds, thousands. The Living Gods who'd stayed behind to defend their homes and their temple were slaughtered. Lohengrin would probably have died there, too, given the chance. A lot of people went when they lit the New Temple itself on fire. His armor is pretty kick-ass, but I don't see it stopping him from crisping up. The way *they* did.

Horus. Nice guy. Wings, but can't fly. In New York, he'd be just another schulb in Jokertown looking for work. In Egypt, he was a god. And now he's dead. One of the last things I saw there before I pulled the last of my wasps in was his body being paraded around on a stick. Lohengrin still thinks we should have stayed. Fortune says it was better to move on. To live long enough to protect the people we still can.

I'm not sure anymore who those are supposed to be. We're on the road south to Aswan. The local folks are under the impression we might be safe there, but every day that hope looks more and more like a pipe dream. The attacks are coming daily now. Not full-on, we're-taking-you-out *Götterdämmerung*, but skirmishes. At a guess, we lost about a hundred people yesterday. We'll lose that many more today. And the day after that. And the day after that.

Think I'm making this up? Bug boy sounding a little histrionic? Well, I've still got my cell phone, and it's still good for shooting video. It took all night to upload this – a 28.8 line from an abandoned trading post or convenience store or whatever that was – and now you can watch it *here* and *here*. Make your kids leave the room first. Seriously. Do it now.

These are real people, folks. Children, dads, moms,

husbands, wives. They're the wrong shape, they think the wrong things, and they're really dying. Some of them have guns. A few of them are aces. Lohengrin is doing what he can. Fortune and his new girlfriend Sekhmet are doing what they can. I help out. But we're up against tanks and helicopters and guys who know how to use AK-47s. We're fucking amateurs here.

And here's the other thing. Schistosomiasis. Ever heard of it? The Nile is so polluted, it's become a breeding ground for something called *bilharzia*. I looked it up on-line. Liver flukes, or something. The upshot is, if you drink this water it will kill you, just not right away. Explain to an eight-year-old who's burning from thirst that she can't have a drink. The part where you tell her it'll kill her really doesn't have the same oomph you'd expect when she's just watched her brothers get shot. Funny how that works.

We're low on food. We're low on water. I can count the number of Westerners here trying to help out on one hand when I'm missing two fingers. And when you turn on your TV sets, are you seeing this? Are you thinking about it when you order your delivery pizza? Honest to God, people, are the things going on here really less important than the latest challenge on *American Hero?*

Fuck.

I gotta go. They're coming.

◆

Back now. It's about eight hours later. I forgot to hit the post button, so let me give you a little update. The army flew a helicopter over a bunch of refugees who were walking south at about three this afternoon, when I was writing that last part. The alleged human beings up in the copter dropped a couple dozen grenades on them and strafed the survivors when they ran. We lost twenty. Another ten will probably be dead by morning, and about that many are going to be too injured to travel. Which means leaving them here. Which is pretty much the same thing as dead.

It's still maybe a week before the first of us reach Aswan. Maybe another two days before the stragglers get in. Everyone's looking to it like it's the Promised Land or Oz or something. Me, I keep getting the feeling that the army's herding us there. There was about twenty minutes when I was sure they were going to wait until we were all on Sehel Island and then blow the High Dam and kill us all. Fortune or maybe Sekhmet pointed out that blowing the Aswan High Dam would also kill everyone else in the country and wash Cairo into the sea, so I might be getting a little paranoid.

Any way you cut it though, we're in trouble here. I need to sleep. I'm afraid to sleep.

If anyone out there knows someone in the Egyptian army or if you're one of the folks in Ikhlas al-Din, listen for a minute, okay? This is the part where I beg.

I know someone killed the Caliph, and I know that's a very big, very bad thing. I know that someone attacked you, and you're pissed. But please – *please* – stop this. Because I'm here on the road with the people you're killing. I've talked to them. I've eaten with them. And here's the thing. Killing the Caliph?

They didn't do it.

2934 COMMENTS | POST COMMENT

♠

THE TIN MAN'S LAMENT

Ian Tregillis

... They didn't do it.

What's worse than being hated for what people think *you did?*

Wally Gunderson, aka Rustbelt, aka Toolbelt, aka You Stupid Tool, aka Hey You, aka Racist, sat in the darkness of his bedroom in the Discard Pile, scrolling through Bugsy's blog. It chronicled cruel people doing senseless things to others. Harmless and undeserving others who hadn't said or done anything wrong.

The monitor cast a sickly hue across his cast-iron skin, tinting the midnight blue-black with green, like he was a nat mottled with half-healed bruises. It fit the ooky feelings that he'd carried in his gut since he got kicked off *American Hero*. Sadness. Confusion. Shame. Anger.

The blog didn't help matters any. As confusing as this Egypt thing was – Wally didn't really understand the details – it was depressing, too. Innocent people were dying for no good reason; he got that much.

But reading still beat venturing outside. The place was awful crowded; all but five of the *American Hero* contestants had joined the Discard Pile. (Twenty-three aces. Four bathrooms.) Of those not living in the overcrowded mansion, two had up and left the show: Bugsy was in Egypt, and Drummer Boy had decided he'd rather be a rock star than a discard. The other three – Curveball,

Rosa Loteria, and, of course, Stuntman – were still competing.

Oomp-thump-oomp-thump ... Somebody cranked up the bass downstairs. Tonight, the others were holding a knockdown, drag-out party to welcome the arrival of Dragon Girl, Jade Blossom, and the Candle, whose team had been eliminated in the most recent challenge.

Wally didn't much care for Joker Plague. Not because of Drummer Boy himself (although he wasn't all that swell) but because their music was so angry. He would have used headphones to drown out the noise, but he'd never found a pair that fit around the massive hinge joints on his steam shovel jaw. Not that he had anything to listen to. His Frankie Yankovic CDs had disappeared when the others sent Joe Twitch to his room to complain about the polka music.

The scent of grilled meat drifted through the open window. When Wally's stomach gurgled, it sounded like somebody squishing up water balloons inside a soup kettle. Earlier that evening the Maharajah's invisible servants had fired up the grill and laid out one heck of a spread on the long, cantilevered deck suspended over the pool and patio. Wally scooted off to his room as soon as he realized the others were preparing for a party. That had been hours ago.

A splash, followed by peals of laughter and a brief rainstorm. Holy Roller must have joined Diver in the pool.

He tried to put food out of his mind and opened a bookmark for the network's *American Hero* website. Wally had stopped watching the show. At first, he'd tried to watch the dailies in the TV room with the other discards, but he might as well have been ice fishing, it got so cold down there. Even Holy Roller, who seemed like a nice enough guy, had taken to saying things like, 'As you have done unto the least of my brethren,' every time he saw Wally. So Wally stuck to himself and got his information about the show off the web.

Huh. The new arrivals had been close to winning the latest challenge until Rosa got a good draw from that magic picture card deck of hers. They had a picture of the winning card on the website. It was called '*El Tragafuegos*' – whatever that meant – and it showed a fellow with fire coming out of his mouth. Wally didn't know what to make of this, except that it had cleared the way for the final three contestants, Curveball, Rosa, and Stuntman. *Mighta been me up there, but for what he said I said.*

It didn't matter. Curveball was a shoo-in. Lots of people said as much, too. They said tons of stuff on the message boards. Stuff like:

Why is Rustbelt with the other discards at all? I can't believe they're still letting him participate after—

CLICK.

Stuntman might be an arrogant jerk, but Rustbelt is a racist, plain and simple, and—

CLICK.

Rustbelt-Redneck hick.

CLICK.

The New Face of Racism. This one was just the one line, followed by an image of Wally's publicity head shot from the *American Hero* press package Photoshopped onto the cover of *Time* magazine.

CLICK.

The next one started out: *You go, Toolbelt! You got friends out here. ...* Finally. Friends were friends, even if they didn't always get the name right. Drummer Boy had a knack for giving people catchy nicknames. Wally kept reading: *... you done nothing wrong but put that spear-chukkin' jungle bunny in his place—*

CLICK.

What's worse than being loved by hateful people?

Tiffani's throaty laugh came through a lull in the music, just as Wally took a long pull on his glass of pop. Something about the Candle trying to light Toad Man's gas. It startled him. The glass shattered in Wally's fist, dousing his face and hands with sugar water.

'Cripes!'

He'd have to scrub his face before going to bed, otherwise he'd break out in new rust spots by morning. This time he'd try to remember to clean the bathroom sink afterward. Nobody got mad at Pop Tart for leaving her makeup stuff all over the bathroom, but they sure got sore when he left his used SOS pads on the sink.

A guy would think they'd never scrubbed a pot before.

He'd been a pimply kid before his card had turned. Turns out you can have bad skin even when that skin is living iron.

Hunger got the better of him. *I wonder if they got any of them Rice Krispies bars downstairs?* Maybe he could just slip out long enough to fill up a plate.

K-chank! K-chank! K-chank! K-chank!

It's hard to tiptoe when you're three hundred fifty pounds and wrapped in inch-thick iron. But Wally was getting better at it, skulking around the Discard Pile.

Chank. Chank. Chank. Chank.

A little better.

Wally paused at the bottom of the stairs for a deep breath before wading into the fray. It's hard to slip through a crowd unnoticed when your elbows can crack ribs.

'Look at me, I'm big and important!' said Mr. Berman. Jade Blossom, Matryoshka, and a few of the others stood around him, laughing. He waved his arms over his head. 'I'm a rich Hollywood weasel! I'm—' Something crunched when Wally tried to sidle past the group. The television executive howled in pain as he dissolved into a pale-faced Andrew Yamauchi. '*Aaah*! My tail!'

'What?'

'My tail! Get off my tail!'

'Sorry, sorry, I'm sorry.' Wally jumped back. Wild Fox swished his tail around and delicately inspected the tip. The last few inches, where the coppery fur blended into smoky gray, had been flattened. It also had a new kink.

'My tail …'

Wally spun around to get out of there, only to bowl over Spasm, causing him to splash his drink on Pop Tart.

'Damn it, you stupid tool. I was going to swi – talk wardrobe into letting me keep this top, too.'

He tried to apologize, but he couldn't form the words around a very violent sneezing fit that nearly knocked his eyes out of his head. Wally bashed a hole in the wall as he stumbled blindly away, trailing apologies as he went.

'Clumsy oaf! Go crush some rocks or something.'

'Did you hear about his audition?'

'No.'

'Oh, man. It was classic.'

Wally pushed his way toward the kitchen.

Somebody *had* made a pan of Rice Krispies bars. Now, how about that? Wally got the last one, too, until Blrr came zipping past and snatched it from his hand. He found some brownies, but Joe Twitch got those, too. They were having some kind of competition, she and him. *For crying out loud*!

Most of the good stuff was gone, but he managed to fill a plate. He didn't feel up to braving the crowd again on the way back upstairs. Instead, he slipped into the library. Nobody ever went in there, not even for a party. Wally didn't, either. He wasn't much of a reader.

Seated in a leather recliner with a paper plate perched on one massive knee, Wally took his first good look at the library. The first thing he noticed was that the books lining the shelves along every wall weren't actually books. They were cheap cardboard facades with the spines of books painted on them. Up close, there was no mistaking them for the real thing. Maybe they looked real on TV.

He did find one real book, a dictionary at the end of one shelf. Fanning through the yellowed pages released a cloud of dust and the mustiness peculiar to books.

They didn't do it.

The entry on Egypt was short. 'A country in northeast Africa, bordering the Mediterranean and Red seas and containing the Nile Delta. Capital: Cairo.'

Not exactly what Wally wanted. Then again, he wasn't sure what he wanted. Thinking about those people in Bugsy's blog felt like an itch he couldn't scratch.

It was a long time before the party quieted down enough to let a guy sleep.

He woke around dawn to the loudest sound he'd ever heard. It was like a couple of freight trains, loaded up good and heavy with taconite ore, colliding head-on in the middle of the room. Over and over and over again. It shook the house so badly that he almost tumbled out of bed. Instead, the bed just collapsed underneath him.

A *whump*, and then from the floor, Hardhat yelled: 'Ouch! God-fucking-damnit!'

Back home in Minnesota, summer thunderstorms were nothing special. But this was different. First off, thunder was never this loud. Plus, there wasn't any lightning. The house just kept shaking, shaking, shaking. And for another thing, a bad storm came with clouds so thick they turned the sky to ink. But he glimpsed sunrise peeking over the Hollywood Hills as the blinds danced and shuddered over the window. Something dusted his face when he opened his mouth to ask Hardhat about this. He tasted grittiness on his tongue. Plaster, raining down from the ceiling. Boy howdy, was this weird!

Tornados could be pretty loud. Maybe they were inside one, and the whole house was whirling away like in that scary movie with the flying monkeys?

'Um,' Wally had to shout over the rumbling, 'strange weather we're having.'

'Weather? It's a big, motherfucking' – just then it stopped – 'earthquake.'

And then it was quiet again, at least compared to the sound of the house shaking apart. New sounds floated through the near silence. Creaking, as the house settled, punctuated with sudden cracks like gunshots. And a little fainter, but still nearby, moans and groans.

The floor shifted a little bit each time a new gunshot crack ripped through the house. More plaster sifted down, getting in Wally's eyes. He rolled off the mattress and climbed to his feet. The blinds came clattering down in a tangled heap around his feet when he pulled the cord to raise them. The glass in the window was cracked, but it hadn't shattered. Outside, plumes of smoke and dust threaded the hills and canyons, lofted skyward on the beeping of car alarms and the barking of terrified dogs.

Hardhat joined him at the window. 'Jesus, Mary, Joseph, and camel. What a clusterfuck.'

The floor shifted again.

Hardhat rattled the doorknob. 'Door's stuck. Piece of shit.'

Wally tried the door. Yep. It was wedged in the door frame good. 'Some folks might wanna stand back.' Wally gave the stubborn door a good yank. The doorknob snapped off in his hand, but otherwise the door didn't move.

Hardhat laughed. 'Smooth move.'

Wally stuck two fingers through the hole where the doorknob had been, braced his feet on the floor, and *pulled*. The door screeched open a few inches, gouging the floor, then cracked in half when it got stuck again. Wally gave up and smashed the two halves of the door into the hallway.

Apparently they weren't the only ones having trouble. People pounded on doors up and down the hallway. Wally worked one side of the hall, shoving the doors open. Hardhat worked the other side, prying them open with a glowing yellow I beam that he wielded like a crowbar.

Halfway up the hall they met up with King Cobalt. He seemed to be enjoying himself as he ripped the door frames apart with brute strength. Even tossed out of bed early in the morning, he still wore his *Lucha Libre* mask. Wally wondered if he ever took it off.

'I guess we work pretty good together, hey?'

King Cobalt shrugged. 'Doesn't matter to me. I like smashing stuff.' His tone suggested that this was the end of the conversation. Maybe he was black underneath that costume, like Stuntman.

I'm darker than all of them, though.

One by one, people assembled in the big TV lounge on the first floor. The bamboo floor had buckled and warped, and a couple of ihumb-thick cracks in the walls ran from floor to ceiling. The flat screen TV had jumped its mounts on the wall, and was lying facedown on the floor.

Matryoshka took a head count while two of the camera guys went off to disconnect the gas and turn off the water. He came up short until Earth Witch stumbled through the front door. Wally noticed a pile of bricks strewn across the U-shaped drive. Apparently the chimney had collapsed. And from the trickle of blood on Earth Witch's forehead, she'd been out there when it came down. Sweat streaked her face. People cleared a spot for her on a sofa. When she plopped down, Wally saw dirt on the soles of her feet, the palms of her hands, and crusted under her fingernails.

Jade Blossom said, 'Well?'

'This quake was strong and very deep,' Earth Witch said, 'and it caught me by surprise. I was sleeping.' She looked around the room. 'I couldn't stop it, but I did my best to weaken it. I might be able to damp down the aftershocks a little bit.' Earth Witch said this last with her eyes closed, like she was ready to take a nap.

Just then another gunshot crack echoed through the house, making the walls shake. The cracks in the walls widened a little bit, as more plaster sifted down to the floorboards.

Wally jumped.

Bubbles went off in search of bandages and hydrogen peroxide. In addition to Earth Witch, a number of people had bumps, bruises, and cuts.

The others took stock of the damage. If it hadn't been for the cracks in the walls, it might have been difficult to distinguish between earthquake damage and the aftereffects of a major party. As the Maharajah's servants swept up the sizeable pile of glass where the sliding doors to the patio had stood, Diver went outside to check on the pool.

She returned a few seconds later. 'Well, this sucks. The pool is completely empty.'

Wally and a half-dozen others filed outside to see for themselves. The pool technically wasn't empty, because the gas grill had rolled off the upper deck and crashed into the deep end. But it was empty of water. A wide crack had opened along the bottom of the pool, pulling the tiles apart like a long, snaggletoothed grin.

'I think the grill is broken,' said Wally.

Another crack echoed up and down the canyon. It sounded louder out here than it had inside.

'Holy shit.' As one, they looked at Hardhat, then followed his gaze overhead to the long, cantilevered deck, then to the wall where it adjoined the mansion.

And then, also as one, they stepped all the way back to the railing at the canyon edge.

The immense deck wasn't level any longer. Now it sagged, with the far end tilting down over the canyon. It dropped another inch while they watched. The first and second floors of the mansion were cracking apart. And they didn't line up anymore, either.

Wally added, 'I think the house might be broken, too.'

'No shit?'

'Maybe we should get everybody out.'

'On it,' said Blrr. She disappeared.

Hardhat peered over the fence, down into the canyon. 'Yep, we're boned. Used to be a couple support columns at the end of the deck.' He pointed to a pair of jagged concrete buttresses perched on a narrow outcrop on the otherwise sheer canyon wall, about thirty feet below the end of the deck. 'Quake ripped those sonsabitches right off.' Wally tried to see where they had landed, but the shadows and the tinder-dry brush in the canyon were too deep. Hardhat continued, now speaking with the professional authority of a fourth-generation construction worker. 'Now the fuckin' deck is coming down, and that cantilever's prying the house apart like a cheap hooker's gams.'

Wally had no idea what his roommate said. But he got the gist of it: the house was coming down around their ears.

'What kind of moron would build a house that way?' Pop Tart tossed her arms up, clearly exasperated. 'This has got to be the stupidest thing in the world to do in an earthquake zone.'

'Jesus, don't be so goddamn naïve, sweetheart. These old houses get grandfathered in all the time. Grease a few palms and any shithole can—'

CRACK! This time the deck sagged a full foot in one go. Glass shattered on the second and third floors. A quieter 'pop' followed the crack as Pop Tart reappeared briefly on the far side of the canyon. She came back a moment later, after apparently deciding that the building wasn't going to collapse just yet.

A luminous yellow scaffold blinked into existence, extending from the severed buttresses all the way up to the deck. Hardhat grimaced. 'I can't do this all day long, but – OH FUCK—'

The scaffolding suddenly dropped, like it had fallen through a trapdoor. The deck sagged again. An assortment of yellow beams and crossbeams of various sizes flickered in the canyon for several seconds before stabilizing again.

'What happened?'

Hardhat gripped the railing, frowning in concentration. 'Pool water caused a mudslide. Now the goddamn buttresses are gone, too. Gotta build this motherfucker all the way up from the bottom of the canyon. It's the only solid ground.'

Wally peered over the fence again. Sure enough, now the ethereal scaffold extended all the way from the road, sixty or seventy feet down.

Blrr herded the others out of the house. Nobody spoke. They stood on the crowded patio, listened to the wail of sirens echoing across the Hollywood Hills.

Through gritted teeth, Hardhat said, 'I'd appreciate it if you cocksuckers did something besides stand around with your thumbs up your asses all day long.'

'Maybe Ana could help.' Holy Roller shook the unstable structure every time he moved.

'No good,' said Earth Witch, leaning on Bubbles for support. 'I won't move earth up from the roadbed down below – that would make it impossible for emergency vehicles to get through. If I start moving things inside the canyon, this whole house could end up at the bottom. The pool water has made the foundation unstable.'

'Now you're talking my language,' said Gardener, pulling a handful of seeds from a canvas pocket on her belt. She flung them over the fence and down into the canyon. A few fluttered away on the breeze, but in seconds the muddy hillside turned vibrant green, as shoots and vines snaked up the canyon like one of those fast-forward nature documentaries. They burrowed into the soil, too, making little sucking and squelching sounds. The smell of fresh vegetation wafted up on an updraft from the canyon.

Wally looked up at the deck again. Pebble-size chunks of concrete rained into the pool, making a patter like hail on a tin roof. In some places he could see the steel cantilevers that now imperiled the house.

Holy cow.

Still looking up, he said, 'Um, would getting rid of the deck help?'

Silence. He looked down again. Some people rolled their eyes, others shook their heads. 'Yes,' said Joe Twitch like he was talking to a five-year-old, 'the-the-the *deck* is our *p-p-p-problem.*'

Cripes. Why did they have to get so sore at a guy just for asking? He *knew* the deck was the problem.

What's worse than being hated by some of the biggest weirdos you ever met?

He tried again. 'If we got rid of the deck, would that make things better or worse?' He forged onward. 'Because the deck is connected to the house with steel beams.'

More silence.

'So they got iron in them.' Wally held up his hands and wiggled his fingers to make his point.

Through clenched teeth, Hardhat said, 'Son-of-a-fucking-bitch, yes, get rid of the deck!'

The construction worker's approval galvanized the group into action. It was the work of just a few minutes before they had a plan. Most of the discards went out to the street in front of the house, where they'd be safe if things went wrong. Wally, Hardhat, King Cobalt, Dragon Girl, and Pop Tart stayed behind.

Wally went back inside the creaking house and came out on the deck. King Cobalt took a position under one end of the deck, with Pop Tart at his side. If things went wrong she'd whisk them both away to safety. Hardhat kept his temporary scaffold in place at the other end of the deck. Dragon Girl and Puffy circled over the house.

Wally kneeled at the junction between the deck and the house. *Wham! Wham! Wham!* Using his ironclad fist like a jackhammer, he perforated the concrete every two feet. The noise echoed through the hills. Soon a fine layer of pulverized concrete coated his skin. When he scooped away the rubble he found three I beams inside the deck. Two ran along the sides and one went straight down the middle.

He took a deep breath. Then, like a blue collar Midas, he touched the central I beam. Steel flashed into oxide under his fingertips. A creeping stain spread out from his handprint, first in little needles of rust, then in an orange wave that coursed through the beam. Chunks of corroded metal flaked away and danced around his hand as the house shuddered. Wally willed the rust deeper until it sundered the beam. Puffs of red dust eddied up around his fingers, sparkling in the sunshine until a gust of Santa Ana wind carried them away.

'That's one,' he called.

The outer beams were too far apart for him to sever at once. As he weakened the second beam, the deck let loose a high-pitched groan. Then it tipped sideways with much shaking, cracking, and the screeching of tortured metal.

King Cobalt called out from underneath: '*Oof!*'

The last remaining beam was so badly stressed that it tore apart even before Wally could push the rust all the way through. The entire deck dropped several feet to where, presumably, King Cobalt held one end overhead. Wally leapt for the second-floor entrance to the house before the masked strongman hurled the deck into the canyon.

'Yikes!'

Wally was in midair, approaching the doorway, when he noticed the cameraman standing there. He'd been too busy concentrating to notice the guy filming him as he worked. The cameraman saw a man-shaped lump of iron speeding at him. He yelped, dropped the camera, and hit the floor. Wally tried his best to tuck and roll to the side. He came to a clanking halt in the hallway after rolling over the camera.

He helped the guy to his feet. 'Cripes, are you okay?'

The man nodded, but he made little wheezing sounds as he breathed. He looked down at the shattered camera. 'Damn. That was some beautiful footage.'

They watched as Hardhat released the scaffold he'd erected

with his mind. At the same time, King Cobalt used his prodigious strength to hurl the entire deck out into the midmorning air. Puffy swooped down, caught it in his talons, and gently set it down across the canyon.

The house didn't creak anymore.

Wally went back down to the pool. The others started to congregate and congratulate each other. A few even smiled at him, and gave him 'OK' and 'thumbs-up' signs.

A second cameraman was taping 'confessionals' from Hardhat, Pop Tart, Dragon Girl, and King Cobalt about how they had felt as they saved the house. Nobody bothered to ask Wally how he felt about it.

The masked wrestler came over when his stint in front of the camera was over. 'You're not too bad,' he said.

Wally shrugged.

'Have you ever thought about wrestling?'

'Um. No.'

'Give some thought to my Wild Card Wrestling Federation, okay? Because I tell you, once this thing takes off it's gonna be huge. And you could get in on the ground floor. You'd be great. The Iron Giant!'

Wally hadn't given much thought to what he'd do after *American Hero*. Probably go back and work in the strip mines with his dad and brothers. But professional wrestling? Gosh.

'Do I have to wear a mask?'

'If you want to. But I think people would dig your appearance. Oh! I know! Can you do different accents?'

'Accents?'

'Different than that *Fargo* one you're always doing, I mean. Russian would be awesome. Imagine it: Iron Ivan, the Russian Robot.'

Wally wasn't sure he wanted to be a wrestler, but the masked man seemed very excited, and this was the most anybody had spoken to him since the Stuntman thing. 'Well, that's different. I'll sure think about it.'

'Yeah?'

'You bet.'

'Great.' King Cobalt slapped him on the back. It sounded like somebody hitting a gong with a steak. Then he went off to mingle with the growing crowd.

'Nice work, cracker.'

Brave Hawk sidled through the crowd, illusory wings and another cameraman in tow. Simoon tagged along behind the camera, looking uneasy.

'I'm sorry?'

'I said, "Nice work."' His lips curled into a half-smile as he added, 'You must be exhausted. It's hard work.'

'It wasn't so bad. Um, what is?'

The half-smile turned into a full-blown grin. 'Trying to convince people you're not such a bad guy. Pretending you're something you're not.'

'Pretending?'

'It won't work, though. I won't let the others forget that you're a racist at heart.' Brave Hawk turned and went back to the crowd on the patio. As the cameraman followed him, he said, 'Shameful. Just shameful.'

What's worse than being hated for what people think *you are?*

'Just ignore him.' Simoon patted Wally's arm. 'You did a good job today. He's just a jackass.'

Cruel, too. Thing is, I'm darker than Brave Hawk and Stuntman and Gardener and everybody else. Way darker.

He looked down at Simoon.

Darker than Simoon and even those poor folks in Egypt.

'Stuntman made it up, didn't he?' she whispered.

Wally went back upstairs to his room. He didn't come out the rest of the day.

The studio must have pulled some strings, because housing inspectors arrived bright and early the following morning. Wally thought they'd have to move out, but now that the deck wasn't tearing the mansion apart, they were much better off than some of their neighbors.

Electricity was restored soon after that. So while workers from the studio poured over the Discard Pile, patching the cracks and holes, stringing new lights and replacing the cameras that had been damaged in the quake, Wally stayed in his room, rereading Bugsy's blog.

Bugsy had updated his blog with more photos and video clips. The shaky video – as if Bugsy had been on the run while he captured it – showed desert-camouflaged tanks rumbling down dirt roads, tossing up plumes of dust, mowing down refugees.

Wally watched the steel-plated Egyptian tanks.

He glanced outside, to where the deck had been. He remembered how good it felt to help out, how satisfying it felt when the beams crumbled under his touch.

And then he looked at the tanks again.

Holy cow.

He was still rereading the blog, and studying the photos, when Ink, one of the production assistants, called everyone into the TV lounge for a 'special meeting.' Maybe they'd decided to move everybody out of the damaged mansion after all. Without the gas hooked up, the hot water hadn't lasted through one morning of showers.

Wally followed Jade Blossom and Simoon down the stairs. He tapped Simoon on the shoulder. She stopped at the bottom of the staircase; Jade Blossom went on ahead.

'Simoon?'

'What?'

'Do you, I mean, I was wondering—'

She rolled her eyes. 'Oh, no. Look, Rusty, I meant what I said yesterday about you doing a good job saving the house, but you're not my type. You're a nice guy and all, but you're made of iron, and I'm not. I just don't think we're compatible.' She looked him up and down. 'At all.'

'Huh?'

'Don't worry, though. I'm sure you'll meet a nice … metal … girl someday.'

'Oh, cripes, no, no no no. That's not what I meant.'

Her gaze darted sideways, toward the TV lounge. A frown

flickered across her face and creased her brow. She looked back at Wally. 'Then what?'

'Did you live in Egypt a long time?'

'Egypt? No. I've never lived there. Not ever.'

'Oh.' That wasn't the response he'd expected. 'Do you know a lot about it, though? Egypt, I mean.'

It took her a few seconds to answer. She sighed, and lowered herself to sit on the bottom stair. 'I guess. Why?'

'I was reading Bugsy's blog, you know, the bug guy that was on the show with us?' She nodded. 'Since he went over there with John Fortune and that German fella—'

'I never meant for that to happen, I swear.'

'. . . he's been writing about the whole thing, and it's a heckuva mess.'

'I know,' said Simoon, looking down. 'Look, can we talk about something else, please?'

'Well, I was wondering if you knew how a guy might—'

A cameraman sidled closer. Wally stopped in mid-sentence. He wasn't too keen on the cameras.

'Hey!' Mr. Berman stood in the archway to the TV lounge. 'Go flirt on your own time, you two. We've got an episode to film.' He tapped his watch. It probably cost more money than Wally had ever seen in one place in his life. He wondered why the executive was there at all.

Wally helped Simoon to her feet – she looked real unhappy all of a sudden – and followed her to the lounge, where the other discards were sitting in a large circle. He stopped dead in his tracks. Not only was Mr. Berman here, but so were Peregrine and the judges: Topper, the Harlem Hammer, and Digger Downs.

And Curveball.

And Rosa.

And *Stuntman.*

The lying showbiz ace gave Wally a little sneer while the clanking joker hurried to find a seat. All the comfortable spots had been taken. Wally chipped a few bricks as he plopped down on the edge of the fireplace.

If he thought a chill settled over the room when Stuntman watched him enter, the glare that Peregrine gave Simoon was worthy of the worst blizzards back home.

The cameraman that Wally had narrowly avoided crushing the previous day circled the room, panning across the faces of the assembled discards. The cameras swiveled in Peregrine's direction as she stood.

Wally read the monitor along with her. 'Hello, and welcome to all of our current and former contestants. The competition over these past ten weeks has been fierce. Alliances were forged ... and broken. Challenges conquered, and failed. Today only three aces are left in the running for the one-million-dollar grand prize. The final three champions vying for the title *American Hero*.'

The camera panned across the sofa where Curveball, Rosa, and Stuntman sat. Rosa and Stuntman watched the proceedings with a smirk and a look of superiority, respectively. Curveball was unreadable.

Peregrine continued: 'But for those of you already out of the competition, your challenges are not over yet. Today the Discard Pile will choose the final two competitors, by voting to eliminate one of today's three.'

If the announcement bothered Curveball, she didn't show it. Stuntman now looked very serious. And Rosa looked particularly unhappy. Many of Wally's fellow discards, on the other hand, looked smug. Some grinned.

'And since this is the final vote of the competition, we're doing things a little differently this time.' Peregrine looked around the room, one eyebrow cocked. 'We're not letting you off the hook so easily, Discards. Today's vote will be an open ballot. No shuffling.'

The grins disappeared.

Ink handed three oversize playing cards to each of the discards. 'Think carefully about who deserves to become the first American Hero ... and about who doesn't deserve the honor.' Peregrine paused. 'When your name is called, show us who you think is *not* an American Hero.'

Once everybody held three cards, Peregrine tipped an

hourglass-shaped egg timer. 'Discards: you have three minutes to consider your choice, starting ... *now*. Contestants: good luck.'

Wally flipped through the cards. The photos of Stuntman, Rosa, and Curveball looked like the kind of glamorous head shots that all the contestants had submitted with their audition portfolios. His own head shot had been taken on a Polaroid camera in his aunt's kitchen.

Wally hadn't exchanged two words with Curveball, but she seemed like good folk. She even smiled at him once, which was more than he could say for a lot of the current and former contestants.

Rosa, on the other hand, had said – quietly, under her breath, so that only he could hear but the cameras wouldn't pick it up – 'Good riddance, you retard,' after Wally had been eliminated from Team Spades. She reminded him of the crazy Lacosky sisters from back home, and the time soon after his wild card had turned, when they tried pushing him into one of the drainage ponds up near the mine. Just to see if he'd float.

And then there was Stuntman. He looked friendlier in his photo than he did sitting across the room. But Wally found it hard to meet the gaze of either version.

'Discards,' said Peregrine, 'your time is up.' Ink went back around the room again, this time collecting two cards from each voter. After she finished, and each member of the Discard Pile held only one card, Peregrine pointed about a third of the way around the circle from Wally. 'Tiffani: How do you vote?'

One cameraman trained his lens on the finalists, and the other turned his own toward Tiffani. The West Virginia ace held up the Rosa photo. 'I vote against Rosa. Why? I'd pay cash money to see her thrown under a bus. Any takers?' Rosa sneered; the corner of Stuntman's mouth curled up.

By the time Peregrine and the cameras reached Wally, the vote stood at four against Rosa, three against Stuntman, and one against Curveball. Spasm's was the sole vote against Curveball; Wally suspected that was Rosa's doing, in the same way that the Lacosky sisters had gotten Lenny Pikkanen to lend them his car, with promises of a wild time when their parents next went out of town.

THE TIN MAN'S LAMENT

'Rustbelt: How do you vote?'

The cameraman crept closer, the lens glaring at Wally like an unblinking eye. *Don't think about the cameras, don't think about the cameras, don't think about the cameras* ... Stuntman crossed his arms over his chest and looked at Wally with a bloodless, thin-lipped smile. 'I dare you,' it said.

'How do you vote?'

Wally glanced around the room. Not at the dozens of aces, nor at the cameramen, nor the lighting guys, nor any of the others. At the room itself. Carpenters and painters had covered up the earthquake damage. But outside of camera range, they hadn't fixed anything. It was all fake. Fake and meaningless. Just like the books in the library.

Then he thought about Bugsy's blog again, and the image of a little girl crushed into the dirt by men driving around in a steel-plated tank. Dead because somebody said she and her family were dangerous.

What's worse than being hated for what people say *you are?*
Letting them get away with it.

Wally held up his Stuntman card. The air pressure dropped as everybody inhaled at once. The Harlem Hammer cocked his head, watching Wally through narrowed eyes.

'I vote against Stuntman.' He looked Stuntman in the eye. 'That's what you get for being a knucklehead.'

'*Pfff*. Figures.' Stuntman tried to dismiss Wally with a wave of his hand, but Wally saw his words hit home.

'That's all I said that day, and you know it. I didn't do anything wrong, but you made everyone hate me. Even people that never met me, for cripes' sake. You don't deserve to win. You're too mean.'

Stuntman looked away.

Wally stood. 'There's lots of people like you these days. Some of them even have guns – and worse stuff, gosh damn it.' Hardhat was a bad influence. Nodding to the three judges, Wally added, 'I don't think I want to be on the TV anymore.' Then he turned and walked out of the room.

'Hey! Where's he going? He can't leave!'

As Wally clanked up the stairs, he heard Simoon saying, 'I … I think he's going to Egypt.'

Hardhat blurted, 'Why in fuck's sake would he do that?'

Curveball, very quietly: 'To be a hero.'

Back in his room, Wally dug his suitcase out from under his bed. He filled it with the few belongings he'd brought to California: his britches; a few shirts; the photo of Mom and Dad and his brother Pete up at the lake cabin; a box of lemon-scented SOS pads.

He didn't own a cell phone from which to call for a taxi. They had a tendency to crumple up in Wally's hands, unless he was extremely careful. So he went back downstairs to use the kitchen phone.

Simoon sauntered in and laid her finger on the disconnect button as he was jotting down the number for a taxi company. 'What do you think you're doing?'

'I need to call a taxi.'

'Why?'

'I need to go to the airport.'

'I mean, why not take the studio limo?'

'That's for the show.'

'But it's nicer. And we won't fit into a single taxi.'

Wally looked up. They weren't alone. Simoon had been joined by Holy Roller, Earth Witch, King Cobalt, Hardhat, and Bubbles.

'We had a little vote of our own,' she said.

King Cobalt added, 'I join you in Egypt, and you join my wrestling federation.' He stuck out his hand. 'That's the deal.'

They shook on it. 'You betcha.'

Dragon Girl squeezed in between Bubbles and Earth Witch. 'Don't leave without me! I have to get my stuffies.'

Bubbles shook her head and waved her arms. 'Oh, no. Absolutely not. No way are you coming to the genocide with us.' Dragon Girl frowned, and stamped her foot. 'Maybe when you're twelve,' said Bubbles.

Simoon had been right about them not fitting in a taxi. Truth be known, they barely fit into the Discard Pile's stretch Hummer, either. Wally felt sorry for their driver. On the one hand, Mr.

Berman didn't want him driving the rogue discards to the airport, and suggested that doing such would be a bad career move. On the other hand, seven aces wanted him to drive them to the airport, and suggested that not doing so would be an even worse move.

They wove through the Los Angeles traffic in silence. It went on a long time. Long enough for Wally to wonder if people were sore at him again. Just to break the ice, he said, 'So, a fella might wonder who got voted off the show. Just saying, is all.'

Earth Witch sighed. 'Rosa got knocked out. So it's Stuntman and Curveball in the final round. Sorry, Rusty.'

Wally shook his head. 'Sounds like a good deal to me. She'll clean his clock.' The others nodded in agreement.

They rode the rest of the way to LAX in silence, but Wally didn't mind so much.

A taxi pulled up alongside them as they unloaded their luggage and argued about how much to tip their driver. (The way Wally figured it, he was probably out of a job now, the poor guy.) The back door opened, and out climbed a slim blond woman in a tank top with a duffel bag slung over her shoulder. The taxi pulled away.

Holy Roller squinted. 'Praise be – is that Curveball?'

King Cobalt flashed him a thumbs-up.

Hardhat smiled. 'Fuckin'A, Rusty. Fuckin'A!' He'd been more inclined to talk to Wally after the events of the previous day. Which was nice, except that he swore so much.

Curveball dropped her duffel bag on the curb. 'Room for one more?'

Before anybody could collect their wits enough to speak, yet another car pulled up alongside the group. This one was a silver BMW, and it screeched to a halt. Mr. Berman jumped out. 'Kate! Are you out of your goddamn *mind*?'

Curveball ignored him.

'Think carefully about what you're doing. You're pissing away the opportunity of a lifetime, just to join some half-baked publicity stunt with a bunch of rejects. Listen to me. You don't need them. A month from now your face can be on the cover of every magazine in America.'

'I have thought about it. And I choose to do something meaningful.'

Mr. Berman pressed his hands to his temples, and ran his hands through his hair. It hardly moved, it had so much mousse in it. 'Kate,' he said, pointing at Wally, 'just look at these freaks. You're the most popular character on the show. You're a shoo-in. You're walking away from a million dollars. You'll win if you come back. I *know* it.'

Earth Witch stepped between them. 'She made her decision. You need to leave now.' The others joined her.

The network executive stared at them for several seconds. His lips moved, but no sound came out. Wally didn't think it possible for somebody to turn so red in the face. Finally Mr. Berman said, quietly, 'You're making a huge mistake, Kate. The worst fucking mistake you'll ever make.' He got back in his car. Through the open passenger-side window, he yelled, 'I'll slap you assholes with lawsuits so hard your ghosts will be lonely!'

Wally reached out. He rested one finger on the roof of Mr. Berman's car. The BMW peeled away. An ochre pinstripe appeared under Wally's fingertip. Mr. Berman tumbled to the pavement thirty yards away in an explosion of orange dust.

The others stared at him, wide-eyed.

Wally shrugged. 'Steel-frame construction. Them Germans sure do make some nice cars.' Then he hefted Curveball's bag in one hand, his suitcase in the other, and entered the airport.

The metal detectors would be a problem. The last time he flew, the studio had handled everything. But his friends would figure something out, he was pretty sure.

♣

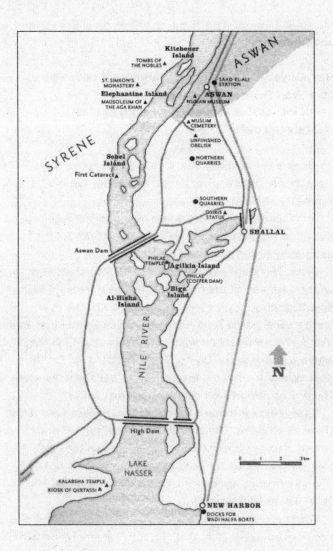

ASWAN

Kitchener
Island

TOMBS OF
THE NOBLES ▲

SAAD EL-ALI
STATION

ST. SIMEON'S
MONASTERY ▲

Elephantine Island

ASWAN

NUBIAN MUSEUM

MAUSOLEUM OF
THE AGA KHAN ▲

MUSLIM
CEMETERY ▲

SYRENE

UNFINISHED
OBELISK ▲

NORTHERN
QUARRIES ●

Sehel
Island

SOUTHERN
QUARRIES ●

First Cataract ▲

OSIRIS ▲
STATUE

SHALLAL

Aswan Dam

PHILAE
TEMPLE

Agilkia Island

PHILAE
(COFFER DAM)

Al-Hisha
Island

Bigа
Island

NILE RIVER

N

High Dam

0   1   2   3km

LAKE
NASSER

KALABSHA TEMPLE ▲
KIOSK OF QERTASSI ▲

NEW HARBOR

DOCKS FOR
WADI HALFA BOATS

Jonathan Hive

Hey, Guys. My Dad's Got a Warehouse! Let's Put on a War! Posted Today 8:16 pm
GENOCIDE, ASWAN | EXHAUSTED | 'WHO BY FIRE' – LEONARD COHEN

It's been a hell of a day, but I'm still standing (in the metaphorical sense, since I'm sitting on my ass in a bar in Syrene).

I'm falling asleep on my again-metaphorical feet here. But I'll do the best I can to catch you folks up. A little geography first. You'll need it.

Okay. There are two cities at Aswan. Aswan itself is on the east side of the river, near the train tracks. The Egyptian army's over there. In the middle of the river, there's Sehel Island (and Kitchener's Island, and Elephantine Island, and Amun Island with, I shit you not, a Club Med), where a bunch of the Living Gods are holed up. On the west side of the river, there's Syrene. That's where we are. The Aswan airport's on our side. Got that so far?

Okay, next (and much to my surprise), there's not a dam. There's two dams. The Low Dam is older, farther north (which is to say downstream – up and down the Nile's confusing when you're used to reading north as up) and nowhere near as apocalyptic as the High Dam. The High Dam? That's to the south.

When you were a kid, maybe you heard about how the Nile flooded every year. Well it doesn't anymore. Because that whole goddam flood is stuck back behind the High Dam. I mention the dams not only because if they blow, a whole lot of people die, but also because they're the only

« II next »

two ways across the river that don't involve boats. So if you had a big infantry force bent on killing a shitload of people like, say, me, the dams are pretty much where it's going to be an issue.

We knew that when we got here. It also became pretty clear that the Egyptian army really wanted to get across the dam – what with their helicopters and tanks and guns and bombs and their whole fucking *army*, we weren't going to be able to stop them.

Funny thing happened, though.

The cavalry arrived.

♥

The war council met at a restaurant about three blocks from the Monastery of St. Simeon. The place smelled of baked raisins and garlic, and the light from the windows made the air seem cleaner than it was. The Living Gods sat at a huge table, arguing, planning, debating, and despairing. Jonathan had picked up enough of the language to catch a word or phrase here and there, but for the most part, he and Lohengrin were excluded. Fortune – Sekhmet, really – was shouting and pounding the table, or nodding, or shaking his head and pointing east.

'There are still the helicopters,' Lohengrin said.

'We are aware,' Sekhmet replied, using Fortune's throat. 'But on the island, there is some protection from the ground troops.'

Fortune didn't look good. The whole not sleeping thing was eating at him like a cancer. And Jonathan was quite aware that neither Fortune nor Sekhmet was going to rest until the refugees were safe, or everyone died. Lohengrin was looking pretty tired, too. Sobek had lost a couple teeth. No one was doing well.

'The problem here,' Jonathan said, louder than he'd intended to, 'is that we're fucked.'

To his surprise, the table went quiet. He blinked. All eyes were on him.

'Well,' he said, 'we can hole up here and hope that they all just go away, but when you get right down to it, we're fucked, right? The island is a pain in the ass for the ground troops to get to, but if they take the west bank, they can starve us out or do some kind of pincer attack or nuke us from orbit. Whatever. And everyone we move to the island because it's safer there means one less we have to defend the dams. We don't have scorpion lady. We don't have Horus. So, I'm sorry to say it, but I think we're *fucked.*'

'God,' a voice said from behind him. 'You are such a loser, Bugsy. No wonder we voted you out.'

Slowly, he turned.

Curveball, a duffel bag over one shoulder. Earth Witch beside her, frowning with her arms folded. The wheelchair-bound minister, Holy Roller, smiling and avuncular even now. Hardhat, grinning. King Cobalt, maybe grinning; under the mask, who could tell? Simoon and Bubbles looking more like runway models than warriors. Rustbelt standing in the back like an old-time locomotive with self-esteem problems.

'Uh,' Jonathan said.

Curveball stepped forward, her duffel bag sliding to the floor. She walked past Jonathan and Lohengrin, straight to Fortune. For a moment the pair were silent. Then Fortune – Fortune, not Sekhmet – nodded.

'So,' Curveball said, 'what's the plan?'

◆

« II next »

They talked all night. It was epic. I slept through a lot of the last part, and more than a little, because getting a little hope can make you realize just how tired you've been up until then.

« II next »

The strategy was pretty basic, since none of us really knew what the hell we were doing. But we had a plan, and we had a bunch of aces and some guns and the determination that the killing was going to stop.

And it would. Either because we'd turn them back, or they'd run out of people to slaughter. One way or the other, it was coming down there.

We'd picked the place to make our stand.

♠

The moon was beautiful, a crescent of silver floating in the black sky. The city lights of Syrene and Aswan were dark, each side keeping information from the enemy. Jonathan sat on the street, his hands on his knees, looking up at the stars.

'Hey,' Simoon's voice said. 'Bugsy.'

He looked over his shoulder. The woman stood in the doorway of the restaurant. The voices raised in debate behind her sounded oddly joyful for a council of war.

'How's it going in there?' he asked.

Simoon stepped forward, letting the door close behind her. The voices didn't vanish, but they grew distant.

'It'll be a while before anyone decides anything,' she said. 'But I think it's going well. What about you?'

'I could sleep right here in the gutter,' Jonathan said. 'Seriously. Just stretch out and snooze off.'

'Probably should. Rest, I mean. Not the gutter part.'

'Yeah. I'll get to it,' he said.

'I wanted to say thanks.'

Jonathan looked up at her. She was prettier than he remembered. She'd been good-looking, but now in the moonlight, with her hair down, she was beautiful.

'Thanks?'

'For butting in,' she said. 'For listening in on my phone calls. For getting John Fortune involved. All like that. I wouldn't have had the balls.'

'I'm not sure I really did you any favors,' he said. Simoon shook her head, her gaze lifting to the buildings, the horizon, the sky.

'No,' she said. 'I'm glad. I've never actually been here, you know. But I'm *from* here. So, you know, thanks.'

'Anytime,' Jonathan said.

♣

« II next »

There's a real problem playing defense. We didn't get to pick when the shit came down. That was all them. The Living Gods took their aces and a bunch of guns across to Sehel Island. Hardhat went too, the theory being that he could build a temporary bridge with his girders to evacuate if the army managed to land there.

Then we got ready.

♥

'Harder!' Bubbles said.

Rustbelt raised his balled fist, and then lowered it. 'Ah, cripes. This is just … I mean …'

Bubbles, now looking like a woman of a healthy hundred and seventy pounds, put a hand on Rustbelt's arm and tried to keep her temper.

'Sweetie,' she said. 'We have to get these bubbles in the air, or it's only going to be Simoon's sandstorm to stop all the planes and helicopters they throw at us. So it's not really me you're hitting. It's them. Just think of it like that, okay?'

Rustbelt smiled, but the expression seemed forced.

'You ready to try again?' Bubbles asked.

'Sure,' Rustbelt said. 'Let's try it.'

'Okay. Beat the shit out of me.'

Rustbelt closed his eyes and swung. The impact sounded like a car wreck. Bubbles put on another thirty pounds.

'Much better,' Bubbles said. 'Do that again.'

'Okay,' Rustbelt said. 'You know, this is really uncomfortable, though.'

Bubbles nodded. 'That speaks well of you, sweetie. Now hit me.'

◆

« II next »

Well, folks, we didn't know what dam they'd cross at, only that we had to hold them off at the places where they'd only be able to get at a few of us at a time. Lohengrin, Curveball, Earth Witch, and Simoon were south with almost a hundred of the followers of the Living Gods, ready to get to the High Dam if they came across there. Holy Roller, King Cobalt, Fortune, Rustbelt, and Bubbles were at the Low Dam where they actually attacked. I went with all of them.

The Egyptian army came at us right at dawn. I always thought that was a cliché, you know? 'We attack at dawn.' Turns out there's a reason. The sun really does get in your eyes. Well, not mine, since I was mostly bugged out by that point.

♠

The boats chugged out from the east bank, dark marks in the sun-bright water. Hardhat and Sobek squatted by the shore. The croc-headed joker hunkered down, his hand shading his eyes.

'This could be a problem,' Sobek said. 'If they reach the island—'

'Those dick-lickers have about as much chance of getting out here as I've got of ass-fucking Mother Teresa,' Hardhat said cheerfully. 'Watch this shit.'

The first girder appeared across the bow of the first boat, forcing the craft lower into the water. There was the distant sound of voices raised in alarm. A second girder appeared. The boat rode lower, water lapping up over its sides.

The other boats hesitated as the lead craft tried to turn back to the shore. A third girder appeared. The boat sank. The boats idled and then turned back.

Sobek chuckled.

'Elegant,' he said. 'Could you do that to all of them? If they all came at once?'

'Probably not,' Hardhat said, folding his arms, 'But I could fucking sure get the first two cocksuckers, and then let the pussies fight it out who gets to go third.'

'They'll have to come by land, then,' Sobek said.

♣

« II next »

It started with a few boats putting out from the east, back toward the islands. That was just a distraction. The big push was at the Low Dam.

It's eighty feet from the top of the Low Dam to the river north of it. The top of the dam is about as wide as a two-lane highway and about two miles long. We'd put some barricades across it – an old bus parked at an angle, a pickup truck Rustbelt tipped on its side, some cars we'd commandeered. Every hundred yards or so, out to almost the middle of the dam, we had something to hide behind. And on the far end, the army was making cover of its own.

That was where they came.

We didn't keep everyone. You should know that now. We lost one right off. But he didn't die a stupid death. Honest to God.

♥

320

'It's a bulletproof shield,' King Cobalt said, leaning against the upended pickup truck. 'Like riot police use. I just hold it toward them like this, charge in, and when I get there, I'll rip 'em apart.'

Rustbelt raised a hand, shielding his eyes from the rising sun. The dam stretched out before them and behind them, water calm and glittering to the right, empty air to the left. King Cobalt crouched down behind his shield.

'Stay behind me,' King Cobalt called out. 'All of you just let me get in there and soften them up.'

'Now, son,' Holy Roller called out, 'I think you had best come on back for a bit, the both of you. We may be seeing some enemy movement. At the far end – over there.'

'I don't see anything,' Rustbelt said, and a bullet ricocheted off his chest with a sound like a piston blowing. King Cobalt lowered his riot shield, sighed, and slid to the ground. Blood poured from the back of his neck.

'*Medic!*' Holy Roller yelled, pushing himself toward the fallen ace. '*Get a medic over here!* We got us a man down!'

'Oh, cripes,' Rustbelt said, rubbing the shiny spot the killing bullet had left on his skin. 'I'm sorry, King. I didn't … we'll get someone … it'll be …'

Holy Roller reached the fallen ace, felt desperately for a pulse, and then shook his head. Leaning over carefully, the minister hooked a finger under the wrestler's mask and gently pulled it free. The thick body thinned and diminished.

'He's just a *kid*,' Fortune said.

'Dear Lord,' Holy Roller intoned. 'I don't know if this poor boy believed in you. I don't even know his name, or if he was a Mexican, but he was a brave boy and he tried to do something good. I know you'll find a place for him in Heaven, wrestling with your angels. He did so love to wrestle.'

They all cast their eyes down for a moment. When he looked up across the dam, the old minister's eyes were hard. On the far side of the dam, the sun was glittering off metal. A sound came like distant thunder that never stopped. Tanks were coming.

'Time's come,' he said. 'Get on the horn to the others. It's started.'

♦

« II next »

The tanks came first, single file. Their guns were blazing, trying to keep us back while they pushed past or through the obstacles we'd placed in their way. It turns out if you send a bunch of wasps up the barrel of those things, it just gets you closer to the shell when it goes off. It wasn't pleasant. But then Rustbelt was in there, howling like a banshee, and the tanks started falling apart. They shot him. They shot him a lot. When the helicopters came, the detonations began. There was so much smoke in the air, I lost some wasps just to that.

The Living Gods put down suppressing fire, and Sekhmet and Holy Roller made a push of their own. I did what I could, stinging and moving and generally making sure the bad guys couldn't keep it together. No matter how hard they tried, there wasn't room for enough men to get onto the dam to overwhelm us. The whole thing was more or less even until a sandblasting wind kicked up, courtesy of Simoon, and Lohengrin in his armor showed up at Rustbelt's side.

When the army started falling back to the east, we pressed them. We were all a little drunk, I think. We were winning. Simoon's wind was vicious. It was enough to rip skin, not that it bothered Lohengrin or Rustbelt. Together the three of them moved slowly across, all the way to the far side, driving the army before them. Bubbles and Curveball made a second wave, shooting down any aircraft stupid enough to try to break through. The rest of us – all of us – came in ranks behind them. Jokers with pistols and ancient rifles and Kevlar vests that were state of the art in the 1970s. American aces who couldn't speak a fucking word of Arabic or do anything more eloquent than give

« II next »

thumbs-up signs all around.

We were overconfident. The Egyptian commander was smart. We didn't figure out what he was doing until it was too late.

♠

Curveball crouched, a stone the size of a golf ball in her hand. Rusty and the German ace were still advancing, but it wasn't easy to see much beyond that. The blowing sand obscured most of what lay ahead, and smoke and flakes of rust swirled madly, making the air taste like blood.

Earth Witch plucked at her sleeve and pointed out to the right, over the water. A boat was just visible, pushing out from the eastern shore.

'Got it,' Curveball said, and sidearmed the stone like she was skipping it. The detonation sent a wave across the surface of the water. Someone – John Fortune? – pressed another rock into her hand.

'It's turning back,' Earth Witch said.

'Good work,' John said. His hand was hot, like a man with a fever. 'Keep going.'

The angry chop of helicopters cut through the noise. They'd crossed the river somewhere else and were circling back to come up behind them. 'Mine! I've got 'em!' Bubbles yelled. 'Take cover!'

Machine guns spat, fire blazing from their muzzles, as two huge, iridescent bubbles rose gracefully into the air. The transparent skins swirled with colors like oil on water, trembling in the wash of the propellers. When they detonated, the concussion was like a blow. The burning hulk of the copters arced down to the water and sank.

'Forward!' Fortune shouted. 'Come on! Let's go!'

Curveball nodded, looking ahead to the battle, to the sky for an attack from above, to the water. Time didn't mean much. They might have been doing this for ten minutes or an hour or a day. No one noticed anything had changed until she looked out to her right and the water was gone. To her left, there was no clifflike drop.

They were on the other side. They'd crossed the dam; it lay ten or twelve meters behind them. Without being aware of it, they'd fanned out into the road. John called out for Simoon to let her storm slacken. As the sand began to fall from the air, half a dozen streaks of green buzzed past.

'Does this mean we won?' Bubbles asked. 'I think this means we won.'

'I don't think so,' Curveball said.

On the dam, the battle had been restricted. Rustbelt, Lohengrin, Holy Roller, Sekhmet. They'd been able to hold a line. No more than eight or ten soldiers could reach them at a time. But the Egyptians had fallen back slowly, drawing them on. Drawing them to the shore where they could be surrounded and overwhelmed. The streets ahead were packed with men, with tanks, with guns.

They'd screwed up. They were dead.

No one noticed the sound at first. When the rumble penetrated, they realized they'd been hearing it – a deep, bone-wrenching sound. Holy Roller was craning his thick neck, trying to spot the source. The Egyptians, across the small no-man's-land of the street, seemed confused as well.

'What's happening?' Simoon shouted over the growing cacophony. 'What is that?'

And the earth opened before them. A great chasm yawned, sand and stone sliding down into an abyss that seemed to go for miles, though it probably wasn't more than a few hundred feet. Egyptian tanks and men slid down into the gap, rifles firing impotently. Buildings cracked and fell apart, walls tumbling end over end in the air.

Curveball turned. Earth Witch was on her knees, her hands grasping the medallion at her neck, her face red with effort. With a thump like an explosion, the chasm closed. The first wave of the army was gone, buried alive, dying under their feet. The soldiers that remained stood agape. The first of them turned and fled.

'Oh, God,' Earth Witch said. Her voice was thin and unbelieving. 'Oh, God. I did that. Did I do that?'

Curveball knelt, wrapping her arms around her friend. Earth Witch shook. 'It's okay, Ana,' Curveball said. 'It's okay.'

'I killed them,' Earth Witch said. 'I killed them, didn't I?'

'Yeah,' Curveball said. 'You did.'

Earth Witch stared out at the rubble, her breath in gasps. Her eyes were wide and round, caught between elation and horror.

'Excuse me, ladies,' Holy Roller said. 'I don't mean to intrude.'

'What's the matter?' Curveball asked.

'The dam,' John Fortune said, appearing at their side. 'Doing that weakened the dam. It's giving way. We need Earth Witch to shore it up. Now.'

Earth Witch sagged into Curveball's arms.

'She can't do it,' Curveball said. 'She's too tired.'

'I can,' Earth Witch said.

'Ana,' Curveball began, but Earth Witch shook her head. A voice called out from the shore – some stray Egyptian soldier surrendering himself to Lohengrin. Curveball stood, drawing her friend up with her.

'I can fix it. Just … stay with me,' Earth Witch said.

'I will,' Curveball promised.

♣

<< II next >>

So to all the folks who said we were fucked, here's the news: We won. The genocide stopped at Aswan, and we didn't even drown all the folks we were trying to save in the process. And no, I don't know how it's going to play out from here. International pressure's going to have to be placed on the Ikhlas al-Din and the government of Egypt. They may have to partition the country. That's all

« ‖ next »

complicated and nuanced and may take years to figure out. The United Nations will almost certainly have to be involved, and the caliphate. And yes, that may be a pain in the ass for some people. Live with it.

The killing stopped. And we stopped it. And that, ladies and germs, is just plain good.

12,338 COMMENTS | LEAVE COMMENT

♥

'Bugsy,' Fortune said. 'Wake up. There's someone here wants to see you.'

Jonathan rolled over on his bed, blinking up into the light. Fortune looked slightly better. Still cadaverously thin, still with the deep, bruiselike bags under his eyes. He and Sekhmet apparently hadn't quite settled on a schedule for sleep yet. And still, the poor bastard looked better.

'Someone wants to see me?' Jonathan asked.

'You should come.'

'Beautiful blond entomologist with no boyfriend and a webcam?'

'CNN,' Fortune said.

Jonathan took in a deep breath and let it out with a sense of growing satisfaction. The traditional media finally there to agree he'd scooped them.

'A close second,' Jonathan said. 'I'll be right there.'

He washed his hair, considered shaving, decided that the stubble was a decent manly touch – you never saw Indiana Jones breaking out a safety razor – and headed out for the lobby of the hotel that had become the aces' barracks. The camera crew had set up shop by one of the big couches designed for travelers to lounge on in times of peace. The reporter looked familiar; black guy in his late thirties, close-cropped hair with a little gray coming in at the temples. He was wearing a khaki shirt with epaulets, like he'd been trekking through the desert instead of driving in from the airport.

'Hey,' Jonathan said, 'I heard you boys were looking for me?'

Hands were shaken, admiration was expressed, someone got Jonathan a cup of coffee. Five minutes flat, and he was sitting on the couch, klieg lights shining in his face, sincere talking head leaning in toward him with an expression built to convey gravity and concern.

It was fucking sweet. Right up until it wasn't.

'How do you respond to the accusations that you've sided with terrorists?'

'That's stupid,' Jonathan said. 'And anyone who says it doesn't understand anything about how international politics works.'

'But you have come to the defense of a group that's been accused of sheltering the Twisted Fists.'

'Well, accused, sure …'

'And the assassination of the Caliph.'

'These people didn't assassinate the Caliph,' Jonathan said. 'There were kids dying out on the road. Kids! You think some eight-year-old joker kid killed the Nur?'

'Right, and you also said in your blog that these people didn't kill the Caliph. You have investigated the alleged link between the Living Gods and the Twisted Fists, then?'

Jonathan tapped his fingers on his knee. 'I've been a little busy being shot at,' he said. 'But I am perfectly comfortable that no such connection exists.'

'And how would you reply to the critics who say that Westerners – especially self-styled crusaders like Lohengrin and religious leaders like Holy Roller – represent an unacceptable Western interference in the internal affairs of Egypt?'

'I probably wouldn't,' Jonathan said.

'So you don't think there is an issue of national sovereignty here? You *are* a group of aces not affiliated with any government entering into armed conflict with the military of a legitimate state. How do you see that as different from a terrorist organization?'

'They were killing people,' Jonathan said. 'Okay? Innocent people were dying. And we stopped it.'

The reporter seemed to sense an unpleasant stinging sensation in his future. He smiled and nodded as if he were agreeing with something, then changed the subject. 'Will your forces remain in Syrene when the army of the caliphate arrives?'

'We are going to stay here until we're sure that ...' Jonathan held up a finger and licked his lips. The klieg lights seemed hotter than they'd been at the start of the interview. The couch had developed some uncomfortable lumps. ' ... *army* of the caliphate?' he asked.

'You didn't know the new Caliph has sworn his support for Kamal Farag Aziz and his Egyptian government? His troops have been on the move for days.'

'Army. Of the caliphate. Ah. Well. That's probably a pretty big army, huh?'

The reporter shrugged. Jonathan got the feeling that the guy might be enjoying this opportunity to make the blogger look dumb.

'About three times the size of the Egyptian forces. And the Caliph's aces Bahir of the Scimitar and the Righteous Djinn,' the reporter said. 'The Caliph says that this kind of Western adventurism is a threat to all sovereign nations of the world, and that your defense of terrorists places you in violation of international law. The Caliph also says he's taken the secretary-general of the United Nations into protective custody to prevent his being attacked by the citizens of Cairo who are outraged by his apparent support of *your* cause.'

'Ah,' Jonathan said. 'Huh.'

'Do you have a response to that?'

Jonathan blinked into the lights. He wished Fortune was nearby; they needed to talk. They all needed to talk. A lot. And right now.

'Jonathan,' the reporter said. 'This is your chance to make a response.'

'Oops?' Jonathan suggested.

INCIDENTAL MUSIC FOR HEROES

S. L. Farrell

The world roared around Joker Plague: a barrage from the stage amplifiers; the black boxes of monitors taking the roar and hurling it back; the massive cliff-wall ramparts of the sound system thundering to either side of the stage; the crowd screaming; slapback from the rear walls of the auditorium a second assault; the insistent rhythm of the song a hammer pounding at them.

To stage left, Bottom thumb-slapped his Fender Precision, his ass's head nodding aggressively in time to the music. Michael felt rather than heard Bottom's bass, a solid minor pattern caught in lockstep with the subsonic pounding of Michael's bass drum, the lowest of the tympanic rings set on his body. Shivers, his appearance that of a demon snatched directly from the fires of hell, stalked stage right before a wall of Marshalls, his blood-red guitar screaming like a tortured soul in hands of the same color.

Next to Shivers was S'Live, floating behind the ranks of his keyboards like a garish hot air balloon painted with a face, multitudinous tongues flickering from a too-wide mouth to punch at the keys. And, in the gel-colored clouds of dry ice fog drifting at the front of the stage, there was *something*: the ghost of a thin body caught in the floodlight-colored wisps and gone again, a wireless Shure SM58 microphone floating in the air before it, though no hand seemed to hold up the black cylinder. There was a voice, though – *The* Voice: a powerful baritone that alternately growled and purred and shrieked the lyrics to 'Self-Fulfilling Fool.'

She says she loves you
And you – you wonder why
You can't see how could that be
When you don't love yourself
For you're the only one who could
At night when there's no one else there
At night when the walls close in
You're the only one who might care

You want to believe them
You don't want them to be cruel
But when you look in the mirror
What looks back is a self-fulfilling fool

Michael – 'DB' to his band mates and most of his friends, 'Drummer Boy' to much of the world – heard mostly The Voice. He wore earpiece monitors to dampen the 120+ decibel hurricane, with only The Voice's vocals coming through his monitor feed. He could hear his drumming quite well, resonating through his body, and no earplugs could entirely shut out the unearthly cacophony of the stage equipment.

Michael loomed at center stage, pinned in spotlights, his six arms flailing as he beat on his wide, tattooed, and too-long torso with his signature graphite drumsticks, the multiple throats on his thick muscular neck gaping and flexing as they funneled and shaped the furious rhythm. He wore a set of small wireless mics on a metal collar around his upper shoulders. While the gift of his wild card talent gave him more than enough natural amplification to be heard throughout the auditorium, the volume would have been uncomfortable for everyone on stage and in the first rows: it was easier to let the sound system do the work. He prowled the stage as he drummed, the actinic blue of the spots following him as he danced with The Voice in his cold fog, grinned at Bottom's driving, intricate bass line, screamed his approval of Shiver's searing licks, or swayed alongside S'Live's saliva-drenched tongue-lashing of his keyboards.

For the moment, he thought only of being *here.* It was what Michael loved about being on stage: for those magical few hours he could leave the rest of the world behind. For that time, there was only the music.

La Cavea, the outdoor venue at Rome's Auditorium Parco della Musica, could accommodate 7,000 spectators. There were that many and more packed into the seething mass of humanity in front of him, a dark, fitfully lit sea of heads bobbing in time to the song, fists pumping their approval back to the stage, their energy fueling Joker Plague's performance in an endless feedback loop. The pit in front of the stage was a tight crush; out in the auditorium, everyone was out of their seats and standing. Against the night sky, the beetlelike shell of the Parco della Musica loomed, caught in blue and red spotlights beyond the tall ranks of the upper balcony.

It reminded Michael uncomfortably of an Egyptian scarab.

The song – their third and last encore – ended in a flourish of riffs and cymbal crashes from Michael, a final power chord from Shiver, and an explosion of pure white light from a bank of floodlights behind the stage. The audience roared, a deluge of adulation that swelled and broke over them. 'Fuckin' yeah!' The Voice screamed at the audience through the Italian night. 'Thank you! *Grazie! Buona notte!*' They shouted back, a wordless, thousand-throated monster's voice. Michael underhanded his half-dozen sticks into the audience as the stage lights went dark and house lights came up at the rear of the auditorium. The audience seemed to be split nearly evenly between jokers and nats, judging from the faces Michael glimpsed, but it was the jokers who were nearest the stage, the nats mostly lurking to the rear.

Roadies swarmed the stage, hooded flashlights guiding the band off to the tunnel behind the stage. 'Fantastic show, DB! Great job! *Esposizione eccellente!*' they said, as he passed them, leading the way. He nodded, but he could already feel the stage adrenaline rushing away, and with it any sense of pleasure. The malaise and subdued anger he'd felt since leaving *American Hero* wrapped more tightly around him with every step he made toward the dressing room, the energy and pleasure of the performance fading.

'Fuckin' A, that was *tight,*' Shivers said as the door closed behind them. He tossed his ancient, scarred Stratocaster into its case, grinning – with his red-and-black-scaled face, it looked more like a leer. 'Better than the Paris show. Shit, DB, those new kicks in "Stop Me Again" were killer. Just killer. S'Live, you and me gotta catch those next time.'

'Yeah,' Bottom added. He'd popped one of the champagne bottles and upturned it into his horselike snout. More of the bubbling liquid seemed to escape the sides of his mouth than went down his throat, soaking his already-sopping T-shirt. 'Let's listen to the board tape. If I punch those bass drum hits with you, it'll be monster. Wish we'd recorded it that way in the studio. DB, man, you listening?'

He wasn't. Michael dropped onto the couch, multiple arms sprawled out, his eyes closed. The remnants of the show still rang in his ears. The cushions at the far end sagged a few moments later under an unseen weight and Michael felt the springs move in response.

''Sup, big guy? You ain't yourself,' The Voice said from the air: low, sonorous, a cello bowed by a master. 'You were playing *angry* out there – sounded nice and aggressive, but it ain't the usual fun-lovin' you. 'S matter, man?'

Michael shook his head. The searing adrenaline high he'd felt during the concert was gone, as if someone had pulled a handle and flushed it away. 'Nuthin',' he said. 'And fuckin' everything. When we're playing, it's cool. But after …'

'Bad shit goin' down in Egypt.' Michael glanced over to where The Voice's head would have been and could almost see the raised eyebrows. 'Hey, I ain't fuckin' stupid, man. I seen what you kick up on your laptop: CNN and Yahoo News instead of porn. Shit, how boring is that?'

Michael shrugged with all six arms. 'Hey, I've been—'

The door opened and their manager came into the room: Grady Cohen, a nat the label had hired as part of their contract. 'Kiss-Ass Cohen,' DB had dubbed him early on. He wondered if Grady knew why the band usually called him 'KA.' Michael thought that if Grady was ever infected with the wild card, he'd turn into an empty suit. Behind him, in the theater's backstage corridor, Michael could see the groupies waiting to be let in.

There were always women waiting, nat or joker, whatever he wanted. Only ...

Grady was grinning and applauding as he strode into the room. 'Hey, KA!' The Voice said loudly. 'You look happy – you snag a blow job on the way back?'

Grady ignored The Voice. 'Great show, boys. That's all I need to say. The promoters are contentedly counting the ticket sales, and the label tells me that *Incidental Music for Heroes* shows up as number-one on *Billboard* next week. *Numero Uno*. It doesn't get any better than that. So congratulations all around, eh? Don't need to say more.' He clapped his hands again. He looked at each of them as if he were counting bills in his wallet. 'All right, here's the schedule. Wake-up call is at noon, and the limo will be at the hotel to get us to the airport two hours later. It's Berlin tomorrow night, then London, then right on to New York – the label's added Cleveland, Dallas, and Denver to the American tour. Boys, Joker Plague is hot. Hot. Enjoy the ride.' He grinned again. 'And speaking of rides ...'

He went to the door and opened it. 'Come on in,' he said to those waiting outside. He gestured sweepingly toward the band. '*Entrato. È tempo di celebrare ...*'

◆

She had the face of a cat and her skin was blanketed with silken fur mottled like an orange tabby, but the body was very much a young woman's. The name she'd given Michael was *Petit Chaton* – little kitten – and she was French, not Italian, having followed the band from Paris. She was beautiful, even in sleep. Michael could swear she was purring as she slept curled under the covers. He slid his several arms from under her, stroking her face gently with his top hand: yes, she *was* purring; he could feel the vibration in his fingers. He slipped out of bed and, naked, padded into the other room of the suite. The clock said five A.M. local time, but Michael's internal clock was blurred by travel and he wasn't sleepy at all. He picked up the remote and turned on the television set, tapping the mute button, since he knew about a half-dozen words of Italian. The channel was still set to the news where he'd left it, and Egypt evidently remained the big story, as it had been for a few days now. He watched the images flickering by: jokers with heads that he vaguely recognized as those of Egyptian gods; jerky, confusing footage of a battle; bodies strewn across a sand-rippled landscape; and ...

Curveball ... Kate.

Michael sat up abruptly, entirely awake now. The camera panned away and he cursed doubly, since fucking Captain Cruller was standing next to her, looking like he hadn't slept in a week, the scarab that had possessed him sitting under the skin of his forehead like the world's largest pimple. Fortune was talking to someone off-camera. Michael fumbled for the mute button, but he couldn't hear Fortune over the Italian translation. The camera panned back again, showing Kate, Ana, Lohengrin, Holy Roller, Fat Chick, Hardhat, Toolbelt, Simoon, and Bugsy all clustered around Fortune, with desert in the background and what looked like a dam structure in the middle distance. Michael watched only Kate. She was solemn, her face dirty with a streak that might be dried blood along one cheek. She looked like she would collapse the moment the camera was turned off, as if it were only force of will keeping her upright. They all looked the same way. And Kate was standing right alongside Fortune. He saw her fingers link with his as the camera panned back.

Light shifted in the room as the program went to a split screen, with a commentator speaking on the left while on the right was promo footage of King Cobalt from *American Hero*. ' ... King Cobalt *morto*. ...' the commentator intoned, and the last word jumped out at him. *Morto*. He could figure that one out. Michael suddenly knew why King Cobalt's picture was on the screen.

He felt as if someone had punched him in the stomach.

The scene switched abruptly to a reporter interviewing a crocodile-headed ace who looked like he'd just stepped from a mural in a pharaoh's tomb, standing outside one of the restored temples.

Another shift, and a new reporter was placing a microphone in front of the fierce scowl of the Righteous Djinn, the former strong right arm of the Nur and now the primary weapon in the new Caliph's arsenal. He glared into the camera as it focused on him, and Michael found himself scowling back.

'Fuck,' he said aloud.

'If you would like.' The answer came in French-accented English. Chaton was leaning sleepily against the doorway to the bedroom, illuminated by the shifting light of the television. Her belly was cloaked in soft orange, her tail curled lazily around a knee, the end of it flicking restlessly. 'But you left our bed.'

'Can't sleep,' Michael told her.

A shrug and a smile. *'Bon.* Then—'

'Not right now. Go back to sleep. I'll be in later.'

Her gaze drifted over to the television. 'The problems in Egypt? That is bothering you? You know them, *oui*? From *American Hero*?'

He didn't answer. With his middle left hand, he tapped at one of the tympanic membranes on his chest – a low, steady *dhoomp-dhoomp-dhoomp* that reverberated through the room and his body. The sound was somehow comforting. Chaton finally shrugged and padded back into the bedroom. A few minutes later he heard her purr-snore again.

'Michael, you're a great guy,' Kate had said with her soft, quiet voice, not long after they'd met. 'But I don't think I'm ready for this.' He started to protest, but she cut him off with a smile. 'Maybe when this whole thing is over. When we're not so distracted.'

But it would never be over. The cameras would always be there for both of them, no matter where they were or what they did. And Fortune … goddamn John Fortune had somehow managed to say the right things that she wanted to hear. Kate saw Michael as the lightweight, the entertainer, the womanizer.

He'd slept with a dozen of the contestants and staff of *American Hero* after his stupid affair with Pop Tart, after it was apparent that Kate was never going to forgive him for the slip. It was stupid and he knew it, but if she thought of him as the slut rock star, then he'd play the role to the hilt. The tactic earned him the response it deserved. After he'd been 'drafted' by the Diamonds, after Fat Chick had been voted off the show, after the show had revealed that he was sleeping with Tiffani, he'd tried again to patch things up with Kate and she had stared at him as if he were a stranger. When he'd persisted, things were suddenly flying at him very hard and very fast, and he was too busy ducking and shielding himself to make any reply at all. The other Hearts took judicious cover.

'You're an ass, Michael!' Kate shouted in the midst of the barrage. 'Go bang your drums!' A vase exploded on the wall nearest him, scattering water and petals and china shrapnel and leaving a hole he could have put his head through. 'Go bang your groupies, too!' A pencil caught him on the ass, punching through his jeans and embedding itself point-first in his buttocks. He gave up trying to cover himself and retreated entirely. He heard glass hit the wall beside the door and shatter. 'Stay away from me!' he heard her say as he fled.

Fortune was serious; he had a vision that included more than CDs and concerts and screaming fans, even if that vision was driven by the goddamned bug inside him. Fortune was also dangerous. Michael felt that instinctively; but Kate ... Kate didn't see him that way, just as he felt she couldn't see beyond the persona of Drummer Boy.

Hell, sometimes he couldn't do that either.

He'd been sent to the Discard Pile after the Blacks had lost their challenge, and that's when his growing fury and discontent couldn't be contained any longer. He lasted a single day there, listening to the stupid prattling, the ego games, the posturing all of them did for the cameras. It was stupid, all of it – fake drama and fake heroism. That same evening, he packed his clothes and headed for the door, only to find his way blocked by King Cobalt and Hardhat. Other discards watched the confrontation: Ana, standing in the middle of the huge living room with hands on hips, shook her head as if she'd been expecting something like this; Toad Man lurked in the archway to the kitchen like a wart-ridden VW Beetle; Brave Hawk, his arms folded on his chest, gazed down stoically from the balcony above them; two five-foot-tall Matryoshkas huddled against the wall. And the cameras. Always the cameras.

'Where the hell you going, DB?' King Cobalt said.

'I'm outta here,' Michael told them. 'Fuck this shit. I got music to play with people I actually like. I'm done with this crap.'

King Cobalt shook his masked head, the silver lightning bolts sewn there glistening. 'Uh-uh. That ain't how it works, and you know it.' Hardhat gestured, and a crosshatch of glowing steel beams barred the door of the mansion.

'You think that shit's gonna stop me from leaving?' Michael told him. He flexed his six arms, looking at all of them. 'It's gonna fucking take most of you to do that, and it's gonna be real. No stuntmen, no dummies, no breakaway furniture, no pulled punches. Real.' He wanted them to try, in that moment. He wanted to lose himself in blind rage. All it would have taken was a word or a movement. Hardhat glared. King Cobalt's eyes glittered behind the blue mask, but then King Cobalt stepped to one side. He waved at Hardhat; the barrier at the door vanished.

'Michael,' Ana said as he stalked past them to the door and wrenched it open. 'All you're proving is that you're still an ass. Kate—'

He hadn't allowed her to finish the sentence. 'Fuck Kate. Fuck you. Fuck John Fortune and Peregrine and this whole goddamn show.' He doubted that they would play those exit lines on the weekly wrap-up, and the slamming of the door behind him was entirely unsatisfactory. He took some small pleasure in ripping the locked steel gates of the driveway from their hinges and tossing them aside. He gave a sextuplet of fingers to the cameraman filming his exit.

As he walked down the street looking for a taxi and drumming irritated riffs on himself, his anger slowly cooled. He wondered what Kate would think when she heard, and how he could ever apologize, how he could ever apologize to any of them.

He would never be able to apologize to King Cobalt. Not now.

The news program had turned to another story now – floodwaters and boats rescuing stranded people in some local city – and he picked up the remote and channel-surfed, looking for Kate or Fortune or anything to do with the escalating crisis in Egypt. Nothing. He tapped on his chest with his free hands as he pressed the channel button with his lower left hand. Drumbeats surrounded him, fast and hard. He focused the sound through the open throats on his thick neck, tightening the muscles there and shaping the sound – he could feel it in his own body, though someone standing five feet to his side would have heard very little. But a person standing right in front of him, where he was staring ...

The television set vibrated in its wooden cabinet.

Tighter yet. Tighter ...

A jagged crack ran quickly across the screen, from lower left to upper right. The television hissed, sparked, and went dead. Michael tossed the remote across the room.

He rose from the couch and went into the bedroom. Without waking Chaton, he dressed quickly and packed a small duffel bag with underwear, jeans, T-shirts, and a bundle of his signature graphite drumsticks. He left the room and took the elevator down to the lobby. The night staff looked up with surprise at his appearance. '*Scusilo.* There's a young lady in my room,' he told the woman at the desk as he placed a hundred-euro note conspicuously on the counter. 'Make sure someone sends breakfast up to her around eleven-thirty. I need a cab, also, and I'd prefer that no one knows that I've gone out.' He tapped the note for emphasis. 'Oh, and there's a slight problem with the TV – just put it on my bill.'

The woman blinked. 'Surely, Mr. Vogali,' she said, her English accented with the Roman lilt. 'The concierge will help you with a cab.'

A half-hour later, he was at the airport.

♠

The call on his cell phone came about 8:30 – hours earlier than he'd been hoping it would come. It seemed that a hundred euros wasn't as much of a tip as he'd thought, or maybe Grady just tipped better. At least it was Cohen and not one of the guys in the group; that would have been much harder. 'Hey, KA,' Michael said as he flipped open the phone. 'I figured you'd be calling eventually.'

'DB, where the hell are you and what the fuck are you doing?'

'I'm just taking a walk, Grady. Enjoying the scenery. Y'know, the Coliseum, the Parthenon ...'

'The Parthenon's in Athens.'

'It's been a long walk.'

He heard an exasperated huff. 'The desk clerk from the hotel called me. I've talked to the concierge and I've been to your room, DB. I've talked to the girl, I've seen what's missing, and I'd appreciate it if you'd treat me like an adult. Now, where are you?'

'At the airport,' Michael told him. The private prop-jet was idling on the runway a hundred yards from him. He could feel the prop wash whipping his pants legs and whistling past the throats on his neck. From the open door of the plane, a hand gestured toward him.

'Please tell me you're going to Berlin,' Cohen said.

'I'm going the other way, actually.'

'You can't do that, DB. You can't cancel this concert at the last minute. Forget that it violates your contract, it's not fair to the rest of Joker Plague. It's not fair to your fans.' A pause. 'It's not fair to me.'

'This is more important right now. To me.'

Cohen's exasperation rasped the phone's speaker. 'What? What's more important? You think you're fucking Bono, off to save the goddamn world?'

'Wow, KA. Didn't mean to touch a nerve.'

'Fuck!' The blast of fury made Michael lift the phone away from his ear. 'DB, you blow off this tour and Joker Plague is finished. The label won't touch you again. Your career – and everyone else's – gets flushed down the toilet.'

'Bullshit,' Michael spat back. 'Let's cut the crap. You're just worried about your own ass, KA. The label still has a best-selling CD, and they're not going to flush that. It's all about the money, Grady, and we both know it. You'll be getting plenty of publicity to sell CDs and concert tickets by the time I get back. I promise you that.'

'When? When are you coming back?' Another pause, and a long sigh. 'Look, maybe I can do something with Berlin, even London if

I have to. But when are you getting back here? By New York? Tell me it will be by New York.'

'Talk to you later, KA.'

'DB! Goddamn it—'

Michael closed the cover. With his middle hand, he sidearmed the phone at the concrete wall of the terminal. It shattered. He strode quickly toward the open door of the plane and hauled himself inside. The pilot was checking off instruments. He glanced back at Michael as he strapped into the nearest seat.

'Let's get the hell out of here before I change my mind,' he told the pilot.

♣

The long road from the Aswan airport was drifted with sand, and the air above the asphalt wavered and rippled. The wind through the open windows of the taxi only seemed to stir the heat. 'It has not rained here in six years,' the driver said, glancing over his shoulder to where Michael was crammed uncomfortably into the rear seat. His eyes widened slightly, and Michael figured he must look like a large spider stuffed into a too-small box. 'When our people weep, we save the tears.'

The car seemed ready to shed side panels like a snake's discarded skin with every pothole and bump. The vehicle shuddered from badly out-of-alignment tires, every inch of the interior was coated with a fine layer of sand, and the driver – 'Ahmed,' he said. 'It is like "Bob" in your language. A common name, but I am a man of uncommon talent' – used his horn at every possible opportunity, or simply as punctuation. Ahmed spoke English well enough, but he also spoke it constantly. 'The Living Gods, they say "Ah, we will take us back to the old ways, the right ways, the way it should be for us." Egypt, she is ancient and that's why she likes them, but these Ikhlas al-Din and the Caliph …' He shook his head and swerved violently around a slower car, horn blaring, as Michael's head banged first against the roof, then the side.

'*Ta'ala musso*!' Ahmed shouted from the window. Michael assumed it was a curse. Ahmed wrestled the car back into its lane and continued his monologue. Michael wished that Ahmed would look more at the road and less at him. 'You are what they call a "joker," yes? Myself, I have many friends who are jokers and a few even in my family, so I am not offended to look at you. Here, so many with the virus take on the shapes of the old gods – it is the very land that does this. Their forms are in the sand and the stones and the air. The waters of the Nile flow with it. You, in your United States, you take on whatever shape you wish, like you with your many arms to make much noise, but *here* – here the old gods use the virus to allow their shapes to return to their ancient home. These Ikhlas al-Din, they believe that Allah has cursed the deformed ones for their sins, but even though I am Muslim I am not so certain. I wonder if the Old Ones aren't truly attempting to return. When you go see the temples and the places of the gods here, you'll wonder, too. Go to Philae, or even to Sehel; I will take you.'

Michael grunted, his head slamming against the roof of the car with every bump, his legs folded up against his chest, his several hands clutching at any hold he could find. The heat made him sweat, which made the sand stick to his bare skin, and he could taste the gritty stuff in his mouth. They drove rapidly east, through a village where people watched the taxi from open doorways or behind shuttered windows. The market they passed was closed and deserted; Michael suspected that most of the inhabitants had already fled the area. The driver turned onto a four-lane highway, and Michael saw ahead the curve of the massive dam that held Lake Nasser. 'Sadd el Aali,' Ahmed said, pointing through the sandblasted windshield. 'The High Dam. And there, that is our memorial, celebrating the cooperation of Egypt and the Soviet Union which allowed us to build such a wonderful dam.'

The memorial was monumentally ugly to Michael's eyes: five huge pillars like the petals of a concrete flower holding up a concrete ring at the summit. There were tents erected in the open space around the memorial. As they approached, guards with automatic weapons waved the taxi to the side of the road. All of the guards appeared to be jokers. Ahmed honked at the men and appeared prepared to run them down, but Michael reached over the seat with a muscular top hand and pulled the wheel hard to the right. 'This is my stop,' he said, and Ahmed shrugged and braked. Michael opened one of the rear doors and managed to unfold himself from the car without quite falling down. He rummaged in a pocket and tossed several bills onto the passenger seat of the taxi. '*Salam alekum*,' he said.

'*Wa alekum es salam*,' Ahmed replied, glancing at the bills – that he didn't bother to haggle told Michael he'd drastically overpaid. 'Though I doubt that you will find much peace here,' Ahmed said solemnly. 'Here, my number if you need me again.' Michael took the crumpled business card as the guards approached, their weapons trained on his bare chest. He put down his duffel bag and raised his many hands.

'Hey, Drummer Boy!' one of them said in Arabic-accented English. He lifted an iPod from the breast pocket of his fatigues, and Michael saw the white cord of headphones running up to a hairless head that looked more like a skull, the buds stuffed into earless holes. 'Joker Plague – love your music. I have all your CDs.'

They slung their weapons over their shoulders and Michael lowered his hands. Ten minutes later, he knew the joker fan's name was Masud, the other guard had taken their picture together, and Michael picked up his duffel bag again. 'I'm looking for Lohengrin or John Fortune,' he said.

'I'll take you to them,' Masud said. He inclined his head toward the monument. 'This way. Would you mind giving me an autograph, too?'

♥

There was a rusting and decrepit motorcycle parked outside the tent. Fortune was inside, standing alongside a table with maps spread out and held down by rocks against the furnace-like wind off the desert. The armpits of his white shirt were stained a pale yellow and his normal *café au lait* skin was tanned darkly; his blond, curly hair was bleached by the sun, so that the contrast between skin and hair was stark. Lohengrin – looking more like a pudgy, badly sunburned college student than a warrior without the white armor – stood next to him, along with Jonathan Hive. Three of the Living Gods were gazing at the maps as well; the one called Sobek, who bore the head of a crocodile, the hippopotamus god Taweret, and a dark-haired teenaged girl Michael remembered from her brief stint on *American Hero*: Aliyah Malik, also known as Simoon.

He'd never been to bed with her. Not that he probably wouldn't have tried, if she'd stayed in the game long enough.

Fortune touched a finger to the jewel of Sekhmet embedded in his forehead, as if trying to massage it. The lump was far too prominent for Michael's comfort. 'What's left of the Egyptian army has pulled back north of Aswan, but all the reports we're hearing say that Ikhlas al-Din and the army of the caliphate are advancing southward along the road from Daraw and Kôm Ombo – the Djinn's with them, and so is the Caliph. Some are coming by rail, some in vehicles. They have C-130 transport planes, too. That means that taking out the airport is a priority, to keep them on the east side of the river and away from Sehel Island and Syrene. They're moving quickly. It'll be the same tactical situation we had with the Egyptians: they're on the east side, and will be looking to cross the Nile at the British dam, or maybe here at the High Dam where the road is wider. We don't know where they'll make their initial attack, or how ... '

Fortune lifted up his head as Michael stepped under the shadow of the open-sided tent. He grimaced and his voice changed slightly. 'Well, the Little Drummer Boy shows up,' he said. 'What are you doing here? Your tour cancelled already?'

Michael held back the anger that surged through him at the hated nickname. 'I figured you could use more help.'

Fortune snorted. 'You know what? This isn't a goddamn television show and I'm not your Captain Cruller anymore. We don't need a guest star appearance, especially from someone who's only here for publicity. You just want to see your face on CNN so you can sell a few more CDs. This is serious. People are *dying* here.' His face twisted, and for a moment Michael wondered who was talking, Fortune or Sekhmet. 'We just buried King Cobalt. The Caliph intends to wipe out all the rest of us, along with the Living Gods and all their followers. This is war, and it's real. I – we – don't need dilettantes strolling in at the last minute.'

A wasp shrilled by Michael's ear. He ignored it. 'That's what I figured you'd say. But you ain't the only one here. What would Kate say? Or you, Lohengrin? Bugsy? You know what I got to offer.'

Lohengrin neither smiled nor frowned. Sweat beaded on his forehead, but evaporated before it could slide down his pale, doughy features. 'He's strong enough, *ja*? We shouldn't turn down allies, John. We need every ace.'

'I'm a joker, not an ace,' Michael told him.

Lohengrin shrugged. Bugsy only stared. Sobek and Taweret were conferring sibilantly with Ali in Arabic, and she said something quietly to Fortune. Michael waited.

Finally Fortune looked down at the map again. 'Fine. I don't give a damn one way or the other. Just stay the hell away from me.'

'Not a problem,' Michael said. He waited a beat. 'Where's Kate?' he asked.

That brought Fortune's head up again. 'You'll leave her alone.'

'I'll let her tell me that.' Michael glanced at the map. 'When you figure out where I can help you, let me know.' He turned to leave the tent. 'No, you ain't Captain Cruller no more,' he muttered. 'You're fucking Beetle Boy.'

He didn't particularly care if Fortune or his companions heard him. He was tapping at his chest as he left, and the sound of drums echoed from the low hills around Lake Nasser.

◆

'Ana! Earth Witch! Hey, I heard you saved the day with the dam.'

The woman, wearing a wide-brimmed straw hat, glanced over her shoulder at him. Her eyes widened as she recognized him, then narrowed tightly. 'I thought I was "Earth Bitch" to you.'

'Ouch.' Michael spread his lower hands. The lines of his tattoos crawled over his abdomen and biceps with the movement. 'Hey, I was just pissed off when I said that, Ana. I really didn't mean it to stick.'

'It did.'

'I'm sorry.'

'Yeah. I'll bet you are.' Ana took a breath, looking away from him to the nearest tent and back. 'Kate doesn't need you here. Your being around is only going to stir things up again, and that's dangerous for Kate. You've hurt her badly enough. Distract her here and you could kill her.'

'C'mon, Ana, lighten up.'

Her dark eyes glittered under the hat. She glanced again at the tent. 'I'm not joking.' Michael could see a deep sadness in her eyes, a grief that had never been there before. 'You care about Kate? Then stay away from her. She won't say that to you because she's too polite for her own good, but I will.'

'She's in there, isn't she? Why don't I just ask her what she thinks?'

'I can't stop you. You always get what you want, don't you?'

'Not always,' Michael told her. 'Not with—' He stopped.

The tent flap flipped open and Kate stepped out. She looked tired and worried, the skin pouched and brown under her eyes. If she was startled to see him, she didn't show it. He wondered if she'd been listening and for how long. 'Michael,' she said, and a faint smile brushed her lips. She tossed a marble up and down in her right hand. Ana sniffed loudly and Kate glanced at her. 'Take a walk with me, Michael?'

'Sure.' He extended his middle left hand to Kate. Her head moved from side to side faintly and he let the hand drop back down.

'We need to get you a hat,' she said. 'And something over your torso and arms. You're going to burn up here.'

She said little else, and Michael was content to walk alongside her. She led him across the road to an observation tower on the northern face of the dam. The guard there, a joker whose face was silver and reflective, nodded to Kate and opened the door. Beyond was a set of metal stairs. When they reached the first platform, she stopped and pointed north – downstream. The water on that side lay a few hundred feet below them, a winding lake held back by another dam several miles north. 'That's the Low Dam, Aswan Dam, built by the British,' Kate said, seeing where he was looking.

'Four miles away, maybe a little more. The island just this side of it, the smaller one over to the right, is Philae; some of the Living Gods are there right now, but mostly they're on Sehel Island, just on the other side of the dam. The Gods and their followers restored the ruins of the temples and rebuilt the town over the last several years. Philae's really gorgeous, truly breathtaking. You should go see it if you get the chance, before …' She didn't finish the phrase. Her voice was strained, dispassionate, and too quick. Michael thought she was talking mostly so he couldn't.

'The main city of Aswan's maybe another four or five miles past the Low Dam on the east bank,' she continued. 'Syrene's on the western bank, directly across from Sehel – again, just a bit north of the dam. Right now there's a quarter million or so of the followers of the Living Gods living there, most of them refugees from downriver – from Alexandria, Cairo, Karnak, and Luxor. They can't go any farther. There's nowhere else in Egypt where they could survive except along the Nile. So they'll stand here, with their Living Gods.'

Kate touched his arm, pointing behind them. Michael turned, feeling the lingering touch of her fingers on his skin. South of the dam, a gigantic lake pooled behind the curved ramparts of the dam out to the horizon, its water crowding the top of the structure. 'Yeah, Lake Nasser,' he said. 'I know. I looked at the maps.'

Kate smiled. 'You knew all this?'

'Pretty much. Figured it might be useful.'

A nod. 'If it weren't for Ana, we would have already lost Syrene and Sehel Island, and I don't know how many people. We won the battle but almost lost Aswan Dam in the process. That wouldn't be as catastrophic as if *this* dam were to rupture – that would send a wall of water rushing all the way down to the Mediterranean – but it would have been bad enough. Controlling the dams is the key to controlling Egypt.' She took a breath. 'Some of the Living Gods are afraid that Abdul-Alim might just try and take out the High Dam if things get desperate. He's a fanatic, Michael. He means to destroy the Living Gods and all their followers.'

Michael stared downriver. On Philae, the sun glinted on gilded columns. Feluccas dotted the waters of the Nile, moving from island to island, shore to shore. He tried to imagine it all gone in a roaring fury of white water.

'Why'd you come, Michael?'

He knew she'd ask. He'd formulated a hundred replies to the question on the way, but they'd all evaporated in the heat and sunlight and her presence. He licked dry lips. 'I wanted ... the way things happened back on *American Hero* ... I don't know, Kate. I really don't. It's all fucking mixed up in my head. I wasn't happy where I was. Even playing with the band wasn't helping. I felt like if I came here – if I showed up ...' He tapped at his chest; a mournful, low *dhoom* answered. 'Y'know, back in L.A., we talked about doing something genuine, something that wasn't faked and artificial. I've been on stage most of my life; I worked my ass off to get where I am. But I know I could do more. The fame, the money – I have all of that I need. I can either play with it all, or I can *use* it. The visibility, the publicity, the money – they can be tools, just like what the wild card gave me. Sometimes they're better.' He flicked his fingers over his chest; a rapid drumbeat answered as the throats along his neck pulsed – a quartet of paradiddles, followed by the splash of a cymbal. 'I've always been able to get what I want if I work at it hard enough.' He found her gaze, held it. 'Every time but once. I really hate fucking up. With you, I fucked up worse than I ever have, and I'm not even sure why. I know I've regretted it every day since.'

'Sometimes you can't have what you want just 'cause you want it.' She hefted the marble; her arm arced back and forward almost too fast to see. He heard the hiss of the glass ball through the air. A moment later, far out in Lake Nasser, a fountain of white water erupted. 'I like you, Michael. I do. You can be charming and funny and empathetic, and when you drop the rock star act there's actually a great person underneath.'

'But?'

'I can't trust you. You've proven that.'

He spread all six hands wide. 'How can I show you you're wrong, Kate?'

'You can't. And ...' She stopped.

'And you're with him. Fortune.'

One shoulder lifted. 'I'm not here because of John. I'm here to stop the genocide. You should understand the difference.'

'You can trust *him*, with that thing in his brain? That's not even Fortune talking half the time. What if he's just a marionette dancing on Sekhmet's strings? Remember how he was when we first met him? Just Berman's toady, Momma Peregrine's little fetch-it boy. We all thought that he was a joke. Even you, I bet.'

'Shut up, Michael.' Her cheeks flushed. 'Look, I'm – I'm glad you're here. I'm sure we can use your strength.'

He flexed his arms reflexively. 'My strength. But that's all.'

She caught her lower lip in her teeth, as if trying to stop herself from saying more. 'We should get back,' she said finally. 'We'll need to find you a place to sleep. Maybe you could share a tent with Rusty.'

'Toolbelt? The iron bigot? No fucking way.'

'He's not that. We wouldn't be here if it wasn't for him.'

'If you say so.'

♠

'No. Here. Hold it like this.' Michael demonstrated the proper way to hold a drumstick to the child, a dark-skinned, dog-headed boy. He was thinking that Ahmed the cabdriver had been right: animal-headed jokers were common as sand among the followers of the Living Gods. He gave the drumstick back to the kid and a loud percussive *crack* followed as the boy slammed the stick onto Michael's chest.

Michael lay on the ground outside his tent, his top arms under his head, the others set close to his body as a crowd of joker children gathered around him, laughing and jabbering excitedly as they played him as if he were a drum set. Parents and other adults watched, smiling from the periphery. Masud, his soldier fan, stood nearby, clapping and smiling. A joker with eyes set on long stalks and press credentials draped around his neck pulled a heavy, professional video camera to his shoulder and put his eyestalk to the viewfinder. A red light pulsed next to the lens.

The racket was incredible, and Michael's neck throats yawned open as he let the sound boom out. There was a definite beat – the two kids kneeling by the lowest of the tympanic rings on his abdomen poured forth a subsonic *phoom* that was more felt than heard, a steady rhythm that struck the onlookers like invisible, soft fists. The children playing the higher-pitched, smaller rings above unleashed a cascade of varied tones as Michael shaped the noise with the matrix of vocal cords layered in his thick neck.

The noise radiated out, forte.

Rustbelt came out from the tent, yawning with a groan like ancient hinges. One of the kids rushed to him and began tapping at his leg with a drumstick. 'Hey, you're not a half-bad cowbell,' Michael said to him, half-shouting.

Rustbelt glanced at the knot of kids flailing at Michael's body. 'Cripes,' he said. 'What are you doing, fella?'

'Getting to know the locals. Kids are kids, no matter where you are.'

Rustbelt glanced at the joker with the videocam. 'Yeah.'

Some of the aces and the Living Gods had come to investigate the racket as well. Through the crowd, Michael could see Lohengrin and Fortune standing several yards away, looking at the scene as Fortune shook his head and whispered something to Lohengrin. Slightly behind them, he glimpsed Kate and Ana. He lifted a middle hand to wave to Kate. She nodded. Michael glanced over at Rustbelt, who was also looking in Kate's direction. '"I like kids" can't be a bad message.'

Rustbelt grunted. It sounded like a dump truck farting. 'Not so long as it's true.' Eyebrows lifted above the rust spots on his face. He stepped away carefully from the child banging on his leg and walked toward the other aces. Kate glanced back once, but through the arms and the blur of drumsticks, Michael couldn't see if she was smiling or not.

♣

He awoke to predawn explosions – a stutter of blasts muffled by distance and reverberations, sounding almost like a distant thunderstorm. He blinked, wondering if he'd dreamt the sound, but as he dressed quickly and splashed water over his face, Rustbelt came clanking into their tent, his massive steam shovel jaw half-open. 'What the fuck's the racket?' Michael asked him.

'The Living God fellas are blowing up the airport so the Caliph can't land his soldiers in airplanes,' Rustbelt replied.

Michael blinked, rubbing at sleep-rimed eyes with his top hands. 'They could have waited until daylight.'

'They could have.' Michael wasn't sure what that meant. Rustbelt hooked a thumb toward the entrance of the tent. 'Come on. Lohengrin said to get everybody up.'

Fifteen minutes later, most of the aces were gathered in the command tent, Michael wearing a long, loose white shirt with holes torn in it for his multiple arms and a blue scarf turbaned around his shaved head. The scene reminded Michael of the tryout sessions for *American Hero*, with so many of the former contestants standing there: Curveball, Earth Witch, Rustbelt, Bugsy, Holy Roller, Fat Chick, Simoon, Hardhat ...

Most of them ignored him after a glance his way.

Fortune looked worried, but he looked up when Kate entered, nodding to her. Michael saw her give him a tightlipped smile in return – so it was Fortune and not Sekhmet running the body at the moment. 'Here's what we know,' he said. 'The army of the caliphate is still advancing along the Nile. Right now they're within thirty miles of Aswan, just leaving Kôm Ombo. They have Chinese WZ-10 attack helicopters providing cover and ground troops in APCs in the vanguard. The Djinn is back with Abdul, but we can't assume he'll stay there.'

'What about the fucking Egyptians?' Hardhat asked. 'Is one ass-kicking enough for them, or do they want a fucking encore?'

'The Egyptians are staying out of it,' Jonathan Hive spat. A cloud of small green wasps detached from his cheeks and flittered around his head. One of them landed on Michael's neck, and he felt a stabbing between two of his throat openings.

'Ow! Goddamn it,' he said, slapping at the thing. He looked at his hand and saw green goo on his palm. Crouching, he wiped his hand ostentatiously in the sand.

'Enough!' John Fortune's voice cut through the rising hubbub under the canvas. Michael wondered who was really talking. 'The Egyptian army no longer matters. The Caliph is our problem now. Him, and the Djinn. If any of you are having doubts...' He glanced at Michael. '... too bad. It's too late to leave now.'

Lohengrin stepped up alongside Fortune. 'Where they will attack first, we don't yet know,' he said, his accent more pronounced than usual: '*vair zay vill ...*'

'Jonathan is watching them with his wasps. The Low Dam is most likely, *ja*, but some of us must remain here at the High Dam, if they come this way instead.'

Fortune nodded. 'Sobek will be on Sehel and will handle things there; Hardhat, you'll be with him. Taweret will cover Syrene and the river. Jonathan, DB, you'll stay here at the High Dam with a full platoon of jokers – DB, you'll prepare roadblocks every few hundred yards. Take anything you can find that'll serve. The Living Gods and their people are doing the same right now on the Low Dam. All the rest of you, be ready to be in one of the trucks in an hour – on the west end of the dam, by the monument.' He turned.

'*Hey!*' Michael shouted. 'I didn't come here to babysit a dam!'

Fortune scowled. 'I told you what we need you to do. Are you telling us that you won't do it?'

Michael could feel them all watching him. He could especially feel Kate's gaze, and he wondered what she'd said to him. 'I'm saying that I could be more help elsewhere. You want to keep an eye on me, fine. Then keep me with you.'

'I want you *here*,' Fortune said flatly. 'We can't afford mavericks, Drummer Boy.' He drew out the name, and Michael tried in vain to stop the scowl that twisted his face. 'Everyone needs to cooperate. Everyone needs to do the job they're asked to do, or we fail.' He stared at Michael.

At the side of his vision, Michael could see Kate standing next to Ana, both of them watching. *I can't trust you. You've proven that.*

He let out his breath through his nose. 'Fine,' he said, his teeth pressed together.

Fortune nodded, and it was impossible to miss the look of smug satisfaction on his face. 'Let's go over things, then. There's not much time. Lohengrin, if you'd give us what's known about the Righteous Djinn …'

♥

War was simultaneously nerve-wracking and boring.

After Fortune and most of the aces left, Michael and the jokers spent several hours driving cars, trucks, and buses onto the four-lane road atop the High Dam, starting from the east side and working their way west. Once a vehicle was in position, Michael would turn it on its side. Michael wrapped metal bars around them while the jokers piled on truck tires and chunks of broken concrete and bricks.

Around noon, he and the others went back to the tents near the monument to rest and eat. Hive was there, in one of the gun emplacements built into the dam. Four guards armed with Russian Kalashnikov submachine guns were with Hive, all of them jokers of the Living Gods, all of them grim as they stared out over the dam's spillway toward the north. Michael thought Hive was sitting on a ledge near the antiaircraft gun mounted there, but only the top third of Hive's body was there. Below the chest, there was nothing at all.

The guards had set up a radio on a rickety card table, with the orange cord of an extension cord trailing off toward the tents around the monument. The voices were spattered with static and interference. In the distance, Michael could hear the faint rattle of gunfire, and once or twice the sound of explosions. In the air, there were a few dark specks hovering far downriver: helicopter gunships, perhaps.

'It's started,' Hive said. 'Doesn't appear to be any end run from the town toward us yet, though. Thank god, 'cuz *we* ain't got enough firepower here to stop four hillbillies in a pickup truck.'

'I'm wasted here, Hive. The action's up north at Aswan. Goddamn Beetle Boy—'

'Did you ever consider why John put you here?' Hive interrupted before Michael could launch into a tirade. 'Oh, that's right, thinking isn't your strong suit. Look, we already lost King Cobalt – and he was strong and fast and tough and always wanted to be in the middle of the fight, just like you. And, just like you, he couldn't do anything about bullets. John was doing you a favor.'

'Yeah?' Michael snarled. 'He's just fucking looking out for me, huh? Seems to me that Kate can't stop a bullet either, or Ana. Or Holy Roller, for that matter. Funny, I don't see them here. Do you?'

Hive just shook his head. Wasps came and went from where his body met the ledge. 'What are you seeing?' Michael asked him. 'Tell me.'

Hive sniffed. 'Well, the Caliph's holed up in this damned mansion in Aswan, and I could tell you exactly what he's got planned if I could speak Arabic. He's got Bahir with him – and I'll tell you, that fucker's fast: he cut my wasp in half with that scimitar. Poor Abdul was badly stung, though—'

'The fighting, Bugsy.'

Hive sniffed again. He closed his eyes momentarily, as if resting. Wasps fluttered away from his sleeves, his hands gone. 'There's fighting on the east side of Sehel Island – the Caliph's people are pumping mortar rounds onto the island from the east bank of the river, and they're trying to cross over the channel to the island in boats. Sobek, Taweret, and Hardhat are doing what they can.'

'And Kate?'

Hive's eyes opened. 'She's with John, trying to hold the dam. They've pushed back one assault already, most of it, anyway. The Djinn hasn't shown up yet, though – so far it's just been the regular troops.'

'I should be there.'

'You should be building roadblocks. And sitting here chatting with me isn't helping anyone at all, is it?' Hive smiled. 'Just a suggestion.'

'Fuck you, Bugsy.' Michael drained his bottle of water. He stalked away, and for another half-hour assuaged unfocused anger by flinging cars into place. The jokers working with him whispered to each other in fast Arabic, pointing at him. The racket from the fighting northward continued to crackle over the water, growing louder and more intrusive by the minute. Michael kept looking that way, wondering at every plume of smoke. When a particularly loud explosion thundered in the north, he plunged his lower hand into the pocket of his jeans and found the piece of crumpled cardboard there. 'Hey, any of you got a cell phone?' he asked his companions.

♦

Ahmed chattered nonstop as they careened down the western Nile road behind a troop carrier laden with jokers. 'I have no fear for myself, you understand, but my wife and my children, they would be lost if I were gone ...'

They were stopped as they approached the western terminus of the Low Dam. 'I'm trying to get to the front,' Michael had shouted to the nervous, armed jokers at the checkpoint, followers of the Living Gods. 'Fortune's orders. Sobek has called for me. Sobek ... ? Sekhmet ... ?' Eventually, through Ahmed's Arabic and the guards' pidgin English, he'd made himself understood. Ahmed's taxi had been commandeered, however. A jackal-headed joker with an automatic weapon sat in the passenger seat, with three more sitting on the trunk and two on the hood. Yet another duo held onto the open rear doors, standing on the car's frame. All the jokers were dressed in ragged uniform pants and shirts that didn't match; most had animal heads or other body parts. They looked more like escapees from a zoo than soldiers, and they looked suspiciously untrained. Ahmed cursed and honked his horn endlessly.

As the noise of gunfire grew louder across the river, Michael heard the *thrup-thrup-thrup* of copter blades, followed by a low, sinister *whoomp* and an explosion of dirt and sand. A troop carrier two vehicles ahead of them lifted its front end high into the air and dropped back again on its side. Ahmed's brakes squealed in protest and locked; the jokers clinging to his car went tumbling, as trucks lurched to one side or the other to avoid hitting anyone.

The air rained blood-spattered sand and truck parts. What had to be someone's hand slapped dully against the windshield, a watch strapped to the wrist and the tattered dun camouflage remnants of a uniform around it. Ahmed stared, momentarily speechless. He made a warding motion toward the severed forearm on the hood. The chopper screamed overhead, heading north toward Syrene. A raging tornado of sand erupted from the ground ahead of it and bent its dark funnel – Simoon. The chopper turned sharply to avoid her vortex, but the rotors were caught in the swirling winds, flinging the craft down like an abandoned toy. They saw the flash as it exploded on the ground, then a second later came the shrieking howl of the crash.

Smoke poured from the wreckage ahead of them. Through the haze, Michael could see figures moving over the sand, rushing toward the dam. 'No further! I go back now!' Ahmed's mouth was opened wide, but Michael could barely hear him through the roaring in his ears.

'No further,' Michael agreed. Crawling from the rear compartment, he ripped bills from his wallet and tossed them to Ahmed. 'Thanks, man. That was definitely over and above,' he said. 'Go find your wife and kids and get the hell outa here. *Salam alekum.*'

'Peace to you' sounded like a stupid thing to say, in context, but it was the only Arabic salutation he knew. Ahmed nodded furiously. He put the taxi into reverse, gears grinding, and fishtailed backward until the car was pointing south. The arm slid from the hood, smearing a line of blood over the rust-flecked paint. Ahmed, with a blare of his horn, spat sand from under the wheels, scattering running soldiers of the Living Gods as he fled.

Michael faced south. *You wanted to come here. You wanted to come because Kate was here.* The smoke made him cough and cover his mouth and nose with a hand. The sand was bitterly hot through the soles of his sneakers. He could barely see through the haze of dust and smoke. Armed jokers were running past him. He joined them, jogging past the fuming wreckage and trying not to look at the carnage inside the twisted steel.

A battle between armies, he discovered quickly, was no clean, discrete thing, but a whirl of individual scenes which made little sense.

… Michael ran through the smoke toward the dam and the sounds of struggle, slipping near the smoldering hulk of a bus, on its side at the western end of the dam. There was the loud *tink* of a bullet striking metal not two inches from his head, and his shaved scalp was peppered with hot flecks of steel. He threw himself facedown onto the sand as a line of metallic craters dimpled the sheet metal where he'd just been. He felt warm blood running down one of his arms, and he realized he'd opened a long, deep slice in his middle left arm on a sharp corner of the wrecked vehicle. The pain hit him then, and he rolled on his side, clutching at the wound.

He stopped. Someone was staring at him from alongside the bus, no more than four inches away from his face: Masud, the Joker Plague fan. His eyes were wide in his hairless skull and his mouth was open in a soundless scream, his temple a gory red crater. Gray brain matter and blood were sliding thickly down the bus just above him. Masud's earbuds had fallen from his earholes, the white cord trailing back to the pocket of his uniform, and Michael could hear Joker Plague's music playing shrill and thin. Michael's stomach lurched, unbidden, and he vomited loudly and explosively. His stomach still knotted, he ran again …

… he was on the dam itself, still running and trying to find any familiar faces in the chaos. Through the smoke, he saw Rustbelt as he came around another cluster of overturned vehicles barricading the roadway. Three soldiers in the uniform of the caliphate were firing at the ace from point-blank range, and Michael could hear a metallic *ting-wheep*, as bullets bounced from Rustbelt's body and ricocheted away. Rustbelt, shouting, reached out to touch the nearest weapon. The barrel crumpled to red dust. Rusty was bleeding as badly as Michael. His right shoulder displayed a sickening red crater; he might be immune to bullets, but something had punched through his natural armor. Michael saw the soldiers backpedaling as they continued to fire at Rusty, retreating and clustering together. The weaponless man reached for a canvas belt bandoliered around his shoulder and fumbled with a grenade there.

Michael crouched; the roadway was broken, and he snatched up a two-foot hunk of concrete curbing with his lower hands, and flipped it to his upper set of arms. Grunting, he heaved it overhead with all his considerable strength toward the soldiers. They went down hard as Michael dove for the ground, trying vainly to cover his head with all six arms. The gunfire stopped. When he glanced up, Rusty was looking down at him, nodding his riveted head and clutching at his wounded shoulder. 'Thanks, fella. That would've been a bad deal.' Michael sat up: The grenade had rolled away from the crushed soldier's hand, the pin still attached. He could see it on the pavement, not two feet away . . .

. . . *people were running westward past Michael and Rustbelt, all of them jokers, some of them with weapons clutched in their hands, many of them bloodied and injured.* 'What's going on?' Michael shouted, catching one of them in his hands, but the man replied in fast, frightened Arabic, pushing at Michael's arms to get away. 'Djinn,' was the only word Michael caught. Rustbelt shrugged and pointed northward over the edge of the dam. There, maybe a mile down the river, Michael could see a large island. Bright girders glowed as a bridge between the island and the town of Syrene on the west bank, with the black dots of hundreds of people hurrying across the improvised span. Then smoke obscured the scene again. 'Hardhat. Good fella.' Rustbelt grunted and started walking eastward, and Michael followed behind him.

. . . *it seemed like he'd been running along this road forever, dodging around the roadblocks and ducking behind any cover he could find whenever he heard gunfire.* He'd lost Rusty during one of those moments. Craters erupted in the edge of the roadway as an automatic weapon fired, and Michael flung himself behind a stack of burning tires. 'You never hear the one that hits you,' he muttered to himself. He thought he'd heard that somewhere. He was close to the middle of the dam, the arrow-straight roadway stretching out in front of him. A hundred yards ahead of him there was another roadblock, this one piled high with the burning, motionless hulk of a caliphate tank perched atop the rubble, stretching entirely across the two-lane road. To the north, there was an eighty-foot sheer drop to the Nile; to the south there was water, only a few feet below the stone retaining wall.

And on this side of the improvised roadblock: Kate.

She wore a hodgepodge uniform: The helmet of a WWII German soldier, a bulky Kevlar vest over her T-shirt, camouflage pants tucked into heavy boots. Several joker soldiers were gathered around her. Ana, similarly attired, was with them, as was Rusty, Lohengrin clad in his shining ghost steel, and Holy Roller. Ahead of them all, prowling from side to side of the road, was Sekhmet, glowing brightly even in the sunlight. The huge lioness's fur was spattered with blood, her claws were snagged with tatters of cloth and raw meat, and smoke coiled from her mouth as she roared defiance.

Michael wondered what Sekhmet was growling at. He wondered at the shuddering of the roadway under his feet. The answer to both came immediately. The Righteous Djinn loomed up behind the barricade – a scowling giant who looked to be three stories tall, a nightmare with black tendrils of smoke curling about him. Fear struck Michael at the sight, a mindless, unreasoning fear that stole the air from his lungs and clamped hands around his throat, a fear that sent his bowels grumbling and bile burning in his stomach, a fear that made his muscles quiver. He shouted with alarm, the cry lost because it was echoed by them all. All but a few of the joker soldiers dropped their weapons and fled past Michael as he gaped up at the Djinn.

'All is lost,' Michael heard Lohengrin proclaim, his sword down. 'We cannot stand against this ...'

Holy Roller shrieked. 'It's Satan himself!' he shrilled. 'The devil walks the earth!' And he was gone, rolling westward and heedlessly bowling over fleeing soldiers in his rush. All of the rest of them except Fortune had backed up several paces. They looked ready to follow Holy Roller. Michael had to fight the compulsion to put his back to this horror.

'*Fear is his greatest weapon,*' Lohengrin had told them yesterday. '*He radiates terror, and his enemies often flee from him without fighting.*' Michael believed that now.

The Djinn glared down at them. His monstrous hands came down and plucked the tank from the barrier. He lifted it high, and

Michael and the others scattered like roaches. There was no place to go – but the Djinn flung the tank effortlessly sideways over the side of the dam. They heard it hit the ground far below, as the Djinn flicked his massive hands as if brushing away crumbs, sweeping aside the rest of the barricade. Behind the Djinn, Michael could see troops in the uniform of the caliphate. One of the soldiers held a banner of red on which a crescent moon enclosed an eight-pointed star made of scimitar blades, both symbols yellow against the blood-hued backdrop: the Djinn's personal banner. They were advancing at a walk, the Righteous Djinn behind them, the roadway shuddering under his step, the army behind him.

The lioness of Sekhmet stood her ground, her tail lashing furiously, her glow almost blinding.

Michael remembered Lohengrin's other warning: *You can't get near him. If he touches you, he will steal your power entirely away.*

Looming above ranks of his elite guard, the Djinn extended his huge hand, palm-up, toward Sekhmet, his fingers curling back toward him in unmistakable invitation. The elite guard pressed to either side of the roadway, leaving an open path to the Djinn. Michael could hear the sounds of the army of the caliphate advancing relentlessly behind the Djinn and his guards – part shouts, part the chatter of tank treads and the growl of diesel engines, part stones tumbling and timbers cracking, part the varied barks of weaponry. All of it the sound of death.

'Kate!'

She glanced over to him. Her eyes widened slightly. He wondered what she was thinking, what he must look like – one arm hanging and bloody, his clothing torn and filthy with gore. He could not read her face. She looked quickly back to Sekhmet. 'John!' she called loudly. 'Don't!'

The lioness roared, and searing flames erupted from her mouth. Some of the caliph's soldiers, their uniforms afire, fled as the lioness bounded toward the Djinn, claws extended. She looked like a kitten attacking an adult. Sekhmet's fire seemed not to affect the Djinn at all, her claws left red scratches on the hand the Djinn lifted to send Sekhmet tumbling back. The Djinn reached for the stunned lioness, but Sekhmet's attack had broken the stasis of fear that held them. Kate was flinging rocks, making the Djinn bring his hand back as though it had been bee-stung. Lohengrin lifted his sword. '*Yield!*' he shouted. 'Yield, Righteous Djinn, and you may yet live!'

And Ana ... she had dropped to the ground. On her hands and knees, her head down, she looked as if she were praying. A rumbling shivered Michael's feet from the roadway beneath him.

Laughing, the Djinn made his gesture of invitation once more, as Sekhmet shook her head and stood once more. The lioness snarled, smoke curling around her snout. Her claws tore furrows in the concrete of the road, and Michael knew that Sekhmet would renew her attack in a moment. The rumbling under Michael's feet grew, and the roadway lifted up and fell under him like a concrete wave. 'Cripes,' Rusty grunted, nearly stumbling. Michael could see the ripple growing higher, as it knocked Kate and Lohengrin from their feet entirely, as it raced toward the Djinn.

The elite guard had responded to the attack on their leader also. Their weapons opened up – Lohengrin rolled in front of Kate; Rusty moved to shield Michael. Tiny puffs of dust erupted all around; concrete chips flew. Sekhmet leaped toward the prone Ana. Most of the bullets struck the lioness as she roared and spat flame, but Ana gave a cry, rolling over and clutching her side below the short Kevlar vest.

Michael could see blood.

The low grumbling beneath them ceased. Ana's wave stopped sluggishly, but there was enough of a slope under the Djinn's feet that he fell backward. The impact of his body on the dam sent reverberations through the entire structure and sent clouds of dust skyward. The mound of Ana's earth wave collapsed noisily, leaving a deep and jagged fissure separating the groups. Water rushed in to fill it, pouring over the north side of the dam. The Djinn's guards continued to fire wildly over the gap as they moved back quickly from the breach, as the Djinn picked himself up.

'Ana!' Kate ran to her friend. Rusty and Michael ran to her also.

'I got her,' Michael told Kate, who was crying and trying to lift the young woman. 'I can carry her.' He took Ana in his lower set of arms; she fought him, crying out in pain with her eyes closed, her flailing arms striking the tympanic rings on his chest, so that wild drumbeats sounded. He tried not to look at the wound that gaped just above her right hip or the blood that poured from it. He cradled Ana and ran, crouching low. Terror gave him speed. Sekhmet roared, the guns of the Living Gods' people chattered. Several green wasps went zipping past Michael's head. 'We'll stand at the western end,' Lohengrin shouted. 'Simoon and Bubbles will meet us there.'

They retreated, Lohengrin, Rustbelt, and Sekhmet at the rear.

The Djinn's mocking laughter pursued them.

Michael panted, carrying Ana, who had gone terribly still in his arms. To the north, Hardhat's girdered bridge still gleamed, wreathed in greasy smoke and filled with refugees fleeing Sehel. On the island's eastern shore, a fleet of landing boats clustered while helicopters hovered like carrion birds overhead. The tornado of Simoon was racing south from Syrene on the western shore of the Nile, in their direction. A flotilla of bubbles was hurrying west to east across the river toward a squadron of WZ-10 attack helicopters, all with the black, green, and white insignia of the caliphate on them.

'Curveball!' Lohengrin shouted, gesturing with his sword. One of the WZ-10s emerged from the dust and smoke behind them, its black snout bristling. Its nose dipped and Michael waited for the guns to open up, or for a missile to gout fire and race toward them. But Kate had turned at Lohengrin's shout, and, with that softball pitcher's windup, she threw.

The stone shattered the windshield and buried itself in the pilot's face. The chopper wailed like a wounded beast, its nose tilting straight up so that it seemed to be standing on its rear rotors, which sliced at the ground and shattered. Bits of rotor flew; Michael heard one of the followers of the Living Gods grunt and fall, his body nearly severed through. The chopper fell backward, the main rotors thrashing at the roadway. They all ran for cover. Michael heard the shrill scream of tortured metal and felt the heat of the explosion as the fuel tank went. The world was bright yellow and red, then black – the concussion sent him to his knees as he cradled Ana in all six arms.

A larger explosion came as he tried to rise; the ordnance on the craft exploding. Michael was flung down entirely, and he rolled to avoid going down on top of Ana. A series of smaller detonations followed.

He struggled up again, clinging to Ana with two arms and using the others to lever himself up. Bits of unidentifiable things were smoldering all around him. He couldn't hear anything; the explosions still roared in his ears. Sekhmet was rising from where she had been flung. Kate was shouting something to Rusty and Lohengrin, both still on their feet. She was pointing. There was pure fright in her eyes.

A crater, twenty feet across and far deeper than that, was gouged in the dam where the chopper had been, ripping entirely through the two-lane road. The wound seemed to be widening as they watched, white foam lashing at the tumbled, broken lip. Lohengrin waved his sword, his mouth open below the helm though Michael could hear no words. Lohengrin and Kate started running; gesturing at Michael. Sekhmet spat flame, but then she, too, turned. The followers of the Living Gods, those who could, ran with them.

The dam shuddered like a living thing.

They were within sight of the western end when the dam failed.

'*Scheisse*,' Lohengrin breathed. Michael heard the curse. He stopped and looked back, pressing Ana to his chest with four arms.

In the center of the long, straight span, the dam bulged, broken now in two places. Water boiled, spewing wildly from twin rents in the wall. As Michael watched, the bulge sagged entirely. The confined waters of the Nile burst free, tearing away concrete and earth, ripping away the tanks and trucks and soldiers of the caliphate caught on the roadway, and hurling it all northward in a tsunami of white water. The entire middle third of the dam was gone, and still the water poured through, tearing away more of the dam every second, an endless deluge. People were screaming on both sides of the river; feluccas and other river craft were tossed and tumbled under; houses crushed and ripped from their foundations on the islands and along either bank. The Nile, which after millennia of annual floods had been tamed since the first decade of the 1900s, flooded once more. A century's worth of pent-up fury rushed downriver as the lake behind the dam emptied – toward Hardhat's bridge, unstoppable.

The freed Nile reached Sehel Island and bore it under.

There was no sound, not from that distance. Michael saw Hardhat's bright girders lift, black specks of people falling from them. The girders swayed and twirled, lifting higher and higher above the flood, as if Hardhat were trying to use them to rise above the water, to find something to hold onto and survive this watery assault.

They watched silent, helpless.

The girders vanished. They were present one moment, towering above the foaming torrent, a flickering hope. And in the next, they were gone, as if they had never been there at all.

♠

Michael watched as Kate wiped Ana's face with a damp cloth while a nurse injected a syringe of morphine into her arm, before moving down to the next cot in the crowded field hospital. The chill night air under the canvas roof was laden with the plaintive cries of the wounded. Michael doubted there was enough morphine in all of Egypt for this.

'... and you saved literally thousands of lives today. We held them to the east side of the river, and most of the people got off Sehel before the dam went, thanks to Hardhat. We've certainly hurt the Caliph's army.'

'The Djinn?' Ana husked. Her voice was barely a whisper.

Kate lifted a shoulder. 'Alive.'

Ana tried to sit up, but fell back even before Kate could stop her. 'Don't,' Kate said.

'Listen to Curveball, Ana,' Michael commented. 'You've lost enough blood for one day.'

Kate looked over her shoulder. Michael smiled at her. Kate bore a long cut down her right cheek, taped closed, and a smaller one over her left eye, and there were bruises on her arms. The corners of her mouth might have moved slightly in response. 'Hey,' she said. 'They patch you up okay?'

Michael rubbed his middle left arm, wrapped in white gauze from shoulder to elbow. 'A couple dozen stitches. The doc said I'll have a nice scar. How you holding up, Ana?'

'Fine,' Ana mumbled drowsily. 'Thanks, Michael. You got me out of there.'

'Hell, I figured grabbing you was the best excuse to get the fuck away from that dam.' He tried another smile; neither woman returned it. 'I just … I thought I'd see how you were. Any news about Hardhat, Kate?'

She shook her head. 'Nothing. Even if he survived, he could have been swept miles downstream. …' Her voice trailed off.

'He's strong enough. You never know,' Michael said, and knew neither one of them believed it. He wondered if they'd ever know how many hundreds or thousands had died, on Sehel, in the lower sections of Syrene, or at Aswan and on downstream, as the flood rampaged north. 'Ana, you just take care of yourself for now …' he began, and noticed that she was asleep. 'Kate, you want to grab some food? I'm told they got the mess tent going. Ain't much there, but—'

Kate shook her head. 'I'm going to stay here for awhile.'

'If you'd like some company …'

'No,' she said sharply, then tried to soften the words. 'I'd really rather be alone right now,' she told him.

'Yeah.' He tapped at his chest; drumbeats answered. 'Sure.'

♣

They gathered at the top of the High Dam, all the aces and several of the followers of the Living Gods – at least all of them who could be there. A few were missing: Kate was still with Ana, and Holy Roller was also in the infirmary – after his panicked flight from the Djinn, plowing over and through everything in his path, his body looked as if someone had scoured him with a divine file.

As Michael glanced around, he could see few aces who were unscathed. Lohengrin appeared none the worse for the battle, untouched through his armor; Aliyah was tired but uninjured, and of course Hive looked just fine, though he was currently missing everything below his hips, his torso propped on the ledge next to Fortune. But the rest ... The least wounded, like Michael, bore scabbed and stitched wounds from the battle. Fortune's body was visibly bruised and battered. Rustbelt's arm was wrapped and in a sling; Bubbles looked decidedly anorexic, her pupils nearly lost in the caverns of her eye sockets. The two Living Gods present appeared little better. Sobek was missing teeth, and the great bulk of Taweret's hippopotamus body was mummy-wrapped in red-stained bandages. They had been among the last to escape Sehel.

Feluccas patrolled the waters between the Low and High Dams, and on the western side of the Nile the banks were dotted with campfires from the refugees who had fled from Syrene and Aswan. Lines of them clogged the roads leading south. Michael had been told that there were at least five thousand camped on the road between the High Dam and the airport, mostly the elderly, the infirm, and the very young. In the middle distance, the island of Philae was ablaze with lights: some natural; some, Michael suspected, wild card driven. Farther out, past the remnants of the Aswan Dam, there were few lights burning where once villages had lined the banks of the Nile. The old Nile channel had been scoured clean of life.

'... we must prepare for tomorrow,' Fortune was saying. 'The Low Dam is gone and we've taken out most of their air power – they now *have* to cross the Nile here at the High Dam.'

Sobek grunted his agreement. 'The Caliph will send his army south again as soon as it's light, pursuing those our resistance saved.'

'Maybe, but those bastards took huge losses yesterday,' Hive interjected. 'If I were them, I wouldn't be quite so anxious.'

Sobek's crocodilian snout wrinkled, as if he were scowling. 'They took losses, yes, but that will only anger them. They will come, and they will be crying for revenge.' Next to him, Taweret shifted her immense weight almost daintily. Sobek translated. 'Taweret says we could retreat to Abu Simbel – we might still reach there.'

'They'll just follow us out into the desert and kill us there, where we have no cover at all,' Fortune answered, and other voices murmured agreement. 'At least here we know the ground, and we have the advantage of the river.'

'Then send a team to Aswan. Kill the Caliph,' Sobek told him. 'It's *his* army.'

'Yeah, there's a great idea,' Hive grumbled. 'Wasn't killing the Caliph what started this shit in the first place?'

Taweret and Sobek both started to answer angrily, but Fortune's voice rose over theirs. To Michael's ears, it didn't sound like Fortune at all. 'Enough of this. There's no other way for them to go, and we will make our stand here.' Fortune paused. No one spoke. 'Good. Now – here's the crux: we need to deal with the Righteous Djinn. He's the real head of the beast, not Caliph Abdul – if the Djinn is removed, the loss would demoralize the army. They'd break. I'm certain of it.'

'And just how do you propose to do that?' Michael asked. Heads turned toward him. 'Maybe some oracle told you about a fatal weakness? Maybe a poison arrow in the heel?'

Fortune scowled at Michael's interruption. 'We could start by making sure that people obey the orders they're given,' Fortune answered. 'We were lucky yesterday that the Djinn didn't decide to cross here at the High Dam, because there wasn't anyone to stop him if he had.'

Yeah, like I'd have been able to stop that guy, Michael wanted to retort. He wanted to rage and fume at Fortune, at his combined arrogance and hubris. *Who the fuck elected you God?* Michael swallowed the bile, and it burned all the way down. Fortune glared at him, but now there was a smirk hiding in the corners his mouth.

Lohengrin spoke before Michael had decided what to say. 'If the Djinn touches you, you are lost. He will slay you and drink your powers. We all know that. But he can't touch *me*. My ghost steel will protect me. The Djinn should be mine.'

Simoon gave a bitter laugh. 'The Djinn is killing *my* people,

Klaus. If he tries to grab me, I'll rip the flesh and muscle right from his hands. Believe me, I can take him.'

'Look, none of you know what powers the Djinn has stolen from those he's killed, what he can do, or what his vulnerabilities might be.' That was Fortune again.

Michael had heard enough. He turned and walked away as the debate went on.

♥

He set the bottle down on the wall around the memorial. High above him, concrete petals held a ring encircling the half moon. Stepping back from the bottle into the center of the memorial, he pulled out the sticks he'd crammed into his back pocket and started to drum. The cadence was fast and rapid, the beat from his six hands so quick that it was difficult to hear the individual strokes at all. He ignored the painful objections from his wounded arm; instead, he focused the sound with his throat openings, shaping it until the bottle started to shiver. He tightened his throat, moving the sound up just a quarter step.

The bottle jumped an inch into the air and shattered. Glass shards sparkled jewel-like in the moonlight and rained down on the concrete with a sound like sand thrown against a window.

'Beer?'

Michael shook his head. 'Water,' he answered. 'Couldn't find any beer.' He glanced over his shoulder. Kate was standing at the entrance to the memorial.

'Great talent you got there,' she said. 'I thought only sopranos could do that.'

'I'm pretending it's the Djinn's head. Or maybe Fortune's. I haven't decided which yet.'

She didn't laugh.

'How's Ana?' he asked finally, when the silence threatened to swallow them both. 'She gonna make it?'

'She's stable, they tell me. But they need to get her to a real hospital soon.'

He nodded. He didn't say how unlikely he thought that possibility to be.

'I talked to John,' she said.

Michael gave a bark of a laugh. 'Did Beetle Boy give you my "assignment"? What am I doing tomorrow? Kitchen help? Bandage detail? Maybe I should sweep the sidewalks so no one dirties their sandals while running away from the Djinn?'

Kate let out her breath through her nose. She was wearing jeans and a long-sleeved denim shirt with a large leather pouch around one shoulder, bulging with what Michael suspected were smooth, polished stones from around the riverbank, perfect for throwing. 'You know what? John's right about you, Michael,' she told him. 'You refuse to listen to anything he has to say because you don't like him, and that's stupid. It really is. We can't win here without taking out the Djinn, and we can't take out the Djinn without everyone's cooperation. Sobek, John, Lohengrin, and Bugsy are making those plans now; maybe you should be with them, helping.'

'The way you'll be with Beetle Boy when he goes after the Djinn?'

Kate grimaced at the name, but only shrugged. 'If that's what he thinks is best,' she said, 'yes, that's where I'll be.'

'Then that's where I want to be, too.'

'Why?' she asked. 'You think I can't take care of myself, Michael? You think I need your protection?'

He walked over to where she stood. She watched his approach with near-defiance in the tilt of her head and the narrowing of her eyes. He towered over her as she looked up at him. 'I want to be there because *you're* there. No other reason. I'd think that would be obvious by now.'

'Michael—'

'No,' he said. His arms, moving, sent bars of shadows flowing over her body. 'Listen to me. I can't change what I did back in L.A., Kate. I was an asshole, I'll admit it. It was a fucking game and I treated it that way. But there was something genuine between us, and I really craved the feeling I had when I was with you. You felt it too, at least at first; but that feeling's never left me. Maybe what

I did, being with Pop Tart and the others, killed it for you. I don't know. But I can pray that something's still there.'

When she didn't answer, he allowed himself to hope. He hurried into the silence. 'I can't change what I've done, but *I* can change. I can. I have.'

She stopped him with a lifted hand that seemed to shake slightly against the moon-shimmer of Lake Nasser. 'Michael, I really don't know how I feel about any of this.' She stopped, shook her head again. 'I can't think about it now. I won't. The truth is that it's not important. Not here, not now. Maybe afterward, if ...' She wouldn't finish that sentence. 'I've already told you: I'm not here for John, not at the core. And if you're here for me, then you're here for the wrong reasons. So why are you here, Michael? Tell me.'

Her eyes scanned his face, the question held in them waiting for his words like a knife. '*Maybe afterward* ...' He clung to the words, playing them over and over in his mind.

He opened his mouth. He tapped his chest nervously, sending the sound of a low drum into the night. His arms flexed and broken glass ground under the soles of his sneakers, but the words wouldn't come.

'I thought so,' Kate said. 'I'm sorry for you, Michael. I truly am.'

◆

Fortune didn't put him in the reserves. Michael wondered if that was Kate's doing, or simply because there were no reserves. But he wasn't with Kate, Fortune, and Lohengrin. He was teamed with Bubbles and Rustbelt.

Hive's wasps had warned them that the Djinn was leading Ikhlas al-Din and the army up the eastern bank of the Nile from Aswan, though the Caliph himself remained cocooned in the mansion he'd commandeered in the city of Aswan. 'If they manage to cross the High Dam, if we can't stop them here today, we've lost everything,' Fortune told the gathered aces in the predawn dark. 'All that matters is this moment.'

By the first hour after dawn, they had moved north on the eastern bank, the High Dam towering two hundred feet over them as they marched away. Michael, Rustbelt, and Bubbles accompanied a battalion of the Living Gods headed by Aliyah, positioned on the Aswan Road nearest the dam's eastern terminus, holding the newly drained slopes between the Aswan Road and the Nile. Fortune, Kate, and Lohengrin joined with Sobek, Taweret, and the rest of their joker followers – farther north on the road and blocking it entirely. Hive ran communications from the High Dam, his wasps already placed.

All of them – aces and jokers – rested behind sandy earthworks erected hastily the night before, as the shadows shortened and the day's heat began to rise. Michael's bald head was encased in an Egyptian army helmet painted a sandy orange, and he wore a Kevlar vest, far too small, that was bound to his torso with elastic bandages. Rustbelt, his right arm still bandaged but out of the sling, was pounding on Bubbles with his left hand, as she glanced at Michael, her face rounding with new weight. 'You, too,' she said. 'Hit me.'

He punched her in the arm. She sneered at him. 'That all you got, Little Drummer Boy? Now I see why Kate dumped you. You're weak, pathetic, and useless.' This time, when he hit her with an anger that surprised him, she staggered backward but grinned fiercely. 'More,' she told him. 'Don't hold back. We don't have much time.'

She was right.

It started with machine gun fire to Michael's right – a rough cough answered by a sibilant, fast stutter. Somewhere close, a voice screamed in Arabic. An invisible giant's boot thumped against the artificial dune sheltering them; a moment later sand dusted the sky in a thundering spout of orange and black. Michael could hear the sinister, grinding clank of tank treads; the ugly snout of one drifted over the crest, the tricolor flag of the caliphate painted on the side. Michael could see a soldier standing up in the turret. The man shouted down into the tank's interior, reaching for the machine gun mount as the turret swiveled toward them. But a bubble the size of a beach ball had formed between Bubble's outstretched palms, and it floated away from her toward the tank.

The metallic shriek when it struck the vehicle was tremendous. Caterpillar tracks broke like rubber bands; the lopsided frisbee of the turret went spinning away, and the chassis split open raggedly, as if a divine can opener had ripped through it. There were body parts mixed in with the twisted steel.

Aliyah stood. The dark-haired young woman lifted her arms and a hot wind roared around her, sand lifting and swirling like a cloak encircling her, a tornado coiling, lifting and rising, the wind a shriek and howl: Simoon, the terrifying wind of the desert. The sand devil widened and thickened further, so that Michael had to shield his face from the blowing sand. The orange-red tornado, howling, went twirling northward toward the enemy. The Living Gods shouted and began running up the sandy slope in pursuit.

'Okay, fellas,' Rustbelt said. 'Here we go.' They ran, Michael staying behind Rusty and Bubbles for the protection they could provide. By the time they reached the summit of the dune, Michael could hear the occasional bullet pinging from Rustbelt's riveted skin, and Bubbles had gained back all the weight she'd lost.

From the top of the dune, Michael could glimpse the panorama of the sandy battlefield, the scene before them spread out like a movie set.

… Figures spilled down a low rise just to the north, black against the sand. The horde seemed uncountable despite their losses from yesterday, and Michael despaired. Banners fluttered among them – most with the black, green, and white flag of the caliphate, though he also glimpsed the eight-pointed Islamic star of Ikhlas al-Din. The Caliph's forces had evidently given up on air support – the sky was empty. The followers of the Living Gods rushed toward them, with some of the Living Gods themselves among them. The insistent chatter of small arms fire and the sinister *ka-thump* of mortars and RPGs rattled the air as they began their descent.

… Across the Aswan Road and ahead, clouds of green wasps swarmed. Lohengrin's armor gleamed white and cold as he charged toward the enemy, and just behind the German ace, Sekhmet had taken Fortune once more. The great lioness roared and flame spouted from her mouth as she leapt into the fray, claws tearing at the ranks of the caliphate. Kate, farther back, flung rocks that struck the Caliph's soldiers like missiles.

... and there wasn't time to see more, as Rustbelt and Bubbles, with Michael close behind, were suddenly in the midst of fighting themselves. Rustbelt's massive arms swung like pistons, as those nearest him retreated with curses in Arabic. Michael swung around Rustbelt's left; a soldier fired at him, the burst hitting the center of his vest. The tremendous impact drove Michael to the ground. The soldier stood over him, and he was too dazed to react. He saw the muzzle pointed at his face ...

... but a bubble the size of a orange wafted past above him, and the soldier went tumbling back in a spray of blood. Michael stared at the body for moment before pushing himself up, bruised and sore but intact, the vest hanging from a few shreds of bandages. 'Thanks, Bubbles!' he shouted, but he couldn't see her anywhere. The followers of the Living Gods were flowing past him, charging into the fray, and it was suddenly hand-to-hand combat. A bayonet-tipped rifle emerged from the crush, stabbing at him. It was all he saw, but Michael managed to grab the muzzle. He pulled with all his strength. A man came flying from the press around him, and Michael flung the man screaming back into his own people. There were weapons on the sand, and Michael picked up four of them with his lowest hands ...

... 'DB!' he heard Rustbelt call, and saw the ace swarmed with soldiers, like a praying mantis beset with fire ants. Michael ran toward him, firing his quartet of AK-47s without bothering to aim, feeling the furious kick of the automatic weapons as they bucked in his hands. Bullets sparked against Rustbelt's body, and whined as they caromed away, but bodies were falling from him as well. Rustbelt rose with a groan and a cry and shook off the rest.

He pounded the last few of the soldiers heavily into the sand, leaving red craters. Michael looked away, trying to gain his bearings again.

They were in a valley between low dunes. The wind devil of Simoon scoured the top of the dune ahead of them. He didn't know where Bubbles or the rest of the followers of the Living

Gods had gone. 'Come on, fella,' Rustbelt said, 'we're done here.' He lumbered up the dune with Michael struggling after him. The sand dragged at his feet and filled his sneakers, clinging to his sweating body and chafing at the belt of his jeans. He was bleeding; the bandages wrapped around his wounded arm were soaked, and there was a long, ugly gash on his right side between his top and middle arm, the blood mixed with gritty sand. Michael hadn't felt the bayonet that had left that mark, but now he felt the pain and the stitch in his side.

Rustbelt reached the top of the dune. He stopped, and Michael heard the ace grunt.

'Shit.' Michael saw the issue as he scrambled up next to Rustbelt. For the moment, they were alone in an oasis of relative calm. The main force of the army was focused on the road snaking through the landscape a quarter mile to their left, on the east bank, north of the dam. There, smoke rose from the twisted hulks of personnel carriers and tanks. The troops of the caliphate and the armed jokers of the Living Gods were engaged in a fierce firefight. In the midst of it, in the smear of the tracer rounds and the explosions from mortars, the aces of both sides had come together.

The banner of the Djinn waved, bloody and threatening. Around him, the armies swarmed, but the Djinn stood untouched, a tower in the midst of the plain, his hands lifted to the sky as if in praise. The followers of the Living Gods were running away from him in wild retreat, firing their weapons over their shoulders to no effect. Even from this distance, Michael could feel the tinge of fear radiating from the ace. Uncertainty burned in his stomach. This would be a quick and brutal assault. The Caliph intended to take the High Dam and end this, and the Djinn was going to make certain that the job was accomplished swiftly.

Michael didn't see any way to stop it. The Djinn dwarfed everyone, and the fear he produced was spreading outward in a wide crescent in front of him. Taweret was among those fleeing, running over her own people in her panic. Michael watched the Djinn reach down and pluck a trio of jokers from the running troops behind Taweret. His fist squeezed, and he flung the broken bodies at the Living God and her priests, chortling in his bass voice.

'If we only had Ana,' Bubbles said, and Michael started to see her standing next to him. 'We'd see how that bastard likes being buried under a hundred feet of sand.' Rustbelt grunted in answer.

But they didn't have Ana. They didn't have King Cobalt or Hardhat or Holy Roller. They didn't have the hundreds of jokers who had died yesterday. Those who were still standing were exhausted and injured, and there would be no Peregrine to call 'Cut!' when it was obvious they had lost.

The wind devil of Simoon raged to the Djinn's left flank, her sands tossing tanks as if they were toys, her fierce winds ripping flesh from bone and leaving skeletons on the sand in her wake. The funnel cloud bent toward the Djinn and he opened his arms as if to welcome her, unmoving. 'No!' Michael heard Lohengrin's cry even from where he stood. 'Simoon, *don't!*' But she ignored the warning. The tornado tossed aside the Djinn's guards. Her funnel touched his outstretched hand and he roared as if in pain, snatching his hand back as blood rained on his troops. Simoon curled her winds toward him; they whipped the Djinn's robes, they lashed his face and body and he retreated a step back. For a moment Michael felt hope. But he braced himself in the sand, reaching for her again, this time with both hands as if he were grasping something hidden in the twisting column of the tornado. The winds abruptly ceased to howl and sand fell like rain; the Djinn's massive hands were flayed and bleeding, but in them was Aliyah, naked. They could see her mouth open in a scream. 'Bubbles—' Michael said. 'Can you ...?'

'I can't,' she said. 'Not while he's holding her.' Michael could see Kate with a stone in her hand, evidently with the same doubt in her mind. Lohengrin called challenge and Sekhmet roared, but the Djinn's huge fingers closed over Aliyah's head and shoulders, around her hips. With a grimace, the Djinn twisted his hands as if he were snapping a dry twig.

'Oh God,' someone said, and Michael didn't know if it was Bubbles or Rusty or himself.

The Djinn tossed the halves of Aliyah's corpse to either side, trailing gore. He laughed. New skin slid over his wounded hands, as if painted on by an invisible brush. He pointed at the cluster of Sekhmet, Kate, Lohengrin, and Sobek. He took a stride toward them that covered yards.

Rusty started to lumber down the dune toward the others. Bubbles and Michael followed, stumbling through the sand. They were going to be too late, Michael knew. Already he could feel the fear clogging his throat and making each step more of an effort.

Lohengrin ran toward the Djinn, armor gleaming and sword shining; Sekhmet roared, flames jetting from the lioness's mouth; Kate brought her arm back and flung stones at the giant ace; Sobek, crocodile mouth gaping, snarled as he advanced, his finger holding down the trigger of the AK-47 he held; a clot of wasps arrowed toward the Djinn.

'Hurry!' Rustbelt shouted over his shoulder as they ran. He stumbled, over-balanced and went rolling down the slope of the dune. Michael and Bubbles slid through the sand behind him.

The Djinn took another step and was within arm's reach of Fortune's group. Shadows played around him even in the brilliant sunlight, as if he were surrounded by unseen figures; he loomed over them like a god. Sekhmet was slapped down in midleap; Kate's stones went careening away; Sobek was down, bleeding from a head wound; a puff of breath from the Djinn banished the wasps. The giant reached toward Lohengrin, ready to pluck him from the sand. '*Deus Volt!*' they heard the German ace cry, and Lohengrin's sword slashed at the hand that curled around him – two massive fingers fell like tree trunks to the sand. The Djinn roared, and the sound drowned out everything else. His other hand came down and struck Lohengrin open-handed. The ace went flying, slamming hard into a disabled tank.

The glow of ghost steel faded. Where there'd been a warrior drawn from myths and legends, a pudgy blond boy now sprawled, unconscious.

'*Fuck.*' Michael spat out the word along with a mouthful of sand. They'd reached the bottom of the dune. Bubbles was helping Rusty to his feet. 'Hit me!' she shouted at him, at Michael. 'Hit me now!'

Ahead, Kate and Sekhmet were the only two still standing. Kate reached into her bag of stones; Sekhmet roared defiance. The followers of the Living Gods were fleeing the confrontation, while the Djinn's elite guard spread out around the giant once more. Between Michael and Kate, there was little but open sand. 'Come on,' Michael said, as Rusty slammed a fisted hand into Bubbles's stomach. 'We gotta get there.'

They ran. As they did, Sekhmet roared once more, the sound louder even than the Djinn's laughter. Fortune bounded in one leap toward the Djinn; Michael saw Kate shout at him – 'No!' – and desperately begin to fling stones. The Djinn stood calmly. Shadows pulsed; his figure shimmered. Kate's stones slid harmlessly through and past the Djinn.

And Fortune: the lioness of Sekhmet leapt toward the Djinn, and he rushed forward to embrace the Living God. He was too slow this time. Sekhmet twisted in midair, slipping past his maimed hand. She slashed at his bearded face with her claws, ripping a quartet of bloody lines down his cheeks. Strips of flesh curled back from the wounds. The flames from her mouth set his beard afire.

The Djinn pulled her from his face as more flesh tore. He held Sekhmet in one hand; his fingers tightening around her body. The lioness screamed, an awful shrill of torment. The flames gushing from her mouth went to smoke as he threw her hard to the ground.

The lioness fell, but it was Fortune, naked and unprotected, who lay crumpled on the sand. The Djinn crouched and picked him up again, a smile twisting under his dark beard, his cheek bloodied and torn. As he held him tendrils of smoky vapor began to curl from the scarab embedded in Fortune's forehead toward the Djinn, wreathing around his body and sinking into his flesh. Fortune screamed in his hands, wordless and horrible. Kate, weeping, flung stones.

Michael, Rustbelt, and Bubbles were fifty yards away. It might as well have been as many miles. Rustbelt bellowed; the Djinn glanced in their direction. Michael felt as helpless as he had the night he'd seen Kate and Fortune on the television set in Rome. As helpless as he'd felt during the first challenge when none of them knew how to work together, as outmatched as he'd been when Golden Boy tossed him aside as if he were a child.

'*If the Djinn touches you, you are lost. He will slay you and drink your powers.*'

But if they didn't have to *touch* him at all ...

'*I'm pretending it's the Djinn's head ...*'

Michael blinked, fighting the despair flowing from the Djinn. He tore away the remnants of the Kevlar from his chest. 'Rusty, you gotta go after that fucker – make him pay attention to you somehow, just don't let him touch you; Bubbles, can you keep him distracted, too, maybe put him off balance, the way you did Golden Boy?'

'And what are *you* gonna do?' Bubbles asked.

'Play,' Michael answered. Grimacing as aching muscles protested, he began to tap on his body with his open hands, playing on himself as if he were a set of living congas – softly at first, then louder and harder. The sound welled out from him, unfocused, echoing from the ruins of houses along the road and the ramparts of the High Dam. The Djinn turned, noticing him as his dark eyes narrowed. Michael tightened the throats of his neck, forcing the sound of the drumming into a narrow pattern, all of it aimed toward the Djinn. The Djinn grimaced as waves of percussion hammered at him. He seemed to stagger a step backward, but that was all. The wispy shadows continued to flow darkly from the screaming Fortune toward him ...

... as Rustbelt charged blindly at him; as Kate redoubled her efforts; as Klaus shook his head groggily and rose, clad again in Lohengrin's ghost steel. They were not going to be enough, Michael knew. The shadows faded and Fortune's screams fell to whimpers as the Djinn laughed.

... a torrent of bubbles broke over the Djinn, crashing down on him, the impact sending his guards tumbling, as well as Rustbelt and Lohengrin. Michael struck his body harder than he ever had, as he forced his multiple throats to close even more tightly so that his own skull ached with the sound – he forced his vocal cords to contract yet further, as he imagined the bones of the Djinn's skull vibrating and shaking, rattling in the fleshy envelope that held them and slamming the brain against its bone prison, again and again and again.

The Djinn screamed a shrill, high cry. He dropped Fortune's body and clapped his hands over his ears; thick, bright blood poured from his nose and mouth. He sank to his knees. Shadows whirled chaotically around him, a hundred smoky figures of those he'd consumed. Michael continued to drum, to pound at the man with sonic fists. The Djinn wailed. His head shivered, a frantic quivering that rendered his features blurred and unfocused. Blood gushed from his mouth and into his dark beard. The violent motions of his head sent droplets splattering everywhere.

His eyes rolled back. The shadows around the Djinn fled. He collapsed, a stricken tower, crushing his guards beneath him.

The fear that had held them all evaporated in the same moment. The guards, those still standing, gaped at their stricken commander – now just a man laying on the sand, swaddled in yards of cloth that no longer fit his entirely normal stature. A breath later, they fled, pursued by the Living Gods' followers, who had turned with a desperate hope rising in them.

Kate was staring at the fallen Djinn. Then her gaze moved to Michael, his hands now down at his side. In his mind, he saw the way she would smile, how the realization would dawn on her face, how she would run desperately and gratefully to him.

She did run. She sprinted to Fortune and sank down alongside him, cradling him in her arms as they gathered around her: Lohengrin, Bubbles, Rustbelt. Several of Hive's wasps quivered on Lohengrin's shoulder. 'He's really hurt,' Kate said, her voice breaking slightly. 'Help me. Help me get him away from here.'

Lohengrin moved, kneeling to help her pick up the moaning, half-conscious Fortune. 'No,' Michael called to the ace. His throat openings ached and the words grated. 'I'll get him for her.'

He lifted Fortune in his many arms. With Kate alongside him, stroking Fortune's bloodied hair and crooning encouragement, he walked from the battlefield with the rest of the injured, his own great wound invisible.

BLOOD ON THE SUN

Melinda M. Snodgrass

Golden light strobed across the white plaster walls as Bahir teleported into the room. The young soldier, his cheeks downy with the fragile growth of his first beard, gave a grunt of alarm, and the machine gun dropped from his nerveless fingers. Bahir caught the weapon before it could hit the floor and discharge. He handed it back to the boy, and felt the stitches in his right shoulder twinge.

'Go,' Bahir said. He had to repeat the command to be heard over the panicked shouts from the street below, the whine of a helicopter engine ramping up, the occasional chatter of gunfire, and the moaning wail of the wind tugging at the eaves of the mansion. The boy gulped and left.

The bedroom looked like the erstwhile ace Simoon had swept through. Carpets were missing. The silver coffee set that had been Abdul's pride – and the source of so many tantrums when the coffee had been poorly prepared – was gone. The Caliph himself lay on the wide bed shrouded by the white mosquito netting, writhing and rolling, biting at the corner of a pillow, and emitting shrieks of rage and grief.

The door to the room flew open, and slammed against the wall. A panicked officer rushed in. 'Caliph, we must flee. The aces may come.' He broke off and blurted, 'Bahir. The battle ...?'

'Lost.'

There was a moan from the bed.

'We're safe for the moment, but I would not linger.'

Abdul quailed before the burning gold eyes.

'Retreat?' the officer said.

'Yes,' Bahir said, and waved him out. He crossed to the bed. A broken mirror on the floor gave back a crazy kaleidoscope image of himself. The usual brilliant gold and red luster of his hair and beard were dimmed by a coating of sand, and the edge of his golden cloak was stained with blood and dirt. Blood also stained the front of his shirt where the cut from Lohengrin's sword had broken open again. Bahir dropped onto his knees at the side of the bed. The rank smell of fear-driven sweat stung Bahir's nostrils.

'Lost. Lost. Allah turns his face from me.' The Caliph's voice held the same moaning wail as the wind that shook the windows with a booming hum.

'The Djinn was powerful, but you are the son of the Nur. Let us exact vengeance on the West.' It was a subtle push. It was never wise to let the Caliph think you were instructing him.

Abdul-Alim sat up and mopped his face on his sleeve. He was an unlovely sight, with his swollen, reddened eyes and red nose dripping snot. There were painful welts on his cheeks where he had been stung by the American ace's wasps. 'The UN secretary-general,' he said. 'You said to invite him. If he hadn't been here I couldn't have seized him.' Abdul's tone was querulous.

'Well, now we can use him. You can show them the justice of the Caliph.'

Abdul stood up and paced. The broken mirror cracked beneath his booted feet. 'Yes. Yes. I warned them what would happen. His blood will be on their heads. I think I should kill him, yes?'

Bahir bowed his head. 'What is your command?'

'Yes, yes, kill him.'

Bahir felt a momentary flare of joy. *At last.* 'It will be done. But, my lord, you must tell me where you have hidden him. When last I checked, he had been moved. I hope at your command.'

The narrow lips stretched in a cunning, self-satisfied smile. The Caliph rested a hand on Bahir's head, then slid it down and across his cheek. The palm was moist with sweat. Bahir felt his own sweat trickle like an insect crawling through the hair at his temples, and burn in the sword cuts. Each throb of his pulse counted the passing seconds. 'I hid him in the burial chamber of the Great Pyramid.'

And as Bahir swept his golden cloak around himself, and felt that nerve-deep stretch and pop, he reflected how the choice of hiding place exemplified everything that was wrong with Abdul-Alim.

♠

His arrival never made a sound. When he left a space there was a faint pop, like the bursting of a soap bubble as air rushed back into the space previously occupied by his body, but the arrival was soundless. There was no warning for the four guards who sat around a card table on folding chairs. Their Uzis leaned against the legs of the chairs or were slung by their straps. A softly hissing propane lantern threw its yellow glow across the massive cut stones. Jayewardene sat on the floor. His hands were tied behind his back, his ankles bound, and his head was covered by a hood.

Bahir drew his scimitar. The soldiers scrambled to their feet, and one tried to hide the hip flask. They salaamed. Bahir thrust the point of the sword at the man fumbling in the pocket of his fatigues. 'You ... will be dealt with later. Now bring me the prisoner.'

They rushed to obey. The cords around Jayewardene's ankles were cut and he was pulled to his feet. The secretary-general almost fell again as he tried to balance on feet gone numb. Bahir sheathed the scimitar, and threw his arm around the Indonesian. Oddly, there was no comment from beneath the hood.

But perhaps as a precog he was expecting this, Bahir thought.

'Turn around,' he ordered the soldiers. The sand gritted on stone as the men shuffled around until their backs were to him. Bahir drew his pistol, and shot them in the back of the head with two quick double taps. There were shouts from up the corridor. Bahir flung the cloak around himself and Jayewardene, concentrated, and teleported. They were gone before the reinforcements arrived.

♣

He dropped the secretary-general in an auto graveyard in New Jersey, across the river from Manhattan. The air held the tang of brine and oil from the passing ships, and the rusting hulks of old cars loomed all around them.

The hood covering Jayewardene's head fluttered as he sniffed. 'I do hope you've left me reasonably close to the UN,' he said mildly.

'Reasonably,' Bahir said in English. 'You show an admirable calm.'

'This was a time I saw true. May I know my rescuer?'

'Sorry. No.' Bahir laid his hands on the man's narrow shoulders and turned him a hundred and eighty degrees. 'You'll get wet and muddy, and perhaps fall a time or two, but if you walk straight ahead you'll come to a road. Someone will stop. Eventually.'

'You have a low opinion of people,' Jayewardene said gently.

'They so rarely disappoint me.' Bahir teleported away.

♥

There were more people in the room when he returned, and Abdul-Alim was regaining his swagger. One of the Egyptian generals was arguing that the Caliph should stay in Cairo while the Baghdad advisors stuttered their objections. Abdul pushed through the crowd. There was an eager light in his brown eyes.

'Is it done?' he asked.

'Almost,' Bahir said. He gripped Abdul on the particular pressure point on the elbow that delivers paralyzing pain, swept his cloak around them, and teleported away.

♦

The wind that cried like the souls of the dead in Aswan also blew in Cairo. As Bahir and Abdul-Alim appeared in the center of the marketplace, Bahir heard the dry clacking of the fronds on the palm trees that clashed and shook under the wind's assault.

Open-air stalls filled the dusty square, but the sellers of Egyptian souvenirs were absent. There had been no tourists in Cairo for many weeks. Instead, the stalls held foodstuff and cooking oil. The smell of overripe melon mingled with the pungent, oily smell of kerosene, and that of coffee. The shrouded figures of women with baskets over their arms glided between the stalls. In cafes, men in *keffiyehs* drank the thick coffee, played dominos, and argued.

Their sudden appearance stopped every conversation, and pulled a few screams from the heavily veiled women. Bahir transferred his grip from Abdul-Alim's waist to the nape of his neck. With his other hand he drew his scimitar.

'What are you doing, fool? Take me back at once!'

Bahir ignored him. He filled his lungs so deeply that he felt pressure against the waistband of the trousers that he wore beneath his *dishdasha* and *jalabiya*.

'Hear me! Abdul-Alim has led the armies of the faithful to humiliating defeat at the hands of Western crusaders and abominations! His foolishness has cost the life of our great hero. The Righteous Djinn has fallen.' A moan ran through the listening people. 'The caliphate will fall, the oppressors will return ...' The moan became a roar. '*Unless* ...' The roar was muted. ' ... we unite behind a true leader, a great leader. Not this weak and useless man.'

Bahir gave Abdul-Alim a hard shove. The Caliph staggered a few steps, struggled to keep his footing, failed, and fell forward onto his hands. Bahir ripped away Abdul-Alim's *keffiyeh*. Gripping his scimitar in two hands, he spun in a dervish's dance and swung the blade. It whistled through the air. Bone and sinew offered momentary resistance, then blood jetted from the severed neck. Abdul-Alim's head fell with a meaty *thwack* onto the flagstones.

There were screams and wails. Bahir thrust the bloodcoated blade into the air. '*PRINCE SIRAJ! LEADER OF THE ARAB PEOPLE! SIRAJ!*'

For a moment there was confused silence, then a few tentative voices began. *Siraj. Siraj. Siraj.* More and more people took up the name. Soon it was being shouted, and people went sprinting away down the narrow streets to spread the word. People still loyal to Abdul the Idiot drew knives and flung stones.

Bahir swung his cloak and teleported away as the riot began in earnest.

♠

He reappeared on the grounds of the Mena House Hotel. The long shadow of the Great Pyramid fell across the date palms and jasmine-scented gardens. Bahir looked up at the rough sandstone blocks marching toward the pinnacle. The westering sun sent the shadows of the palm trees across the manicured golf course and up the walls of the hotel. The way the shadows fell created the impression of lines on paper waiting for a mighty pen to write a message.

And the message is – Britain is back, Bahir thought.

He closed his eyes and prepared himself. If teleporting left him feeling as if every nerve, bone, and sinew in his body had been plucked like a violin string, the transformation was even more disturbing. It burned along his nerve endings as he watched the skin on his hands lose the golden tan and the blond hair on the joints of his fingers turn brunette. His hair now brushed at his collar, and his face felt vulnerable as the beard vanished. He felt his body lengthening, as if invisible hands pulled at his flesh like the hands of a potter coiling soft clay. It pulled at his wounds and hurt like the very devil. Finally it ended.

Noel pulled off the cloak, folded it into a small square, and tucked it beneath his arm.

He sauntered toward the hotel accompanied by the whirr and clack of the sprinklers anointing the grass of the golf course with the waters of the Nile. He chose a service entrance, picked the lock, and slipped inside. The generators rumbled with a sound like the breathing of a massive beast, as they pushed the air-conditioned air through the hotel.

Back in his room, he washed away the dirt and blood and laid a sulfa-coated bandage over the wounds on his shoulder and belly. He hissed at the medicine's bite, but felt satisfied. He had been hurt worse and for a less successful result.

He made a few phone calls and then dressed once more in his signature black leather jacket, black silk shirt and tie. Noel strolled down the main staircase. In the lobby, the desk clerks continued their work, answering the phone with soft voices, writing down messages, and placing the notes in room slots. A waiter paced cat-footed across the lobby, carrying a scotch and soda balanced on a tray. Only a few miles away Cairo was in flames, but here wealth buffered all.

Noel used a house phone to call Siraj. A few moments later one of the prince's bodyguards appeared to escort Noel to the royal suite. Noel pushed past before the guard could knock, and entered without waiting for permission.

Siraj stood frowning at the television screen where Al Jazeera ran a constant kaleidoscope of changing images: the battlefield, the riots in Cairo, the fleeing armies of the caliphate, the great glowing lion, the jokers dancing on the ruins of Philae. Their twisted forms made it look like a scene from *The Inferno*.

'Hello, President,' Noel said, and he flashed a smile at Siraj. The prince's frown didn't fade. Noel walked to the table that held an array of bottles. He picked them up one after the other. Not one of them held an alcoholic beverage. It made him oddly uneasy, but Noel shook it off and continued. 'A BBC camera crew is on the—'

'I prefer to announce that I've taken control on Al Jazeera.'

Noel pushed down the flare of annoyance that roiled briefly in his gut, then threw up a hand. 'Fine. I'll push back the time with the BBC.'

'You don't understand me. I will not speak to *any* Western media outlet.' The prince's tone was flat, and devoid of emotion. The anger was gone, replaced with a flutter of concern. Not in their years as roommates at Cambridge or in the years subsequent had Noel ever heard such a tone out of the Jordanian.

Noel decided to change the subject. *Let Siraj have his little glamor fit.* 'You've got an ally in Bahir,' Noel said. 'He killed Abdul the Idiot and declared for you.'

'That's an ally I'm not sure I want,' Siraj said. 'Isn't he driven by religion?'

Noel shrugged. 'Oh, here's something else you should announce. Agents of the Silver Helix freed Jayewardene, so do take a bow for that as well when you assume control.'

'You should not have done that. He was our hostage. *My* hostage.'

'It would have been incredibly stupid for you to hold him. Look, old boy, I know—'

The rigid control broke. '*Don't* call me boy!' Siraj thrust his finger at the screen. 'For two days I've watched Arab soldiers dying beneath the blade of a Teutonic knight. An American ace burning them in fire, another crushing them, presumably in the name of his god. These were normal men whose only offense was to serve their god …'

And massacre jokers, Noel thought, but he kept the words behind his teeth.

'… and follow a fool,' Siraj concluded. Bitterness hung on the words. 'I would have protected those frauds, the Living Gods, and left their deluded followers in peace, but these mad children have made that impossible now.'

Softly, Noel said, 'We're not behind the aces. In fact, I tried to stop them.'

Siraj's implacable expression did not change. 'That doesn't absolve you. You are still a Westerner, and one could say the worst offender. For a hundred years Britain has destroyed our governments …'

'What governments?' Noel drawled.

'You have drawn countries in the sand, all in pursuit of our oil. And the UN has stood by while refugee camps have festered and children have starved. I would have done nothing for Jayewardene.'

It left Noel breathless. He had spent years cultivating this friendship. He had killed for this man. 'You're Cambridge educated, for God's sake, you know how the world works. This is *realpolitik*. We've given you Arabia. It's time you remembered where your loyalties lie.'

'I have.' A weight of decision was carried on the words. Geography, culture, and religion formed a vast chasm between them, and as if to physically drive home the gulf, Siraj took another few steps away from Noel. 'For a thousand years we've staggered under the rule of despots. That changes now.'

Noel gave an elaborate shrug. 'I'm sure you'll be a paragon, but reality does intrude, and here's one for you to consider – ruling with our support would have been much better than what you're about to attempt.'

'Your problem, Noel, is that you don't give a damn about anything. You never have. It's all a game to you.'

The words stung in a way he hadn't expected. *No, you bastard, it's about crown and country, and doing what's necessary to protect them both.*

Siraj said, 'I've found my soul, and it's Arab. A hundred million of my people are looking to me to lead them. I will deliver neither them nor their patrimony into the hands of Western imperialism and paternalism – whether it wears a corporate face or not.'

'Listen to yourself,' Noel said. 'You sound like a street Arab.'

The slur hit home. Siraj stiffened, and Noel realized he had allowed his anger and pique to override his ability to read others and calculate every word and gesture he made. 'I think you will not be leaving.' The words were forced between the Jordanian's clenched teeth. 'You will be revealed as a spy, and the courts will mete out your punishment.' Siraj raised a pudgy hand. From behind the elaborate carved wood screens four guards stepped out.

Noel glanced out the window. The sun was down, but the last light had not yet faded from the sky. He was trapped. Twilight had robbed him of his power, and there was no escape. Two of the guards grabbed his arms. A third one stuck the barrel of a rifle in his back. The final soldier quickly lifted the Browning out of its holster. 'Take him to the Kanater Men's Prison,' the prince said.

They weren't gentle as they bundled him into the back of a car. Noel looked back through the dust-covered back window at the receding angles of the Great Pyramid. He glanced surreptitiously down at his watch. He had at least eleven minutes until full dark when he could become Lilith. But he didn't dare reveal her in front of the guards. He would have to wait for the cell. He resigned himself to an unpleasant hour.

It began almost immediately when one of the guards shot Noel a grin. His front tooth, a stainless steel rod, flashed in the last spill of light over the horizon. He had noticed Noel's glance at his wrist. He grabbed and yanked off the expensive gold Baume and Mercier watch. Next his cufflinks went, and then the small ring he wore on his little finger that served as a distraction for audiences.

Noel realized that the soldier in the front seat was eyeing him oddly. *Of course, they expect the British spy to do* something, *and not behave like limp prey. Yes, this is going to hurt.*

Noel lunged forward and grabbed the man's chin in one hand, wrapped his free arm behind his head, and yanked. The stitches in his shoulder tore free. The muscles in Noel's back burned as he braced and pulled the soldier over the backseat. The man's flailing legs kicked the driver and sent the car careening in a mad serpentine back-and-forth across the road. Everyone was shouting. A fist took Noel in the kidney, and he gagged from the pain. The muscles in Noel's arm tensed. A quick twist would break the neck.

No, better not to kill one of them. I don't want them too *angry.*

Instead, he tried to claw for the soldier's pistol, and the men on either side of him piled on. As best he could, Noel covered his head and endured the drubbing. He lost interest in the rest of the drive, and only returned to his surroundings when he was dragged across the flagstones in the courtyard of the prison. It was full dark and still very hot. Noel was so thirsty that his mouth tasted like he'd been sucking on iron filings.

Finally they dumped him in a cell. It reeked of shit, urine, and sweat. There were no mattresses on the metal cots, just coiled steel frames. A small, ferretlike man lounged on a cot, but he scrambled to a back corner and huddled by the stainless steel and overflowing toilet as the soldiers dragged Noel in and flung him down on the concrete floor. There were a few farewell kicks, and Noel wasn't able to turn fast enough and not take the blows on his abused gut. One boot did connect with his ribs, and he heard a *crack*, and pain flared.

Transforming was not going to be fun. He eyed his fellow prisoner. And of course he couldn't be observed.

'Lucky for you I hurt too bad to kill you,' he said in English.

The man grinned at him ingratiatingly. Noel groaned and got to his feet, crossed to the man, and held his breath against the stench from the toilet. He lashed out with a foot, and kicked the man in the head. Pain made him less precise. There was a chance he'd just created a breathing, shitting vegetable.

Slowly, painfully, his body burned and shifted, flowing like hot wax. Breasts pressed tightly against the fabric of his shirt, and the pants were suddenly far too snug across his hips. Lilith's long hair brushed at his back. Noel concentrated and teleported away.

♣

Captain Flint set aside the pages of Noel's report and leaned back in the stone chair that had been carved to accommodate his massive stone body. The commander of Her Britannic Majesty's Most Puissant Order of the Silver Helix, the ace division of British Military Intelligence, was almost eight feet tall and weighed more than three thousand pounds. He rubbed his eyes, momentarily masking the flames that formed his pupils. '*Not the result we had hoped for.*'

Noel leaned forward to better hear his commander's whispered words, so incongruous, coming from the gigantic gray stone body.

Rains sluiced down the outside of the tall windows of this Whitehall office. It was decorated in Flint's unique style. He made no nod to faux intellectualism. There were only a few volumes on the bookshelves. Instead the polished wood displayed a collection of British arms and armaments ranging from neolithic arrowheads to Enfield revolvers.

'*I've never seen you so badly misread a situation before,*' Flint continued.

'Yes, well, sorry about that.'

'*You allowed a personal relationship to interfere with your judgment.*'

'Yes, thank you, I rogered the pooch. I get that. Shall we move on? What do you want to do about Siraj?'

'*Nothing yet. Let's observe for a little while. You're in a unique position to do that.*'

'Yes, to think it was me – well, Bahir – that put the son of a bitch in power.'

'*He's still better than the Nur, or Abdul-Alim.*' Flint shifted the papers and studied another section for a long moment. '*Interesting that he named a caliph and didn't take the title for himself.*'

'He's not such a fool. He can never be sufficiently ardent for the fundamentalists, and he can wring our nuts more effectively if he's perceived as a secularist.' Noel hesitated, and the memory of Straight Arrow's condescension replayed for a gut-tightening instant. He knew it was childish of him, but he wanted to have one small thing about which to crow when next he met his American cousins. 'Are we going to take credit for rescuing the secretary-general?'

'*Yes, I suppose so. But I don't know if I ought to let you take the bow.*'

'But you will.' Noel added just a bit of wheedle to make it less demanding.

Flint sighed. '*You got the poor bastard kidnapped in the first place. I do wish you'd stop improvising.*'

'I get results.'

'*Just not always the ones we expect.*'

'Touche. What do we do about Fortune and these baby aces?'

Flint snapped his fingers and watched the flame dance briefly on his fingertips. '*Have you any suggestions?*'

'Is this you setting up for plausible deniability, or do you honestly want my opinion?'

'*You've been around these children. I expect your insights are better than my own.*'

'Then let me have a presence in all camps. Bahir with Siraj. Noel can continue to liaise with the Yanks. And Lilith can join their little club. Lohengrin will forgive her if she asks prettily enough. After that I'll just ...' he flashed Flint a smile, '... improvise.'

Flint snorted to cover his amusement. He pointedly pulled out another file. '*Keep me informed,*' he said, without looking up.

Noel let his body shift. Felt the whisper of Lilith's long hair across his hips. Soon he would measure his dark against Curveball's gold, and find out if John Fortune really was a hero.

He doubted it.

LOOKING FOR JETBOY: EPILOG

Michael Cassutt

The last day of *American Hero* begins with the phone chittering in Jamal Norwood's apartment in Sherman Oaks. It is Eryka, the cute female production assistant who replaced John Fortune – 'Hi, Stuntman! We're picking you up at nine A.M.!'

Jamal blinks, not sure what time it is, where he is. 'I'll be ready,' he mumbles, or something close to that.

Showered, somewhat fed, Jamal finds himself on Moorpark Street, waiting for the *American Hero* Humvee. Today is to be the last challenge. Today is to be the big live broadcast. What will he be tomorrow? Winner of *American Hero*? A million dollars richer?

Or the answer to the trivia question, 'Whatever happened to the ace who came in second?' At this moment, he wishes the earth would open up and swallow him.

♥

Stuntman has had zero contact with Rosa Loteria since the penultimate vote that named them the Terrible Two. As he follows Eryka into the gym of Carpenter Avenue School, he sees Rosa arriving with her escort at the same time. She actually smiles and offers a toss of the head by way of greeting. In fact, as they find themselves waiting at the entrance, she says, 'Do you have any idea what this is all about?'

'None,' Jamal says. 'Which means this is no different than any other day on this show.' And she laughs.

Peregrine and a camera crew are in the auditorium, along with three hundred grade-school kids who go wild when the aces enter. Jamal and Rosa look at each other with *what the hell*? faces. 'You've seen them for the past couple of months! Now, here they are, the two finalists for *American Hero*, Stuntman and Rosa Loteria!'

And the applause grows even louder. The kids seem genuinely happy to be in the presence of real, live aces. As they climb up to the stage, Rosa says, 'They must have us mixed up with the ones who went to Egypt.'

And what appeared to be a long day looks to be even longer.

◆

While Jamal bounced back from the penultimate challenge, all hell had broken loose in the Middle East with the former Discards from *American Hero* making actual history, while Stuntman, Gardener, Jetman, Tiffani, Rosa Loteria, and the others were nothing but tabloid fodder.

Then came the visit with Mom and Big Bill Norwood.

His parents still lived in Baldwin Hills; not in the same house Jamal grew up in, rather, in a two-bedroom condo a few miles away. It was another dislocation that made Jamal feel as though he were visiting strangers.

His mother fussed more than usual, proud to have a celebrity in the family. More precisely, a wild card celebrity. 'It was so strange to see you ... being hurt like that!' Mom had never really accepted Jamal's wild card. 'You didn't have it as a child!' she had protested the first time he gave his parents a demonstration of Stuntman's powers. (Okay, maybe he was showing off, leaping from the fourth-floor roof of their condo building and going *splat* on the parking lot below.) But Jamal's appearance on television – the sort of thing the neighbors could see – somehow made his condition more real to her. Being an *American Hero* made it okay for Jamal Norwood to be an ace in his own home.

That was Mom, of course. Big Bill Norwood was a whole different matter. When Jamal entered, Big Bill was in his easy chair, remote in hand, detached. He nodded a response to Jamal's greeting, then let his eyes flick back toward a basketball game. (It always amazed Jamal that his father could follow four sporting events simultaneously on television, but couldn't sustain a conversation longer than a few sentences.)

'Mom says you saw the show,' Jamal said, knowing there was no reason to postpone the inevitable conflict.

Big Bill grunted. 'Yep.'

'What did you think?'

'Seemed kind of dumb to me.'

Jamal felt stung. He pointed a finger at the TV screen. 'Dumber than Division III girls' volleyball?'

Then Big Bill did a surprising thing. He clicked off the TV and set down the remote. 'Yes, your show is dumber than those girls, because no one's setting up phony challenges to make them look like fools.'

'You think I look like a fool?'

'Bill.' That was Mom, using her warning voice.

'You know what you are, Jamal.'

That hadn't been the end of the visit, of course. Visits with Mom and Big Bill never had dramatic endings, they always faded out like a song that goes on too long. It was one low point in a season of low points ... as Jamal did, indeed, find himself being recognized ... as he wished he had never signed up for the program in the first place.

♠

The second phase of the final challenge takes Stuntman and Rosa to the Los Angeles Police Department's training academy for a challenge that turns out to be a photo op. Peregrine explains that this challenge is designed to show how Stuntman or Rosa – whoever wins – can relate to law enforcement. 'After all,' she says, 'no matter how easily you crush crime in your new city, you're going to be dealing with cops.'

Stuntman and Rosa, the two L.A. natives, both laugh out loud at this. 'As if either of us would leave L.A.,' Rosa says.

'As if either of us would get anything but shit from the LAPD,' Jamal says. He finds himself liking Rosa for the first time. Well, they are in this thing together.

Here, at the Academy, at least, the aces get to be aces. Their challenge is to simply race through a modified version of the LAPD obstacle course – along with a group of LAPD rookies. Rosa is especially good at this, pulling one card after another out of her sleeve. One second she's *El Valiente*, beating the department's hand-to-hand combat instructor, the next she is *La Bandera*, leading her squad of rookies up the last hill. Stuntman simply has to hump it, running, climbing, and jumping like the other nats, though he is able to take a beating from the hand-to-hand instructor without breaking a sweat.

The whole event is merely to create footage, not to prove anything. 'Where the hell are we going now?' Jamal asks Eryka. He is in low-level bounceback, panting, bent over, cranky.

'Network Center on Beverly. It's the broadcast.'

The biggest challenge of all.

♣

Jamal and Rosa travel in separate Humvees that are directed to different entrances. Jamal emerges, with Eryka, at the door normally used by the network staff. He sees no cameras, no fans. The parking lot is full, but the stark hallway is empty, as if quarantined. Jamal is quick-marched from a well-lit passage through one turn, then another, to cold, shadowed steps, emerging several floors down, in what would – in any city other than Los Angeles – be called a basement.

He is left in a dressing room used by actors on the network's soaps, complete with chairs for makeup, the usual mirrors, a decrepit couch. The only sign that anyone has been here for days, possibly weeks, is a basket of fresh goodies – more than six people could consume. Typical for television.

Jamal has barely collapsed on the couch when he hears, 'There you are!' His agent, Dyan, is in the doorway to the Green Room. A large, enthusiastic, essentially ineffective woman, she is nevertheless a welcome sight, given the circumstances. 'Aren't you excited?'

'Trying to be.'

Dyan tilts her head, like a schoolteacher with a mischievous student. 'Don't be like that.'

'Where's Rosa? What's going on?'

'She's in another dressing room,' Michael Berman announces as he enters. 'We thought it was better to keep you apart.'

'Are we supposed to be fighting?'

'It would help.' Berman's voice is bitter, even by the standards of a network executive.

'We'll do what we can, Mike. What is the last challenge, anyway?'

'If I had to give it a title, it would be "Facing the Music."' Berman does not hide his juvenile satisfaction at this.

Jamal looks at Dyan: no help there, none expected. 'Which tells me nothing.'

'You'll find out everything you need to know in fifteen minutes.'

'Too bad the challenge isn't to rescue your ratings.'

Berman's only response is a microscopic raise of his right eyebrow. 'If only your wit had been more apparent on camera. I'd wish you good luck, but why be hypocritical about it?'

The exec is out the door before Jamal can press him. He can only turn to Dyan, who is staring, eyes wide in shock. 'Wow. I knew Michael was a tough customer, but ...'

'Well, we've had our moments.'

'Thank God he can't control the voting.' The final winner on *American Hero* will be selected by votes from the global audience – texted calls that, in the best American tradition, will be charged by the call. The ace with the richest fans around the world would win.

'Can't he?' Jamal says. *American Hero* was television, not politics. The producers could rig it any way they wanted.

'Just remember,' she says, putting her hands on his shoulders in a very manly, almost coachlike way, 'this is nowhere near the worst experience of your career. Remember *Riders to Las Cruces*?' His only Western, a low-budget nightmare.

'I've been trying hard to forget it for the past two years.'

'Well, no matter what happens, you'll have serious heat.' The agent's kiss of death. As if unconsciously literalizing the idea, Dyan gives him a friendly peck on the cheek, and leaves him.

All Jamal can do now is pace. He thinks back on the appearance at the school and has no memory of anything he or Rosa said. Back to the last few challenges – back to that day on the road to Griffith Park Observatory.

Don't look back, look forward!

♥

Wearing the headset that has by now become a permanent part of her head, Eryka knocks on the door to the locker room. 'Show time.'

Feeling like a prizefighter headed for the arena, Jamal emerges. The hallway is still empty, but he can feel vibrations through the floor. Only now does he realize he will be in front of a live audience. Odd to think that in five years as a stuntman, two years as a film and theater major, he has only performed in front of a group larger than a production crew three times – all today.

You'd think he'd be used to it.

Music blasts as Eryka opens the door. The noise has heft, like a strong wind, an effect no doubt heightened by the difference in air pressure between the claustrophobic hallway and the open stage and theater.

With the sharp rise in noise comes a corresponding loss of light: it is dark backstage. Jamal blinks, stumbles, feels a hand grabbing his arm. 'Careful!'

It's Rosa, visible now as Jamal's eyes adjust. He nods a thank you as he feels the flurry of activity around them – production assistants, grips, stagehands, all in motion, a voice penetrating the curtain that separates them from the set and hundreds of fans.

'God, I hate this,' Rosa says. The simple admission wins her Jamal's eternal gratitude and affection. They are soldiers in the same foxhole. He actually feels – fleetingly – that it would be okay if she won. 'I'd rather be trying to lift Holy Roller.'

'Yeah,' Jamal says, 'or trying to get Spasm to shut up.'

The curtain opens. They are blinded by the light.

When Jamal can see again, he finds himself on a platform with Peregrine and Rosa. All around the platform are life-size Jetboy statues. There is a flat-panel television screen the size of Vermont to his right, facing the audience. In front of him, behind Peregrine and Rosa, is a low set of bleachers. And sitting there, wearing what can only be described as shit-eating grins: Pop Tart, Toad Man, Brave Hawk, the Candle – at least ten of the discards. Jamal can't be sure, because his vision is still being blasted by lights, and Peregrine is talking, commanding him to turn his attention to the audience.

The stands are filled. In the front row, Jamal can see his mother and Big Bill – God only knows what lies Berman had to tell to get his father here.

Peregrine is demanding his attention. He turns, catches Jade Blossom's eye – and quickly turns away. Their fling turned out to be as mutually unsatisfying as it was brief.

'Our on-line voting is open now. The number is on your screen. Text "R-O-S-A" for Rosa Loteria, "S-T-U-N" for Stuntman.' Jamal is still boggled at knowing that all over America, people are clicking on their computer screens or using their thumbs to send text messages. 'But first,' Peregrine says, 'we take a look at our fallen friends who have become … true American Heroes.'

On the monitor, a montage of events from the earlier episodes … King Cobalt … Simoon … Hardhat … God only knows how long it took the editors to find footage that made these guys look that good.

They have managed to score the tribute with a tune that recalls the Navy Hymn. Strangely, surprisingly, Jamal finds tears forming in his eyes. He didn't even like these aces – the ones he knew at all – yet they really did something. They weren't playing games for the amusement of people living in trailers in Oklahoma or crammed into high-rise boxes in Yokohama, they were risking their lives.

Losing their lives.

The tribute ends. The camera finds Peregrine again, as she says, 'Let's have a moment of silence.'

Jamal bows his head, even as he hears Toad Man – ten feet

away – saying just loudly enough to be heard by the finalists, 'Great television, isn't it?' For an instant, Jamal wishes he could slam the Toad. But the impulse passes. Whether it is the sudden tide of good fellowship flowing from the tribute to fallen aces, or an athlete's Zen state inherited from Big Bill Norwood, Jamal feels confident. The game is in its final minutes.

Then he hears Peregrine announce, 'In addition to the votes cast by our viewers around the world, the aces here with us tonight will also have a major say in deciding the real *American Hero*. Their votes, cast here tonight, will be equal to a *thousand* viewer votes.'

This news hits Jamal like a blindside tackle. It's one thing for the contest to be decided by viewers who have only watched the shows. It's a whole different deal to let the contestants – the same aces who lost the challenges or otherwise screwed up – take out their resentments on the finalists.

American Hero has just become a popularity contest – and Jamal's big problem is that, while Rosa Loteria annoyed the hell out of the other aces, she never played the race card.

Jamal and Rosa are forced to sit, smile, and react – knowing the damn director will be pulling extreme reactions from the footage – as the Candle arches his eyebrows as they watch the first challenge, aces against flames. ('God,' Rosa mutters, 'I've heard about people being so gay they're on fire, but give it a break.')

He votes for Rosa. No justice.

Then the underwater safe under the lake – and Diver's throaty laugh. She, too, votes for Rosa.

Then there's a double whammy: Brave Hawk stands to vote, and the big screen reminds the world how Stuntman turned aside the Apache's offer of an alliance. Jamal can't help meeting his father's eyes, it's clear that Big Bill never saw this episode. He just shakes his head.

A surprise, though – Brave Hawk votes for Stuntman!

But that bright moment is followed by the darkest of all. Jade Blossom, clearly – if the hoots of the men in the audience are any indication – the most popular *American Hero* contestant of all – pointedly refuses to look at Jamal as she approaches the ballot box.

Even as the big screen shows footage of them kissing (how the hell did Art and his team get this?) Jade Blossom votes for Rosa.

Toad Man votes – Stuntman! Then Pop Tart, Joe Twitch. Who did they go for? 'Can you believe this? I'm losing count!' he says to Rosa.

'Don't worry about what's happening here,' she says, looking baffled herself. 'This is only a few thousand votes. The audience is *half a million*.'

Jamal doesn't even see the footage of the hostage challenge, or hear Dragon Girl, or have any idea how she voted. He sees one of the Jetboy statues looking down at him. Now, *there* was an *American Hero* – he didn't ask for it, he just did the job that had to be done.

Jamal tries to look at the scoreboard for the audience votes, but can't see it. Of course, Berman and his team don't want the Terrible Two to know what's coming. Jamal can only look sideways at Rosa, as Peregrine goes into a torturous spiel about how these votes are now being integrated with those of the viewing public, and offers a tortured word: 'Congratulations.'

Then he hears Peregrine say, 'And the winner of *American Hero* is …' Jamal knows this will be dragged out, as if time weren't already stretching. It is that endless moment between the football leaving the quarterback's hand and its descent into the receiver's – the hour it takes for a curveball to sail, spin, dive …

Suddenly the studio explodes with sound – clapping, laughing, cheering.

He didn't hear the name!

But Rosa Loteria has her arm around him. 'Congratulations to *you*, Stuntman. You played the game just right.'

He won! Jamal Norwood, aka Stuntman, is the *American Hero*!

The others are around him now, hands thumping him on the back (it can't really hurt, can it?), the women kissing him (even Jade). He only registers a strange, slick, smooth hug from Tiffani before he is with Peregrine at center stage. 'Are you surprised?' she's saying. The crowd is still making noise.

'Yeah.' Feeling more awkward in public than he has since fifth grade, he can only blurt the word. But he remembers being at the school earlier today, talking about being a hero – and he forms a speech that will dedicate this award to the aces lost in Egypt.

But before he can speak, he sees Berman flinging his arms around like a child of six in midtantrum. 'What do you fucking mean "we're not on the air"?'

The information strikes Peregrine at the same moment. Frozen smile on her face, still conscious of the cameras on her, she turns to Eryka, the production assistant. 'Did I hear that? We're not on the air?'

'Look,' Rosa says.

On the monitor showing the network feed, the *American Hero* finale is gone. In its place a middle-of-the-night scene in some European city – the hot, young South African reporter from NBC standing in front of some ornate building.

'What the hell is that?'

'The Hague,' Berman says. He reminds Jamal of a tire deflating.

'What's the Hague?' Rosa asks.

'Home of the World Court.'

The reporter is saying, ' … brought the strong man leader of Egypt, Kamal Farag Aziz, and his whole leadership, here to the Hague …'

'Who brought them?' Jamal can't see or hear.

'Your friends,' Berman says. 'Our discards.'

'Michael, what are we doing?' Peregrine says. 'Do we start over?' Berman shakes his head. 'Well, fine,' she says, completely flustered. 'This was going live to the East Coast. What about three hours from now?'

'You think that's going to be over? Look at it!'

On the screen a group of men in chains, with CIA-style hoods, is being marched right to the front door of the Hague. Suddenly the camera finds John Fortune, grinning like … well, to Jamal, like Tom Cruise. Harrison Ford. Jack Nicholson. And there's Lohengrin, Bugsy.

And Rustbelt, looking more sure of himself now than he ever did during *American Hero*.

They are the real heroes now.

Rosa turns to leave. 'Where are you going?' Jamal asks her.

'Home, baby. Like everyone else.' She nods toward the audience. Those who aren't staring at the screen, openmouthed in admiration and wonder, are jamming the aisles, talking on cell phones, clearly thinking only about the events at the Hague.

Jamal searches for his parents. They, too, are rising from their seats, shaking their heads. All this work! All this time! And he was ready, not just to accept the money, but to be the *American Hero*.

He will. It is the role of his lifetime.

But no one will care.

JONATHAN HIVE

Daniel Abraham

GIVE THE WOOKIE A MEDAL

The Sri Lankan guy was short. He had a small frame and moustache that looked like an apology perched on his upper lip. His hair was close-cropped and thinning. Everyone else around the table was an ace – Fortune, Lohengrin, Drummer Boy, Curveball, Earth Witch, Holy Roller, Bubbles, Rustbelt, and of course Jonathan Hive himself. Ten people, only one of them a nat.

And yet, when United Nations Secretary-General Jayewardene spoke in his soft, thoughtful voice, it was his room. He owned it. He could have been an actor.

'The world, in its present condition, is not acceptable,' he said the way another man might have said *we should paint the house.* 'You here are, I think, among the most aware of this fact. The injustices committed by Abdul the Idiot were outrageous and unacceptable, and I was as aware of them as each of you. Possibly more so. Like you, I tried to intervene. Unlike you, I failed.'

Jayewardene paused for a moment to let that sink in. Jonathan looked down at the table, suppressing a smile. It was hard not to be smug. Ever since they'd come to the Hague, they had been treated like celebrities, cheered and feted in a way that none of them had experienced since the first days of *American Hero.* Only it was different now. The half-hidden stares at restaurants, the strangers approaching them to ask for autographs or shake their hands. It all looked the same on the surface, but it felt different.

Because, Jonathan thought, this time it meant something. This time they maybe actually deserved it.

'The United Nations is, I firmly believe, a force of reform,' Jayewardene said. 'The idea of universal human rights, of the dignity of life, and of the power of law and consensus cannot help but make the situation of the world community better. However, here, on my first assignment, I found myself playing the role of hostage.'

Jayewardene smiled gently and shrugged.

'I am not an ace,' he said. 'I was, perhaps, overzealous. I have, however, learned from my error. I have been reminded that the organization I oversee is in essence powerless. I have been made to appear weak in the public eye, and appropriately so. I went to stop the genocide of Egypt, and the task was beyond me.'

Jayewardene's gaze traveled around the table. Jonathan thought he knew what was coming.

'There are other atrocities in the world besides this one,' Jayewardene said. 'There are dictators who traffic in slavery. There are governments who shelter terrorists and preach hatred. There are genocides. Many nations, even those that are members of the United Nations, ignore its decisions. And until now, my predecessors have relied upon the consensus of the governments of the world to take action. It has been a dull tool.'

'You said *until now*,' Fortune said, leaning forward. It was the important phrase. Jonathan noticed how much better Fortune was looking now that he and Sekhmet had agreed to let his body sleep from time to time.

Jayewardene smiled. Curveball and Earth Witch exchanged glances. Lohengrin's chin was already sticking out about half a foot from his neck, and he was practically glowing with noble sentiment and pride. They all knew.

'I have called you all together to make a proposal,' Jayewardene said. 'Through your actions, you have become symbols of something greater than yourselves. Men and women of the West and of the East, black and white, Arab and Christian and Jew, joining together to protect the defenseless.'

'Jew?' Jonathan said. 'Who's Jewish?'

Bubbles raised her hand. 'My mother's side,' she said. 'They're pretty secular, though.'

'Huh,' Jonathan said. 'Well, who knew?'

'I would like you all to consider the good that you could still do,' Jayewardene said. 'I have had a proposal drawn up for the creation of a special committee. The Committee on Extraordinary Interventions. It will function through my office, answering directly to the secretary general. And I wish to extend the invitation to each of you, in recognition of your service to humanity and to myself, to join as charter members.'

'You want us to go back out there?' Earth Witch asked. Jonathan could see the distress in her expression. He didn't know if she was seeing King Cobalt, Simoon, and Hardhat, or the Egyptian soldiers she herself had killed. Curveball, he noticed, was looking mighty thoughtful, too.

'I want every dictator in the world to fear justice,' Jayewardene said. 'I want every soldier ordered to slaughter innocent children to hesitate. I want every trader in slaves to sleep less peacefully. I will not ask that you place yourselves in danger if you do not wish it. Certainly, I cannot compel you.'

Lohengrin was on his feet, armor shimmering into being, sword appearing in his hand, raised in salute.

'My sword is yours to command,' Lohengrin said.

There was a moment's silence. And then Jonathan watched as they slowly rose, each of them. He tried to understand why.

From the need to justify his father's death, Fortune stood. From guilt over her success in burying men alive and despite her wounded body, Earth Witch. To keep her friend from standing without her, Curveball. From idealism and a competitive heart, Drummer Boy. From a belief in goodness that transcended reason, Holy Roller – well, his hand at least. Christ only knew when the last time was he'd stood up without assistance. From delight at not being discluded, Rustbelt. Jonathan didn't know why he and Bubbles stood up. Maybe just because it seemed like the thing to do.

'Excellent,' Jayewardene said. 'This is excellent.'

It occurred to Jonathan for the first time that the meeting table was, in point of fact, round.

◆

The hall was like something from an old movie. Huge curtains lined the walls, and the crowd in the seats was bigger than a rock concert. The constant flashes from the press section would be the front pages of newspapers and magazines all across the world by tomorrow.

They were all sitting in surprisingly comfortable chairs on a dais. The slow ritual of presenting them with medals was over, but the ceremony itself promised to drag on for hours. While they waited for the next speaker to say more or less the same things, they fell – as bored people will – into conversation.

'Yeah,' Bubbles said, 'now that you mention it, I was bothered by that. I mean, he did as much as Han or Luke, right? So why *wasn't* he on the dais in the last scene?'

'Sidekick syndrome,' Jonathan said. 'Whole rebellion was prejudiced against Wookies.'

'Oh, whatever,' Earth Witch said.

'You guys all know he's just using us, right?' Jonathan said.

'Who?' Curveball asked.

'Jayewardene. I mean, he said it himself. Here he is, it's his first day of work, and what happens? He gets kidnapped. I mean you have to figure he lost huge credibility there. And so now he has to make it up somehow, and we're the most convenient way.'

'Does it matter?' Lohengrin asked. 'Whatever drives him to do what is right, it is not important. Only doing what is right.'

'I find you charmingly naïve sometimes,' Jonathan said. The German bristled visibly, then laughed. 'I'm just saying Jayewardene is posturing. He's using us to seem more effective than he is.'

'Even if you're not totally full of shit, so what?' Drummer Boy said. 'I'm good with it. You can back out anytime you want, Hive. We won't call you chickenshit. Honest.'

Curveball and Fortune both chuckled at that. Jonathan frowned.

'I'm not saying I want out,' he said. 'I'm just saying that this whole committee thing is a publicity stunt. It's not like we're actually going to put on uniforms and run around the planet stopping bad guys and hauling them into the World Court for trial. We're figureheads. We're just for show.'

'You know, Bugsy,' Fortune said. 'We're *really* not.'

The crowd roared as Secretary-General Jayewardene took the podium. He smiled, nodding to the left and to the right. The room grew quiet. The cameras continued to flash.

'Ladies. Gentlemen,' he said. 'I hope you will all find this as worthy of celebration as I myself do. I have come before you now to announce the formation of the Committee ...'

COMMITTEE, POLITICS, AMERICAN HERO | REFLECTIVE | 'CHILDREN OF THE REVOLUTION' – VIOLENT FEMMES

The Committee.

Yeah, there's more after that; but when you get right down to it, we're really the Committee. Say it, print it, post it. Everyone knows what you mean. The Committee.

I have a new job now. I'm one of the poor bastards going out there to help save the world now. But at least they don't want me to put on Spandex or a cape or some shit like that. It's great, but it also has the feeling of something ending. I'm going to keep this blog going as long as I can, but I don't know how much I'll be able to keep up with it. There are only so many hours in a day, after all. There's already talk about maybe going in to this shithole in Africa where a guy is encouraging half the people in his country to take machetes to the other half. I don't know what we're supposed to do about it, but I guess if they send us, we'll try. What else could we do?

I started this thing because I wanted to talk about what it was to be an ace. Here we are, with powers other people dream of having. We're the cool kids. The heroes. The ones who get celebrated. And it's not because of what we think or what we do. It's because of what we are.

I don't think there's anything more toxic than that. To be celebrated – or condemned – for *what* you are instead of *who*.

We're aces. And some of us are petty little fucks. Some of us are pretentious asses. Some of us can rise to the occasion, and some of us can't.

So, if I did write my book – and honest to God, folks,

I don't see the free time anywhere in the immediate future – what would I say with it? That Hollywood's ideas of heroism are shallow and cocaine-driven? Yeah, there's big news.

That genocide is bad?

That sometimes people do honorable, good, right things for all the wrong reasons? Or stupid, destructive, short-sighted things for all the right ones?

The problem with a cliché is that it starts in truth. So when you dig down, fight and scratch and bleed and sometimes even die for the truth, sometimes – not always, but *sometimes* – you end up with something you could have bought on a greeting card.

Do the right thing. Cherish your friends; you don't know how long you get to have them. You're flawed and weak, but that's okay; just do the best you can.

For that, I went to Hollywood and Vegas and Egypt and Hell. Hardly seems worth it, except that maybe I understand better what the Hallmark cards mean.

And I understand they're looking at another season of *American Hero*. Good luck with that, guys.

I don't know how you're gonna top this one.

COMMENTS DISABLED

♠

THE
WRITERS AND CREATORS
OF THE WILD CARDS
CONSORTIUM

George R. R. Martin	Lohengrin, Popinjay, the Turtle
Melinda M. Snodgrass	Double Helix, Dr. Tachyon, Dr. Finn
John Jos. Miller	Carnifex, Yeoman, Wraith
Victor Milán	Cap'n Trips, the Harlem Hammer
Stephen Leigh	Puppetman, the Oddity
S. L. Farrell	Drummer Boy
Walton (Bud) Simons	Mr. Nobody, Demise, Puddleman
Lewis Shiner	Fortunato, Veronica, the Astronomer
Walter Jon Williams	Golden Boy, Black Shadow, Modular Man
Roger Zelazny	The Sleeper
Leanne C. Harper	Bagabond, the Hero Twins
Edward Bryant	Sewerjack, Wyungare
Chris Claremont	Molly Bolt, the Jumpers, Cody Havero
Michael Cassutt	Stuntman, Cash Mitchell
Kevin Andrew Murphy	Cameo, the Maharajah, Rosa Loteria
Pat Cadigan	Water Lily
Gail Gerstner-Miller	John Fortune, Peregrine, the Living Gods
William F. Wu	Lazy Dragon, Chop-Chop, Jade Blossom
Laura J. Mixon	Clara van Renssaeler, the Candle
Sage Walker	Zoe Harris, Diver
Arthur Byron Cover	Leo Barnett, Quasiman
Steve Perrin	Digger Downs, Brave Hawk, Mistral
Royce Wideman	Toad Man, Crypt Kicker

Howard Waldrop	Jetboy
Daniel Abraham	Jonathan Hive, Spasm, Father Henry Obst
Bob Wayne	The Card Sharks
Parris McBride	Elephant Girl
Christopher Rowe	Hardhat
Caroline Spector	The Amazing Bubbles, Tiffani, Ink
Ian Tregillis	Rustbelt
Carrie Vaughn	Earth Witch, Curveball, Wild Fox